Karin Baine lives in Northern~~ ~~
husband, two sons, and her ou~~ ~~
collection. Her mother and her ~~ ~~~~ast~~
collection of books inspired her love of reading and
her dream of becoming a Mills & Boon author. Now
she can tell people she has a *proper* job! You can
follow Karin on X, @karinbaine1, or visit her website
~~ ~~ ~~latest news~~—karinbaine.com.

Sue MacKay lives with her husband in New Zealand's
beautiful Marlborough Sounds, with the water on
her doorstep and the birds and the trees at her back
door. It is the perfect setting to indulge her passions
of entertaining friends by cooking them sumptuous
meals, drinking fabulous wine, going for hill walks
or kayaking around the bay—and, of course, writing
stories.

TEMPTED BY HER OFF-LIMITS BOSS

KARIN BAINE

WEDDING DATE WITH THE ER DOCTOR

SUE MacKAY

MILLS & BOON

First published in Great Britain 2025
by Mills & Boon, an imprint of HarperCollins*Publishers* Ltd,
1 London Bridge Street, London, SE1 9GF

www.harpercollins.co.uk

HarperCollins*Publishers* Macken House, 39/40 Mayor Street Upper, Dublin 1, D01 C9W8, Ireland

Tempted by Her Off-Limits Boss © 2025 Karin Baine

Wedding Date with the ER Doctor © 2025 Sue MacKay

ISBN: 978-0-263-32500-3

03/25

This book contains FSC™ certified paper
and other controlled sources to ensure responsible forest management.

For more information visit www.harpercollins.co.uk/green.

Printed and Bound in the UK using 100% Renewable Electricity
at CPI Group (UK) Ltd, Croydon, CR0 4YY

TEMPTED BY HER OFF-LIMITS BOSS

KARIN BAINE

MILLS & BOON

For my own older hero xx

CHAPTER ONE

ELOISE CARTER WAS in the middle of nowhere. Nothing but darkness lay ahead. Of course, that was exactly why she was moving to the village of Bruce Valley in Ayrshire for peace and quiet. Though she hadn't counted on driving up this narrow, twisted lane in the pitch dark *en route* to her new home next to Loch Bruce, not realising there were no streetlights

With no Internet signal, she couldn't get the sat nav to direct her either. The stress was making her blood pressure rise—something she didn't need when perimenopause was already wreaking havoc inside her. She switched on the air conditioning as her body temperature went into overdrive despite the cool night. Another lovely symptom of being almost fifty years old was a completely banjaxed internal thermostat.

'This is hopeless!' She hit the steering wheel in temper, when leaning closer to the windscreen didn't prove useful.

Suddenly, she was blinded by the glare of headlights as another vehicle came straight for her. She swung the car to the right and into a shallow ditch, narrowly missing a head-on collision. Hyperventilating, gripping onto the steering wheel so hard her knuckles were white, she sat stunned in the driver seat, realising her new life had almost been over before it began.

This move from Glasgow was supposed to be her new start, a shift away from all the bad things in her life. She'd only left the city a matter of hours ago and she'd already nearly got herself killed.

Someone rapped on the window and she nearly jumped out of her skin. 'Are you okay?'

She wound down the window, not about to open the door to a strange man in the middle of nowhere. 'I'm fine.'

'You're going to have trouble getting out of that ditch. Let me help you.'

'I said I'm fine. Now, leave me alone.' She couldn't quite see the man who'd almost run her off the road, but he was backlit by the high beam still blazing in the darkness, and it was obvious he was tall and broad. Despite Eloise's apparently ever-expanding waist these days, she would still be no match for him.

'I'm not going to leave you out here all by yourself...' He was persistent, and did nothing to assuage her anxiety.

Ignoring him, Eloise stuck the car into reverse and put her foot down, succeeding only in making a lot of noise and polluting the air with exhaust fumes as the car refused to move. It was hardly surprising when it had been overloaded with all of her belongings. Her entire life was packed into the ancient black car.

'You might need to lose some of the weight bogging your car down,' he suggested with a sigh.

'I know that *now*.' Eloise bristled as she undid her seat-belt. She had no choice but to get out or she'd be stuck here all night. All she could do was hope that, since he sounded more ticked off than she was right now, it meant he wasn't some psycho serial-killer. Not that it excused his terrible driving, which had forced her off the road in the first place.

'This is your fault, you know. If you hadn't been hogging the road, I wouldn't have had to take evasive action,' she griped, as she got out of the car and began untying the large canvas bag attached to the roof of the car, which contained most of her clothes.

'I wasn't expecting anyone else to be out here at this time of night. I was on my way back from an emergency call. Sorry.'

The tall, dark stranger sounded apologetic and helped her undo the straps attaching her luggage to the car. If he'd been out on a call it suggested he was part of the emergency services—a doctor, perhaps, someone she could trust, though she wasn't going to satisfy him by asking what he did. This wasn't a social event. Eloise just needed to get her car back on the road so she could get to her new home and hopefully she'd find something in her belongings that would constitute dinner.

Today had been a whirlwind trying to get the car packed and saying all her goodbyes at work, then she'd got caught in the city rush-hour traffic. She'd expected to get here earlier.

Actually, she'd hoped to be here days ago, since she was supposed to be starting her new job in the morning, but they'd been short staffed at the veterinary clinic where she worked as a nurse. Soft touch that she was, she'd agreed to stay on to relieve some of the pressure. That meant leaving herself short on time. She hadn't even stopped for anything to eat and, though she could stand to lose a few pounds, she needed some sustenance when she was already feeling a little lightheaded.

Once her roadside assistant had heaved the heavy bag to one side, Eloise got back into the car and tried again to manoeuvre it out of the ditch. There came more revving, wheel spinning, clutch burning, swearing and not much else.

'OK, stop, before you dig yourself in completely.' The stranger tapped on the roof to get her to stop.

Eloise just about managed to hold in a scream as she got out again for another look at her predicament. Whether she got out of her seat too quickly, or the uneven earth knocked her off-balance, she had a little wobble. A little lightheaded, she fought hard to regain her composure.

Strong hands caught her around the waist and steadied her. 'Are you okay?'

'Yes,' she insisted, brushing away any offer of help.

This past year and a half she'd had no choice but to do everything on her own, and she certainly didn't need outside interference now from someone she didn't know. With her girls having flown the nest to start their own lives, and her husband, Sam, doing the same—deciding he didn't love her enough to stick around after thirty years— she hadn't had much choice but to go it alone.

The breakdown of her marriage had come as a shock at the time, as she'd believed they were comfortable and happy, if not as in love as they had been in the beginning, but she'd had time to come to terms with it. And the fact she'd probably be on her own for the rest of her days. She couldn't imagine putting all that time and effort into another relationship only to have it thrown back in her face when she needed support more than ever.

A mishap with her car wasn't going to be the end of the world compared to all she'd gone through. Except, when she stepped away from him, her head began to spin again, her skin felt flushed and she suddenly felt very clammy. She stumbled, fighting the darkness which was threatening to close in.

'I've got you.' There were those big arms around her again, catching her, saving her from collapsing onto the ground.

And, oh, he smells so good...

'I said, I don't need your help,' she grumbled, though made no attempt to push him away this time.

'I know, but humour me.' She could hear the smile in his voice. 'Why don't I take you back to my clinic and make you some sweet tea? I'll make a few calls and get someone to pull your car out.'

'I just haven't had anything to eat today. It's probably my blood sugar...' She really should have known better; she'd have to start taking better care of herself. No one else was going to do it.

'Well, I'm sure I can find you a snack at my office.' The stranger guided her to his car and, though she probably should have resisted, there was something about him that made Eloise feel safe. Perhaps it was his calm demeanour, or the mention of his clinic—it could even have been the promise of snacks—but she trusted him and went with him willingly.

'Is there anyone I can call for you?' Daniel was desperate to hand over responsibility for this woman to someone else. The last thing he wanted was to bring her back to his practice out of surgery hours without his receptionist to run interference.

As well as his business, it was his home, and he wasn't used to sharing that part of his life any more—not since he'd lost Anne five years ago. She'd been his soul mate, the only person who'd understood him. Without her he'd regressed back to the person he'd been before she'd barged into his life: a loner who only associated with the outside world when he had to. Though the nature of his job made that unavoidable, he did at least have control over who did, or didn't, come into his home at night... until now.

However, it was his fault she'd ended up on the side of the road and he couldn't leave her here alone. He hadn't taken as much care as he should have on his way home, not expecting to meet any other traffic. There were so few people who lived this far out, most of them at an age when they didn't venture out after dark, so he hadn't imagined seeing anyone else. He should've known better, and was lucky there hadn't been a more serious incident.

'There's no one. I've just moved here from Glasgow.

Hence the overloaded car...' His passenger settled herself in his car as he tied her bag to the roof and got in next to her.

'Ah. I heard someone had bought the old place near the loch. It's going to be quite the change of pace, moving here from the big city.'

'That's what I'm hoping,' she mumbled, staring out of the window into the darkness.

'Is your family joining you?' It wasn't any of his business, and if he was honest he wasn't really interested; he was just trying to make small talk, something he had to do a lot of during clinic appointments.

She shook her head, apparently not wishing to divulge any further personal information. That was fine by him. As soon as he was sure she was okay to send on her merry way again, he'd be washing his hands of this spiky stranger. He was glad when they finally pulled up outside the surgery to end the awkwardness of the situation.

'Well, this is us. I'll get you settled with something to eat and drink and make a couple of calls.' Then hopefully he could lock the door on the outside world again.

Eloise sat down with a heavy sigh once her host had illuminated his small office with bright fluorescent light. She felt a little safer, knowing he was a medical professional and not just some opportunist murderer who'd got her to come with him under false pretences. In a village this small, the likelihood was that he'd end up being her local GP anyway, so she should probably stop being so defensive around him. She was going to need his assistance for the foreseeable future for all the joys which came with being an older woman.

'I'll just go and make us some tea. Make yourself, er, comfortable.'

He disappeared out through the door again, leaving her to take in the sparse surroundings of brilliant white walls, a couple of chairs and laptop on the desk. It didn't exactly scream, 'homely, village doc'. Some doctors she knew liked to decorate their work space with a few personal mementos to give the room some personality: a family photo, a whimsical mug, or an inspirational quote on the wall. Not so here; she couldn't get a feel of the man at all.

Although, now she'd seen him in the light, she could tell he was handsome. His black hair was threaded heavily with strands of silver, and long dark lashes framed his deep-brown eyes. He had an outdoors tan and broad shoulders which tapered down into a narrow waist. She was sure more than a couple of his patients must harbour a crush on the doctor, especially given his sympathetic bedside manner.

The opposite sex hadn't held much interest for her since the divorce, or the realisation that she was apparently past her prime—invisible to most, now that she was approaching fifty, and apparently holding no appeal for any man, including her husband. That didn't mean she couldn't appreciate a handsome older man. This one was striking and very much in his prime.

He came back in clutching two steaming mugs of tea and handed one to her, before taking the seat opposite.

Their knees almost touching created an intimacy between them which made Eloise's pulse flutter.

'How are you feeling now?' he asked, presenting her with a chocolate-covered, caramel wafer biscuit.

Her rumbling stomach, and need for a sugar rush, bypassed the usual polite refusal in response. She unwrapped it and savoured the sweet treat as he finished his in two bites.

'Better now,' she finally offered. Though it wasn't strictly true. Perhaps in all the chaos to get here she'd been avoiding all of the issues which had weighed her down lately and, although this little interlude was giving her body a boost, her mind was just as burdened as ever.

'Really?' He cocked a dark eyebrow, seemingly not fooled by her pretence. The sign of a good doctor, she supposed, who could see beyond the façade and was willing to take the time to discover the truth—vital in getting to the heart of what ailed his patients.

She supposed there was no harm in being honest. It might do her good to get some stuff off her chest, and he might be able to help her move forward in this new chapter of her life.

'No. Not really.' She leaned back into her chair with a sigh, as though the weight on her shoulders of having to keep it together had finally been lifted. This felt like a safe space, somewhere she could actually open up about everything.

Besides, by pouring out her heart to him, she'd absolutely have to ditch any romantic notions towards this man. It would be a strictly doctor-patient relationship in the future. There'd be nothing romantic about a middle-aged woman having an emotional breakdown in his office, and she'd only embarrass herself to think otherwise.

Eloise took a sip of the sweet tea and the floodgates seemed to open.

'I'm a forty-nine-year-old woman who's peri-menopausal. My husband has just divorced me rather than stick around to support me, or "waste any more of my life with someone I don't really love".' She couldn't help the accompanying tut and eye-roll.

It seemed like such a ridiculous thing to say after thirty years of marriage. It was as if it meant nothing to him, and their whole time together had been a sham. They'd had some good times together, and Eloise had imagined they'd have some more. Apparently her husband had other ideas. It had left her feeling worthless, a burden, surplus to requirements. She didn't know how she was ever going to get past that, knowing she no longer had a place in the world as a wife or mother. No one needed her any more and, after having looked after others for half of her life, she didn't know what to do with her life now.

'I'm sorry.' The doctor frowned and she was convinced he genuinely empathised with her situation, given he probably dealt with this story every day of his working week: middle-aged women who'd outlived their usefulness being nursemaid, cleaner and cook suddenly finding themselves on the scrapheap for the crime of getting older.

'It's not your fault, is it?' She flashed him a wobbly smile. It wasn't hers either, but her ex had firmly laid all the blame for their marriage ending at her door, taking no responsibility or making any effort to save it.

'Perhaps you're better off without him.' Daniel shrugged.

'Oh, I know I am now, it just took a while to get used to the idea. But it's not just about that… I suppose it's the end of my life as I know it. My girls have both moved out, I've left my job and my home I've had for decades, never mind what my poor body is going through: insomnia, sweating, bloating, never knowing when my period's coming or how long it's going to last for. It's no wonder my husband doesn't find me attractive. I revolt myself these days.'

She gave a brittle laugh, because all of it was true. Out of the blue, her comfortable, predictable life had suddenly been turned on its head, and there was nothing she could rely on these days, not even her own body.

He cleared his throat. Eloise knew she was over-sharing, but he was a doctor, he could take it, and he was going to know what he was dealing with sooner or later. She was a mess and she was going to need his help to manage this next stage of her life.

'I'm sure you'll get through it.'

It seemed an odd thing for a doctor to say, not offering any solution or counselling. She didn't know what she'd been hoping for other than sharing her burden, but she was sure it was more than that. He hadn't struck her as the kind of doctor who'd tell her she was making a lot of fuss over nothing, but he wasn't giving her any practical advice on how to deal with her physical ailments at least.

'Is this it, then?'

He looked at her in bewilderment. 'Pardon me?'

'Is this just going to be my life for ever now—an endless round of unpleasant symptoms I have to put up with until eventually I turn into a dried-up old hag?'

A touch overdramatic? Perhaps. But that was how it felt these days—that she had no hope, or prospects, other than eventually her womanhood would completely be taken away from her. It would be nature reminding her that she was well past her 'best before' date. As though she was in any doubt.

'I'm sure it must feel like that now, but it won't last for ever. There are different things you can take to ease the symptoms. My wife went through it all too, and I know how rough it was for her. You have my sympathies.'

His affirmation that this wasn't all in her head was appreciated. She found herself looking at his ring finger for signs that he hadn't just made up a wife in order to sympathise with her. Although there was no glinting gold band to signify that he was indeed taken, there was a telltale pale ring of skin around his finger to suggest he had been married once upon a time.

Eloise couldn't help but wonder if that was the point at which his married life had ended too. Had he been unable and unwilling to cope with his partner's physical changes, and sought a new life away from her? She suddenly found she no longer wanted his sympathies if he hadn't been able to extend them to his poor wife when she'd needed them.

'I had hoped for something more than your sympathy, like hormones, or whatever it is you usually prescribe…'

With everything that had been going on at home, she'd put a lot of her medical issues down to stress, but she couldn't ignore the fact any longer that her body was changing and she would accept whatever help was out there.

'I'm not sure you'll want the usual hormones we prescribe here.' His hearty laugh was out of keeping with her impression of the caring local GP, as well as their current conversation.

'What do you mean? You're the doctor here. I thought that was what's recommended for women going through menopause.'

Eloise was beginning to think they were having two very different conversations here. Especially when he wore a puzzled frown in response. 'I'm not sure what that has to do with me.'

'You're a GP. Given the size of this town, I assume you're soon to become my GP. Okay, so I haven't officially joined the practice yet, but I would've thought you'd take some interest in a potential patient.' All the stress was beginning to build up inside her again, as she'd apparently opened up to someone who had no interest in her problems.

'What on earth made you think I was a GP?'

Now she seemed to burn from the inside out as she realised she might have got this whole scenario wrong. 'The clinic…'

'Well, unless you have four legs or wings, you're not likely to be one of my patients, I'm afraid. I'm the local vet. I'm sorry if you thought otherwise.'

The bell of shame rang loudly in her ears. She'd just bared her soul to a complete stranger because she'd assumed it was a confidential conversation with a medical professional! Someone who worked in human medicine, at least.

Now it was apparent she'd simply humiliated herself in front of one of her new neighbours…and worse…

'Is this the Loch Bruce Veterinary Practice?' she asked, her soul about to leave her body.

'Yes. Why?'

'You're my new boss…'

CHAPTER TWO

DANIEL WAS ON tenterhooks waiting for his new employee to arrive, so he could only imagine how she would feel after their unfortunate introduction last night. The misunderstanding over his job, which had caused her a great deal of embarrassment, had been entirely down to her, though perhaps he should have interrupted when she'd shared such deeply personal information, should have realised something was amiss. He'd simply assumed she needed to get her problems off her chest and he'd provided a listening ear. It was clear she'd been through a lot, and he'd never intended to make life even more difficult for her, but they'd got off to a very shaky start.

He didn't know which of them would be more embarrassed to see the other this morning. Actually, he did, and he was sorry her start here would be on a sour note. His concerns were affirmed when she turned up at the main entrance looking rather sheepish.

'Hi.' She was biting her lip, her pale-blue eyes fixed on him, probably waiting for him to address last night.

'Hi. Come in, come in. The others shouldn't be long.' Daniel was hoping Brooke, his receptionist, and Debbie, his fellow vet, wouldn't be too far behind to welcome her.

She might feel more comfortable with others around to break the tension between them.

It was probably that need to keep some sort of barrier between the outside world and him which had caused the confusion in the first place. He'd left it to the other members of staff to hire his replacement nurse. If he'd done the job himself, he'd have known exactly who he was dealing with last night and vice versa.

'I'm Daniel Grant.' He introduced himself to the curvy brunette—a little too late, as it turned out.

'Eloise Carter. Can we talk about last night?' She got straight to the point, which he appreciated. After the misunderstanding last night, she'd left in such a hurry there hadn't been much opportunity to apologise.

'Of course.' He led her into his office and could see her cringe at the memory of everything she'd shared with him in that room only a matter of hours ago.

'I take it Gary got you sorted out last night?'

'Thank you for the tea and arranging help to recover my car.'

They stumbled over each other's words, then exchanged embarrassed grins. It was going to be difficult working together if it continued to be so toe-curling and awkward between them.

'Gary was a great help, thanks.'

Daniel had wondered if she'd got home okay, but she'd fled the building the minute the local farmer had arrived with his tractor to help tow her car. Daniel had considered phoning her, certain that he would've found her contact number on her job application form if he'd bothered to look at it. In the end, he'd thought it best to give Eloise some space from him to recover.

'And is everything okay with the house?' Here they were, back to making small talk, but he was reluctant to be the first to confront the elephant in the room.

'Yes. It'll take some work, and I still have to unpack everything, but I'll get there eventually.'

'Good. Good.' He nodded, and spent a long time staring down at his shoes.

'Look, I know last night wasn't your fault…'

'A misunderstanding.'

'Yes, well, it's all very embarrassing for me to have poured my heart out to you. Especially given that I'm going to be working for you for the foreseeable future.' She was clutching her bag and coat so tightly, he worried she might run out again and cancel the whole job contract.

'All forgotten, and I promise I won't say a word to anyone.' That was all he could do. They couldn't change what had happened and he couldn't unhear her troubles. Nor, he supposed, would he forget everything she'd confided in him, but he could assure her it wouldn't go any further.

'Thank you. It would be great if we could just put it behind us.'

'Done,' he said, with a clap of his hands. He hoped that they could start over as work colleagues, with Eloise as his new employee he knew nothing about. Except deep down he knew it was going to be impossible to forget the strength it must have taken this incredible woman to pick herself up and move here on her own to start again. Goodness knew he hadn't managed to do it in five years.

* * *

'Ah, the rest of the team are here. Let me make the introductions.' Daniel seemed as relieved as she was to hear the sound of other people in the building, opening the door to usher them both back out into the public domain.

It hadn't been easy, coming in to face him this morning, and sleep last night had proved impossible. She didn't think she'd ever get over the humiliation, and had spent most of the time since her outburst recounting every very personal detail she'd shared with her new boss. The best she could hope for was that they'd both pretend it had never happened, and that he wouldn't think it was some amusing anecdote he could trot out at parties. The disaster which was her personal life was not for dinner conversation, and something she wouldn't have shared at all if she hadn't been convinced he was a doctor.

'Hi.' She waved nervously at the two young blondes who'd walked in together.

'This is Debs and Brooke, and this is Eloise, our new recruit.' Daniel made the introductions, though they weren't strictly necessary, since they were the ones who'd done the interview process with her over numerous video calls.

'Hello again.' Debbie and Brooke stepped forward to shake her hand.

Eloise was able to relax a little, seeing some familiar faces. They'd hit it off immediately when they'd spoken before, despite the twenty-year age gap. However, she couldn't help but think that if Daniel had been more involved in the recruitment process, rather than delegating the responsibility to other members of staff, then they might've avoided her complete humiliation last night.

'It's good to finally meet you in person,' Eloise said, genuinely meaning it.

The enthusiasm and camaraderie which had been apparent from these two had been enough to convince her once and for all to pack up what was left of her life and move here. Again, if Daniel had done the interview himself, the outcome might have been very different.

'I'll let you get acquainted and show Eloise around while I get ready for the clinic.' Daniel didn't bother waiting around for anyone to agree. It was clear who was boss around here. It helped her breathe a little easier when he disappeared back into his office, out of sight.

'You know, he's not what I expected…' Eloise ruminated aloud, watching him walk away. From the way they'd spoken about the surgery owner, she'd imagined him to be some old man, out of touch and relying heavily on the youth of his staff. Although there was an age difference, Daniel was not some past-it old fogey—far from it.

'Pay no mind to him. Daniel prefers the company of animals to people.' Debbie had clearly misunderstood her comment, thinking she was in some way disappointed.

Concerned was the word she'd be most likely to use. She'd been expecting someone on the brink of retirement, perhaps leaving the running of the place to the youngsters, not a handsome older, very capable man. She realised she'd been using the word handsome a lot to describe Daniel in her head, and that alone was a warning sign. Uprooting and coming here hadn't been about re-discovering an interest in the opposite sex, especially in another troubled divorcee, and her boss. Hopefully it was a passing phase and she'd get over the fact he was good-looking soon enough.

'What about his family?' she found herself asking, despite telling herself his personal life was none of her business. It would help her better understand the man she was working with, she told herself. And, since she'd spilled her guts about her background, it seemed only fair she should know something about him too. Perhaps then she wouldn't feel quite so much as if she was starting here on the back foot.

'He doesn't have any. At least, none of his own, and I've never known of any other relatives. Other than Anne, of course.' Debbie dropped her head as though it was a subject she shouldn't be talking about, which only increased Eloise's curiosity.

'Anne… Is that his wife?'

Both women nodded solemnly.

'I never knew her,' the receptionist was quick to point out.

'And I started after she'd gone,' Debbie added.

'Gone?' There was obviously some sort of scandal surrounding Mrs Carter that she wasn't aware of, and Eloise felt she had a right to know if her new boss was somehow to blame for his wife's departure. She didn't want to work with someone who might have a temper, or other issues which had caused his wife to leave him. This was supposed to be a slower pace of life for her here, and she didn't need to get involved in any messy domestic situations. She'd had enough of her own to push through lately.

'Anne had brain cancer. Daniel was devastated after she died, obviously. They ran this clinic together. It was their baby, since they hadn't had any children. I don't know what he was like before he lost his wife, but I think he kind of withdrew into himself. He doesn't go out much and work seems to be his life.' Debbie clearly thought a lot of her colleague and seemed genuinely concerned for him.

'That's terrible.' Eloise had to admit, he hadn't given her the impression he was a sad, reclusive widower.

Then again, she'd been good at hiding her pain during the worst part of her life, not wanting her daughters to see it, or give her husband the satisfaction of knowing how much he'd hurt her. So she'd packed it all away inside and plastered on that brave face too—at least, until last night. Something had triggered the floodgates to open and she'd finally expressed all of her frustrations and fears which she'd bottled up all this time. Although it had been epically cringeworthy at the time, perhaps it would prove cathartic in some way, finally to have got it off her chest.

She supposed Daniel still had to deal with his grief and loss in his own way too.

'Yes, but he wouldn't like to think we're gossiping about him, I'm sure. I just thought it would be good for you to know, to try to avoid any misunderstandings.'

Eloise just about managed not to tell Debbie it was too late for that.

'Okay, I'll get your uniform sorted, and Debbie can

give you the quick tour.' The receptionist disappeared out the back and left Eloise with the pretty vet.

'Obviously, this is the waiting room.' Debbie gestured round the bright, spacious room peppered with several chairs and posters of special dog-food and warnings about ticks.

Eloise followed her behind Reception, bypassing the small room which she knew was Daniel's office.

'We have a couple of examination rooms, our own theatre for minor surgeries and our pet hotel for overnight guests.' The whirlwind tour revealed the usual steel tables and medical equipment Eloise was familiar with.

If there had been a few more open doors or lights on last night, she might have seen inside and figured out for herself that Daniel was a vet, not a doctor. Though, perhaps she'd seen what she'd wanted to see. After everything she'd been through, the dam had been sure to burst at some point, and both she and Daniel had simply been unlucky that he'd been the one to witness it.

'I guess I'll pick up everything as I go along, though I'll probably have to get you to walk me through how you do things here.' Every practice had its own procedures, and she didn't want to overstep anywhere. She was probably going to have to work even harder to impress her new boss, now he knew what a disaster she was behind her immaculate CV.

'No problem. We're one big happy family here.' Debbie gave her a wide smile, reminding her why she was here. She liked these people, and the area. It was perfect for her new start, and she was going to have to get over last night's very vocal *faux pas* to make it work. She'd gone through a lot worse than oversharing with her new boss and survived. This was simply a blip.

'I'm looking forward to getting into the swing of things.' Maybe then she could relax.

'It won't take long. We're not exactly swamped. It's not like a big city vet. You'll probably spend more time chatting to the locals about the weather, or the rubbish the tourists have left behind, than treating their pets.'

'Suits me. I'm not cut out for long hours without a break. I'm hoping to wind down a bit at my age.'

Debbie turned and frowned at her. 'You're not old. Why does everyone over forty think they're past it these days?'

'Um, because we're made to feel that way.' If she hadn't already embarrassed herself with one work colleague by spilling the details of her personal life, she might've been tempted to do so now just to prove a point.

Neither Debbie nor Brooke were aware of the exact reasons she'd moved here, other than her daughters had moved out and she was on her own. She supposed 'why are you single again at your age?' wasn't on the list of approved interview questions these days. Though she was sure it wouldn't be long before they'd extracted the details, given that she'd already had the rundown on Daniel's circumstances.

One thing she'd neglected to factor in when moving to a small town was that gossip was the local source of entertainment. Boy, did she have some juicy tales with which to fuel the conversations around here!

'Well, you're not. You're shiny new around these parts and everyone will want to know all about you.'

Debbie confirmed her worst fears, making her shiver. It was bad enough that her boss knew how undesirable she was without the whole town knowing too, though they'd be able to see for themselves without having to strain their eyes too much. Her expanding waistline, hair in need of a wash and blow-dry and her hormonal acne breakouts would tell that story soon enough.

She made a note to unpack her hair straighteners and make-up bag as soon as possible. Today she'd had to make do with the powder compact, lipstick and eyeliner she carried in her bag for emergencies.

'First off, though, tea!' The receptionist handed her a uniform before directing her back towards the small staff room.

'We start every day with a cuppa.' Debbie flicked on the kettle, and Daniel appeared in the doorway the second it boiled.

'Who's turn was it today?' he asked.

'Yours,' the girls chorused, and he swore under his breath.

'Sorry, I forgot. I was out on a call last night and, well, I got distracted...'

He slid a glance at Eloise and she wondered what she was to blame for other than making them both uncomfortable.

'It's just as well we keep emergencies...' The receptionist opened the cupboard and reached in for a plastic tub, which when opened revealed a whole selection of yummy biscuits.

'We take turns buying, but Daniel has a habit of forgetting,' Debbie explained, giving him the side-eye.

He reached into his pocket, pulled out his wallet and produced a five-pound note. 'Here, that should cover me for my next turn too.'

He set it on the counter before helping himself to some chocolate-covered digestives.

'Let me know when it's my turn to contribute,' Eloise insisted, accepting the cup of tea and biscuits offered to her. She had a feeling she was going to like working here, already being made to feel part of the family.

'We'll add you to the rota.' Debbie leaned against the kitchen counter, sipping casually, as though they had all the time in the world.

Eloise was used to a much more frantic pace of work, with a constant stream of pets and emergencies. This was what she needed—time for herself. She had to make herself a priority for once, and this place seemed perfect for that.

'How's the house?' Brooke asked.

'Good, although I've a lot of unpacking to do. I was lucky to get it fully furnished, but now I just have to find everything I brought with me.' She'd realised that this morning when she'd overslept and had had no idea where were her toiletries, kettle or any other morning essentials.

'We could all go over tonight and help you unpack,' Debbie suggested.

'I couldn't ask you to do that.'

'You didn't. Besides, we want to have a good nosy at the house, don't we, Debs? Daniel can put those muscles to work and do the heavy lifting and we could order a wee takeaway.' The receptionist was planning everyone's evening for them, and Eloise couldn't find a way to get out of it when she was being so kind.

'We don't want to steam-roll over Eloise when she's only just got here. She might have plans, or not feel up to having visitors just yet.'

There was something about Daniel's interference which got Eloise's back up, even though he was probably only trying to help. She couldn't help but think her revelation to him about her personal circumstances and health issues might have contributed in some way to his decision to pour cold water on Debbie's idea. Either that, or he was reluctant to spend any time with her outside of work again.

'I was just trying to help.' Debbie sniffed, her nose obviously out of joint at having had her idea shot down.

'I appreciate it. It would be lovely to have some help, and I haven't had time to do a food shop yet, so a takeaway sounds perfect. Only if Daniel wants to, of course.' She batted her eyelashes as she tossed the ball back into his court.

There was a flicker of reticence in his eyes before he responded. 'Sure. Dinner's on me.'

Eloise swallowed hard as she realised she'd just agreed to another night in her boss's company.

CHAPTER THREE

DESPITE THE FACT her new work colleagues were coming to help her sort out the house, Eloise found herself fussing around, trying to make it look as tidy and clean as possible—not an easy feat when everything was piled high in boxes. She had at least managed to locate the dishes and cutlery, unwrapping and washing them ready for use.

Her working day hadn't been too taxing, and she supposed they were breaking her in easy. Everyone had been very kind and patient with her as she got to grips with where everything was kept. She and Daniel hadn't interacted a whole lot unless it was work-related. He'd called for her assistance with a particularly difficult feline patient who'd objected to having its temperature taken, but between them they managed to coax it into co-operating. She'd taken blood samples, helped administer vaccinations and had even cut a pet rabbit's over-long front teeth, all whilst chatting away to the locals and getting to know their patients. Overall, it had been a fun, if tiring, day.

The doorbell rang and her stomach clenched, as though her date had just arrived, which was a silly thought. It was just nerves about opening up her new house to people she hardly knew. Of course, she'd also made sure to locate her favourite jeans, which hugged her ample butt, and her wrap-over black shirt with the red roses on it, which showed off her cleavage. Daniel had seen and heard her at her worst; it was only natural she should want to look nice. It didn't mean any more than that.

'Hi!' She opened the door to the trio, who all appeared to have travelled together.

'Well, give us the tour,' Brooke demanded the minute she set foot inside.

'Give her a minute,' Debbie insisted, following in behind.

Daniel was last in and simply gave her a nod in acknowledgement.

As he walked past she caught a whiff of his peppery aftershave, saw the crisp, ironed crease of his pristine pale-blue shirt and the shine on his shoes. It made her smile. Whilst the other members of the party had donned more appropriate scruffy jeans and ripped sweatshirts, it seemed Eloise and Daniel had both made more of an effort. At least she didn't appear to be the only one who wanted to make a good impression.

'Let me give you the guided tour first, then we can set to work putting the boxes in the right rooms at least.' After getting in so late last night, post-spilling her guts to Daniel, she'd been too physically and emotionally exhausted to do anything other than dump her belongings in the living room and fall into bed. Thank goodness she'd had the foresight when packing at least to label the cardboard boxes before chucking all of her worldly possessions into them.

'It's a good-sized room.' The receptionist spun round, arms wide like a child, to prove the point.

'Yes. I have to admit that's what sold it for me. The patio doors open out onto the decking with a lovely view of the loch.' She'd pictured herself sitting out there in the mornings with a coffee, enjoying the peace and quiet. It would be a world away from the busy main road where their family home had been. Although, that was how she'd been able to afford this place: a city centre two-up, two-down was in a very different price bracket. And there was something to be said for settling down young and having a mortgage paid out before the age of fifty.

Even after her husband had had his share, there had been just enough left for her to buy this place, and she had no intention of moving ever again. It had been traumatic to say the least, having to get rid of a lot of their things and closing the door on the place she'd called home for over two decades.

'Are you going to use the fireplace?' Debbie asked, inspecting the stone centrepiece of the room.

'I hadn't really thought about it. I have central heating, but it might be nice in the winter.' She could quite cosily curl up in here under a blanket with a book and a hot chocolate with no need for anything, or anyone else, in her life.

'You'll need to get someone qualified to make sure it's safe before you open that up.' Daniel was quick to issue the warning and she was touched that he was thinking of her safety—even if it was more likely that he thought she was daft enough accidentally to burn the place down because she hadn't checked to see if the chimney was blocked in any way first.

'Yes, I'll make sure to do that,' she said diplomatically, rather than start an argument over it.

'What do you need us to move first?' Daniel rolled up his sleeves, clearly ready to start, no doubt wanting to get this over with as soon as possible, since he'd been railroaded into it.

So much for the tour.

'I've already started unpacking some of the kitchen things—perhaps you could carry the heavier items in there for me, please.' The kitchen was her domain, and she'd acquired some expensive equipment over the years. Even though she wouldn't have a houseful of hungry teens, such as when her daughters used to bring their friends round, she might do some baking again if the mood took her. She'd prided herself on making good home-cooked food for her family when they were growing up. It had been sad when her daughters had moved out and she'd just been cooking for two.

By the time her marriage had ended, she hadn't had the same urge to make anything from scratch. Processed ready meals and takeaways probably hadn't helped her weight gain, either. However, she was hoping that out here, where access to supermarkets and takeaways was limited, she'd do more cooking. This new lifestyle out here seemed more conducive to exercise too. Hopefully, instead of simply sitting in front of the TV, she'd enjoy long country walks and maybe even some wild swimming.

Daniel certainly appeared to keep active. For a man

of his age, he was clearly looking after himself. She'd seen the muscles flex as he'd rolled up his sleeves, and he certainly wasn't sporting the same rounded belly her ex had seemed to take great pride in at times. 'All bought and paid for,' Sam used to say, jiggling it.

Of course, her body wasn't the same as when they'd married either, but it hadn't seemed to matter to Sam that she'd birthed two children. He couldn't get past the physical changes in her during their thirty years together. Then menopause had arrived, determined to steal what was left of her femininity, and she hadn't felt very sexy.

Somewhere along the way, she supposed they'd both fallen out of love with one another. It had just taken her longer to realise it, accepting comfort and familiarity over passion, or even attraction—something which had become more apparent after the girls had moved out and it had been just the two of them left in the house. Perhaps Sam had been right to make the break and want something more for the rest of his life. Now Eloise just had to find her new place in the world without him.

'We'll just, er, unpack your books and ornaments for in here,' Debbie said when there was no further instruction.

'Sorry. I zoned out there for a moment.' Eloise blinked back into the room in time to see Daniel shifting with ease her heavy, expensive mixer, her other two colleagues staring at her.

'No problem. I'm sure it's been a long couple of days for you.' The receptionist put a reassuring hand on her arm before beginning to unwrap the more fragile items destined for the room.

'That's an understatement. I'm sure I'll be able to relax once I have all of my own things around me. If you could just unpack those onto the book shelves for now, I'll sort them out later. Thanks.'

'Aww, are these your daughters?' Debbie held up a framed photograph of her girls, which made her suddenly very emotional. It hit home that she was essentially starting this new part of her life without them, and that was very hard to do when she'd been there for them every day of their lives. For some reason this felt different from when they'd made the decision to leave home. She'd still been there, ready to welcome them back at a moment's notice, but now it was just her.

'Yeah: Dawn and Alison. They both live abroad now. If you don't mind, I'm just going to take some of these boxes up to the bedroom.' She needed to get out of the room and compose herself before she made a fool of herself in front of Daniel again by blubbing and feeling sorry for herself.

Without waiting and having to explain why she was here without her family, Eloise grabbed the nearest boxes and hurried out of the room. Hopefully, some day it wouldn't hurt as much as it did right now to be here on her own.

'Where's Eloise?' Daniel asked, noticing her absence when he came back into the living room to collect his next assigned armful of his new nurse's belongings.

'She took some stuff upstairs to the bedroom,' Debbie informed him, continuing to line the book shelves with a selection of romcoms and thrillers. Eloise appeared to have an eclectic taste in reading habits.

It was good news for him that everyone was working away. He might have let himself be roped into this but that didn't mean he intended to make a night of it. It shouldn't take him long to shift a few boxes and, if the others wanted to stick around, he was more than happy to pay for a taxi to take them home. This was already more socialising than he usually did and he didn't want to give anyone the impression that this could be a regular thing—especially Eloise, when this was the second night they'd spent in one another's company. He'd already learned more about her personal life than he knew about those of the employees with whom he'd worked for years. He kept a distance from people for a reason.

After losing his mother when he'd been just thirteen, he'd gone into the care system. He barely remembered his father, who'd abandoned them when he'd been just four years old, so his whole adolescence had been spent moving from one foster home to another. He'd been too old for most people who wanted to adopt and create their own little family. No one wanted a troubled teen, so he'd learned to be self-sufficient, not getting too attached, because eventually he'd be separated from anyone he got close to.

It was only Anne who'd persuaded him to share his life with someone else. They'd met at a veterinary conference. Though she'd been older, they'd had the same focus on work, neither of them keen on starting a family. It had seemed logical to set up a practice together, as well as a new life.

They'd been happy living and working here, then Anne had been taken from him too. He'd learned his lesson and, since losing his wife, he'd lived a solitary existence outside of work. Last night Eloise had crashed into that existence, and now here he was, returning the favour. Hopefully after she was moved in he could get back to normality.

'Yeah, she seemed a little upset when we asked about her daughters,' his receptionist added, pointing out the framed photograph of Eloise and her girls.

Eloise was smiling, happier than he'd seen her so far, dwarfed by her tall, dark-haired clones. He could only imagine what it would be like to have a family of his own, but he did know how it felt when a family was no longer there. Okay, so her daughters hadn't passed away, but they weren't currently in her life, and she'd told him last night how sad she was. They had that in common.

Despite his wish to get out of here as soon as possible, he couldn't in good conscience leave her to wallow on her own. He was the only one who knew what she was going through, who understood to some extent how she felt. At the very least he should check on her.

'I'll go and see if she needs a hand,' he told the others, resigned to the fact that he was probably the only person she could talk to about the things that were troubling her…whether he liked it or not.

Eloise took a moment to look at the contents of the boxes she knew were guaranteed to bring a tear to her eye. As well as the family photo albums she couldn't bear to part with, even though her husband was in most of the pics too, were the girls' toys and baby things.

She hoisted the box onto the un-made bed she'd fallen into last night, before she'd even had the chance to unpack the bedclothes, and peeked inside. There were the well-loved teddy bears, and the dolls who were now partially bald and covered in pen marks. There were the school reports and primary school paintings. All of them held memories of a better time, yet somehow it still seemed like only yesterday.

She supposed soon enough there would be grandchildren and other family get-togethers, and eventually she'd feel part of their lives again. Until then, she simply had to keep going on her own. They had their own lives to live now. Dawn lived with her husband in Australia, and Alison worked in Canada—too far away for a hug.

With a sigh, she closed the box back up. The best place for this was probably in the loft out of sight for now— at least until she could look at things without wanting to weep.

'Eloise?' Daniel knocked on the open door.

'Hey.' She did her best to compose herself again. As tempting as it was, falling into Daniel's arms in a sobbing mess wasn't going to do either of them any good. She was probably lucky he hadn't employed her on a trial basis or he'd be looking for ways to get rid of her, if she kept dragging him into her personal affairs. By all accounts he was a private man, and would likely prefer it if she kept her business to herself too.

'Debbie thought you seemed a bit upset. I just wanted

to check that you were all right.' It was a kind gesture, though he was hovering in the doorway, apparently ready to make his escape at any moment. The girls had probably forced him to come up here and see how she was.

'I'm okay. Just missing my daughters, that's all.' She plastered on a smile and got up from the bed, lifting the box with her.

'It'll take a while to get used to. Not that you'll get used to being without them but you learn to adapt.' Although he was trying to comfort her, there was a sadness in the tone of his voice and a faraway look in those deep-brown eyes. He was thinking about his wife.

Eloise's heart went out to him. At least she could still talk to her daughters and see them every now and again, even if it was just on a video call. Daniel truly was on his own, and seemed unprepared to change that. She didn't want to end up the same, shut away completely from the rest of the world. Eloise simply wanted to come to peace with the fact this was her new life now, not become a recluse.

'Thanks. I'm just being silly and reminiscing over their childhood.'

As she shifted the weight of the box in her arms, a small teddy bear fell out at his feet. Daniel picked it up and smiled. It was a strangely sad expression which made her heart catch at the sight of it. 'It must be nice to have so many memories and mementos. I don't have anything like that. Mum died when I was thirteen and no one thought it was important to keep any of my childhood for me.'

'That's terrible. Don't you have anything?' She doubted the insight he was giving her into his background was a privilege he gave willingly to many, and it painted a bleak picture. Although both of her parents had died before she was married, she'd at least had a wonderful childhood and a lifetime of memories to cling onto.

'A few worn photographs, and my mother's sweet tooth.' This time the smile did reach his eyes, and it transformed his face completely, making him look like a little kid. It was the mischievous grin of someone who'd been found too often with his hand in the biscuit tin—something she could definitely relate to.

'I'm glad you have something to remember her by. It's important, even if it hurts to remember sometimes.'

Eloise tried to ignore the cute look, or the feelings she was beginning to have for her new boss, and reminded herself she hadn't even moved in to her new house. The last thing she needed was to jeopardise her job and her place here with an ill-advised, ill-timed and unwanted crush on someone she was going to work very closely with.

Apart from the fact he knew intimate details about her problems, she wasn't exactly in her first flush of youth. Daniel could probably have his pick of anyone around here, and someone still young enough to give him the family he seemed to have missed out on, even if he was ready to move on from the death of his wife. Which, given that it had been five years, and he didn't seem to leave the house unless it was an emergency call out, seemed as likely as him being attracted to her in return.

'Where do you want to put the rest of these?' He lifted another couple of the smaller boxes and followed her out onto the landing.

'I'm just going to put them in the loft for now. I'm not sure what it's like up there yet, but there's supposed to be a ladder for access at least.' She grabbed the pole propped up nearby which had a hook on the end, pulled on the steel ring attached to the trap door on the ceiling and let it fall back. The ladder immediately crashed down, sending her toppling out of the way and boxes flying everywhere.

'Easy,' Daniel said, as she stumbled straight into him.

For a moment they were locked in one another's arms, eye contact unwavering, breath held. It was as though time had somehow stood still and they were frozen in the moment. Eloise's mouth was dry as she gazed up into his heavy-lidded eyes, acutely aware of the strong hands which had caught her by the waist.

'I…er…let me take those up for you.' Daniel broke through the tense silence first, his voice hoarse, suggesting she hadn't imagined something happening between them.

'Be careful. As I said, I haven't been up there yet.'

She didn't argue with him. Ladders and dark places weren't her favourite things in the world, and a little personal space from him might help her to think clearly again, so her brain wouldn't be completely taken up with how long and pretty his dark eyelashes were, or how his lips looked so full and soft. Although, these new thoughts about a member of the opposite sex were a revelation that apparently she wasn't dead from the waist down—even if the discovery was at an inopportune time with the completely wrong person.

Maybe she wouldn't have to spend the rest of her days alone…if there was a middle-aged man somewhere out there desperate enough for company to settle for an overweight, menopausal divorcee.

With the first of the boxes tucked under his arm, Daniel climbed up the ladder, leaving Eloise unashamedly to ogle his backside: 'athletic', she would call it, not chunky or flat, and it filled his trousers nicely…

'Is there a light up here?' he called down after disappearing into the hole in her ceiling.

'They said there was… Try feeling along for a switch or a light pull.' She really ought to have paid more attention, but she'd been so excited by the forest view, the blue skies and the tranquil loch that things such as a light in the attic hadn't seemed important…until now.

Daniel's footsteps sounded above her, on what she hoped was floorboards. It would make storage so much easier if there was a fitted floor. She still had things such as luggage and her Christmas decorations to hide away up there. As she mused over the extra room she might have, there was a crashing sound, followed quickly by a very masculine, expletive-filled yell.

'Daniel? Are you okay?' she called up into the darkness.

'No. I think I've just fallen through your ceiling.' He sounded extremely calm, considering…

Eloise rushed into the bedroom, half-expecting to see

Daniel lying there with debris all around, with a great big hole in the ceiling, but there was nothing. She checked in the spare room too but could see no sign of him there either.

'Daniel? I can't see you.'

'I'm definitely stuck here…' He sounded more ticked off than injured, so she hoped the damage both to him, or her ceiling, wasn't too great.

On impulse, she finally yanked open the doors to the built-in wardrobe in the spare room, only to be greeted with the sight of Daniel's legs hanging in the top of the closet. 'Oh, my goodness!' She hadn't meant to laugh, but really, it was like something out of a farce.

'I'm glad I'm amusing you, but apart from being stuck this is also kind of painful.' Though she couldn't see his face, Eloise could imagine the sardonic look on it.

'I'm coming,' she yelled up through the Daniel-shaped hole in her ceiling.

Despite her own anxiety about the ladder and the dark attic, she bounded up to go and help him. With the light still unlocated for now, she used the torch on her phone to guide her steps over to Daniel, who was wedged in between the joists.

'I'm so sorry,' she said, setting her phone down so she could use both hands to try and dislodge him from the plaster board.

'It's my own fault. I should have known better than to try and walk between the joists where there's nothing to support my weight.'

As Eloise hooked her hands under his arms and pulled,

he pushed down until he finally came unstuck. He fell back on top of Eloise, his body crushing her.

'Daniel…' she croaked.

'Sorry.' He rolled off her, so they were lying side by side, her phone providing the only light.

Both were panting heavily, and for a moment she imagined that they could have been two lovers lying in post-coital bliss. A ridiculous notion, of course, but that was the sort of image this man conjured up in her fevered brain. Working together was going to prove a bigger challenge than simply pretending he didn't know about all the skeletons in her closet. At least she'd managed to keep this one to herself so far.

'Are you okay?' she asked, once she'd recovered from her physical exertion and her wandering thoughts.

He pulled up his shirt to reveal where he'd been battered and bruised during the escapade. 'It stings a little, but I'm sure I'll survive.'

Seeing the red marks on his skin, and the deep grazes he'd sustained while trying to help her, Eloise felt bad.

'I think we need to get you patched up. Everything else can wait.' She held out a hand and helped him to his feet, though he had to stoop under the eaves of the roof so he didn't knock himself out.

They gingerly came back down the ladder, and she led him into the bathroom.

'Sit here and I'll go and see if I can find a first-aid kit.' Eloise directed him to take a seat on the edge of the bath in the small bathroom.

'I'm sure I'll be fine. There's no need to put yourself to any trouble on my account.'

She ignored his protest, sure she'd seen the contents of her bathroom cabinet in a bag somewhere.

'Hey, Eloise, what was all the noise? Is everything all right?' Debbie asked when she walked back into the living room and began to rummage in the boxes again.

'Daniel had a bit of an accident,' she said, not prepared to go into details and give them any ammunition with which to tease him when she was sure he just wanted to forget about it.

'Is he okay?' Brooke piped up from behind the book she was currently reading instead of unpacking alongside Debbie. Not that Eloise could criticise, when they were all doing her a favour.

'A few scrapes. Nothing serious. I'm just looking for my first-aid kit… Ah, got it!' She grabbed her supplies and made a hasty exit before they could quiz her any further.

'Should we order dinner? I'm starving,' the receptionist called after her plaintively.

'Sure. My credit card is in my bag. Just use it to order whatever you want. My treat for helping.' It was the least she could do, and might keep them busy enough until she had Daniel sorted out and save a few of his blushes at least. She reckoned she owed him one when so far he'd kept her secrets for her.

He was still sitting where she'd left him, examining the grazes marring his side.

'The girls are ordering food. I reckoned that would

keep them out of our way until I get you patched up.'
Eloise gave her hands a quick wash then pulled out an
antiseptic wipe to clean the badly grazed skin on his
torso.

Daniel sucked in a breath through his teeth. 'I guess
I should think myself lucky you didn't bring them up to
film my mishap and find myself on one of those "funni-
est home video" shows.'

'Damn it. I could have made myself two hundred and
fifty quid if I'd thought of that,' Eloise joked, ignoring
the flash of his taut torso she was enjoying, and the feel
of his warm skin beneath her fingers.

'Ow. Don't make me laugh. I think I bruised a couple
of ribs on the way down.'

'Poor baby!' She pouted, before breaking out into a
grin.

'I know. I'm being a brave soldier, you know.' Daniel gave her a brief glimpse of the jovial character she
hadn't seen much since first meeting him, and she had
to say she liked it. It was a sign that the man knew how
to have fun, and wasn't as serious as he seemed on outward appearances.

'Just don't expect me to kiss it better,' she said, gently
applying some antiseptic where the skin had been broken.

Only when she looked into his dark eyes, which were
no longer twinkling with amusement, did she realise what
she'd said. Now he was looking at her as though that
was exactly what he wanted her to do and it was a jolt of
lightning she hadn't been expecting, mostly because she
didn't know what to do about it.

Of course she wasn't going to kiss him anywhere, but the fact that he might want her to wasn't something she'd anticipated. It was one thing being attracted to her new boss, but something else if he might actually feel it too. That was something neither of them could really afford to follow up. She stepped back and packed away her first-aid kit, quickly letting the moment dissipate.

'I'll owe you one.' His voice was even deeper than usual and Eloise was afraid to let her thoughts linger on what that 'one' could be.

'I think that makes us even,' she said, shutting down whatever this was happening in the confines of her small bathroom.

'The food's here!' their colleagues chorused from downstairs. She'd never been so relieved for food to take her away from an attractive man.

Daniel forced down several slices of pizza and the low-alcohol beer bought especially for him, regardless that he had no appetite. All he really wanted to do was get home to his safe space, his sanctuary, where he'd be content in his own company and wouldn't think about his new nurse kissing his bare skin...

'Would you like a taste?'

As three pairs of eyes turned to look at him across the living room, it occurred to him that Eloise had spoken and was now waiting for an answer.

'Excuse me?'

'I can see you staring at the Texas barbecue dip I'm

hogging; would you like some?' She held up the little pot and he dipped the last bit of crust in it simply for appearances' sake.

'Thanks.'

It wouldn't do for anyone in this room to realise his head and thoughts had somehow been turned away from his late wife and onto the woman he'd just helped to move in. Although, Anne would've wanted him to move on— she'd always chided him for being so withdrawn from society—it felt like a betrayal even to be attracted to another woman. The two didn't even look alike—Anne a tall, slender blonde compared to the voluptuous woman with chestnut hair currently occupying his thoughts. He clearly didn't have a type, but there was something which he was drawn to. Of course, she was attractive but, more than that, he'd felt an instant connection to her from the moment she'd spilled all her personal problems out to him in his office.

Perhaps it was that recognition of her loneliness that had bonded them together. Though he hadn't admitted it to himself, life without Anne had been rather…quiet. He'd told himself he didn't need anyone else in his life. Anne had been a huge part of his every day and, now she was gone, no one could replace her. He wasn't prepared for anyone to fill that space, only for them to be taken from him again too. However, it was possible that he needed to expand his world beyond his practice.

Anne had been the one who'd thrown dinner parties for friends and colleagues, because they'd had no family to socialise with. It was she who'd accepted invitations to awards ceremonies, or booked the occasional weekend away. Daniel had never cared where he was, as long as he was with her. Once she'd gone, there'd seemed little point in pretending he wanted to be part of anything else. It wasn't long before the invitations had stopped coming, and he'd got used to being on his own again. As though he'd reverted back to that self-sufficient teenager no one had been interested in.

Tonight was the most sociable he'd been in five years, and it had served as a reminder why he didn't venture far from his own door. Making a fool of himself falling through the ceiling aside, he'd let his thoughts drift some-where they shouldn't—to another woman. And not just any woman—his new nurse who, by her own admission, had problems of her own to work through.

Those few moments they'd shared alone, when she'd stumbled into his arms, and when she'd touched him in the bathroom, had wakened something in him. It wasn't just an attraction; he realised how much he'd missed that physical connection. He was sure he'd had moments when he'd brushed against other people in passing, and he shook a lot of hands in the context of his job, but there'd been something more to it when he and Eloise had touched. He'd wanted more, as though it had awak-ened a hunger in him that only she could satisfy. None of which had been the plan when he'd only agreed to move a few boxes for her.

'If it's okay, I'm going to head home.' Daniel broke

through the quiet lull which had descended onto the room once they'd eaten their fill of carbs.

He'd organise a taxi for the others if they weren't ready to leave yet, but he didn't want to stick around in case any more little 'incidents' occurred between Eloise and him. Hopefully, if they kept their relationship strictly on work premises, he wouldn't misinterpret any close contact for anything likely to jeopardise his current peace of mind.

'Me too. Sorry, Eloise, I'm shattered.' Thankfully Debbie also got to her feet, with a yawn, so he didn't look as if he was being the party pooper.

'Maybe we can pick this up at the weekend?' Brooke suggested, though Daniel hoped she was only being polite. The last thing he wanted to do was spend the weekend dodging whatever this was building between Eloise and him.

'No, you've all done plenty. Thank you so much.' She saw them to the door and, though Daniel felt guilty about the empty pizza boxes and cans they'd left behind, he was glad to leave. Glad to go back to his quiet, empty home where he didn't have to worry about anyone else but himself.

Daniel opened the car for the other two to get in, social etiquette requiring he at least showed his appreciation to his host for dinner before he scarpered.

'Thanks for dinner. My turn next time.' To his horror, he found himself offering an invitation to do this again. Worse, he leaned in and kissed her on the cheek, as though his body had been taken over and he had no control of his actions.

He walked back to the car, eyes wide, heart pounding, a small part of him looking forward to doing it all again.

CHAPTER FOUR

'HELLO.'

'Lovely day, isn't it?' Eloise gave a nod in passing to a couple walking hand in hand past the lake in the opposite direction, taking in the view.

The one thing she hadn't counted on when choosing her slice of solitude to live on was how many other people came to visit. For the most part it didn't interfere too much with her day-to-day living, but there was the odd inconsiderate tourist who left their litter at the side of the road, or the bikers who used it as a race track.

At least she lived on the other side of the road from the loch so it wasn't as though she had bus-loads of day-trippers parked in her driveway. It was still a relatively quiet spot compared to where she used to live. Here, she could walk across the road without fear of being run over by an articulated lorry, and breathe in fresh air that wasn't polluted with diesel fumes. There were designated camping areas and laybys further on round the loch which people used.

People liked to come and enjoy an uninterrupted view of the sky without the light pollution of the city, which she had to admit was spectacular. She couldn't be selfish about sharing this place when she was just a blow-in from Glasgow herself. It was a good place to go for long walks to clear the head, especially on her day off after a week of awkward tension between her and Daniel.

The night everyone had helped her move in had been overwhelming in ways she could never have dreamed of. Apart from them being the most people with whom she'd spent time in company since her marriage had split, there had been those intimate moments alone with Daniel—not that they'd done anything other than exchange a couple of intense looks. Okay, so she might have taken more than a passing interest in his body when he'd lifted his shirt for her to tend to his injuries after his mishap, but that was only natural, wasn't it? He was a good-looking man and she'd been curious. And she had not been disappointed...

Eloise gave herself a mental shake, trying to dislodge that particular memory and the feel of his hard body beneath her fingers. Easier said than done when he'd ended the night kissing her on the doorstep. It might've been nothing more than a thankful peck on the cheek for dinner, but the touch of his lips on her skin had been branded there ever since.

She raised her hand and traced the very spot, as she did absent-mindedly when she recalled the event. She thought it had surprised both of them, it had been so out of the blue, and certainly hadn't been mentioned since, along with the offer of dinner. An invitation which she'd lain awake at night veering between wanting to accept, or run away from, should it ever come to fruition. In the end she needn't have worried. It had become clear by the next morning that nothing could've been further from Daniel's mind than spending any more time with her.

He'd been careful since not even to end up alone in the break room with her. That didn't mean he wasn't professional and courteous when they were working together, but somewhere along the way a line had been drawn between them. It wasn't a bad thing, when the feelings she'd begun to have towards a man she hardly knew were confusing and making her new life difficult. This was not what she wanted, or what she'd come here for.

'Should've known it was too good to last.' The couple who'd passed her earlier were now rushing back the way they'd come, pulling the hoods of their rain coats over their heads as they ran towards their car.

Eloise had been so lost in her own thoughts she hadn't noticed the rain, but now she could see it dapple the water in the loch, hear it pitter-patter through the trees, feel it soak her skin and smell that fresh, earthy aroma it brought with it. Instead of rushing away from it, she embraced the downpour as a baptism of her new life here. It was a reminder that she was still alive, even if at times it had felt as though she'd died inside and she'd just kept going for the girls' sake. Slowly, she was beginning to live again.

She was sure this awkwardness around Daniel was simply part of the process of coming back to life. A realisation that she was still a woman, with feelings and needs which had lain dormant for a while due to everything going on in her chaotic life prior to moving. Things would settle down, and she was sure whatever her hormones made her think about her new boss would pass too. For now, she should concentrate on her, and getting her new house into some kind of order.

As Eloise made her way home, the beautiful purple and green hues of the landscape turned a muted grey. A heavy fog began to descend, cloaking her pretty view. She could just about see the road and the glow of car fog-lights ahead.

Suddenly, a deafening thud filled the air, quickly followed by the screech of brakes and an awful canine yelp. Eloise rushed to the side of the road just in time to see the car speed off again into the gloom, leaving the dog it had hit lying in the middle of the road. Making sure there were no other cars coming, she ran over to check on the poor pooch. Even though it was whimpering and in obvious pain, it was trying to lick her face.

'Oh, you're a sweetie, aren't you?' It was covered in dirt and blood, its fur matted and body emaciated, and it was hard to tell what breed it was, but it needed help regardless.

She scooped the dog into her arms, which for the size of it wasn't as heavy as it probably should've been. There was no collar or tags on its neck, and she doubted if they'd find a microchip. The poor thing looked as though it had been living rough for quite a while.

Although it was Sunday, the clinic closed and the staff enjoying their day off, she knew there was one man who'd still be on site. She reckoned Daniel would forgive her for crashing in on him, since this was an emergency, and he was always on call when it came to work.

'Don't worry, we'll get you sorted.' After laying the dog on the back seat of her car, she gave him a gentle stroke and was rewarded with a lick of her hand. Her heart broke for him, and at the same time rage was building up inside her that he'd been left in such a state. Now it was down to Daniel and her to make a difference to him and show that not all humans were capable of such cruelty.

Daniel turned off the shower, certain he heard a noise. He waited, suds still in his hair, listening until he heard it again: a desperate, rapid thumping on his front door. It wasn't unheard of for worried pet owners to turn up at his door out of hours but he couldn't very well greet them like this. He quickly rinsed off and grabbed a towel.

'Daniel? It's Eloise.' She sounded panicked.

After the strained atmosphere between them this week, he knew she wouldn't have come here unless something was seriously wrong. He wrapped the towel around his waist and padded, wet and barefoot, to the front door. The last thing he expected was to see her carrying a bleeding dog in her arms.

'He was hit by a car.' The anguish in her voice was reflected in the worry lines across her forehead.

'Bring him through to the surgery. I'll run and put some clothes on.' He let her into the house and unlocked the adjoining door into the clinic.

As he left, he heard her whispering soothing assurances to the injured animal. She was a great addition to the team, good with animals and their owners. It was only the vet who was having issues with her appointment.

He didn't know what on earth had come over him the other night when he'd kissed her on the cheek and casually thrown out a dinner invitation. It was almost as if his body had been possessed by someone who did that sort of thing all the time—not a grieving widower who'd been hiding away from the world for five years.

Thankfully, neither incident had been mentioned since. They'd both seemingly been resigned to things they would never speak of again, along with what had happened that first night they'd met.

However, it didn't mean he hadn't thought of that doorstep goodbye, and what might've happened in other circumstances—if he wasn't still grieving, so afraid of getting close to someone else. It might be nice to have dinner out with Eloise, like a normal man. Even if there was a possibility she'd be receptive to the idea when she'd obviously been scarred by her past relationship too. The fact that she hadn't even mentioned the matter in passing suggested that she thought it better forgotten too. Though, for a brief moment when he'd seen her on his doorstep, he'd thought it might be a social call, and the thought hadn't been as frightening as he'd have imagined.

'He's not microchipped. I think he's a stray,' Eloise told him when he came into Theatre.

He'd had to dress quickly and his clothes were still clinging to his wet skin. Not ideal conditions to work in, but this was clearly an emergency.

'We'll need to X-ray him and probably open him up

to fix the fracture. I can already see the bone sticking out through the injury sight so I'm going to need to set that.' An open fracture like that was a high risk for infection and could cause complications if not closed and reset properly.

'Even if he's a stray?' It was clear Eloise was already attached to the dog, and her likely concerns about costs were understandable.

'Even if he ends up in the dog home, I'll still do whatever it takes to have him back on his paws.' Daniel gave her a smile to reassure her that this was more than a business to him. He would never turn away an injured animal. It was the one area of his life over which he had any control, where he could make a difference without getting too attached. Although the animals sometimes held a piece of his heart, the best part of his day was seeing them go home happy and healthy. Though he didn't relish the idea of sending a dog to be rehomed, it had a better chance of being adopted if it had been seen and treated by the vet first, without passing on those costs.

They both donned their protective green scrubs. The X-rays showed a fractured femur to the front right leg, and Daniel was keen to operate straight away. Eloise shaved the area which was going to require surgery so Daniel could better see what he was doing.

'They always look so vulnerable, lying there,' Eloise remarked as she monitored the anaesthesia, preparing for surgery. Sometimes anaesthesia was the most dangerous part, depending on the dog's age and health.

Daniel couldn't argue. Head back, tongue lolling out

of the side of its mouth, this little dog was completely at their mercy. At least they weren't going to let him down. By the look of it, the dog hadn't been cared for properly in a long time, and now it had been left for dead. It was Daniel's job to make sure that didn't happen.

'Hopefully, he'll be up and running around soon.' Daniel made the first incision and set to work trying to locate the piece of bone which needed to be put back in place.

'And then what? The dog's home?' Eloise's tone was accusatory, but if he kept every stray animal that came through the doors he could be a local tourist attraction.

'Well, we can put some posters up—see if anyone's missing him or willing to take him in. We'll cross that bridge when we come to it. For now, I just want to make sure our little friend recovers from his trauma.'

'He'll have to stay in for observation for a while, won't he?'

'I expect so.'

'Good. It's about time someone took care of him.' Eloise stroked his paw and proved again what an asset she was to the practice.

Although she was very capable at assisting him here in surgery, it was important that she was empathetic with the pet owners who needed their help. Everyone who came in through the door wanted to be sure that their well-loved fur babies were in good hands, that they were being treated by people who cared for them and thought of them beyond the bill at the end of the treatment.

Eloise was that special kind of person with room in her heart for everyone—human and animal. He was already enjoying working with her. She brought a new element to the place, a bridge between the other staff and him, as well as the patients. He was able to relate to her more than he had to anyone else in five years, even if that was bringing its own challenges.

'Can you hold that in place for me?' he asked Eloise as he prepared to drill into the two bits of bone, reconnecting them with the aid of some metal screws.

'Of course.' With a steady pair of hands, she held the fracture together until he'd finished pinning, then he was able to close up the site and wrap a bandage around the area.

'I'll keep an eye on him through the night just to make sure there's no infection.' There was always a risk post-surgery and, like a lot of the animals which were kept overnight, this dog would have to be monitored closely. High temperature or vomiting would require immediate treatment, so he kept a close watch on any overnight boarders. It wasn't as though he had anything else to do with his time, and it was a routine he and Anne had got used to along the way. It was as though these animals which had passed through had been their own little family, if only for a short while.

'Thanks,' Eloise said absentmindedly, as though he'd personally offered to do her a favour. She'd already bonded with their patient; she was a natural nurturer, which he was sure made her a great mum to her daughters. It was a shame for her that they didn't currently seem to be in her life, and he could only imagine the pain it caused her. They were both alone, but knowing she had family out there that she couldn't be with must hurt too.

'OK, we'll try and bring him round again. Careful, in case he's a bit disoriented.' Sometimes animals lashed out when the anaesthetic wore off, and stray dogs were the most unpredictable. The last thing he wanted was for Eloise to get hurt when she'd likely saved this pooch from dying a horrible death in the middle of the road.

'I think the only danger is that he might lick me to death.' Even as they carried him to one of the crates to settle him in bed for the night, he was nuzzling her. Clearly the infatuation was a two-way deal. Perhaps Eloise was going to be the one who'd end up with a house full of waifs and strays when she had so much love to give.

'He'll probably sleep for most of the night but I'll check in on him periodically to make sure he's all right,' he assured her when it became obvious she didn't want to leave the dog on his own.

Eloise made sure there was water for him and tucked a blanket around him. She probably would have read him a bedtime story if left to her own devices too.

'I think he needs a name.'

'I'm not sure that's a good idea. You don't want to get too attached, Eloise.' Regardless that it was already a lost cause.

'But it doesn't seem right, leaving him here in the dark and not even giving him a name.'

Daniel didn't know what difference it would make but if it kept Eloise happy, and more importantly got her to leave, he was happy to go along with it.

'Dan's a good name.'

She gave him a scathing look. 'No human names; it's weird. And nothing boring like Rex, or Prince.'

'Lucky?'

She gave an exasperated sigh.

'No, hear me out. Not only did he have a lucky escape, but he was lucky you were the one to find him and bring him here.' Regardless of his insistence that neither of them should get too attached, Daniel had already put some thought into the idea too.

'Hmm, I suppose so. What do you think, Lucky? Do you like that?' She put her hand into the cage to give him one last stroke and the dog licked her in approval.

'Lucky it is, then. At least until we find him a permanent home somewhere else.'

The look she gave him was of utter betrayal on his part and he knew that Lucky was going to stick around for some time to come.

CHAPTER FIVE

'MORNING.' ELOISE BREEZED into the clinic and straight in to visit Lucky, as she had done every morning since his arrival.

Daniel no longer seemed surprised to see her this early, always dressed and ready to greet her, unlike the night when she'd first brought the dog to his door. The sight of him clad only with a towel around his waist, body wet, was an image not easily forgotten.

'Do you want some breakfast?' he called through from the annex. It had become almost commonplace now for her to be in his private part of the building before work. He usually had the kettle on for her arrival, and Lucky had somehow managed to help them bypass the awkwardness of being alone. They had something else to focus their attention on.

'I don't want to put you to any trouble.' She insisted every morning that she didn't want to intrude, she was only here to check on their patient, but as usual Daniel dismissed her protest.

'Tea's ready and I've got some toast on anyway. You can bring the mutt in with you, if you want...' His invitation would have been more of a surprise if she hadn't already spotted some dog toys lying around, evidence that he'd been keeping Lucky company outside of his usual working hours. It seemed she wasn't the only one with a soft spot for the dog.

'He's looking good this morning,' she commented as Lucky ran as fast as his bandaged leg would let him, straight from the surgery onto the sofa in the living room. She suspected he'd come to think of the place as his own, right in front of the television.

He'd also had a makeover of some kind. His coat was no longer matted with dirt and blood and was now a shiny golden mane, making him look cared for. Apart from the shaved patches where they'd operated on him, and the bandage on his leg, no one would know the trauma he'd been through.

'I...er...gave him a quick shower. Didn't want him stinking the place out.' Daniel dodged eye contact as he set to work buttering the mountain of toast on the breakfast bar in front of him where they'd taken to having their first cuppa in the morning—the one before the others came to work which no one else knew about.

Eloise grinned. Bathing the dog was something he could easily have tasked one of them to do during working hours. She suspected he was simply enjoying the company, as was she.

'I think he's put on a bit of weight too. He doesn't look as skinny as when he first came in.' Eloise was glad to see it. Ribs shouldn't be visible on a dog this size; it was a clear indication of malnutrition. Goodness knew how long the poor thing had been wandering around out by the loch, with very little to live on. Unlike the city, there wasn't the abundance of rubbish or leftover takeaways for him to rummage in for sustenance.

'That'll be down to the chicken breast you cook for him every day, on top of the meals he's getting.' Daniel pushed the cup of tea and plate of buttered toast towards her, and she sat on one of the high stools at the counter.

'And those have nothing to do with it, I suppose?' Eloise nodded towards the open bag of dog treats sitting on the kitchen worktop.

'Guilty as charged.' Daniel's blush was endearing.

'I suppose he'll be moving on soon.' Breaking off a piece of toast to feed to Lucky, who was patiently waiting at her feet, she broached the subject she'd been dreading.

'I'm afraid so. He can't take up a bed in the clinic indefinitely, but no one has come forward to claim him.'

It wasn't surprising, really, that whoever owned him hadn't admitted to the cruelty he'd obviously suffered, but it did mean that he'd have to be sent to the dog's home, with no guarantee that he'd be adopted. She didn't want to contemplate the alternative.

'You could keep him,' she suggested, since he appeared to have a home here anyway. Daniel seemed to enjoy having him around too.

He shook his head. 'There's a reason I never had a pet here. It wouldn't be fair to leave it alone all day. I get a lot of call outs. What about you? Couldn't you give him a home?'

'I'd love to, but I've got work too. You're right, it wouldn't be fair to keep him locked up all day.' Although, she supposed it wasn't going to be much different for him if he went to the dog's home.

'I guess I have no choice but to contact the dog warden to come and pick him up.' Daniel's heavy sigh, along with the half-eaten toast he pushed to one side, suggested he wasn't looking forward to that happening any more than she was.

'It's a shame when he seems to be thriving here. He's such a lovely guy.' Eloise stroked his soft fur, knowing he'd be great for cuddles when he wasn't so tender. It would be nice to share a sofa with him at night, like having a great big teddy bear to keep her warm. Having a dog in the house might make the place seem a lot less empty, and she wouldn't be talking to the walls the way she was now.

Except there was the problem of what to do with him during the day. It had been the same when the girls were little and they'd begged to have a puppy. She just hadn't had the time to spend at home; she'd always been working. There'd been bills to be paid, after all.

'I think we had a dog when I was little. I don't remember a whole lot, but I think he used to sleep in bed with me.' A half-smile crossed over Daniel's lips as the memory sprang to mind.

'What happened to him?'

'I'm not sure. Maybe my dad took him when he left. I've no one to ask. For all I know, he's nothing more than a figment of my imagination. I would've done anything to have a pet. Probably for that feeling of being loved, and having someone in my life. We weren't allowed any in the foster homes.' It was another sad glimpse at the lonely life he'd had as a teen, apparently with no family or friends to keep him company.

Eloise supposed it explained a lot about the way he interacted with people now. She could see it would be difficult for him at times when conversation with pet owners strayed beyond the realms of animal care. He didn't like to give a lot away about himself, and she knew even her being here in his home was likely a great test of his strength. He'd only agreed to it so that Lucky would benefit from having both of them to look after him.

'It's a wonder you don't have a house full of them now,' she mused. There was plenty of space, and opportunity, for him to have as many pets as he could ever want. She had to admit it was tempting for her to fill the house with replacements in her affections now that she didn't have her family around her to fuss over.

'Why do you think we made it our first rule when Anne and I set up the clinic not to literally bring our work home with us?' He grinned, and she could see he'd been trying hard to keep that particular impulse at bay for a long time too.

'What if…we both take him on?' Eloise couldn't believe she was suggesting this when, until Lucky came on the scene, they'd been trying to keep their relationship strictly professional. However, she couldn't bear to think of their canine companion going back into a world where he wouldn't have special treats or evenings in front of the telly.

Worse, she wouldn't have anything to look forward to

in the mornings. She was referring to seeing Lucky, not having breakfast with Daniel, obviously.

'How's that going to work?' It wasn't an outright 'no', at least. Though neither of them clearly wanted to commit full-time to the responsibility of having a dog, this compromise might be a less intimidating prospect.

'Well, he could come to work with us. I'm sure he wouldn't be any bother. We can take turns walking him on our down time. One of us could take week nights and the other could take weekends,' she suggested with a shrug. It was all the same to her when she didn't have anything of a social life anyway.

'Like shared custody?'

'I guess so. At least until we decide otherwise. Circumstances might change, or one of us might decide we're ready to be a full-term pet owner further down the line.' She could see that full-time owner being her, once she was settled into her house properly, and having a dog might make it feel even more like a home. It was just too soon in her chaotic life to be fair to Lucky when she still had a lot to sort out in her head, as well as her house.

Daniel studied the dog, who was looking at him adoringly, as though deciding whether or not he was worth the risk. It was no wonder he was still single if it took him this long to ponder whether to let a dog into his life on a part-time basis, never mind another partner. Not that Eloise could say anything when she was in exactly the same predicament. A dog wouldn't tire of her, or decide she wasn't worth loving any more. As long as she kept feeding it, at least.

'I suppose we could give him a trial, and if it doesn't work out...' Daniel didn't have to say any more. They both knew what the alternative was, and the thought of abandoning Lucky again sent a chill up her spine. After all, she knew how it felt to be rejected, found wanting and left on the scrap heap. If she could help a creature feel loved again, it would give her a sense of achievement. Even if she wasn't likely to experience that feeling for herself again.

'Best behaviour, buddy,' she warned Lucky with a wagging finger. Then felt guilty when he looked at her with those big, sad eyes. She gave him a cuddle so he knew she wasn't mad at him, though he'd never comprehend just how much she and Daniel were putting on the line to give him a home.

For a man she worried was already disrupting the new life she'd planned for herself here, she'd just made an arrangement which would bring them closer than ever. Hopefully, she could forget those feelings she'd been having for her boss in favour of caring for this little dog who so desperately needed a home.

Eloise wondered if she did just need something to focus her attention on, and she'd latched onto Daniel first. She'd spent her whole life looking after her family; it was only natural there would be a void in her life now she was living on her own. Hopefully, Lucky would fill that hole in her life, now her children were off exploring the world themselves. Then perhaps she'd get over this crush on her new boss and she could find the peace she was looking for.

* * *

'So, what, you're Lucky's parents now?' Debbie was clearly amused by the information, and no wonder when Daniel had spent years denying that he needed the company any time she'd tried to foist an abandoned pup or kitten onto him as though he was some sort of sad case desperately in need of a friend.

'Sort of. We've agreed to take care of him between us, that's all.' He tried to downplay it, even though it was the biggest commitment he'd taken on since he'd lost Anne.

It wasn't just because the stray needed a place to call home; goodness knew his heart strings had been tugged by many similar sob stories over the years and he'd managed to remain resolute. He didn't think it was even because he was now used to having a TV buddy in the evenings to share snacks with and watch football. No, a big deciding factor was Eloise. He could see how much the dog meant to her, and how torn she was about potentially having to say goodbye.

After everything she'd been through, he reckoned she could do with something nice happening to her for a change. Yes, initially it was going to mean being in each other's lives more than he'd been prepared for, but he hoped ultimately that Lucky would prove a distraction for both of them from the loneliness which was obviously drawing them together.

A pet was just something else for him to love and lose. He'd seen the devastation the death of his patients caused their owners. It could be like losing part of the family. That was the primary reason he hadn't been able to bring himself even to commit to a four-legged companion in the wake of Anne's death. His hope was that Eloise would eventually take over sole ownership once she was ready. She was the one who wasn't used to being alone, not him.

'It'll do you good to open up and share your life again,' Debbie said, casually sorting through her files on the reception desk, but Daniel cold hear the implication there.

'It's just a dog— a stray. For all we know, the owner will turn up next week looking for him.' He purposely focused on Lucky, rather than the fact she was alluding to Eloise, not wanting to fuel any workplace gossip.

'Uh-huh. And if they don't?'

'Then Eloise and I will continue to look after the dog the way we have been doing. It's no big deal. We both have a lot of spare time on our hands and it seemed logical to offer assistance, rather than see him go to a rescue centre.' Sometimes he wished their little country practice had a bigger clientele so he didn't have to stand around discussing his personal life in between patients.

'Where is he now? I haven't seen him around this morning.'

'Eloise took him out for a walk whilst it's quiet. She'll be back soon, once she's settled him back in the house.' Despite Lucky's injury, it was necessary to take him out for restricted, slow walks to help him recover. They'd agreed to take turns, but Daniel would likely have the heavier workload during the day. At least it meant in any down time they had would most likely be spent apart and he could stop worrying about being in close contact with her all day, every day.

'She has a key to your house?' Debbie's eyes couldn't have been any wider than if he'd told her they'd eloped to Las Vegas over the weekend and got married.

'For the dog,' he reiterated with a scowl.

'For the dog,' she repeated with an annoying grin.

Daniel grabbed up the file for his next patient.

'Pinky Patterson,' he called to the one elderly lady sitting in the waiting room, with a shivering chihuahua in her handbag, ignoring Debbie's sniggering behind him.

He didn't mention Debbie's comments to Eloise when she returned. It would only annoy her. This arrangement was between them, nobody else's business, and he would've told his colleague that if he hadn't thought it would pique her interest in their deal with the dog even more. It was better just to let the matter drop than make a bigger fuss.

'Lucky's doing really well. He was obviously house trained wherever he started out, and he's walking to heel. Now we just have to get him to stop him trying to jump on people.' Eloise was flicking through the photos she'd taken of him on the short walk, like a proud parent.

'He might need some obedience classes once he's healed.' Daniel stopped short of volunteering to take him personally. That would be a step too far into commitment.

'Aww, it's not his fault. He's just desperate to be loved. It's his version of a hug.'

There was no doubt he was a loving dog, but not everyone would appreciate his attention at full force.

'Well, we can't run the risk of him knocking anyone over in his enthusiasm to say hello. I'm sure we have some details of local classes somewhere.' Daniel began rifling through the contents of the reception desk, Brooke being on her lunch break.

'Help me. Someone please help.' A young woman suddenly burst in through the surgery doors carrying a clearly distressed ginger cat in her arms, a trail of blood dripping onto the floor in their wake.

'Come on through.' Daniel opened the door to let her straight into the operating theatre, so he could have a good look at what was going on, with Eloise following behind.

'What happened?' she asked the woman gently, taking the cat from her arms to put him on the examination table.

'It was a dog, off the lead; it attacked him in the front garden. Marmalade was just lying enjoying the sun, and the next thing this devil dog was shaking him like a rag doll in its mouth. I had to fight him off myself until the owner eventually turned up and took him home. Not even a word of apology.' The woman was shaking, her arms covered in scrapes and grazes, clearly in shock.

'Well, he's in the best hands now. Why don't I get you settled with a nice cup of sweet tea and Daniel will check him over?' Eloise took her by the arm and led the woman out of the room. He knew she'd come back to assist him once she'd calmed down Mrs Gillies, as much a help to the concerned pet owners as she was to the animals, and to him.

The injured cat was uncharacteristically subdued and, though it made it easier for him to do an examination on his own, it was a clear sign that there was something seriously wrong. Cats in general weren't known for co-operating, and he'd suffered many a deep scratch in the line of duty. He managed to clean away some of the blood one-handed, whilst searching for the wound site. Unfortunately, he discovered several, deep and extensive, meaning there could be muscle or nerve damage as well as the possibility of infection.

'I hope you don't mind, but I've tucked her up in your office for now with a blanket and a cup of tea. I've asked Brooke to keep an eye on her until we're done here.' Eloise washed her hands and donned a plastic apron before joining him, holding their patient in place so he could do a thorough examination.

'That's great. Thank you. I think we can suture these more superficial wounds, but I'm worried there's some internal damage. We might need to open him up.' It was risky for an animal this age to be put under anaesthetic and he would have to get Mrs Gillies' consent before he did that.

'Shall I give him some pain meds?' Eloise was already preparing with the vial and needle, always thinking ahead.

'Yes, please.' He let her do that first, then set to the task of closing up some of the puncture wounds caused by the dog bites.

Even when the cat was sedated, Eloise was stroking it, murmuring words of comfort. She worked differently from Anne and the veterinary nurses he'd employed in the past. This was obviously more than a job to her: she cared. Not that this was a profession a person could be in if they didn't have that empathy with the animals they treated, but Eloise took it to a different level, treating every pet with the same kindness and respect that was normally reserved for human patients.

He imagined the problem with having a heart that big was how painful it was when it was broken. She didn't deserve what had happened to her, and he hoped she found some peace here. As long as it didn't interfere with his.

'Mrs Gillies should probably report the incident to the police. Once we're finished here, I'll have a chat with her, make sure she's okay to do that.' Eloise was noticeably still worried about the owner, as well as her cat.

'Good idea. If a dog capable of that sort of attack is on the loose, there's always a chance it could hurt something, or someone, else.' Although the chances of finding the dog responsible or its owner were slim, it would still be advisable to report the incident in case it happened again.

'This sort of thing happened all the time in the city. I don't know why people take on dogs if they're not prepared to put the hard work in to train and look after them properly.' Eloise didn't talk much about her life in Glasgow, at least not since that first night when she'd mistaken him for a GP. It made Daniel curious about why she'd given that life up to move here on her own.

For him, it had been a compromise. Anne had wanted to open a practice, but he hadn't wanted to do so in a well-populated area. Although he'd grown up in and around Ayr town centre, he much preferred the quiet country life: less people, traffic and noise, as well as the space he needed for himself.

Growing up in care had been claustrophobic at times. Sharing rooms with others had made it difficult to have any personal space, regardless that he still felt emotionally isolated from those around him. A constant stream of house mates—different faces, each with their own issues and demons—hadn't provided him with any sense of stability or belonging. Opening up, showing any vulnerability, would only have made him prey for those who sought to exploit anyone who showed weakness. He'd seen it for himself: those who'd been abused in their own lives going on to repeat the pattern and become the abusers themselves, taking advantage of anyone they deemed inferior, using fists and words to pummel their victims into submission.

So he'd kept himself to himself. He'd put his head down and concentrated on his studies so he could break free of the system and make a life for himself. Except it had been difficult ever to escape that protective shell he'd wrapped around himself. Anne had been the only one to coax him out of it every now and then to join the real world. Although, somehow, Eloise had already managed to get him to agree to take on a pet…

'It must be a big change to come here. In general, I mean. What made you decide on this place?' He understood that need for change, to start again, but it didn't explain why she'd specifically come to this town. For him, it wasn't too far from the place he'd known his entire life, yet offered him the tranquillity he craved. Eloise was used to the bustling city, a house full of family, and this didn't seem the obvious place to start over. If anything, she would feel the loneliness more. He should know.

A soft smile lit up her face. 'I used to come here with my parents when I was little. We had some great camping holidays at Loch Bruce.'

'Ah, the old rose-tinted spectacles...' It was easy to look back and think only of the good times. He was probably guilty of doing that where his marriage to Anne was concerned, skipping over the difficult parts to hold onto the good stuff, lest those memories of lost loved ones be tainted in any way.

'Perhaps, but I needed something positive to cling onto. There were too many bad memories for me in the city. I tried to carry on, living in the same area, doing the same job, but I was unhappy. This is where I remember being happiest.'

Daniel met her sad eyes, recognising that longing to go back, but knowing deep down it could never happen. 'I hope you find the contentment you're looking for.'

'So far, so good. I think Lucky will help keep me from wallowing too much in my own misery.' At least now there was a ghost of a smile on her face, and Daniel knew he'd made the right decision concerning the dog, regardless that he'd had second thoughts from time to time.

'He's certainly a distraction.' Daniel chuckled. His daily schedule had changed dramatically simply trying to keep him fed, entertained and keep the tumbleweeds of dog hair at bay.

'If it's okay, I'll collect him and his things when we're done here.' It was clear she was looking forward to having him to herself over the weekend. Their arrangement was very much like a divorced couple sharing custody of a child, only without any bad feeling or history.

'Of course.' Though Daniel had a feeling it was going to be a quiet weekend for him without his new charge around the house.

CHAPTER SIX

ONCE THEY'D FINISHED the surgery on Marmalade, they informed Mrs Gillies they'd be keeping him in overnight for observation. Eloise made sure she had someone to come and collect her after the shock of the attack, then they were able to lock up for the night.

'We'll see you two tomorrow,' Brooke said, looking pointedly at Eloise and Daniel.

Eloise felt herself blush, even though she'd done nothing wrong, and saw the dark look on Daniel's face at the suggestion there was anything going on between them. Thankfully Debbie appeared, waving a leaflet in Daniel's face to break the tension in the air.

'Don't forget the fete at the village hall tomorrow afternoon, either.'

'I haven't said for definite I'm going. I have a clinic to run.' Daniel snatched the piece of paper from her hand.

'What's this?' Eloise tried to see what the fuss was about.

'It's just a fair in the village. They do it every year. There are stalls and competitions, and Daniel has been asked to judge the pet show.' Debbie made it apparent she was delighted at the idea with her wide smile in contrast to Daniel's pursed lips.

'No. The clinic has been asked if a representative will assist. That doesn't have to be me,' he insisted.

'You're the owner and a long-term resident. It's you that they want. I can mind the clinic for a few hours.' Debbie folded her arms, preparing for battle, and Eloise imagined this was a scenario which played out frequently, both of Daniel's colleagues trying to convince him to step out into the real world every now and then.

'I don't really want to spend my afternoon drinking tea, eating home-made cake and watching pups on parade.'

'No? Sounds like my idea of heaven,' Eloise teased, wondering why he was so against it. The community was reaching out to him, keen for him to be a part of the day. If he wasn't careful, he'd become the feared local hermit instead.

'You go, then,' he said petulantly.

'Maybe I will,' she spat back. Then common sense kicked in. 'Except, no one knows who I am.'

'You could go with him, Eloise. It would be a good way for the locals to get to know you, and take some of the attention from Daniel.' It was Debbie who came up with a compromise which didn't sound like too much of a stretch for either of them.

Eloise looked over at Daniel, who began to move towards the door, ushering them all before him.

'I'll think about it,' he said, which proved sufficient to satisfy Debbie for now.

She and the receptionist waved before getting into their cars and driving off, leaving Daniel and Eloise alone. It was the first time they'd been truly on their own since that moment at her house, without their colleagues, clients or Lucky to provide a buffer. Even now, as he locked up the clinic and led her round to the house, there was a tension in the air, an anticipation that was neither justified nor wanted when she was simply holding up her end of the agreement.

'Hello, gorgeous.' Eloise was equally as thrilled to see Lucky as he was to see her, though her backside was not wiggling with quite the same enthusiasm. When she looked at him closer, however, he was not the same dog she'd left here earlier after his walk. 'Oh, Lucky. What have you done?'

'What's wrong?' Her concern drew Daniel's attention and he immediately came to her side.

'His face is all swollen.' She pointed out Lucky's muzzle, which had ballooned in size, so he looked as though he were a reflection in a funhouse mirror. It might've been comical if it didn't suggest something had happened to him.

Daniel knelt on the floor beside her to examine the dog, close enough that she could almost feel his body heat through her uniform.

'It looks like an allergic reaction to something. He didn't eat anything when you were out on your walk earlier?'

'No. He was fine when I left him. I gave him some water and left the window open so he could get some air.'

She hated to think she was in some way responsible for whatever had happened to him, failing at the first hurdle as a pet owner.

'I think it's a bee sting. I see this all the time. The numpty has probably tried to eat one and got stung for his trouble. He doesn't seem to be struggling to breathe but we should take him through and give him some antihistamines.'

If there was one thing to be said about owning a pet, it was that there was never a dull moment. Certainly there was no time to sit around moping, when her thoughts were taken up with his wellbeing as much as any of her children.

The trio traipsed back into the surgery and Lucky, who looked very sorry for himself, sat quietly whilst Daniel took out a pair of tweezers to remove what was left of the stinger in his muzzle. Eloise held a cold compress to the area, trying to reduce some of the swelling.

'I think he's going to need close observation to make sure the antihistamines are doing the job. There's always a possibility of a delayed allergic reaction. Do you want me to keep him here?'

'I suppose it's for the best, but I was looking forward to having him round.' It was silly, especially in the circumstances, but she'd been longing to curl up on the sofa with the dog and a good book tonight. Just having that company made her feel safer, more comfortable, and less as though she was alone in the world.

Daniel paused, seemingly deep in thought. 'You could stay here.'

'In the clinic?' As much as she would miss having Lucky, she wasn't prepared to give up her comfortable bed for a night on the floor.

'At my house, silly.'

'Oh.'

It was a proposition she hadn't seen coming, which made her heart flip and her stomach clench. A night with Daniel was something which both appealed and terrified at the same time. The prospect would satisfy her curiosity, and more, for the man about whom she'd been having inappropriate thoughts lately.

However, she'd only ever been with her ex, and her body was entirely different from the one she'd had when they'd first met. If it had been enough to disgust a partner of over three decades, it wasn't likely to impress a new man in her life.

Daniel cleared his throat with a cough. 'I mean, I have a spare room you can stay in.'

'Of course. I knew what you meant.' She forced a nervous laugh so he wouldn't think she'd been seriously contemplating sharing his bed with him—something which apparently hadn't even crossed his mind until now.

'I just thought it might put your mind at rest. I can make us something to eat if you want to go and pack an overnight bag or something.'

Now Eloise knew he had no romantic notions towards her at all, or he wouldn't be so blasé about the matter. She knew what a big deal it would be for him to have a woman spend the night with him when he'd apparently shut himself off from the world since his wife's death. He obviously didn't think about her in any way other than as a colleague, or Lucky's co-owner. She was the one who had to get her head round the nature of their relationship and stop reading things into it that weren't there.

'I might do that. I won't be long.' Perhaps a night establishing that this was a platonic work situation would help her to get over this attraction she felt towards him. Besides, she wanted to be here for Lucky. She wouldn't rest tonight, worrying about him, worrying she might lose him before she'd even had a chance to be a dog mum.

And dinner together would just be sustenance. There was absolutely nothing to read into the fact he was cooking her a meal. And no reason to share that information with their other colleagues.

Lucky was stretched out on the bed Daniel had just made up for his overnight guest. He didn't have the heart to make him get off, and he didn't think Eloise would object. Chances were she'd spend the night with the dog cuddled up next to her anyway. She was clearly concerned about him and he could tell she'd been reluctant to leave without him. That was the only reason Daniel had made the suggestion for her to spend the night. There was no more to it than that.

As for dinner, they both had to eat, and he had food in the fridge to use up anyway. It was no big deal, even if he'd been vacuuming, dusting, and doing everything to make this room which hadn't been used in five years, comfortable for her stay in.

He and Anne had never really used it for anything even

though it had been kitted out as a second bedroom. He supposed anyone else would've used it as a nursery, but since they hadn't wanted children it had never been an option. Anne had used the wardrobes to hold her overspill of clothes from their bedroom, but even they'd long ago been donated o charitable organisations. So he'd had no reason to come into this room until now, though it wasn't likely to be a regular occurrence.

'Daniel?'

He heard Eloise call from the hallway, having left the front door on the latch so she could let herself in.

'I'm just getting your room ready. Come on down.' He finished plumping the pillows, glad he'd still held onto the unopened bedding which had been in the wardrobe, intended for use in this room. It might make it seem as though he had guests over all the time, so this wasn't really a momentous occasion, even though he was already opening up parts of his life to Eloise which had been closed for a long time. He blamed the dog.

'You didn't have to go to any trouble for me.' Eloise arrived at the bedroom door, overnight bag in hand.

'It's no trouble. I think Lucky's claimed it as his room, though.' He directed her attention to the slightly less swollen dog who was now sprawled sideways across the double bed.

'I'm sure there's room enough for both of us.' Eloise plonked her things on the floor and took off her jacket to hang it on the back of the bedroom door.

Daniel was trying not to think about the fact she'd changed out of her uniform and looked much more relaxed in her jeans and loose white silk blouse. Of course she would've wanted to get out of her work clothes as soon as possible. However, it was a reminder to him that this arrangement was outside of working hours, venturing into an altogether different territory—in his spare room of all places.

'Dinner should be ready if you want to come when you're settled.' He rushed out, not bothering to wait for her, keen to be somewhere less confined.

'What are we having?' Her voice sounded behind him as she followed him down the hallway to the kitchen.

'Nothing fancy. Just a lasagne.' Usually a whole lasagne would last him some time. Most meals he batch-cooked and froze to use at a later date. It saved him from having to shop in town every week, with supermarket deliveries not as readily available out in the countryside. At the same time, it was one step up from living off microwave meals for one, which he'd got sick of pretty quickly after Anne's death. Cooking and freezing had become part of his routine as a widower. Tonight he was sharing his food with someone for the first time in recent memory, or someone other than Lucky.

'It's more than I've managed to cook since moving here. I've been living off toasted sandwiches and instant noodles.' Without waiting for instruction, Eloise began opening the cupboards and drawers, setting their places for dinner at the table. It was as if none of this was out of the ordinary at all for either of them.

'It's better to get into a routine when it comes to cooking, before those bad eating habits are here to stay. I should know. When Anne died, I didn't see the point in cooking just for one. Sandwiches and toast were my staple for some time. I was only eating for fuel, and took no pleasure in it.'

'I wish I could say the same,' Eloise mumbled, plating up the salad he passed to her.

'You know what I mean. Grief steals away any happiness in your life. I'm just saying, don't end up like me. You still have a life to live.'

'And you don't?' Eloise looked at him with such pity in her eyes, he had to turn away.

'I had my life with Anne. I was happy. Now she's gone, and I simply have to carry on without her.' He carefully took the tray of lasagne out of the oven and cut two steaming portions, leaving the rest to cool so he could freeze it later.

'Don't you think she'd want you to be happy? I'm sure she didn't mean for you to lock yourself away from the world for ever.'

Daniel gritted his teeth as he poured them each a glass of wine to accompany their meal. This wasn't the conversation he'd expected to have over dinner. It was deeply personal and uncomfortable. Eloise was making him look at his existence through different eyes and he wasn't sure he liked what he saw.

'I've got the practice; that's all I need.'

'Did you and Anne never think about having a family?'

He shook his head. At least on that matter he could confidently defend himself. Neither he nor Anne had seen the point of bringing more lives into the world if they couldn't commit to them one hundred percent. For them, work had come first. It had been their vocation and their security. Nothing was more important than that to them. Even though Anne had grown up in a loving home with both parents, it had been a struggle for her family financially. Stability had been just as important to her as it had to Daniel—part of the reason her illness had thrown them both into turmoil. That hadn't been in their plans for their life together.

'No. We were always focused on work, and putting all of our energy into the practice. It wouldn't have been fair to have children and not give them the love and attention they deserved.' He sat down at the table with his dinner, hoping that the meal would signal the end of this particular conversation.

Unfortunately, it didn't put Eloise off. She simply carried on in between mouthfuls and compliments on his cooking prowess.

'At least you were both on the same page. It would've been worse if perhaps you'd wanted kids and never got that opportunity. Not that either of you could ever imagine what was going to happen...' Eloise seemed to backtrack, as though she was worried she'd offended him in some way, but Daniel understood what she was getting at.

Anne's passing had left him alone in the world, which was a tragedy in itself, but he supposed if he'd wanted to be a father, and that role had been taken from him along with his wife, it would've been a double tragedy. It was bad enough being left to try and look after himself. He didn't think he would've managed it if he'd had to raise their children on his own. It would've meant more loved ones to lose further down the line too, as witnessed by Eloise's current status.

'No, but at least I'm the only one left behind.' It would've been difficult to deal with other's grief as well as his own, forced to put on a mask and carry on as though his life hadn't been completely destroyed. At least he'd been able to be his authentic self, grieving as long as he had.

'It's hard, isn't it, watching everyone carry on around you when you feel as though your life has just stopped?' Eloise was the only one he'd met who seemed to understand that. Even though her family were simply relocated elsewhere, she was grieving for the life she'd had, and lost, nonetheless.

'It can't have been easy for you. Do your daughters visit much?'

'They're very good. They call me most days to make sure I'm all right, but they have their own lives to live and adventures to enjoy. I'm happy they're doing so well for themselves and are confident enough to go out and see something of the world. I don't want them to waste their time worrying about me. I've lived my life, done the things I'd wanted to do—raised my family and had a lovely career.'

'You make it sound as though your life is over, Eloise.'

'According to everyone else, it is. My husband doesn't want me, my daughters don't need me and the rest of the world hardly knows I exist. It's not empty-nest syndrome

I have. It's more like empty life. I don't seem to have a place here any more.'

'You have a place here. We want you. We need you. I'd like to think you've found somewhere here where you can start over again. You still have time.' It wasn't until he said it that Daniel realised he meant every word. He couldn't, or didn't want to, imagine Eloise moving on. She'd already become such a big part of the place, of his life, that it would seem like a huge loss if she was to leave.

It was a startling revelation about someone he'd only really known for a few weeks. If anything, he should be pleased if she suddenly decided that she wanted to move back to the city, or be closer to her daughters. Not having Eloise around would certainly make his life easier. He could return to his days and nights in which he didn't think about her. Then again, he might be lonelier than ever if she suddenly disappeared out of his life as quickly as she'd arrived in it.

'As do you.' She finished her meal and set the cutlery to one side of her plate. 'You could still bag yourself a young wife and start a family. Unlike women, men never appear to be too old to do that.'

The slight tinge of bitterness in her voice was understandable, because she was right—rock stars could go on making babies into their seventies or eighties, their wives decades younger and immeasurably prettier than their male counterpart. Not so much the other way round. For those superficial men who wanted trophy wives and families, a woman past a certain age held no appeal; once she was past child-bearing age she was of no apparent use.

But Daniel liked to think he had more substance than that. To him, a woman, or any human being, was about more than their appearance or what they could do for him. It would take a lot for anyone to live up to Anne, who'd given him a life he never thought he'd have: a house, a home, a business of his own and, more importantly, love. He would happily have spent the rest of his days with his wife, getting old and wrinkly together.

'Like I said, that's not something I'm interested in. You know, when Anne was first diagnosed, one of the first things that people said to us was how it could affect our marriage.' Like most of those afternoons spent in hospital, it wasn't one of the happier memories he had of his time with Anne, but nonetheless an important one.

'I can understand the strain it would put on a relationship. It only took something as inevitable as menopause to end mine.'

'I couldn't believe it at the time. Couldn't understand why they were telling Anne she should prepare herself for facing her treatment alone, and make arrangements for alternative support. It was insulting to me, who'd planned to be there for her every step of the way—though apparently there's an appallingly high number of men who don't stick around when their partners are diagnosed with cancer.'

Once he'd calmed down after the initial sting of what they were saying, he'd realised they were trying to prepare Anne if she had to go through chemo and surgery without him. He couldn't imagine being the sort of spineless human who ran at the first sign of trouble. As far as he'd been concerned, marriage had been for life, till death parted them.

'That's terrible. It was bad enough knowing my husband didn't care enough to see me through a few years of hot flushes and haywire hormones. I can't imagine facing difficult hospital treatment, and such an uncertain future, with someone who couldn't support me. Especially someone I've been with for a long time. Someone I've shared more than half of my life with.'

The sudden passion in her voice and pain in her eyes made him think that Eloise wasn't talking hypothetically any more. Although her circumstances were different from Anne's and his, the betrayal must've felt huge when her husband hadn't loved her enough to stick around when she'd already been feeling so low. He was the sort of man they'd been describing when they'd warned Anne to prepare for the worst.

'Honestly, it never occurred to me. I thought they were making it up when they said a high percentage of men left their wives during cancer treatment, going on to set up a new life with someone else. But apparently there are plenty who can't cope with the idea of being alone, so they plan ahead in the worst possible way.'

'But not you.' Eloise's face softened again, but he didn't want her to think he was trying to appear as some sort of martyr for sticking by his wife when she'd been sick.

'I loved her, and I never had any intention of leaving her, even when we knew she was terminal. But I wasn't afraid of being on my own either. My mother died when

I was thirteen, and I was in care for most of my adolescence. I learned during those teen years not to get close to anyone. Anne was the exception. She showed me that life could be better by sharing it. It just made it all the harder when she was no longer in it.'

That pain, never far from the surface, pierced his heart deeper as he remembered the life they'd once had. One in which they'd woken up together, worked together, talked, made love and done all the other things a couple took for granted. Eloise's husband hadn't realised how lucky he was still to have her.

There was something in that moment, sharing each other's pain, exposing their grief to the other, which Eloise found cathartic. It made her realise that she wasn't just some hormonal, hysterical woman. She was entitled to feel the way she did: hard done by; abandoned; alone. Daniel had experienced those same emotions.

'I'm so sorry for everything you've been through, Daniel, but my opinion still stands. You're too young to give up on life. Hell, so am I. Maybe it's time we both stopped feeling sorry for ourselves and just put ourselves out there. We can start with judging a pet contest at the village fair. Surely that's not too scary? It's not as though I'm signing you up for a round of speed dating or something.'

Despite the fact she was trying to make light of it, the idea of setting him up with other women was something which really did not appeal to her. She had no claim over him, and he certainly didn't owe her any loyalty, but that was one area of his life she didn't want him to move on with. At least, not with someone else.

That revelation made her feel as though someone had just attached jump leads to her heart and given it an extra charge. She hadn't come here with the expectation of meeting anyone or having any sort of relationship. However, deep down, apparently she'd been harbouring something of that nature towards Daniel—a widower, clearly still grieving, who'd be horrified by the notion. Yet who still seemed to draw her closer into his life.

She jumped up from her seat as though she'd just been scalded and set to work tidying away the remains of their meal. Perhaps stepping out into the world wouldn't be so bad for either of them, expanding their horizons and their world, which sometimes only seemed to consist of the two of them and the dog.

'I'll sleep on it.' Daniel was non-committal, but at least he hadn't completely dismissed the idea.

'Thanks for dinner, but I think I'll go to bed if that's okay?' She finished loading the dishwasher and made her excuses as politely as possible.

Staying the night in his house made it impossible to put any real kind of distance between them, but at least if she went to bed now she wouldn't have to find out anything more about Daniel Grant which would only make her like him more. She was privileged that he'd opened up to her the way he had, but reaffirming the fact that he was loving and loyal wasn't going to help her stop seeing him as someone other than her boss.

'Yes, of course. Is there anything you need?' Bless

him, even though she and Lucky had completely derailed whatever plans he'd had for tonight, and imposed on his hospitality, he still thought he should do more to make her feel comfortable.

Perhaps that was why these inappropriate feelings towards him had manifested in the first place. It had been so long since anyone had taken her feelings into consideration, so the slightest kindness had swept her off her feet.

'No, thank you. I'll see you in the morning.' She left him in the kitchen and hurried away, with Lucky limping after her, though she knew sleep would likely elude her. How could she hope to slumber peacefully when they were under the same roof? When her wandering mind would never let her forget the sight of him answering the door to her wearing nothing more than a towel?

Oh, she might have kept herself busy since that moment, but that didn't mean it wasn't imprinted on her psyche. She was with him when he'd said that he was attracted to people based on their character, but knowing he was as attractive on the outside as well as in his heart was a bonus. Or a curse, at least for her peace of mind.

''Night, Eloise.'

There was nothing remotely sexual in his tone, or the sleepy smile he afforded her. Yet, her body interpreted both entirely differently. Parts of her she'd thought numb, desensitised and lost for ever were coming back to life like blooms in spring. It was overwhelming to discover she might not completely have gone to seed at all. That with the right conditions she might just flourish once more.

CHAPTER SEVEN

'WHY DON'T WE just bring him with us, Daniel?' Eloise couldn't resist those soulful eyes pleading with her to change her mind.

Lucky was just as endearing.

'Or…he could go with you and I'll stay here,' Daniel suggested with exaggerated enthusiasm. Sometimes he appeared much younger than his years—playful, even. It was a side to the revered vet she was sure not many got to see. Today she was hoping to change that for both of their sakes.

It would do him good to get out and have a little fun, and she could use an introduction to the rest of the village too. Maybe she could join one of those groups that crocheted cardigans and made their own jam. At least then she'd have different hobbies than thinking about Daniel.

'Nope. I think people might just notice. Now, Debbie is looking after the clinic for a few hours, so we're free to eat as much cake as we can, buy more jumble sale tat than we can ever possibly need and make someone's day by telling them their dog's cute. It's not that much of a hardship, is it?'

'I suppose when you put it like that…' Like a petulant

teenager, he reluctantly grabbed his jacket and followed Lucky and her out to the car.

They'd agreed it made more sense to travel in one car to the event, and she hadn't wanted to attract more attention by suggesting they should go separately. She doubted a ten-minute drive together was going to make much difference at this point. Having dinner together and staying overnight at his house would definitely have caused a few raised eyebrows from anyone at work aware of their antics. Regardless that the only untoward things that had happened between them were completely in her imagination.

'Did you sleep okay?' he asked, once they were in the car and on their way into the village.

'Yes,' she lied. 'Thank you.'

Between thoughts of Daniel lying semi-naked—at least in her mind— a couple of rooms away, and a dog hogging most of the bed, sleep hadn't come easily. At the crack of dawn, once she'd been sure Lucky hadn't suffered any other side effects of his altercation with a bee, she'd gone home. Not before she'd run into Daniel in the kitchen, however, who'd also risen early. After refusing breakfast, and after a quick thank you and goodbye, it had been home to shower and change before coming back to work as though nothing had happened, at least from outward appearances.

Inside, she was a mess—an even bigger one than when she'd first arrived in town, only for different reasons. Now it wasn't just the fact that her husband had left her, her daughters were living their own lives away from her and that she was physically undergoing a transformation which was difficult to terms with. After last night with Daniel, and their previous interactions, her emotions were all over the place. She had to get a grip of them soon, or her new set-up here would be in jeopardy.

'Hopefully, Lucky has learned his lesson about trying to make friends with buzzy insects.' The subtext to that was that hopefully he'd never have cause to have her stay in his house again.

That was fine by her. The next time Lucky got himself in trouble, she might be inclined simply to set up camp in the clinic to keep an eye on him instead. It might feel less like crossing that line between their professional and personal lives that way.

They pulled into the Bruce Valley Community Centre car park, slowly edging past the stall owners setting up around them until they eventually got parked at the back of the small, squat building.

She made sure Lucky had his lead on securely before letting him out of the boot, leaving Daniel to lock up the car. Lucky had yet to be tested socially in an environment with lots of other dogs and she was praying he wouldn't end up causing a scene. That wouldn't do much to convince Daniel this was a good idea.

'The lady I was talking to yesterday, Mabel, said she'd meet us inside. She was thrilled that you'd agreed to do this. It was one more thing off her list, apparently, so you're her new hero.' Eloise was sure he'd be a hero for a few more people by the end of the day. He had that effect.

They walked through the car park and round the side

of the building, where it was already filling up with early birds. Chattering pensioners, excited children and meandering dog walkers hovered round the entrance, waiting for the official opening. It occurred to Eloise that they probably looked like any other couple from the village out with their dog, having a nosey at what was going on today. She was sure Daniel would hate that idea, but she didn't mind someone might think she was with this lovely man. Or that he would have any interest in her.

A matronly, efficient-looking woman holding a clipboard to her ample bosom hurried over to meet them. 'Oh, Mr Grant, how lovely to see you here. I can't thank you enough for agreeing to do this. Otherwise I was going to have to do it myself, and you know I'm already judging the cake show and the gardening section. I mean, we have some guest judges, but I'm Chair of the committee, so my opinion's very important.'

'Of course. I'm honoured that you wanted me here at all. You obviously have everything in hand yourself.' Daniel pandered to the woman's sense of importance, making her blush like a school girl.

'Well, yes, but it's nice to have a new face. And you must be Eloise.' Just when Eloise thought she'd accidentally donned her invisibility cloak this morning, the woman peered at her.

'Yes, I think we spoke on the phone this morning.' Taking a not so wild guess, she'd say this was Mabel herself. She had that same efficiency, and 'no time for nonsense' attitude which had made it a very short phone call confirming that Daniel would be in attendance today.

'Indeed. Now, we're setting up the stalls inside at the minute, and the pet show isn't for another hour. I'll give you a shout when you're needed. In the meantime, enjoy the atmosphere, get yourself a cup of tea and I'll look forward to having a conflab with you later.' With that, the whirlwind which was Mabel spun off again.

Eloise looked at Daniel, who had one eyebrow raised, as if to say, *what on earth have you got us into?*

She didn't want to give him any reason to retreat, to go back to thinking that his life was better without this level of socialising, so she hooked her arm in his and directed him towards the stalls outside.

'You heard the woman. Let's go and get a cuppa. We can scout the potential winners from a distance, as long as Mabel agrees to giving us final say on the best in show. I've a feeling she doesn't defer to others easily.'

'Well, since you roped me into this, you're buying.' Daniel didn't argue, or try to shake her off as they headed to the little van selling teas and coffees, so Eloise took that as a win. Hopefully today marked the start of them both spreading their wings a little.

'Lucky would hands-down win this if we were allowed to participate,' Eloise whispered to Daniel as the dogs were paraded in front of them.

As fond as he was of their joint charge, he couldn't bring himself to agree. Lucky was sitting obediently at their feet watching the others, tail wagging and desperate to join in, but he wasn't cover-model material. With his shaved patches, leg bandaged and still underweight, he wasn't the picture of health, even if he was a survivor. It was too bad they'd already given out the award for Pet Most Like Its Owner to the scruffy-haired guinea pig and his human counterpart who looked as though he'd just woken up. Daniel reckoned he and Eloise had a lot in common with their dog—they'd been through the wars but were still here to tell the tale.

'I think he deserves a participation rosette at least.' Daniel slipped her one of the blue ribbons they'd been handing out like candy, and she proudly attached it to Lucky's collar.

The two of them looked so pleased with themselves that Daniel couldn't help but smile at the scene. He didn't remember smiling so much until Eloise had come into his life. There hadn't been a lot to make him happy. Perhaps he'd believed he didn't deserve to smile when Anne hadn't been able to carry on with her life too. In a few weeks of being in his life, Eloise had changed that. Now, not only had he adopted a stray dog, but she'd convinced him to judge a pet show. And he was enjoying it—most likely because she was here with him.

'You've got to make a decision, Daniel,' Eloise whispered to him.

For a moment he didn't realise she was talking about picking a winner of the best dog in show, and thought she meant about her, him and whether or not he should let her into his life.

It was a bigger decision for him than choosing a husky over a dachshund. Part of him wanted that comfort, support and companionship that being with Eloise offered, not to mention the emotions she was able to rouse in him. Although having desires towards someone who wasn't his wife felt like a betrayal in itself. But Anne wasn't here, he could have another twenty or thirty years of life ahead of him and, recently, facing that alone seemed like a very dark future—even if he hadn't thought that until Eloise had come into his life.

She offered him a new way of living, a future to look forward to. He just had to decide if he was ready for that. If he could risk the chance of getting close to someone again, when fate had a cruel way of taking everyone away from him.

Then, as Eloise nodded her head towards the eager pet owners watching him, he remembered what he was here to do. He strode forward and shook the hand of the woman who was wearing a pink bow around her neck to match that tied around her little long-haired dachshund's neck. Until that moment he hadn't known which to pick, but it had been Eloise's clear favourite. She quickly helped him distribute runner-up rosettes to those who'd made it into the final to pacify the disappointed owners.

'Congratulations on being a finalist. Thank you for participating.'

Whilst she appeased the others, Daniel found himself swamped in a hug, enveloped in a cloud of sickly-sweet perfume, the delighted winner embracing him tightly to the point where he thought he'd have to push her away so he could breathe again.

'I think the photographer from the local paper wants a photo of you and little Pixie.'

Thankfully Eloise came to the rescue, tapping the woman on the shoulder and directing her towards another man. Clearly keen to get her five minutes of fame, she unceremoniously dropped Daniel and rushed off, fixing her hair as she went.

'Thanks for that.' He could feel the heat in his face and it wasn't just from being almost smothered in someone's chest, although Eloise seemed to find his discomfort amusing, failing to hide the smirk on her face.

'I thought you might need rescuing.'

'You thought right. See, this is exactly why I don't come to these things.'

'Because women can't help but throw themselves at you?' She was teasing him, something he was used to with his other colleagues who were always trying to get him to come out of his shell. He usually didn't get drawn into it, but it was different with Eloise. He liked seeing the twinkle in her blue eyes, knowing she was getting a kick making fun of the situation. If anything, he was inclined to keep the banter going, finding his own pleasure in her enjoyment.

'Yeah, it's an awful hazard of the job. That's why I had to lock myself away at the practice. Traffic would come to a standstill, no one could get anywhere or get any work done.'

'So, really, you were doing everyone in town a favour by staying away?'

'Uh-huh. And now...'

'Everyone is being reminded of what they're missing and can't control themselves.'

'Exactly.'

'Then perhaps we should go inside before we cause a riot of stampeding admirers out here.' Eloise offered him her arm and he took it gladly. Although they were joking about a fan club, he did think people would be less likely to approach him when he was with Eloise. They presented a certain image of togetherness, which was only true because of their work relationship, but nonetheless hopefully deterred anyone approaching.

A hope which tempted fate as a harassed looking Mabel met them at the door.

'Mr Grant, can I have your assistance please? One of our contestants appears to have been in the sun too long.'

Daniel, Eloise and Lucky followed her over to a man holding a little pug in his arms. The pug was panting heavily and clearly in distress.

'Pugsley's been sick, but he won't drink any water,' the worried owner told them.

Dogs with flatter faces and shorter muzzles often had breathing difficulties, and it made them vulnerable to overheating in the warmer weather.

'The first thing we need to do is get him somewhere cool. We should take him inside. Eloise, there are cooling pads and a spray bottle. Could you get them please?' He tossed Eloise the car keys and rushed inside the community hall in search of a cooler space.

'There's a small room at the back with a fan. We can take him there.'

Mabel led them through the main hall to an office where a free-standing fan was already whirring away.

Daniel suspected Mabel had been using the room in between commitments to cool herself down.

'Could we get some fresh water please?' he asked, sending Mabel off to locate it.

'Is Pugsley going to be okay? He's my daughter's dog. I'm just exercising him for her.'

'The important thing is to get him cooled down first, then we can take to the clinic for a more thorough examination. Has he had any seizures?' Daniel checked the pug's gums, the grey discoloration showing that there wasn't enough oxygen getting around his system. The excitement of the day, combined with the heat, would increase oxygen demand, resulting in the heavy panting.

'No, but he was having trouble standing.'

When Eloise returned with the cooling mat he kept in the car for Lucky, Daniel instructed the man to set the dog down on it in front of the fan. Although they were in a cooler area now, there was still a chance that Pugsley's increased effort to breathe could cause a collapse of the inner walls around his larynx and prove fatal—a horrible way to end the day for everyone involved.

'Good boy.' Daniel stroked him slowly, speaking in a reassuring voice to encourage him to calm down as Mabel set down a bowl of water.

Eloise tied Lucky to the leg of the nearby table and began to spray the pug all over with water, letting Daniel enjoy the cooling mist drifting his way in the process.

'I think his breathing's a bit more normal now,' the pug's guardian noted, probably trying to reassure himself that everything was going to be all right.

Daniel was inclined to wait a bit longer to make sure.

'We'll probably take him back to the clinic with us to keep an eye on him.' Eloise knew as well as Daniel that damage may well have been done to the little dog's organs already. They would have to run some tests to make sure, even though he might seem fully recovered.

It was nice to have her support. Although other nurses had worked alongside him, it had been very much a job to them. They clocked in and out, their home life very separate from the clinic. Perhaps that was why he had more of a bond with Eloise, because she seemed as invested in the practice, and the patients, as he. Maybe that would change if she should ever find herself in another relationship, but she was such a kind-hearted soul he didn't think so.

It was also a disturbing thought that she might pair off with someone new and leave him behind after opening up his world. Despite telling himself not to get too close, to have her too involved in his personal life, it was too late. She was part of it now, permeating his work space and his home. He didn't want to think of either without Eloise in it.

'Would you be happy to drive us back to the clinic, Eloise? I'd like to keep Pugsley with me, just in case anything were to happen.' He wanted to have his hands free and be totally unencumbered if the little dog stopped breathing altogether and needed resuscitating.

'Of course. You could follow on behind us,' she told the man waiting anxiously beside them.

'That's fine. I want to phone my daughter and let her

know what's happening. She'll likely want to come over to see you too.'

'No problem.' Daniel took a business card out of his wallet and handed it over, before gathering Pugsley up into his arms, cooling mat and all.

This time Eloise took the lead back to the car, loading Lucky into the open boot whilst Daniel took Pugsley into the passenger seat with him. Lucky gave an excited, 'Woof!', not knowing what was going on, but clearly picking up on the charged energy in the car.

'Back to work, then,' Eloise said with a sigh, starting up the car.

She didn't have to say any more for him to know exactly what she was talking about. For a couple of hours away from reality, they'd enjoyed one another's company doing something normal, as though they didn't have any worries in the world to deal with.

A sick dog had quickly brought them back down to earth and reminded them they had a job to get back to. It also meant they would most likely see each other outside of working hours again tonight, since Eloise wasn't one to clock out just because her shift was officially over. She liked to be personally involved with the animals which might require overnight observation, echoing his work ethic and once again proving how alike they were.

It was good fortune that he'd bought extra chicken for dinner tonight when he'd probably end up cooking for two again—a routine he could find himself easily getting used to.

CHAPTER EIGHT

'YOU REALLY DIDN'T have to do this, Daniel. I could've grabbed something when I got home.' Eloise's protest was weak since she'd just finished the delicious honey soy chicken drumsticks and vegetable rice he'd presented her with for dinner.

'It's okay. I was cooking anyway, and it's nice to have company.'

Daniel cleared the dishes away and came to join her on the sofa. Lucky seemed content lying on the floor in front of the television. It was the sort of homely scene which she hadn't been part of in a long time. She knew she shouldn't get too comfortable, yet it had been lovely these past couple of nights being with Daniel, chatting over a meal together. He cared enough to include her, to think about her needs, at least when it came to dinner.

She didn't remember her ex-husband ever having done that. As a wife and mother, she'd always been the one catering for others, pandering to their wants and needs. Though she'd been happy enough to do it at the time, now she could see no one had ever really thought about her in return. And, when she'd outlived her usefulness, she'd been casually discarded. It had left a great big hole in her life which was increasingly being taken up being in Daniel's company—something which, in itself, wasn't anything to get too concerned about, except for the need now building in her to do it all the time.

'I'm glad Pugsley's going to be all right,' she said, moving them back onto work talk where it was safer.

'Yeah. You can never be too careful, but I think we got to him just in time. I suppose it's lucky we were there. I've got you to thank for that.' Daniel fixed her with his brown-eyed gaze, and Eloise felt her heart melt a little more.

'Me and Mabel,' she said with an anxious laugh, trying to deflect his gratitude.

'If it wasn't for having you by my side, Eloise, it wouldn't have entered my head to go there today—even Anne couldn't persuade me to go to things like that—but I wanted to see you having fun. It looks good on you.'

When he looked at her so intensely, said nice things to her, she was inclined to forget she was a middle-aged divorcee invisible to most people. Daniel made her believe she was someone he wanted to listen to, to be with, and she found that intoxicating. Along with the fact she was beginning to recognise herself again. She'd found a purpose here and was beginning to feel like part of the community as well as the work force.

In the mornings she'd even found herself paying a little more attention to her appearance. For a long time it hadn't seemed that important. She'd probably stopped making an effort for Sam when he never noticed anyway. At the time she'd felt too ground down by life to be bothered.

Since moving here, however, she'd taken more care over how she looked. It gave her a little confidence boost, making her feel better in herself when she'd made an effort. These days she had more of a spring in her step, a reason to get up in the morning, and a lot of that had to do with Daniel.

Of course, moving here, starting over, had given her a new impetus. Here she wasn't just an abandoned wife and mother. She could start over and she wanted to make a good impression.

She liked the appreciative looks it drew from Daniel in the process, along with how it made her feel when he looked at her that way. Except now, sitting so close after an intimate dinner, she was worried her thoughts would take them somewhere neither was ready for.

'Oh, I almost forgot...' She hopped off the sofa and grabbed her bag, pulling out a little lunch box. 'Dessert.'

'Where did you get that?' He sat back and watched with interest as she lifted off the lid to reveal slices of Victoria sponge cake.

'Mabel insisted we take some home with us to thank us for helping out. I think it was from the first prize winning entry in the home baking competition.' Cake was always a good distraction, and she'd often comforted herself with a cup of tea and a slice to get those feel-good endorphins which had been otherwise missing in her life.

In this case, it was her hormones that needed some distracting... She held up a slice and, just when he was about to take a bite, she thought it would be funny to shove it in her own mouth instead. Trying not to laugh and spit crumbs everywhere, she munched on the soft sponge cake, licking the cream from her lips when she'd finished.

'Such a tease,' he said, but his deep and husky voice meant the joke had backfired on Eloise. Far from breaking the sexual tension, she felt it even more as he watched her with hungry eyes.

Enjoying having captured his interest, she leaned into the moment. She scooped some of the cream onto her finger and held it out to him. Without hesitation, he took hold of her hand and directed her finger into his mouth. Eloise held onto her intake of breath as he slowly sucked the full length of her finger, never breaking eye contact.

This wasn't her imagination. There was something exciting happening between Daniel and her. It was both frightening and thrilling at the same time. If this went any further than a flirtation with her boss, she would risk her job, therefore her financial stability and new life here. Yet feeling this way, desirable and womanly, was something she thought she'd never experience again. It was something that might be a one-off, the last chance she might have to enjoy what was left of her femininity.

So, when he leaned forward and kissed her, she put up no resistance. They would come to their senses soon enough so she wanted to enjoy this while this moment of madness lasted.

The cake fell somewhere between them as Daniel closed the small space between their bodies, overcome with desire for Eloise. In the end he didn't know who'd been teasing who, but the inevitable outcome had been the same.

His resolve—and Eloise's too, it would seem—had been stretched to breaking point.

He'd tried holding back, fighting these feelings, but he couldn't seem to stop himself. Probably because she'd given him clear signals that she was just as affected by whatever was happening between them. They hadn't been able to stay away from one another, and this kiss was the consequence of attempting to deny that attraction. All of that pent-up desire was spilling over into this hard, passionate exchange that was blowing his mind. He literally couldn't think straight when her soft lips were moulded to his, her tongue dipping into his mouth, awakening a fire that had taken him by surprise.

It was one thing discovering he was attracted to another woman who wasn't his wife, but he hadn't expected the chemistry to completely take over. All those doubts he'd had about giving into his urges, the thoughts of how it would be a betrayal of his wife's memory, were drowned out by the sound of his blood rushing in his ears. One kiss had made him realise how stale his life had become, and he was reluctant to go back to that situation any time soon.

'Stay with me tonight,' he muttered against her lips.

'In the spare room?' she asked, those big, blue eyes questioning his true intention.

'No…with me.' Daniel needed to be honest with them both about what he wanted. Then perhaps one of them would use the opportunity to come to their senses.

He watched her gulp, saw the slight panic in her eyes

and realised this was as big a deal for her as it was for him. 'Is that a good idea?'

'Probably not.' He made them both smile nervously, but neither of them could look away from the other.

In the end he was the one to take the initiative, getting to his feet and taking her by the hand.

Eloise followed him as he led her to his bedroom, the place where he'd spent every night on his own for the past five years.

'We don't have to stay here. We could go into the other room if you'd prefer?' Eloise apparently understood the significance of him bringing her in here, but he didn't want her to read more into this than it being any more than a much-needed release for both of them.

He shook his head. 'No. I have to move on some time.'

It was becoming obvious that he couldn't spend the rest of his days alone. He wasn't a saint. And, though he'd loved Anne, his feelings hadn't died with her...as his body was strongly reminding him.

He knew he wasn't ready for a serious commitment, but surely he deserved some happiness? It had been in short supply for over five years. And being with Eloise made him happy.

'You're shaking.' He reached out to a trembling Eloise and pulled her into his embrace.

Having her soft form pressed against his revitalised all sorts of emotions inside him. It was comforting and arousing at the same time. His body and his mind were in tandem for once, wanting this, needing Eloise.

'It's been a long time since I've done this with anyone. I've only ever been with my husband, and I… I'm not exactly in my first flush of youth.' She was mumbling into his chest, as though she was too embarrassed to look him in the eye.

Daniel released his hold a little so he could lift her chin up and make her look up at him. 'You're beautiful.'

He dropped a soft kiss on her mouth and she began to relax into him again. It was reassuring to know that they were both venturing into unfamiliar territory, even though he was under pressure to make it good for both of them. This needed to be worthwhile, since they were going against their better judgement.

Eloise's hands were pressed against his chest, her body heat branding him with her touch, and he was suddenly desperate for that skin-on-skin contact. It was a long time since anyone had touched him.

He undid the first few buttons of his shirt, then pulled it over his head in impatience, eliciting a smile from Eloise. The look of appreciation she gave as she swept her gaze over his body did wonders for his self-esteem. Like her, he had some reservations about getting older, his physique not the same as the last time he'd been with a woman. As she traced her hands over his chest, his stomach and down to the waistband of his trousers, it appeared he'd passed muster.

'Is it sore?' she asked, when she grazed over the vivid bruises left from his accident in her house.

'Not now,' he said; he wasn't aware of anything except the feel of her on his skin.

Daniel sucked in a breath when she undid the button

and let his trousers fall to the floor. The graze of her fingers below his waist made him tingle all over in delicious anticipation of that touch everywhere else.

'Someone's been working out.' Her honeyed voice was appreciative and laden with lust, increasing his own arousal.

'Just swimming in the loch.' A cold-water dip was his reminder he was still alive. It connected him with the world every morning and helped him forget his troubles for a little while as he focused on regulating his breathing. It wasn't something he did to impress anyone. Though he was currently reaping the benefits of Eloise seeing the results of his early-morning routine.

'Mmm, maybe I should try it.'

'I'd like that. Though you'd have to wear a lot less clothes than you're wearing now.'

'Oh, really?' Her eyes were shining as he began undoing the buttons on her blouse.

'Yeah. I mean, this top would only weigh you down.' He slipped it off her shoulders, revealing her white lacy underwear.

'And the jeans?'

'Have to go, obviously.' He unbuttoned them and slowly pulled down the zip. Just before he was able to push them over her hips, Eloise grabbed hold of his hands with hers.

'Wait,' she said, panic in her eyes, and sudden tension in her body.

'What's wrong?' As much as he wanted this, Daniel would stop the second she decided it wasn't what she wanted after all. This would only work if they were both in the moment.

'I've had two children, I eat too much cake... I'm embarrassed about the idea of getting naked in front of you.' She had her arms wrapped around her belly, trying to hide it from him. Which, in the circumstances, might seem absurd, except he knew something about those anxieties.

He had his own insecurities about aging; he didn't know anyone who didn't. Going grey, losing hair, not being as fit or toned as he used to be, were all superficial things he thought about these days when faced with an older reflection in the mirror. None of which changed him as a person.

'We're all a little softer around the middle. It doesn't make you any less beautiful to me, Eloise.' He kissed the side of her neck, nuzzling into the crook of her shoulder, and heard her suck in a shaky breath.

As he made his way across her decolletage, dropping tiny kisses, he felt her begin to relax beneath him. He carefully peeled her hands away from her stomach and she let them drop to her sides. It was a sign of her trust in him that she was being so vulnerable in front of him, exposing her insecurities and hoping he wouldn't shame her the way her husband apparently had.

Not that he could see any reason why she should've been subjected to such treatment. Her soft white skin smelled of raspberries and cream and tasted just as sweet on his tongue. He cupped the mounds of flesh rising from her lacy bra and swept his tongue over one, then the other.

She gasped when he undid the clasp and released her voluptuous breasts to his gaze. Daniel plucked her nipples between his fingers until they were tight pink buds ripe for the taking. He flicked his tongue over one tip, enjoying Eloise's little moan of pleasure in response. And when he sucked her into his mouth, grazed his teeth over the sensitive nub, her body seemed to melt against him.

'Can…can we take this slow?' She gasped. 'It's been a long time.'

'Sure. We don't have to rush anything. I want you to enjoy it, Eloise.'

His own body was throbbing with need, and he was severely testing his own restraint, but for Eloise's sake he needed to take his time. He took her by the hand and led her over to the bed, feeling just as nervous as she looked. It had been a long time for him too. Hell, he hadn't even realised he still had such urges when he'd focused all his time and attention on work for the past five years. He thought his libido had died alongside his wife. Since Eloise had entered his life, he'd learned differently. He was still a man with needs and wants. All of which apparently included Eloise.

'Are you okay?' he asked as they lay down together.

Eloise bit her lip as she nodded. 'It's just… I don't know how it's going to feel, for you, or me. You hear all these stories about menopause and how it ruins your sex life. I'm afraid it's not going to be good.'

Daniel understood her fears. He'd been through this with Anne, but there were always ways to make sex enjoyable for both parties. 'I'm sure it'll be fine. We'll take our time, and if something doesn't feel right just let me know. Okay?'

'Okay.'

He silenced her doubts with a hard kiss until she was limp beneath him, totally lost to him. It was a powerful position and one he wouldn't abuse. He began his journey down her body again, kissing, licking and tasting every inch of skin he came into contact with, though when he nudged her legs apart he felt her tense again.

'So beautiful,' he mumbled, kissing the soft skin of her inner thighs, feeling her heat as he licked his way up to her most intimate area.

Eloise let out a small cry but, when he looked up to make sure she was okay, her eyes were closed, her head thrown back, and she clearly enjoyed what he was doing, confirmation that he should continue his endeavours.

He parted her legs, opening her up to him, and lapped her with the flat of his tongue. She trembled beneath him and reached down to tangle her fingers in his hair. With the tip of his tongue he dipped inside her, circling and teasing that swollen sweet spot and making her arch off the bed. Provoking such an immediate, responsive reaction to his intimate touch made him wonder what either of them had worried about. Eloise's arousal was as obvious as his own and, the more she clenched around him, writhed beneath him, the harder he fought to bring her to that final release.

The sharp pain as she tugged his hair was of no consequence compared to the feeling of pride inside as he brought her closer to orgasm. And when she cried out, bucked against him, and let her climax claim both of them, Daniel felt like the king of the world. He'd made her feel good and hopefully brought her some happiness, as well as a sense of achievement for both of them.

'Thank you,' Eloise said breathlessly when Daniel moved back up the bed to lie beside her again. Words could never convey the gratitude she felt towards him for what he'd just done, but it was all she could do for now. Her body was limp from his attentions, unused to the exertion of an orgasm which seemed to have come from her very soul, as though she'd been waiting a lifetime for the release.

Maybe she had. She didn't remember sex with Sam ever prompting such an overwhelming reaction from her body—a body she'd thought incapable of giving her, or anyone else, any satisfaction ever again. Boy, had she been wrong! If she never ever felt this way again, at least she'd have the memory to cling on to for ever: this contented, self-satisfied, cat-that-got-the-cream happiness that Daniel had gifted her.

'Are you okay?' he asked, watching her intently, his concern for her evident.

Everything about the moment made her want to weep with joy, not least the discovery that she wasn't the dried-up old hag she feared she'd become. A life, a sex life, was still possible beyond divorce and menopause. She would never have known that if it weren't for Daniel.

He'd taken his time to make sure she was comfortable, at the same time making her so hot for him she'd been on the edge before he'd even touched her. There was a passion inside her that she hadn't known existed until now. Until recently, sex with her husband had been routine and familiar. Even kissing Daniel was exciting, inciting feelings in her that made her feel shiny and new, much younger than her forty-nine years.

In a lot of ways she felt like a born-again virgin. It was an absurd notion for a divorced mother of two, but she was discovering herself again, along with her new-found sexuality. The day might come when she didn't have the same urges, but until then she was going to enjoy everything Daniel had awakened inside her.

'For now.' She leaned over and kissed him, stroking a hand down his body, keen to give him the same high she was still coming down from.

The stomach Daniel had tried to persuade her had become soft over the years was tight as he flexed at her touch. He gave a sharp intake of breath as she ventured lower and took hold of his long length, then a satisfied grin.

'You're playing with fire…' He growled, his voice hoarse with desire.

'You're the one who lit the match,' she reminded him. He'd been the one to cross that line when he'd kissed her and started this chain reaction.

His mouth tightened into a thin line, and his eyes fluttered shut as she moved her hand along his shaft. She was enjoying watching him fight for control, knowing that she could make him feel this way, that he was responding to her touch as though she was desirable after all.

As he had done to her, she flicked her tongue over his

nipple, watching with glee as the flat disc grew taut with arousal. Before she had an opportunity to tease him any further, Eloise found herself flat on her back, Daniel on top of her. The weight of his body on her was as welcome as his passionate kisses. It felt right, like something she hadn't known she'd been missing in her life.

With her arms wrapped around his neck, she lost herself in those kisses. They were something that might seem unimportant to most people, but was so intimate to Eloise. It was a deep, personal connection, something more than simply the physical act of sex itself. She didn't even know if she would feel this way with anyone else, or if this was merely 'Daniel lust' that had overtaken her body and brain.

'Hold on. We still need some contraception.' Daniel's voice was urgent in her ear, his restraint clearly stretched to breaking point and fuelling Eloise's desire with that knowledge. He reached into his nightstand and took out a packet of condoms.

'I bought these when I was doing the shopping. An impulse buy, just in case. I hadn't planned this.' He seemed embarrassed by his foresight but at this moment in time Eloise was glad of it.

'At least in the future it won't be such an issue. There are some perks to this menopause lark.' Not that there'd be any way of knowing if he'd still want to do this with her when that time came.

Although she was only in the early stages of menopause, it had felt like the beginning of the end: the knowledge that she wouldn't be able to conceive another child, the death of her femininity. Even though she'd never imagined having any more babies, that choice being taken away from her seemed a cruel reminder that she was no longer useful as a woman simply because she'd got older. Thankfully she was making peace with that aspect of the aging process.

Daniel didn't need any further persuasion. He tested her readiness first, dipping his finger inside her and starting that pulsing need for him all over again. She was slick with arousal when he joined their bodies together, but that first contact still took her breath away.

'Daniel...wait...' It felt like losing her virginity all over again, and she needed a moment to adjust and accommodate him.

'What's wrong?' His genuine concern for her was there in his eyes and the tone of his voice. Knowing he cared for her was enough to help her relax a little.

'I just need a second or two to get used to you,' she explained.

'Is there anything I can do to make this easier for you?'

'Just kiss me.' It was ironic that, despite their bodies being forged together, she still needed that extra element of intimacy, that proof that he wanted *her*, not just anyone.

Daniel took his time kissing her thoroughly, teasing and tasting, showing her a tender regard that almost brought her to tears. This was more than sex, though she knew neither of them would admit it. They were discovering themselves, as well as each other. Eloise wasn't sure she would've been able to do this with anyone else, but Daniel made her feel safe...wanted...appreciated.

All things that had been missing in her life too long. It wasn't long before she was a puddle of need wanting more...wanting Daniel.

He waited until she relaxed again, then moved slowly until she got used to the sensation of him inside her. He filled her again and again, driving Eloise to that pinnacle of ecstasy she'd thought she'd never reach again. Every thrust, every groan, was interspersed with tender kisses, reassuring her that he was interested in more than his satisfaction, though she knew this was about more than a physical release for him too.

This was a lot more than a casual hook-up for both of them, regardless that they were reluctant to commit to anything. Even tonight hadn't been planned. Their libidos had apparently taken over, bypassing all those red flags of warning that this wasn't a good idea.

It didn't matter that he was her boss still mourning his wife, or that she was grieving her losses too, when they could make each other feel this good. And why was that such a bad idea anyway? Who said there had to be more to this than enjoying the pleasure there was to be had sharing a bed? They weren't doing anything wrong, and it felt so right she didn't want it ever to end, because then they'd have to go back to the real world and remember why they'd been trying to avoid this for so long.

All the superficial things she'd worried so much about didn't seem important when Daniel was made love to her, making her feel so good. It could get addictive, this enjoyable reminder that she could still be sexual, desirable. Not to mention this building arousal she knew was about to carry her away onto a cloud of bliss.

'Don't stop!' she cried, as he pushed her ever closer to the edge. And, when he growled her name, he pushed her right over. Her orgasm claimed her completely; that out-of-body experience as her soul seemed to drift above her body was a euphoria she hadn't known in an age, and she never wanted to come back down from it.

When Daniel's climax followed soon after hers, it seemed to last an age. The accompanying cry made it sound as though he'd been waiting a lifetime for that release. He crashed down on the bed beside her, both of them grinning and panting for breath.

'I'd forgotten how good that felt.' Eloise wasn't sure it ever had been that amazing with Sam. Daniel seemed to bring out the best in her, in every way possible.

'Me too.' At least he knew what she was going through. Both of them had ventured out of their comfort zone together. It had made it easier for her to admit she was nervous and ask him to make concessions for her.

The care Daniel had taken with her to make sure she was comfortable helped her relax, made her know she was safe with him. It wasn't just his own pleasure he cared about, and that went a long way to making her feel at ease with him.

'Thanks, Eloise.' He leaned across and kissed her, making her heart flutter all over again.

It might have seemed an odd thing to thank someone after sex, except she felt the same thing: gratitude; thankfulness for sharing this experience, letting her know it was still possible to have a satisfactory sex life. More than that, to enjoy great sex.

It was going to be difficult working alongside one another, knowing that this was possible together. For two people who'd been isolated, locked in their own worlds for so long, it was a revelation to find there could be something good again in their lives. Eloise just didn't know if Daniel was ready to accept it, or her, on a long-term basis.

CHAPTER NINE

DANIEL FELT AS though he'd just been hit by a truck. His body was completely spent, and the air had been knocked from his lungs. He didn't remember ever feeling this way after sex, and he didn't think it was just down to his age or the fact he'd been celibate for five years.

This was all about Eloise. About how she made him feel, and how he'd just been able to fully express that. It was where they went from here that was going to be the sticking point.

'Well, that was…'

'Unexpected? Amazing?' Eloise offered when he was at a loss to describe what had just happened.

'Both of those things.' He couldn't take his eyes off her naked body as she gave a languid stretch, providing him with a perfect view of her full figure. He couldn't resist kissing her again, as though marking his territory. For a little while, here in his bed, she was his.

His sex life with Anne had been great, but never so exciting. It was difficult to process his feelings about that when it felt so disloyal to admit it. He wondered if the reason they'd stayed together so long was because he'd been grateful to her for loving him. She'd provided the security he craved, but their relationship hadn't had the same passion he'd just shared with Eloise.

'Do you want me to go?'

'What? No.' The thought of her going now, leaving him alone and perhaps never getting to feel this way again, was something he didn't want to contemplate—at least, not yet.

'I just… I didn't think you'd want anyone to see me leaving in the morning.'

'We've got plenty of time before then. Besides, I don't know about you, but I'm not sure I can even walk at the minute.' His legs were still trembling, his heart pounding and he'd never felt so alive.

'Probably not!' She laughed, then moved over to cuddle into his side.

Daniel wrapped his arm around her shoulder, her head on his chest, and pulled the covers up over their bodies. It was a cosy picture he'd never thought he'd get to be part of again. The contentment of lying in this bed with Eloise was a snapshot he would keep in his heart for ever.

The logical part of his brain, which was just about working, knew she would have to go. They couldn't afford their colleagues to see them together, because that would mean labelling what this was, and that was a step too far just now. However, he wanted to enjoy this moment of peace for as long as possible before the guilt and doubt had time to kick in.

'I never expected this to happen, you know. It's not why I made dinner.' Although, he knew he'd had Eloise in mind when he'd been shopping for the ingredients, knowing dinner would be all the better if he had her to share it with. He hadn't been wrong.

'I know. I didn't even know it was possible—for me, I mean. I don't know what's happening with my body any more...' Eloise's feeling of powerlessness was obvious, and he felt for her. It was bad enough that he didn't seem to have control over his emotions; he could only imagine how it was for her, being a slave to her hormones.

'I know menopause was tough for Anne too. Then we had the cancer diagnosis, and she had to go through chemo too.'

He didn't know if it was insensitive of him to mention his wife after sex with another woman, but he wanted Eloise to know he understood a little of what she was going through. Anne had gone through the mood swings, the sweats and the irregular periods, and he'd seen how she'd suffered. He'd been there to support her through it all, but at the time she'd described it as her body betraying her.

'Menopause is awful. Sorry, I know she went through so much more than me, but still, it sucks. At least I have my two girls. Sorry, that's insensitive of me...'

'It's okay. Children were never on our agenda.'

'Even so, I'm sure Anne struggled with the fact that her chance to be a mother had been taken away from her. We never intended to have any more children either, but that doesn't mean I'm not mourning the loss of my femininity.'

Daniel had never looked at it that way. He'd only seen the physical symptoms and the toll they'd taken on Anne. She'd certainly never mentioned feeling less of a woman when her periods had finally stopped. He supposed she'd been saving him from knowing how much she was suffering on the inside as well as outwardly. It didn't bring him any peace, knowing that.

'You certainly didn't seem any less of woman to me.' He skimmed his hand over the indent of her waist and her hips, luxuriating in her curves.

'It was a surprise to me too. I didn't think I'd ever get to enjoy this again. I mean, this could be a one-off for me—a last hurrah before everything south packs up shop for good. If that's what happens, then I'm glad we've had this tonight.' Eloise reached up and stroked his cheek. He caught her hand and kissed her palm.

'It's not the end of the world, you know. There is treatment: hormones and patches and whatever. You'll get back on an even keel.'

'I haven't had the chance to see a GP yet with trying to sort out the house, so I've still to look into all my options, but it'll never be quite the same, will it?'

Daniel was beginning to see why she'd worried so much. Her future was uncertain, unknown, and he knew how terrifying that could be. All he could do for now was help her enjoy this time together before everything changed.

'We could test that theory…'

'You mean…?'

'I'm game if you are.' He reached for her again, pulling her flush against his body.

She wasn't the only one who'd worried about age catching up with the body. He wasn't the young man he used to be, but thankfully a certain part of him was still able to recover quickly.

'Oh, I'm game. As long as you don't mind me being the games master.' To his surprise, Eloise rolled him onto his back and straddled his lap. Daniel's arousal immediately reached full throttle.

'I'm all for equal opportunities.' He grinned, gripping her hips as she moved against him.

She took control, impaling herself on his erection, making them both gasp at the sudden, intimate connection. Although she felt amazing around him, her new-found confidence was equally thrilling. From someone who'd been afraid to let him see her naked, she was now riding on top, free from inhibition.

If this was the effect one round of love-making had on her, he was content to keep going long into the night. She needed to have a higher opinion of herself, one that matched his own. Eloise was an amazing woman, and clearly not enough people had told her that lately. This seemed more like the real Eloise. The one who hadn't been worn down by life and an unappreciative husband. Her hands were braced on his chest and she was seeking her own satisfaction, taking him with her on the ride.

He watched the ecstasy on her face, felt her tighten around him as her climax built, and when she let go he went with her. That feeling of complete release and peace was something he'd never tire of, yet something he'd denied himself for a long time.

He knew if roles had been reversed, and Anne had been the one left behind, he would have wanted her to find happiness again. As far as he was concerned though, for him that would always bring unhappiness somewhere else down the road. The danger of getting too used to this, enjoying being in a relationship again, was another risk of losing someone who meant a lot to him. Even though Eloise wasn't suffering from a terminal illness, the fact that he was her boss, and she had baggage of her own to deal with, brought different challenges. If being together made things difficult at work, she might decide to move on somewhere else, and that would still mean losing her.

Yet, he knew they would both benefit from continuing to see each other. They were able to remind one another that their lives hadn't ended. Perhaps some time together getting used to being in one another's company would open them up to the possibility of another relationship in the future, even if it wasn't with each other.

Right now, he wasn't sure they were able to commit, or provide the sort of long term stability they needed to move on from their past. That didn't mean he was willing to give up this new, exciting development in discovering more about Eloise and himself. They both needed, and deserved, to have this sort of intimacy in their lives. He hoped this wasn't the one-off she'd suggested, but the start of their exploration together, of finding out about the needs and desires that had been lying dormant and had awakened with a roar.

However, this could only work if they kept their private life separate from work, if they kept things physical without letting their hearts get in the way. He had to go back to being the Daniel he'd been before he'd met

Anne, and shut himself off emotionally from anything that might come back to hurt him. He only hoped it wasn't already too late.

When Eloise woke up and reached over to the other side of the bed, all she found was an empty space. For a moment her sleep-addled mind wondered where she was... if she'd forgotten she'd gone home at some point. She'd expected to find Daniel lying next to her. In fact, she'd looked forward to waking up next to him. Then she looked around the room, at the unfamiliar aqua-green coloured walls and the pine bedroom furniture, and realised she was still in Daniel's bed. He just wasn't here with her.

She couldn't believe the sense of loss she felt already, after just one night with him. After years of separate rooms, even before the divorce, she should be used to sleeping on her own. It was just nice to have someone there again, making her feel safe and wanted. Not to mention that power she'd felt, driving him out of control with lust for her. Being with him had helped her rediscover the old Eloise who didn't have to worry about her weight, medical problems or the distance between her family and her. She'd actually been able simply to enjoy her time with Daniel.

'Morning.' He appeared from the bathroom brushing his teeth, already dressed.

Although her heart sped up at the sight of him, she couldn't help the sense of disappointment that their time together had apparently come to an end. She glanced at the digital clock on the nightstand. It was only six a.m., but he was making it clear he wanted her gone.

'Morning.' Her response was half as enthusiastic as his as she threw back the covers and began retrieving the clothes that had been discarded over the floor last night in the heat of their passion. She supposed her body needed the rest several times over, unused to its exertions. However, she was reluctant to go in case she never had this experience again.

Once Daniel had finished in the bathroom, she ran in, clutching her clothes to her naked body. She wasn't quite so bold in the cold light of day. 'I won't be long.'

Without her own toiletries to hand, she had to make do with soap and water to freshen up, and a squirt of toothpaste on her finger in place of a toothbrush. At least if Daniel was insistent on her going home she'd have time to shower and change before work, though she was a bit miffed she wasn't even being offered breakfast. Okay, so it might be a one-time deal, but they still had to see each other. This wasn't some anonymous hook-up with someone he was never going to cross paths with again. His attitude was the equivalent of phoning her a taxi to get rid of her as soon as possible.

'I guess I'll be on my way.' When she came out of the bathroom, Daniel was sitting on the edge of the bed, waiting. She didn't want to make this any more awkward than it already was when they were going to have to work together in another couple of hours. Goodness knew how she was supposed to carry on as though last night had never happened when it had completely rocked her world.

He'd made her think about what she was missing out on, and if it was possible she might not have to spend the rest of her life on her own after all.

'I—I thought you might like to go swimming with me this morning.' He was fidgeting with his hands, not quite meeting her eye, as though he was asking her out on a first date and they hadn't spent most of last night naked together.

'Swimming? Like, in the loch? What about work?' She couldn't have been more shocked if he'd asked her to stroll into town hand in hand. At least he wasn't trying to get rid of her, so she hoped that meant he wasn't harbouring any regrets about sleeping together. She certainly wasn't.

'We've got plenty of time. I thought we could swing by your place so you could get your swimming things, then head down to the loch. I've made us some tea to take with us.'

It was such a sweet gesture, Eloise was going to ignore the fact that taking an ice-cold dip at this ungodly hour was the last thing she'd ever want to do. Daniel was extending their time alone together and she wasn't going to turn that down. Especially if it meant they might have a chance to continue whatever it was happening between them.

'Sure. What about Lucky?' She didn't want to neglect the other man in her world.

'I've already taken him for a walk. As soon as his leg is healed, he'll be able to go swimming too, but in the meantime I think we should keep him away from the water.'

'I didn't even hear you leave.' Eloise tried not to get too excited about the prospect of this morning routine becoming a full-time arrangement if he was talking about taking the dog once he was healed. Of course, he could be talking about going solo, but why else mention it if he wasn't going to include her?

And this was why she needed to stop reading things into everything he said...

'You were out for the count and I didn't want to wake you. You looked so peaceful. Besides, I kept you up late last night.' His eyes took on that dark, hungry glaze that made her pulse flutter, along with every other part of her.

The mere mention of what they'd been up to into the small hours of the morning made her want to do it all over again. However, with Daniel up and dressed before she'd awakened, it gave a clear indication that he wasn't ready for that. She didn't want to push things too far when she didn't even know what it was she wanted herself. An affair with the boss didn't seem like the smartest move for someone just starting out, and if it turned out to just be a one-time thing it might be easier for them to move past.

'I guess we should go, then, if we want to have time for that cuppa before work?' The sooner they got out of this bedroom, the less likely they were to submit to temptation again. Then they might be able to think a bit clearer about what happened next and what they wanted from one another.

Eloise was almost giddy as they pulled up outside her house. It reminded her of her teenage years when she'd been excited about Sam coming to take her out to the cinema, or an early-bird dinner at the local restaurant.

She rushed upstairs and rifled through her drawers. It took her a while to locate her black one-piece swimsuit. She hadn't worn it in an age, since she'd become paranoid about her rounded tummy. Although she enjoyed swimming, she'd become stuck in that vicious circle—not wanting to be seen in public in anything but baggy clothes, yet the lack of exercise adding to her weight problem. Here it didn't matter, since Daniel had seen her in a lot less and hadn't complained. He'd actually been very complimentary, but she didn't think anyone here was ready for skinny-dipping just yet.

'It's so peaceful here.' As they got out of the car in the layby near the loch, the only sound was the early morning birds chirping in the trees and the rustle of leaves in the breeze.

'That's why I like to come here first thing. It sets me up for the day. Puts me on an even keel before the madness of barking dogs and hissing cats.'

She supposed it was a big adjustment every day, transitioning from the quietness of being in his house alone into the bustling veterinary practice. Eloise, on the other hand, longed for that busy white noise that came with running a family home.

Whilst she didn't miss the city so much, she wasn't used to living on her own like Daniel. She'd gone straight from living with her parents to being married, then being a housewife and mother. It had seemed like a punishment to have all of that taken away from her when she'd spent years looking after everyone else. Maybe she could learn something from Daniel and find the peace she was searching for here.

He took a bag and blanket from the boot of the car and led her down the bank via a small trail where the grass had been trodden flat, most likely worn down from his routine morning swim. Daniel seemed like a creature of habit, which made it all the more remarkable that he was including her.

'It's going to be cold at first, but your body will soon adjust.' He began stripping off, folding his clothes into a pile as he went.

Eloise tried not to stare as she undressed. Somehow it seemed more intimate to strip off here together in the broad daylight, even though they weren't planning anything more than an early morning dip.

Daniel waded into the water first, giving her a quick glimpse of his cute backside in his swimming shorts, before turning to wave her in. It was tempting to rush in so he didn't get a good look at her in her swimsuit, but the moment she stepped into the water the cold took her breath away.

'It's freezing!' She kept her arms and chest out of the water as much as she could, walking out to meet him.

'You'll get used to it. Just take deep breaths.' He held her hands and coached her through some breathing exercises.

Eloise tried to follow his instruction but she couldn't

get past the pain the icy water caused every exposed part of her. It was like needles jabbing at her skin.

'Tell…me…why…this…is…a…good…idea…' It was difficult to get the words out in between gasps of air.

'It's good for the heart—increases circulation. And it wakes you up in the morning.'

'Well, one of those things is true…' She was standing on her frozen tiptoes, trying to keep as much of her body out of the water as possible.

'It's better to just dive in there so your body adjusts to the temperature.' Daniel started by splashing some water on his face and chest, then threw himself onto his back and lay there floating, daring her to do the same.

Eloise could never be called a coward. With a deep breath, she bent her knees and ducked her head right under the surface so she was completely submerged in the cold depths of the loch. It wasn't long before she sprang up again, gasping for air, since it all seemed to have left her lungs. At this stage, though, she had nothing else to lose, so she launched herself forward, keeping her head up, letting her arms and legs propel her towards Daniel.

'See? You'll get used to it,' he said, rolling over onto his belly before swimming away.

'I'm not so sure about that,' she grumbled, unconvinced about the benefits, or the enjoyment he claimed to associate with the experience.

What she did know was that she was doing it to spend more time with Daniel, and that said something about the strength of feeling she had towards him. She wasn't usually the sort of person who'd feign interest in anything to keep someone else happy—at least, not any more.

When she realised that was the reason she'd stayed in her marriage so long, she felt like a fraud. She might have got out sooner, made a different life for herself before she got too old for it, if she hadn't simply tried to play the good wife for far too long. If she'd been honest with her husband and herself, they might've parted ways a long time ago. She supposed she should be thankful to him for finally having the courage to end it for her. Despite how hurt she'd been, it was probably better in the long run to go their own ways than to pretend they still had a relationship. Eloise didn't want to pretend any more.

After a few laps up and down, doing her best to take in the beautiful scenery and quietness, she had to admit defeat.

'Sorry, Daniel. I'm going to have to get out. It's just too cold for me.'

The look of disappointment on his face was apparent, but she knew it was only because he wanted her to enjoy it as much as he did. As she dried off, wrapping a huge towel around her body, he began to emerge from the water too. His skin pink, his hair plastered to his scalp and swimming shorts moulded to him, he was a sight worth coming here for.

'You don't have to get out of the water because of me. I'm happy to sit here and warm up.' *And watch.*

'It's fine, just a quick dip. I'm not a masochist!' He grinned, and she was glad she was forgiven for prematurely ending the swim session.

'Here. You need to get warmed up too.' She handed him another towel, watching as he dried his hair and body before doing a quick change beneath it. The logistics of changing out of her wet things and into her work clothes was a little trickier for her, trying not to flash her bits to unsuspecting hikers who might happen by. Somehow she managed it, just about keeping her dignity intact.

'This will help get some heat back into us.' Daniel rummaged around in the bag and pulled out a small metallic flask and two cups. He poured them both a cup of hot, steaming tea, then produced a spread of croissants, muffins and fresh fruit.

Now this was more like it.

'Do you do this every morning?'

'Pretty much. Although, I've put on a bigger breakfast spread than usual for you.' He took a huge bite of a croissant, flaky crumbs dropping onto the stubble of beard lining his strong jaw.

Eloise supposed it wouldn't be appropriate to lick them off. Instead, she made do with a blueberry muffin, breaking it into small pieces before eating it so she didn't make a mess, even though she was ravenous. Exercise was certainly making her hungry. Between great sex and swimming, she was getting more of a work-out than usual and she had to admit she did feel great.

'It's very much appreciated.' She washed the cakey goodness down with some hot tea, slowly beginning to thaw from the inside out.

'So, wild swimming isn't for you, then?' She wasn't clear if he was asking out of politeness or if it was more of an open invitation to join him again. Eloise wasn't going to turn down a chance to spend more quality time with him.

'I could *learn* to love it. It is invigorating, and I'm definitely wide awake now.' She could see why it appealed to Daniel, but having breakfast together was the bit she was enjoying the most. It was a reward for her effort, and that was definitely something she could get used to.

'I could stay here all day.' Daniel sighed and stretched out flat on the blanket, hands behind his head and eyes closed.

Eloise acted instinctively, leaning over to kiss him. It was a thanks for everything he'd done for her last night and this morning. It was also an urge she couldn't seem to pass up when she looked at him, which was going to make work interesting.

She knew was taking a chance by continuing what had happened last night into today. They hadn't discussed how they wanted to play this: if it was a spontaneous event which should be consigned to the past, or perhaps was the start of something for them. However, since he'd been the one to suggest she join him this morning, she was willing to take the chance that he hadn't tired of her already.

It was one that paid off, as Daniel slipped his arms around her neck and pulled her deeper into the kiss. Only when she began to get a crick in her neck because of the awkward angle she sat at did she break away. 'I wasn't sure if you still wanted that.'

'Did it feel like I didn't want that?'

'You know what I mean, Daniel. What is it exactly we're getting into?' She wanted to be clear from the outset so she wouldn't be blindsided when he dumped her like everyone else. At least if she was aware this feeling of being wanted had a shelf life, she might better be able to prepare for it this time.

He sat up and hugged his knees. 'I have no idea.'

'Helpful.'

At least she made him laugh.

'I'm sure neither of us planned for this to happen, and maybe that's the way we should continue.'

'Aimlessly?' She wasn't sure if that was enough for her. Being held at his whim, waiting for word if he still wanted her or if he'd decided she wasn't worth the hassle of adjusting his lifestyle to include her, was a precarious position she'd been in once too often already. He screwed up his face at that description. Her whole new life, possibly her future, was riding on how this worked out.

'I understand how big of a deal this is, moving on from Anne, and I don't want to put you under any pressure to make a decision. However, I'm a little concerned about where this would leave me in terms of my job if you decide this isn't what you want—that I'm not want you want.'

She swallowed hard. It was difficult to admit that was what was going on inside her head when it sounded so desperate, so needy, but she needed some clarification, some reassurance she hadn't just screwed everything up when she'd started to settle in here.

He was frowning by the time she'd finished. 'One

thing I can assure you of is that I intend to keep my work and personal life separate. I always have—until now, at least. If we'd met anywhere else, this wouldn't even have entered your head. Whatever happens between us, your job is safe. I think we're both old enough and wise enough to figure out the important things in life.'

Eloise wasn't so sure when they'd already failed to acknowledge that last night had probably changed everything for them, but she didn't argue as he pulled her in for another kiss. His hands tangled in her wet hair, his soft lips reassuring her that this was all they needed, and it almost convinced her it was true. Even though, deep down, a little voice was telling her that he'd never answered the question.

CHAPTER TEN

IF DANIEL COULD just have sat there for ever with Eloise, he'd quite happily have done so. Especially when he was kissing her, all thoughts of the real world fading into insignificance. Being with her held so much promise, a future he'd never deemed possible after he'd lost Anne.

Of course, that in itself burdened him with guilt when he'd sworn there would never be another woman for him—no one with whom he'd want to spend every minute of every day, or who'd ever understand him the way she had. Perhaps because he'd thought he'd never meet that woman who'd tempt him from his self-imposed isolation again. It had seemed improbable to be that fortunate twice in one lifetime.

Now that Eloise appeared to have blown that theory out of the water, it was his decision whether or not he wanted to risk breaking what was left of his heart again if things didn't work out. She wanted a commitment from him, or at the very least a definition of their relationship, but he couldn't give her that. At least, not yet. Opening up his small world to include her in it permanently would mean opening up his heart, being vulnerable again, and he would have to dig deep to find that level of courage before he could commit to that.

'What's that?' Eloise broke the silence that had fallen between them as they finished their tea, and he avoided answering the question.

She anxiously looked around, as though something had spooked her. He hoped they hadn't been spotted by anyone he knew or he would have some explaining to do, pushing him into making a call he really wasn't ready to do.

'I didn't hear anything.' He watched on as Eloise got up and walked away from the small clearing to the leafy bushes nearby.

'Shh. Listen.' She stopped, ears pricked, clearly having heard something he hadn't.

He sat still and quiet, until a chirp finally pierced the silence. It immediately spurred Eloise on in her search, parting the branches, ignoring the jagged brush clawing at her legs in her pursuit.

'Oh, Daniel, he's hurt.'

At the sound of her distress, he got to his feet and went to investigate for himself. She kept the branches parted so he could see what she was looking at: a little starling was hopping around in circles, clearly hurt. Every now and then it gave its wings a flutter but only managed to lift himself partially off the ground.

'It looks as though he's got a broken wing.' Daniel knelt down and cupped his hands gently but firmly around the bird, cradling it as he got to his feet.

'Have we got anything to put him in?'

'The box which had the breakfast pastries in should do.' They made their way back to the blanket and Eloise emptied out the plastic container so they could put the injured bird inside.

'Poor baby,' she soothed, stroking the bird as it pecked at the remaining crumbs in the box. 'Can we help him?'

'I'm sure we can try.' The pleading look she gave him was so full of compassion and hope, there was no way he'd deny the request.

It was clear Eloise was the sort of woman who wore her heart on her sleeve, which made her a vulnerable target for someone who didn't appreciate her. No wonder that the end of her marriage had hurt so much. He knew she'd taken it personally, shouldered the blame and retreated into herself as a result. These were all things he could empathise with when he'd done the same after Anne had died. It was the very reason they were both tiptoeing around the idea of a relationship, even though they were clearly benefitting from being together.

'We can try and make him a splint or something, until it heals.' Eloise pouted, clearly upset on the creature's behalf.

It showed just how nurturing she was and gave Daniel an idea of the kind of loving mother she must be. He had no doubt she paid her daughters the same care and attention she did to everyone else, if not more. She needed somewhere to express those motherly feelings which he was sure hadn't disappeared simply because her children weren't in close proximity. Her daughters didn't know how lucky they were to have her. Not everyone got to

grow up in a loving, stable home, which he was sure Eloise had made for her family.

If he was honest, there was a touch of jealousy creeping into his bones at the thought. He would've done anything to have a stable home and family, but it seemed as
though Eloise's loved ones didn't know what they'd had.
Perhaps if his childhood had been different, if his mother
had survived to take care of him, he might've gone on
to have a family of his own. As it was, losing his loved
ones had traumatised him to the point he hadn't wanted
to take the chance of losing anyone else.

Eloise's circumstances had merely cemented that view
given, despite a marriage and two daughters, she'd still
effectively been left on her own. It wasn't fair on someone who clearly had so much love to give. But even he
wouldn't give her the security she needed; he was too
afraid himself, of something happening to jeopardise the
careful existence he'd established for himself here since
Anne had gone.

'We should probably get him back to the clinic with us.
I'll X-ray and bandage the wing and phone a rescue centre. They can look after him until he's able to be released.'

Eloise began to pack away their stuff into the bag he'd
carried down, but Daniel didn't want to go back to work
just yet. It wouldn't be fair to go back to being colleagues,
not discussing what had happened and hope it would all
work out for the best.

He knew he was being selfish by not being upfront
with her about his fears. She needed the same security
he did, but in a different way. From their first night to-

gether he'd known her fears and problems and had held back his own, afraid to let her see inside to that vulnerable part of him. Now it was time that he was honest with her about why he hadn't been able to man up and put a label on what they had together, what they could have.

'Wait.' He grabbed her hand in his, and she simply stared at it, as though she was afraid this was the last time they'd be able to touch. His heart caught, pained by the fact she knew he'd deny her once they were in company, yet still wanted her in his bed.

'We should go,' she said again, her voice barely a whisper on the wind.

'We will, but first I want to be honest with you about what's happening. How I'm feeling.' He was nauseous at the thought of sharing such personal information, but Eloise deserved to know why he was holding back. Especially when it wasn't her fault.

She sat back, listening, waiting for him to open his heart. Even their little one-winged patient had stopped chirping, giving him the floor to speak without interruption. All he had to do was find the courage to use his voice.

'I like being with you,' he started.

'Thank goodness for that.' Eloise attempted to lighten the sudden tension between them and he appreciated that she was trying to make this easier for him.

'You have to understand that growing up in care, constantly moving around foster homes and living with different people, wasn't easy. It was hard for me to feel secure, or to get close to people, because I knew I'd inevitably have to move again. I'd already lost my mother, didn't know my father and it was too hard to keep making friends or getting close to a family, only to move on again. So I learned to keep an emotional distance, preventing my heart from taking another battering.

'Then I met Anne… Up until then, my relationships had been short-term, casual, and work was the only thing I fully committed to. She showed me that we wanted the same things, but we could still have a good time, enjoy one another's company. Anne showed me how not to be afraid to love again. Then she died.'

'And you hid yourself away from the world again.'

Eloise got it. She seemed to understand him in a way no one else did.

'It seems safer that way. I hadn't counted on meeting you. On getting close.'

'Neither had I. I didn't think I'd ever get that lucky.' Her compliment warmed his insides even more than the flask of tea. Yet he didn't want her to think that he was the answer to all her problems. There was a long way to go for both of them.

'The thing is…it's a big step for me to have anyone in my life. It's going to take a while to get used to.'

'I can wait. It's not like I'm going anywhere soon.'

'I just… I need to process the fact that I'm moving on. That I *want* to move on. Until then, I'd like to carry on the way we are—getting to know one another, spending time together, making love…'

Even saying it, thinking about it, made him want her all over again. If it wasn't for the fact they had to get to work, or that someone might see them, he'd take her right this minute. As tempting as outdoor sex was, they had reputations and jobs to protect, and were supposedly mature enough to keep their libidos in check until they had somewhere private to go. It might make it even hotter when they would have to hold back until after work.

'I think we can manage that.' Eloise leaned over and gave him a sweet peck on the lips, which he hoped was something they'd get to expand on later.

Everything he had with Eloise was something to look forward to; sharing his working day, having dinner together, even walking the dog, were all tasks much improved by having her as a partner. In their own way they were becoming a little family, with Lucky and their new little patient to take care of together. It was something he'd always been too afraid to want. All he had to do now was let go of that damaged foster child inside so he could get on with this new life being offered to him.

'Daniel? What are you doing here? I told you I'm out of action for the foreseeable future.' Eloise rubbed her eyes and pulled her dressing gown tighter around her body as the cold air filtered in from the open door.

She'd thought something was wrong when her doorbell had rung at this hour of the morning, but Daniel was standing on her doorstep with Lucky, both looking happy to see her.

'That doesn't mean we have to miss breakfast. It was hard enough not waking up to you this morning. For future reference, I'm happy to just cuddle, as long as that means you'll stay over.' He pushed past her into the house and in the kitchen began unpacking the bag he was carrying, with a loyal Lucky trotting in behind him.

'Well, come on in,' she said, unbothered by the interruption to her lie-in.

They'd got into something of a routine before work: waking up, going for a swim then having breakfast. Of course, the best part of all of that for her was sitting having tea with him, but she was getting used to the ice-cold wake-up call too.

It was difficult, not touching each other at work, but they'd been careful not to let their 'relationship' spill over into the work environment. As far as she was aware, they'd managed to keep it secret from their colleagues, but she looked forward to closing time. Then she'd slip into Daniel's house for dinner, and more often than not she'd stay the night.

Even though she'd prefer to have more of a commitment, to put her mind at ease that he wasn't going to decide he didn't want anything more than a casual arrangement, she was happy enough with the situation for now. It was more than she'd ever expected to have when she'd moved here.

The only fly in the ointment at present was her unreliable hormones, which had sprung some breakthrough bleeding on her. She wasn't due her period for another week, but her bedroom adventures with Daniel had been curtailed for now, along with the swimming. They seemed to be on the same page, though, with being together seeming more important than the physical aspect of their evenings. It was that intimacy she missed.

'Do you want proper cups or the usual?' He waved the little metallic mugs she'd come to know and love, since it was a symbol of their early morning quality time together, rain or shine.

'There's no point in breaking the habit. It almost tastes better out of those.' She stood by and let him fix their usual selection of pastries and fruit, along with their tea. He looked at home in her kitchen, and she loved that he'd even thought to do this for her.

Her problems had been nothing but an inconvenience to Sam; how she was feeling had been immaterial. He'd only been concerned with how it impacted on his life. Selfish—a word that could never be used to describe Daniel. She saw the way he interacted with the sick and injured animals at work, and the owners, who sometimes needed a little more careful handling. He gave a lot, and never expected anything in return. That was something she wasn't used to.

'It's nice to do this in the warmth for once, don't you think?' Daniel handed her a cup and carried their indoor picnic into the living room.

'Do you know what would be even nicer?' she asked, taking a bite of a sugar-glazed donut he must have bought especially, knowing what a sweet tooth she had.

'What's that?' Daniel helped himself to a nectarine, the juice dribbling down his chin as he bit into it.

Everything about this man was a turn-on, which in itself was like getting blood from a stone. Before him, she'd thought her body had given up on the idea of being with anyone again. Now she knew differently…though there was only one man she wanted to be with, who made her feel this way.

Regardless that neither of them wanted to label their relationship, both afraid of their feelings and scarred by the past, she knew she was falling for him. She'd jumped right in at the deep end, and was struggling to keep her head above water, because she knew already that if he decided to end things she would be devastated.

'Breakfast in bed; maybe on a Sunday morning, when we don't have to get up for work.' She could picture it, them cosied up together, spending the whole day in bed, making love and snacking on pastries. *Heaven.*

'I'm sure that can be easily arranged when you're feeling better. If you want to come over tonight, I'm making spaghetti. I've also got chocolate and a hot-water bottle if you want to cuddle up on the sofa and watch a soppy film.'

Eloise watched him through suspicious eyes. 'Have you been typing "perfect man" into a search engine, trying to impress me?'

He was saying all the right things, offering comfort food and emotional support. There had to be a catch somewhere.

'Am I being too OTT? Sorry. I just felt as though I never did enough for Anne when she was going through this and I want to be there for you.'

Even the words, without the gesture, were enough to bring her to tears, just knowing he wanted to help. He never made her feel like a burden, or an inconvenience, despite her crashing into his life and upending his routine.

'I'm sure Anne was grateful to you just for being there. I know I am. You don't have to go to any trouble for me. Although, I'd love some comfort food…and chocolate. I'll take you instead of the hot-water bottle, and there's no need for a soppy movie. I'm a bit too cynical for those these days. I'd settle for a thriller.'

She didn't care what they would watch; it would just be nice to cuddle up with him, with no expectation of pretending that she was up for anything else. There was no telling where their new arrangement was going to lead, but Eloise knew she wanted it to last.

Her phone rang then, the outside world breaking into their morning ritual. When she saw her eldest daughter Dawn's name on the screen, her heart became more full than it had in ages. Those lonely days rattling around the house on her own with nothing to look forward to, no one to talk to, seemed a lifetime away now. Since coming here, she had someone to be with, to look forward to a future with, and she knew being happier in herself would mean being a better mother. Moving here was the best thing she'd done in years and she hoped it would stay that way.

'It's my daughter,' Eloise told him as she grabbed her phone. 'Do you mind if I take this?'

'Of course not.'

She didn't want to be rude by taking the call, but neither did she want to ignore it. As excited as Eloise was to hear from Dawn, she worried that there might be something wrong.

'Hi, honey. Is everything okay?' She paced across the living room floor, that worry clutching at her stomach until she was assured that her daughter was all right.

'Hi, Mum. Everything's fine. I just wanted to call you with some news. Curtis and I are having a baby.'

'What?' That tension lifted, her spirits soaring with the happy news and her daughter's obvious joy at becoming a mother herself. She just wanted to make sure she hadn't imagined it.

'I'm pregnant. I wanted to wait until the third-month scan to make sure everything's okay with the baby.'

'And is it?'

'Yes. Everything's great. We're over the moon.'

'I'm so happy for you. That's wonderful news, so exciting for everyone. I'm sure your sister will be delighted to find out she's going to be an auntie.'

'And you're going to be a granny. Or would you prefer "Nanny"? Maybe "Glam-ma"?' she teased.

'Granny's fine. I'm not bothered about titles. I'm just over the moon that you're going to have a little one of your own.' She turned to grin at Daniel to let him in on the happy news too. He gave her a thumbs-up, and for a brief moment she pictured babysitting her grandchild with him.

Then the pretty picture dissipated when she remembered that her daughter lived in another country and she'd be lucky even to get a cuddle with the new member of the family. As much as she was enjoying her new life here, she was still mourning her old one. Now she'd have even more reason to miss her daughters and her role in their lives. Even Daniel wasn't going to fill that void in her heart that her family had left, and it was only going to get bigger by the day, knowing there would now be a baby for her to miss too.

'I'm going to be a mum,' Dawn whispered, as though she couldn't believe it was true.

Emotion choked Eloise now; she was thrilled for her, but sad for herself that she wasn't going to be a part of that journey with her. If she was lucky, she'd get to be an occasional visitor into their lives—something that wasn't currently working out too well for her.

'You're going to be wonderful.' Her voice cracked, the effort of holding back finally becoming too much. She turned away from Daniel so he wouldn't see her tears, even though he could probably hear them.

'Actually, Mum, it's got me thinking… I want you to be part of this. To be in our lives. I don't want my baby to grow up not knowing you. You'd make such a wonderful grandmother.'

'But I don't know how that would work.' It was breaking her heart already, knowing that she wasn't going to see this baby grow up and be part of all of those firsts that she'd gone through with her own children.

Her ex-husband had always been the main breadwinner and she'd taken care of things at home. That had meant being the more involved parent, attending school meetings and plays, arranging play dates and making sure big occasions such as birthdays and Christmas were special.

The chance to do all of that again, or at least be included in it, was something she'd thought she'd never get to have. Now it was almost within her reach again, it was torture that only distance would keep her from it.

Dawn cleared her throat. 'Well, we've been talking it over, and you know we have a huge house here? I know you're on your own over there and I thought maybe, you know, you might want to move in with us. You could help me with child care when I go back to work, or just be there. I miss you, Mum.'

'I miss you too, sweetheart.' If she'd had this offer a couple of weeks earlier, Eloise wouldn't have thought twice about taking Dawn up on the idea. Now, however, she'd set up a new life for herself. She had someone here she cared about, a job, a house and a future of her own. It was a pity there wasn't a way for her to have it all.

'Anyway, you have plenty of time to think it over. I better go call Dad and share the news.'

Eloise could only imagine how that news was going to go down with Sam when he was so caught up with reliving his youth. Becoming a grandad certainly wouldn't be such an exciting prospect for him, she was sure. It was very telling that he wasn't being invited to help raise the new addition to the family.

'Okay, sweetheart. Congratulations again, and I'll definitely think the offer over.'

'I hope you decide to come. I miss you. Bye, Mum.'

'Talk to you later. Bye.'

She ended the call and flopped down into a chair, emotionally wiped out by the exchange.

'Good news, I take it? Congratulations.' Daniel raised his cup of tea to her.

'Thanks. It's a lot to take in. I'm too young to be a granny,' she protested with a laugh, even though it really didn't bother her at all.

'When's the baby due?'

'You know, I didn't even ask the exact date, but she's three months gone. She's asked me if I would like to move out there with them and be more of a hands-on grandmother.'

'Oh? And that...that's something you'd want to do?' Despite Daniel's carefully worded question, she understood the meaning behind it. He wanted to know if she was going to leave him.

'Yes and no. I have a life here I'm not ready to abandon. But it's something I'm going to have to at least consider.'

'Of course.'

After he'd opened up to her about his past, and why he didn't want to get close to anyone, Eloise understood why he'd be concerned about this new development.

Eloise wished she didn't have to make a decision between him and her family at all, but at least she had a few months to think about it. To see how things went with Daniel and her, and if he'd prove serious competition for her new grandchild when it came to sharing her life and her heart.

CHAPTER ELEVEN

'IT'S BEEN QUITE a day, hasn't it?' Eloise finished wiping down the examination table, then took a handkerchief and mopped Daniel's brow.

He forced a laugh, glad that they'd been busy today so it hadn't left them a lot of time to talk. After the phone call that morning, he'd been somewhat at a loss for words. Eloise hearing from her daughter, and her otherwise happy news, had left him feeling on the outside of her life and it made him uncomfortable.

Things were fine when they were in their little bubble of two, where none of their real worries were allowed to enter. That contact from her family changed everything. Though he was glad for her sake that someone other than he could finally see her worth, it was forcing them to take stock of their relationship—something he'd been shying away from with good reason it seemed.

This was everything that he'd been afraid of. The second he'd opened his heart, fate had conspired to take her away from him...unless he was honest about his feelings for her. He knew he'd fallen hard, and that was why he was so afraid of committing. But if he wasn't up front about how much she meant to him, how much he wanted her in his life, she mightn't think there was anything worth staying here for.

He resolved to have an honest conversation with her over dinner tonight. Then at least she'd have all the facts at hand when she made her decision.

Just as they turned off the lights in the surgery, getting ready for the best part of his day when they were alone in his place, someone started hammering on the front door.

'Can someone help? Please.' The woman on the doorstep looked desperate, clutching the hand of a toddler and cradling something in her other hand.

'I guess the day isn't over just yet.' Daniel wouldn't turn anyone away and immediately unlocked the door to admit one more patient.

'Come on through.' Eloise turned the lights back on and led the latecomers through to the exam room she'd just cleaned down.

'He's just started fitting. I don't know what's wrong with him.' The woman set a rabbit and the blanket it was wrapped in down on the table.

The little boy with her was obviously upset at witnessing his pet's distress, and Daniel couldn't be sure at this stage he could even save the rabbit.

'Hey, sweetheart. What's your bunny's name?' Eloise, who was clearly on the same page, knelt down to speak to the child, distracting him from what was going on.

'Angus.'

'That's a lovely name. Did you call him that?'

The boy nodded.

'I'm Eloise, and the man taking care of your rabbit is Daniel. What's your name?'

He looked at his mum for confirmation it was okay for him to share that information with a stranger. When she gave him the go-ahead, he muttered a shy, 'Frankie.'

'Well, Frankie, why don't we let Daniel and your mum talk in here and we'll go and find something fun to do?' Eloise took the boy's hand and turned to Daniel, mouthing, 'Is that okay?'

He waved her away, keen to get the child out as soon as possible, knowing that there was probably little he could do for the animal except give it pain relief and hope the seizures stopped soon.

The sound of Eloise's voice carried down the corridor as she engaged with the little boy, and his excited response as she took him into the waiting room. Daniel had seen her on occasion, helping the kids colour in when they were waiting for news on their beloved pets, or holding babies for anxious parents trying to juggle animals and toddlers. It was obvious she was born to mother and he could only imagine how happy her family life had made her before everyone had gone their separate ways. It was probably as much a vocation for her as her job, if not more.

He supposed her role here was scant consolation for the one she'd lost, as was he. Going swimming, watching TV and sleeping over wasn't much to offer in comparison to her having that family life again. It wouldn't be fair to keep her here, pretending that he could ever fill that void in her life where her children, and now her grandchildren, had a right to be. It was tempting to beg her to stay so he didn't lose her, but it would also be selfish.

He couldn't promise her any of the things she clearly needed in her life, like children or family. Neither could he be sure that whatever this was would last, or make it worth the heartbreak for either of them. If he couldn't completely open up to her, it would be a betrayal to them both. As far as he could see, letting this thing between them go on any longer would simply end in pain, and they'd both had enough of that to last lifetimes.

At least by letting her go now, on his terms, he'd save himself some of that heartbreak just waiting round the corner when she decided he hadn't been worth the sacrifice after all.

One of them deserved to be happy, and he could go back to the way his life had been before Eloise had made him think he could have something more. Now he just had to tell her it was over and she wouldn't have to choose between a couple of strays and her real family, who still needed her.

'Bless him; little Frankie wanted to make a "get well soon" card for his bunny.' Eloise barely made it into Daniel's house before collapsing onto the sofa. It had been a physical and emotionally draining day. She was glad he wasn't expecting anything more than dinner and a cuddle.

Daniel winced. 'I'm not sure that's going to happen if the rabbit doesn't stop fitting or start eating soon. I've sedated him and he's been given fluids. I'll check on him again after dinner, but given his age I don't think he's going to make it. I explained the situation to the mother so I think she's going to try and break the news to her little boy so it doesn't come as such a shock.'

'Aww, that's sad, but children are resilient. When Alison's hamster, Biscuit, died she was sad until we took her out to get another one—then Biscuit Mark Two became the best thing since sliced bread. It's important for them to learn about death and grief. Although, I hope when I go they'll mourn me long after the next Mrs Carter comes on the scene.'

Losing a pet was the hardest, and the worst part of being both an owner and working at the clinic. Some things were simply out of their control, and Eloise was definitely happier when she had some power over what was happening, although today's events were testing that theory.

She had a big decision to make about her future and it was sure to cause more than a few sleepless nights. Her family had always come first, but that was how she'd ended up alone when they'd all moved on, with no life of her own. It had taken her time, perseverance and Daniel's help to get where she was now. She didn't want to just abandon the life she'd made here for herself.

Yet, the prospect of being part of a family again was exciting, and everything she'd wanted. If only there was a way to have it all, she'd be one very lucky woman. But that wasn't the way life worked out for her. Something would have to give, and it was going to be painful, whatever happened.

No doubt Daniel was thinking the same, as he'd been quieter than usual at work, and even during dinner. Even now, instead of the promised snuggling in front of the TV, they were sitting at opposite ends of the sofa. It was as though by distancing themselves from one another they could avoid the subject she knew had to be addressed sooner or later.

'I'm not sure if I want to be a full-time nanny to my own grandchild.' She hadn't meant to spit it out like that, but she'd been thinking about it all day, and he was the only person she could talk to about it.

'Why not?' He stopped stroking Lucky, who was lying on the floor at his feet, so he could turn his attention to her instead.

'I mean, of course I want to spend time with him, or her, and any other future grandchildren. I just don't know if that's all I want. I have a life here now.'

Deep down, she was hoping Daniel was going to declare his undying love for her and beg her to stay, taking the decision out of her hands. Because she knew where she wanted to be…and that was right here.

'Don't pin all your hopes on me, Eloise.'

He fixed her with a dark stare that she hadn't seen from him before. It chilled her, freezing the blood in her veins that had been pumping with excitement at the prospect of a future with him until now.

'Don't you want me to stay?' She almost couldn't get the words out, she was so aghast. With the way things had been between them, she hadn't really considered that. Yes, she knew they'd have some challenges to work through when they were both carrying so much baggage from the past, but she'd thought they were at least on the same page as far as their relationship went. That they wanted to be together.

As Daniel leaned forward, looking down at his feet instead of meeting her eye, she realised he thought differently.

'It's not about me, or at least it shouldn't be. You know I'm not ready to commit to anything, I've been clear about that.'

'I knew you had concerns about getting hurt—not that you didn't *want* something more between us.' That changed everything. He was right, in that she wouldn't give up the chance to be with her family and have a life including them if all that remained here was an empty house and only herself for company. She'd had that for too long and she needed more to fulfil her.

Except, Eloise thought that she'd found more for herself here: Daniel. She didn't want to pin everything on him, but he'd helped her find herself again. It wouldn't be inconceivable to want that to continue. Though she should have learned her lesson on relying on others to give her existence meaning. She was always going to be left scrabbling to find a life of her own when they didn't need her any more.

'I said I wanted to carry on with what we were doing. If you stay on account of me, instead of going to be with your family, you're asking something of me that I'm not ready to give.'

Daniel shrugged, proving he wasn't as bothered as she was about the whole situation. It was clear cut for him, and perhaps it would be easier if she was no longer in the picture at all. She'd been a fool again.

'And what would I do here in the meantime? It will take a while to sort things out and the baby isn't even due for another six months.'

Now she had no other option but to leave if Daniel didn't feel for her what she did for him. Her feelings were too deep to stick around and see him every day, knowing that he couldn't be hers. Besides, she'd spent enough of her life putting other people's needs and wants before her own, and Daniel had made her see she was worthy of someone's love. If it was never going to be him, there was no point staying and mooning after him, fighting her feelings every day just to keep other people happy.

She'd have to go. That would mean selling up, moving or storing all of her belongings and working out the logistics of moving to another country. They were things she hoped she could sort out sooner rather than later, because she didn't think she could stand months of being around him and being reminded of everything she'd lost. That if he'd been brave enough, or loved her enough, they could've had a future.

Perhaps it was simply because *she* wasn't enough for him. All those thoughts she'd had, that he'd support her through menopause and anything else, had been apparently no more than wishful thinking. No doubt if she'd been one of those sexy, slim, elegant women approaching her fifties she might've had a shot. She'd been fooling herself by thinking otherwise. All she'd been was convenient...until now.

'I told you your job would be safe no matter what happened between us. It'll take me a while to find a replacement anyway.' He was so matter of fact about the end of their relationship, such as it was, she wondered why she'd invested so much in it.

Now he'd taken a step beyond his mourning, at least into a physical arrangement, he might eventually move on to a proper relationship some day. Apparently that wouldn't be with her and it made her think that he wouldn't look for a replacement for just her role in the clinic.

As for her, it would be a while before she put herself out there again. She supposed she should be thankful she'd had one last fling before she'd been completely written off. At least if she moved out to be with her daughter she wouldn't find herself on the scrapheap altogether.

Eloise stared at him, at a loss for words, because those nights together, not to mention their mornings, didn't seem to mean anything to him when it had been everything to her. She knew that companionship, the reason to get up in the mornings and the passion she'd thought had long gone were all things she wouldn't have with anyone else when it had taken her this long to find them.

'So, what was this tonight—a last supper?' She'd been looking forward to everything; now it just seemed like a cruel joke, with her pasta dinner now weighing heavily in her stomach.

'I made you a promise…'

The bitter, 'Ha!' that escaped her lips wasn't planned, but appropriate. She supposed technically he hadn't made her a promise where their relationship was concerned, but it had been implied—in her mind, at least.

Somehow this felt like an even bigger betrayal than her husband leaving her after thirty years of marriage. Most likely, because she'd opened up to Daniel more than she ever had to Sam. It showed the lack of communication they'd had, that she hadn't been able to tell him how she was feeling, or vice versa, before it had been too late. Daniel had never said, or done, any of the hurtful things to her that her husband had at the end of their relationship, but this was still painful, because his strength of feeling for her wasn't enough for him to fight for her, even to ask her to stay.

That was enough to make the tears well up in her eyes, and she knew she had to leave before she made a scene. She could do her weeping and wailing at home, in private, where there would be no one to see or hear her because she was all alone. And she would have to get it out of her system tonight. After all, she would be expected to go to work in the morning as though nothing had happened. As though her heart hadn't just been freshly ripped from her chest.

'I suppose there's no point in drawing this out, in that case. I'll see you at work tomorrow.'

Eloise grabbed her things and walked out without a backward glance. She didn't give him a chance to talk her round. She'd be too weak to resist if he suggested that they carry on until it was time for her to go, and that would only make it even harder for her to leave.

As she got into her car, tears now blurring her vision, it occurred to her that he hadn't even tried.

CHAPTER TWELVE

'I'M SO SORRY I'm late.' Eloise bustled into the clinic, aware that she looked a mess. There'd been no time to do her make-up or do anything more than run a brush through her hair by the time she woke up. Daniel would probably realise he'd had a lucky escape when he saw her.

She'd spent most of the night crying, eating and re-playing every second they'd spent together since she'd moved here. Wondering how she'd got it so wrong, believing they'd had something special when it clearly meant nothing to him. Perhaps she'd just been so desperate for some affection and attention, she'd read more into it than sex with her boss. Perhaps it was a cliché, not some grand love affair, after all.

'I'm just glad you're here.' Brooke handed her some paperwork before she'd even had time to take off her coat.

It had been tempting to phone in sick rather than face Daniel this morning, but she hadn't wanted to let down her colleagues, who were clearly under enough pressure this morning with a full waiting room. Her subconscious had probably decided for her that a lie-in was called for in order to avoid him, but guilt had got the better of her when she had finally woken up. Now she had to face the man who'd kept her awake with crying over him.

She took a deep breath as she opened the door to the examination room, only to find a complete stranger in a white coat injecting a Pomeranian.

'Sorry,' she said, and closed the door again.

When she checked the other room in case Daniel had moved for some reason, she found Debbie working there instead.

'Where's Daniel?' she asked Brooke.

'Oh, he's taken a leave of absence.'

'Pardon?' She'd been working herself up to come here and he'd taken the easy way out? He really wasn't the man she'd thought he was.

'I know.' Brooke leaned forward with a conspiratorial whisper. 'I've never known him to go on holiday or even take a sick day. Apparently he phoned Debbie at an ungodly hour this morning telling her he'd got cover and would be off indefinitely.'

'He didn't say why, or where, he was going?'

Brooke shrugged. 'That's all I was told. I would've thought if anyone would know it would be you.'

She spun round, back to her computer, dropping the bombshell that they hadn't managed to keep anything secret from their colleagues after all. The only thing more humiliating than that would be having to tell them that he was too embarrassed even to be in the same building as her. Although, they'd probably worked that out for themselves by now.

* * *

Daniel skimmed a stone across the loch, watching the ripples as it bounced, causing a disturbance in the calm water before disappearing altogether. Much like Eloise, who'd burst into his quiet life, forced him out of his comfort zone and caused ripples that were going to affect him long after she'd left the country. Yet he didn't regret a moment with her.

Lucky came and sat beside him at the edge of the loch, tail wagging, panting and as loyal as ever.

'You wouldn't be this happy if you knew that it's just me you're going to be stuck with from now on,' he told the oblivious dog.

Daniel supposed at least he would have some company once Eloise had gone to live with her family. Even if he could never hope a stray mutt could give him the companionship or dreams for a better future he knew he would've had with her. He hoped that by letting her go now she'd have a more fulfilling life with her family rather than just plodding along with him. She deserved more than he had to give.

That didn't mean he wasn't in pain, feeling as though he was mourning a lost love all over again. It would probably seem to Eloise that he'd taken the cowardly way out by getting cover in at work, but the truth was that he didn't think he'd be able to hold it together, seeing her at work, knowing that she was going to leave any day. At least this way he had some control. That was what he was trying to convince himself.

He couldn't even bear to be in his own house, his own

bed, without her. Since Anne had died, he'd convinced himself he could go it alone. He'd had his love and, now it had gone, he simply had to get on with his life, such as it was. Eloise had changed that way of thinking, had shown him a different world with her in it, but he'd lost her the moment her daughter had called.

Now he had to try and get back to life the way it had been before Eloise had disrupted his peace of mind. So he'd rented one of the cabins at the farthest end of the loch from the practice for a few days. Usually it was fishermen or couples on a romantic break who stayed here, away from civilisation, but it was just the dog and him.

He didn't know how long it would take for him to get his head straight before he went back to work and faced Eloise. She wasn't happy with him, or the way he'd ended things, but he hoped that would make the decision to leave easier for her. One day she'd see that and forgive him. The best thing he could probably do for both of them was to stay here, away from the memories, until she left—though he knew that wasn't practical. A couple of days' distancing himself would have to suffice for now.

The sound of splashing and laughter sounded nearby and, perhaps bored with only Daniel's company, Lucky took off to find whoever was nearby. He was probably hoping it was Eloise, come to rescue him again. Daniel jogged along the small strip of shore at the edge of the water, calling him. Apparently they still needed to work on their recall training.

'Lucky, get back here.' Following the excited barks, he

found the escapee mesmerised by the sight of a couple swimming in the loch.

'Sorry. I didn't mean to disturb you. He just ran off.' He called to the elderly pair watching bemusedly as he tried to get Lucky back on his lead.

'That's all right. We're just getting out now.' The man, who Daniel guessed to be in his late seventies, began to stride out, grabbed up hooded robes from the shore and handed one to his wife.

'The cup of tea is the best part. Would you like one?' The woman offered up her flask in one hand and a box of cupcakes in the other.

Daniel smiled. 'That's very kind of you, but I didn't mean to intrude.'

The scene reminded him of the mornings he and Eloise had spent doing the same thing. Not the most thrilling adventure of all time to some people, but it had come to mean so much to him. So much, in fact, that he hadn't been able to go swimming without her since.

'Not at all. We're so used to just seeing each other, it's nice to see a different face for once.' She nudged him with the box of goodies and he decided it would be rude to refuse a second time.

'Do you live near here?' He didn't recognise their faces, although that didn't mean much when he didn't socialise a lot outside of work. Unless they were pet owners, he wasn't likely to have met them before even if they only lived down the road.

'Glasgow. We're just staying in one of the cabins for a couple of nights. It's so peaceful here.' She glanced around the vast wooded area around them, and it reminded Daniel of Eloise's reaction when she'd first arrived.

'It's definitely a change of pace.' He had hoped that this space on his own would help him reset, but it no longer held quite the same appeal.

'Don't get me wrong, I wouldn't like to be here on my own, but Matthew is my rock. Without him it feels like I'm missing a limb.' The woman's words struck him so hard, Daniel felt as though he'd been winded.

'Well, I hope you enjoy your break together. I should get this one back for his dinner, and thanks for the cupcake.' Daniel took Lucky and his sweet treat back to his own cabin, with the stranger's comment ringing in his ears.

When Anne had died, he'd had to adapt to life alone, but Eloise had opened the world up to him again. Losing her, and the possibilities she brought to his life, did make him feel as though part of him was missing: his heart.

The difference between losing Anne and losing Eloise was that his current state was his choice. As if he'd willingly, and bizarrely, decided just to chop off a limb and throw it away—something he'd apparently rather do than simply face up to his feelings and take a chance on love again. This lonely existence he faced again seemed scant consolation when she'd be gone for ever.

He'd thought he was content living and working here, but having her in his life had showed him what real happiness felt like. If he let her go without even trying to make a relationship work, then he really would be the coward she likely thought him now.

That was, if she even wanted him. He couldn't make her choose between her family and him, but the prospect of being without her now seemed more bleak than a future here with his heart still intact—never taking that risk.

To win her back, he was going to have to prove just how much he was willing to commit to her.

'Snookie McDaniels, please.' Usually calling out some of the more amusing pet names made a busy day a little bit brighter, but Eloise hadn't found much to smile about lately.

Without Daniel, this place wasn't somewhere she'd looked forward to coming to any more. Though she was still waking up at six every morning, lying awake, missing their swimming and outdoor breakfasts. She supposed she'd have to get used to it. No one seemed to know when Daniel was coming back, and at this point she wouldn't be surprised if he waited until she'd gone. Her exciting new start appeared to have come to a prematurely sad end.

The family with Snookie the sick tortoise came through to the new vet, who was nice enough, but Eloise couldn't bring herself to move past small talk with him. She was missing Daniel too much. Only time would tell if distance would ease that pain in her heart where he'd taken up residence.

The phone in her pocket vibrated with an incoming call: Dawn. Eloise declined the call and turned her phone off. She'd told her daughter that she was going to move out, and ever since had been plagued with calls about getting organised. Understandable, she supposed, except once she put her house on the market it would make it all real. It really would be over between Daniel and her, and part of her still hopelessly wished she could have it all: a life here with Daniel, her job and still seeing her children and grandchild.

'Eloise, can I talk to you next door?' As though she'd conjured him with thought alone, Daniel came striding in through the clinic door and straight to her.

'What? I'm working.' Her mind was filled with a million questions, but her immediate thought was that he looked good with a few days' stubble.

'I need to speak to you.' He grabbed her arm and there was a desperation in his eyes she couldn't ignore.

'Can you...?' She turned to Brooke, who was watching their interplay with fascination.

'I'll tell him you got called away to an emergency,' she said with a smile.

'Thanks.' Eloise's heart was thumping against her rib cage, her stomach like a whirlpool as she followed Daniel, wondering what on earth was so important.

Lucky greeted her at the door with an enthusiastic lick and she bent down to hug him.

'I've missed you.' Words she wanted to say to Daniel but knew she couldn't.

'We missed you too,' Daniel told her, easing some of that pain in her chest.

'Where did you go?' She tried to keep the pain out of her voice, but it made her sound so small.

'I just needed some space to think. Sorry.'

'And…and what conclusion did you come to?' She held her breath, waiting, hoping that, since ending their relationship hadn't been as easy for him as she'd thought, he'd had some regret.

Daniel took her hands and pulled her up from her crouched position on the floor. 'That I don't want to lose you, Eloise.'

It was everything she wanted to hear, but it didn't solve any problems other than soothing her ego. She still had to make a decision about whether to stay here and take a chance on someone who'd just denied her, or be part of her family's lives again.

'I thought you weren't that bothered. In fact, I think you told me to go.'

He flinched, as though she'd just punched him. 'I thought I was doing the right thing by you. And I was afraid I was going to lose you anyway, so I thought…'

'That you'd just speed things along.'

'Something like that.' He gave her a cute smile that made him look like a mischievous little boy who'd been caught after breaking a window with his football.

'So where do we go from here? You haven't even told me how you feel about me. I mean, I need to know that before I go making any life changing decisions…' Before she could finish, Daniel took her in his arms and kissed her hard on the lips.

'I love you, Eloise. I was afraid to admit it until now,

because that means leaving myself open to getting hurt again if you leave.'

All things he'd told her before, but she hadn't realised they related to her until now. It was no wonder he'd got spooked with the possibility of her moving to another country. But, by saying those three words, he'd complicated everything even more for her. Now there was a reason to stay: the future with Daniel she'd been hoping for might actually be within her reach. Except, she'd already told her daughter that she would move to be with her.

'I've told Dawn that I'm going to go and live with her.'

'Is that what you really want?' He wasn't playing fair with her. She wanted to be with him, but he wasn't guaranteeing her for ever, and anything less than that was a risk. At least Dawn was offering love and support she knew she could count on, even if it was of an altogether different kind.

'I want everything. I want to be with you, and my family, but that isn't possible.'

'And I want to be with you.'

'I don't doubt that, Daniel, at least for now, but what if you change your mind again? You can't just disappear and not tell me what's going on in your head. You have to talk to me so we can work through any problems together. That's what people in a relationship do.'

She was putting that out there. She wanted a relationship and everything that came with it. If that wasn't what he wanted too, then they'd be doomed from the outset, and she wasn't going to go through the pain of another break-up if she could help it.

'I know. I'm sorry. I guess I just have to get used to being part of a couple again.' He gave her that half-smile that made her want to forgive him anything.

'You really want to give us a chance?' She was afraid to ask, because his answer was going to change all the plans she'd been making for her future.

'Yes. I know I was an idiot but I was afraid that you were going to leave me eventually and break my heart anyway. I don't want to lose you, Eloise. I love you.'

He was being honest with her, opening up about how he felt and why he'd acted the way he had. It was all she could ask from him. Now it was down to her to decide what she wanted to do about this new revelation. Her heart told her that Daniel was worth taking a chance on.

'Maybe that's a risk we both have to take if we want to be together. I love you too, Daniel. We'll make this work.'

'I've done a lot of thinking over these past few days, and I would rather be with you anywhere in the world than here on my own. I could move over there with you, if you wanted me to.'

Daniel's revelation that he would give up everything that he'd worked so hard for here to go with her was the biggest commitment he could make to her, but she could never ask him to do that. He'd been brave, and now it was her turn.

'I wouldn't ask that of you, Daniel. All I wanted was to know that you felt the same way about me that I do about you. If there's a chance that we can be together, keep on working together, swimming, sharing a bed, I'm never going to give that up.'

'What about your daughter and your grandchild? I can't ask you to just forget about them.'

'That's never going to happen. I can visit and video-call, just like I have been doing. I'm still going to be in their lives. You will be too, hopefully.'

'I think I'd like that. To be part of a family.' He smiled, and Eloise saw the scarred little boy finally realise that he was loved and wanted.

It was exactly how he made her feel too. And neither of them was going anywhere without the other any time soon. They'd found their purpose, and their future, in each other.

EPILOGUE

One year later

'DO YOU THINK there's going to be enough room for them all? Maybe they should sleep in our room.' Eloise was trying to think of everything that Dawn and her little family were going to need to be comfortable for their stay.

'They're going to be fine. Happy just to be here with you.' Daniel put his hands on her shoulders and talked her down from spiralling into a great ball of anxiety.

'I just want everything to be right.' Although she'd been lucky enough to fly out to Canberra with Daniel to see baby Gabby just after her birth, meeting up with Alison out there too, she hadn't seen them in person since. She knew she'd made the right decision in staying here with Daniel, but it didn't mean she didn't still miss being with her family.

'You've gone to a lot of trouble, making the place lovely for them. Stop worrying.' He shut her up the way he knew how, with a kiss.

Since finally facing their fears and committing to one another, they'd gone all in. Daniel had moved into her place, keen for a completely new start away from the marital home he'd shared with Anne. Debbie was renting it now, so everyone was happy with the arrangement.

Life had been good. They spent every day together, working and winding down at home afterwards, which usually ended in some passionate love-making. The mornings were good too, and she even looked forward to the cold dip as much as the outdoor breakfast they shared.

She was just worried something was going to happen to spoil it, even though she knew her daughters were both fond of Daniel and were happy she'd found someone who appreciated and loved her. Alison had even talked about doing some house hunting when they were over. There was a possibility her husband could get a work transfer, and she missed Eloise as much as Eloise missed her daughter and granddaughter. So she had her fingers crossed that she could have everything after all.

'Do you think Lucky should stay outside? I wouldn't want him to upset the baby.'

'Eloise, you know he's great around people. Stop panicking. Everything's going to be okay.'

He was right. Lucky was quite the celebrity at the clinic now, happy to lie quietly at Reception, or entertain the children who came in and liked to make a fuss of him.

'I don't know how you put up with me sometimes.' She wrapped her arms around his waist and laid her head against his chest—her favourite place in the world to be, where she felt safe and loved.

'Because I love you.' He kissed the top of her head and hugged her closer.

Eloise had no doubts on that score. He'd been with her

through everything, including the not so pleasant side effects of peri-menopause. He was always there with a hot water bottle, or a fan, or a cup of tea. She didn't know how she'd got so lucky.

'I love you too,' she mumbled into his chest.

'Hold that thought.' Suddenly, he pushed her away and walked out of the room, leaving her wondering what she'd done to send him away.

Thankfully he came back not long after...though she hadn't expected him to drop to one knee.

'I was going to wait until your family were here to celebrate, but I think this is the perfect time. I just hope I can get up off this floor again.'

He was joking around, but Eloise's heart was in her mouth, waiting for him to get to the point.

'Perfect time for what?'

'To ask you to marry me. Eloise Carter, would you do me the honour of becoming my wife?' He opened a box to show her a beautiful diamond ring inside and she thought her heart would burst with happiness.

'Yes. I'd love to marry you, Daniel.' She knelt down on the floor beside him, throwing her arms around him.

For her, knowing he was going to be there for her in sickness and in health, loving her and honouring her for ever, was an even greater gift than all the jewels in the world.

* * * * *

WEDDING DATE
WITH THE
ER DOCTOR

SUE MacKAY

MILLS & BOON

To Lindsay, without your unfailing support book No. 50
would've been a lot harder to achieve. Love you.

And to the HM&B editors
who've also supported me on this amazing journey
to reach 50. You're all amazing.

And to the Blenheim, NZ, police
for helping me at an awful time.

CHAPTER ONE

'THANK GOODNESS THAT'S DONE.'

Rosie Carter shoved the trolley containing a week's worth of groceries out through the main door of the supermarket and headed for her car. After three long and involved pickups of seriously injured people on the rescue chopper she was ready for a hot shower, followed by dinner without any interruptions on the deck at her apartment.

Melbourne had turned on the best late-summer weather imaginable. A cloudless blue sky, still air and a bearable temperature, which made wearing all the high-vis gear required on the job a bit more comfortable. No bumpy rides today, not that they often bothered her. She loved flying, whether in a chopper or a plane. So much so she was contemplating learning to fly and getting her private pilot's licence. She should stop dithering and sign up for lessons, except there was never much spare time in her life. Whenever she took on a project she gave it her all, otherwise what was the point?

At the car, Rosie pinged the locks and lifted the boot lid to stow her grocery bags.

Vroom. The sound of a speeding vehicle reached her, sounding very close. *Vroom.*

Spinning around, she heard tyres squeal to a stop right beside her. A wide-eyed man stared at her through the open window of a car.

'What the—?'

A hand shot out towards her, snatched her handbag from over her shoulder and pulled hard.

Instinctively, Rosie grabbed at it, touching it briefly before he threw it onto the seat beside him. Shoving her arm through the open window in an attempt to get her bag back, her hand slammed into the man's chest.

He punched her upper arm hard, then spun the car away, sending her crashing onto the asphalt.

Intuitively, Rosie did a three-sixty roll away from danger and came up hard against the back of her car. Immediately she leapt to her feet, feeling endangered and looking for her attacker.

He'd gone. The car sped through the car park, dangerously close to other people and vehicles. He drove straight through the stop sign and across the centre of the roundabout before disappearing out of sight.

People were rushing to her aid. 'Hey, lady, are you all right?'

'Take it easy. You might be injured.'

'I can't believe what he just did!'

Her head pounded and pain tore through her right hip and thigh. Rosie sagged against the side of her car, shaking from top to toe. 'What the hell?'

'Here, sit down before you fall again.' A man took her elbow and opened the back door so she could collapse on the edge of the seat.

'Th-thanks.' What was that about?

A young woman approached. 'I've called the police. They're on their way. So is an ambulance.'

She didn't need that. She was an emergency doctor. She could take care of herself. But she wasn't getting a word in as everyone yabbered on about what they'd seen. Drawing in a breath, Rosie concentrated on her body, wondering what damage had been done. She was hurting but nothing felt broken even though she had impacted damned hard with the ground. Her forehead had also taken a blow against the back wheel but she'd be fine to go home after she talked to the cops. There was no way she wasn't waiting to tell them the little she'd actually seen.

'I'll go over to the supermarket and see if they've got CCTV,' said the man who'd helped her onto the back seat. 'They should do, but who knows these days? They're not always working properly.'

'I saw it happen,' another man said. 'It was lucky no one else was hit by the car as it sped away.'

'I chased after him, which was plain stupid as he was in one hell of a hurry to get away,' another man said with a wry smile. 'What I thought I'd do if I did get him, I have no idea.'

'Glad you didn't reach him,' Rosie said. She didn't want anyone else hurt by that creep. Her head throbbed so hard it felt as though it was going to split in half. 'Like me trying to grab back my bag.'

'You had a wallet in there?' asked the woman who'd called the cops.

If she'd had the energy she'd have sworn. 'My credit cards need cancelling.' She stood up. Her head spun.

'Is there someone you can call to do that?'

No partner to sort this out. No one who had her bank details either. No phone to call the banks with. Her head spun harder. This was one time it would be great not to have closed herself off from men when they'd got too close. But protecting her heart was far more important than having someone to help her through the next few hours.

Someone caught her arm. 'Steady.'

'Cops are here.'

Rosie tried to straighten up, but it hurt too much everywhere. Looking around, she saw one policewoman walking towards her with a grim expression on her face while another was already talking to one of the men who'd witnessed what happened.

'Hello there. I'm Megan Harris from the local station. How are you feeling?'

A bunch of roses. 'I'm okay. Sore, but angry more than anything. I don't know…' The words stopped as her vision blurred briefly. Great. She really wasn't as all together as she'd hoped. Sinking back onto the seat, she said with as much confidence as she could manage, 'I'm Rosie Carter.'

'Right, Rosie. My colleague is going to take short statements from those who saw what happened. Another has gone to see if the CCTV picked up anything. I'd like you to tell me what you can. Can you manage that?'

'Of course I can,' she snapped, then instantly felt bad. This woman was on her side. She wasn't the enemy. 'Sorry. I'd like to get this done and then I can head home.'

'You're not going anywhere until the ambulance crew have checked you out, and then most likely it'll be a trip to the emergency department for a thorough going-over.'

Megan smiled sympathetically. 'I know it's the last place you want to be right now, but they'll have to take you because once they're called they can't leave you. Unless you sign a document releasing them, that is.'

Rosie started to nod and immediately regretted it as the pounding in her head intensified. 'I'm an emergency doctor on the choppers.'

'Then you'll be familiar with the process. Right, fill me in as best you can.'

'It all happened so fast. I don't know a lot.' How embarrassing.

'Not uncommon.'

'I hit him when I tried to get my bag back. I have no idea why I did that.' But at least she had tried and not let the creep think she was a pushover.

'It would've been a reflex reaction and there's not a lot you can do about those. Did you get a good look at his face?'

She shuddered. 'Wide staring eyes that suggested he was drugged to the hilt.' She'd seen it enough when working in emergency departments to know. 'But I doubt I could pick him out in a line-up. Not with certainty anyway.'

'At least you're honest. Better to hear that than be led up the path by details you make up.'

'Who'd want to be a cop?' They had to deal with all sorts of problems from both sides of the case. Easier being a doctor, for sure.

'Some days I'd agree with you,' Megan replied wryly. 'Here's the ambulance. I'll let them see to you and we can catch up later. There're enough witnesses to help us go look for the man who did this.'

Ambulance. Hospital. Poking and prodding of her body. Not so wonderful. But she'd be given something for the pain in her head. That had to be a plus. Bring it on.

'You'll need my address.' She was going home tonight no matter what.

'Who did you say was in cubicle three?' Dr Lucas Tanner asked Chris, the nurse walking beside him in the emergency department. Surely it couldn't be Rosie. He hadn't seen her in ages. Not since his world had imploded three years ago and he'd left town to avoid everyone's sympathy.

'Rosie Carter. An emergency doctor on the choppers.'

Definitely one of his friends from way back when life was exciting and happy and filled with love, or so he'd believed.

'What's brought her here?'

'She was assaulted and robbed in a supermarket car park.'

'Are you serious?'

Of course he was. Lucas shivered. It was hideous just thinking about it, let alone imagining what Rosie must be feeling. One thing in her favour was that she was a toughie. Well, she used to be, anyway. But then he had no idea of what might've happened to her since they'd last seen each other. He knew from all that had gone on with him that life could throw horrible spears at people when they least expected them. Which was why he was a widower. A guilt-ridden one at that.

'Right, I've got this one.' Pulling back the curtain, he strode into the cubicle. 'Rosie, I can't believe it's you. Long time no see.'

She looked almost unrecognisable as the beautiful, funny woman he'd once known. Her face was pale and there was a large bruise covering her chin and another above her eyes. Her hands were shaking uncontrollably as her little fingers bent and straightened, bent and straightened. A tell that she was stressed he recognised from the past.

'Lucas?' Her eyes widened. 'It's really you?'

'Have I changed that much?' he quipped as he reached for the notes the paramedic had left on her bed. He probably had, given all the stress and pain he'd been through. But this was Rosie, part of the group of close friends he'd spent a year with, training in emergency medicine, and she knew some of what had gone down back then.

But not the reason for his guilt. No one knew that. Needing to put distance between them when his wonderful life had turned into a nightmare, he hadn't learned where she'd gone after he'd left Melbourne. He'd deliberately lost touch with everyone in the group except Brett, who'd refused to let him walk away completely. Now here was Rosie and he was pleased to see her, though not with the circumstances that had brought her into the department.

'Not really.'

That answer said more about her state of mind than just about anything could. No repartee today, something Rosie had always been good at. He'd sometimes wondered if that had been to keep people at a distance because she'd never been forthcoming about her private life. He hadn't a clue why that might've been and was probably so far off the mark it would be laughable if she knew his thoughts.

'Are you all right with me taking your case?' Technically, he didn't have to back off as they'd had nothing to do with each other for three years, but if Rosie had any issue with him checking her out then he was okay with it. 'I can get someone else, though you'll have to wait as everyone's tied up right now.'

He really should've looked her up when he'd returned home, along with the other two from the group he'd lost track of. He'd missed everyone and with his wife, May, gone, life got lonely at times. Very lonely, if he was being honest, but then he deserved to be. May would still be here if they hadn't got into that horrendous argument the night she'd died. Another reason to keep to himself—that way, he couldn't harm anyone he got close to.

'No problem at all.'

He hadn't realised he'd been holding his breath until Rosie said that. She had no issues with him. Not that he could think of a reason why she might. He had enough of his own to more than make up for anyone else's.

'Good.' Scanning the paramedic's notes, a relieved sigh escaped. 'You don't appear to have any major injuries, though I will order X-rays of your right hip and thigh to be certain. My biggest concern is concussion.' The notes didn't indicate a major skull trauma. There was a painful-looking area above her right eye where that massive bruise lay. He'd check that out. The bruise on her chin appeared minor. 'From the notes, it seems you took a fair whack on the head.' Her usually pretty face was marred by abrasions and, even more pronounced, shock.

'He hit me. Then I was thrown to the ground when he sped away and my forehead took a slam against my car wheel. I hit the tarmac with my hip and thigh. But really, I'm all right. Just need to get home and go to bed.'

Slow down...take a breath, Rosie.

'No way. We're checking you over thoroughly and if I have the slightest concern about anything, including concussion, you're staying overnight.' Right now, he was her doctor, not her long ago friend, though as a pal he'd still insist on her staying in if necessary. Probably more so, because he found he didn't want anything going wrong for Rosie.

'Bossy britches.'

At least she wasn't arguing, which was more her style if he remembered correctly. And why wouldn't he? They'd been friends before May had died, before he'd withdrawn from the group of people that he'd been so keen to get to know on a deeper level. Especially this person, he remembered with shock. After four amazing years, cracks had started appearing in his marriage. Even so, he'd never overstepped the friendship line with Rosie. He'd still loved May, despite how they'd started going in different directions all of a sudden.

'You bet. Now, let me touch your skull and see what other damage there is.' As his fingers moved across her head, he spoke reassuringly. 'No soft spots, nor anything to suggest a bleed, but I want to be sure before accepting that as fact. We'll get this X-rayed too.'

Rosie's eyes flew open. 'Surely that's not necessary.'

'I'm erring on the side of caution.' Only doing his job. 'As I know you would, if our roles were reversed.' Her neck was tight. 'Move your head left. Right. Any pain when you do that?'

'No.' But she hadn't moved very far, and her fingers were doing their bend, straighten thing again.

He wasn't sure she was being totally honest with him. 'Any pain when I press here?' His fingers touched her neck by the right shoulder. The muscles were taut.

She shivered. 'No.' Then she sighed. 'It's tender but not painful.' So she wanted to pretend she was fine, but couldn't manage it. Hopefully, that meant the doctor side of her brain was coming to the fore.

'To be expected from impacting with anything solid and unforgiving.' Lucas shuddered at the thought of what that had been like. Sudden and hard, it would've been shocking to say the least. How could anybody do such harm to another person? To a complete stranger at that. It made his blood boil. There were some right losers out there. Nasty, even evil, people who thought they could do as they liked with no comeback. The problem being that many got away with it, which only encouraged others. As he felt Rosie's hip and thigh for possible fractures, he asked, 'Are the police onto your attacker?'

'The cop I talked to said they had plenty of witnesses to get started on looking for the car he was driving. Someone got the numberplate details. They were also going to check the supermarket's CCTV footage.'

Rosie didn't wince too much when he pressed on her hip and thigh. 'You've got massive bruising around this area, but nothing to suggest fractures.'

'Thanks.' A tear trickled out of the corner of her eye. Rosie slashed at it impatiently, only for another one to appear.

'Here.' Lucas felt his heart turn over as he handed across a box of tissues from the trolley. She'd know this was a normal reaction as the initial shock wore off, but this was Rosie and she'd hate for anyone to see her cry. Even him. She'd always been a tough cookie. But being assaulted would undermine anyone's strength for a while at least. 'Let it all out. I'll go organise the X-rays. Unless there's something else you need me to check?'

She tried to shake her head but her neck wasn't having a bar of it, remaining rigid. 'No,' she whispered.

If only he could haul her into his arms and hug away her pain, but he was on duty. Plus, she might not like him to be so friendly after all this time. He'd never hugged her, although sometimes when things weren't going quite so well with May he'd wanted to wrap his arms around Rosie for a bit of comfort. Of course he'd resisted, not wanting anyone getting the wrong idea.

'I'm going to prescribe painkillers for you. Chris will bring them through.' While he worked on being sensible and ignoring this warmth he felt for Rosie.

'Those scrapes don't look deep so I doubt there'll be any scarring.' Chris began gently wiping the abrasions on Rosie's cheek to clean away the dirt and blood, something Lucas had an unusual urge to take over and do.

He really needed to get a life if this was how he reacted when catching up with a friend after so long out of contact. He looked around for something else to distract him and found nothing. Which was odd, since the group they'd both been a part of had got along well but there'd been nothing beyond friendship with any of them. It could be that after these past few years of carrying the guilt of letting May down that night, he was feeling relaxed with someone from that time who wouldn't want anything more from him than friendship. He could do that.

'Something to be grateful for, I suppose,' Rosie said to Chris.

The lassitude in her voice alarmed Lucas. He would do anything to take away her pain and shock. Going forward, how would she deal with the fact that a man had attacked her in broad daylight in a busy car park? It wasn't going to be easy over the coming weeks to accept what had happened without letting it interfere with her daily life. Where was the bastard who did this to her? He'd love ten minutes alone with him.

'I'll bring you some water to drink too,' Chris told Rosie.

She wiped her eyes. Her mouth was flat, her hands still shaky. 'Thanks. Can I have a triple vodka with that?'

Lucas didn't know if she was joking or serious; the despair in her voice was so gutting.

'I'll see what they've got at the pharmacy,' he told her around a tight smile. The last thing he felt like doing was smiling, but Rosie deserved better so he'd done his best. He couldn't have been very successful though because she barely looked at him. 'Back shortly.' He had Radiology to arrange and a prescription to organise.

It was hard to ignore how Rosie's sudden reappearance in his life had him standing up and taking more notice of her than he'd have expected, or had ever done before. He'd been totally devoted to May and the future they'd dreamed of: getting established in their careers, then having a home and family. Then May had got restless, started eyeing up the corporate ladder at the international company she worked for, and holes began appearing in their marriage. Problems he hadn't been prepared to admit to.

He'd been aware that Rosie was stunning, but so had

all the men in their group. Today, seeing her in shock and
as pale as his mother's white sheets, he'd felt a wrench
over how lovely she truly was. Or was that his head playing games with him? Quite likely, as he wasn't usually
into noticing women other than as patients, colleagues
or friends. The pain over losing May had held him back
from letting anyone get close again. That and the guilt.
Especially the guilt. If only they hadn't had such a big
argument. If only he'd remained calm and waited until
they were together to talk about what she intended doing.
He doubted it would've made any difference to her plans
to move to Sydney, with or without him, but at least she'd
still be alive.

When he returned to Rosie's cubicle, she was talking
to a policewoman. 'Lucas, this is Megan.'

'Hello, Megan. I hope you catch the slimeball.'

'We're onto it.' Megan turned back to Rosie. 'Here are
the keys to your car, which is still in the supermarket car
park, all locked up.' She placed them on the table beside
the bed. 'Is there someone who can collect it for you?'

Lucas waited for the answer. Was Rosie in a relationship? Was she married? The fact there was no ring on
her finger meant nothing. She might not wear one while
working. He'd heard she and her then partner, Cameron,
had split about the time he'd left Melbourne.

'I could call one of my friends, but since my phone's
gone I'm stuck. I don't know anyone's number off the
top of my head.'

Sounded like she was on her own.

'Want me to collect the car? I'm knocking off any
minute. I could take it home and bring it here tomorrow
if you're staying overnight, which I think you should.

You've got concussion and it wouldn't be wise to go home on your own.'

Was he making doubly sure she was single? No, he was simply being a responsible doctor, he growled to himself.

Rosie blinked. 'You don't have to do that. I'll pick it up tomorrow.' Then she gasped. 'I still haven't done anything about my bank cards.'

'I'll help you with that,' Lucas cut in. 'Whether you stay here or go home,' he added as she opened her mouth. 'It's what friends do.' They'd sort out what to do about the car later. It wasn't as important as cancelling the cards.

Megan beat Rosie to replying. 'Sounds like a good idea. After what you've been through, it would be nice to have someone giving you a hand with notifying the banks. If you're happy to give Lucas your details, that is?' Policewoman to the fore.

'No problem whatsoever. We're old friends.' Rosie's mouth tipped up into a small, sincere smile.

His heart lightened. He'd be useful to her in a capacity other than the medical one. 'Right, that's it. I'm officially done for the day, so let's start getting everything sorted while you wait to be taken to Radiology.'

'I'll leave you to it.' Megan handed Rosie a card. 'Here's my contact number. Let me know when you go home because we need to get a full statement from you and it takes a couple of hours at least.'

Rosie's eyes widened at that. Then she sagged into her pillow. 'Thank you for your support. The whole thing's been a bit of an eye-opener.'

'I'm sure it has. I'll get out of the way now. Take care and we'll talk tomorrow.'

As Megan headed out, Lucas glanced at Rosie and saw

her shiver. 'Hey, you're doing well. If there's anything good to come out of this, it's that we've caught up again.'

'I've often wondered where you'd got to and what you were doing. I miss everyone from our trainee group. We had some great times together, including everyone's partners.'

'A lot of study and a few too many parties,' he replied with a laugh.

Until his wife had died, and then nothing was ever the same for any of them. Everyone had missed her, and went out of their way to support him, but his grief and guilt had been too much for him to bear all the sympathy, so he'd left for Sydney, and then gone out of the country a year later. Sadness welled up. Another of his and May's difficulties had been that she'd thought he spent more time with the group than with her. He couldn't argue with that totally, but she'd spent plenty of evenings with her work colleagues too.

'We had to let go of the tension brought on by dealing with dreadful cases at work somehow. Though I don't seem to need to do that these days. Must be used to the horrors of the job now.' She stared at him for a moment. 'How long have you been working here?'

'I returned from the States two months ago and came on board here three weeks later.'

'You enjoyed working over there?'

'I did, but my contract was up so I figured it was time to come home and make some decisions about my house.' Time to finally face the past, and hopefully move on. He'd hidden away too long and had missed out on a lot with his family. 'The last tenants didn't exactly take care of the place so I'm fixing up the damage and painting the place throughout.' It had turned out to be harder than he'd expected, being back in the house where there were so many memories of May to haunt him.

'How's that working out?'

He hated the sympathy in her eyes. 'Great,' he lied. 'Even if I say so myself, I'm not too bad at replacing dented plasterboards. My brother, Leon, gives me a hand when he's not at work.'

'Go you.' Rosie yawned. 'I want to go home.'

She sounded petulant, nothing like the woman he remembered, but then she hadn't been attacked back then either.

'How's your vision?'

She blinked at him. 'Mostly fine, though every now and then it's a little blurry.'

That sealed it. 'You're staying overnight.'

She sighed in resignation. 'I'd better let Steve know I won't be at work tomorrow.'

'Your boss?' he asked, since there hadn't been any mention of an important other person so far.

'Head of Victoria Rescue. He's available for staff twenty-four-seven.'

That must be a pain in the backside for the man.

'I've met him a couple of times when he's come in here with a patient. He's a good guy. Do you know his number?'

Her face lit up for the first time. 'It's about the only one I do.'

'Want me to call him?'

'Would you? Right now, I just want to curl up and go to sleep, but what if images of that ugly wide-eyed face fill my head while I'm out?'

Lucas felt his heart tighten. She was more shaken than she'd let on and it seemed to be catching up with her. He was surprised it had taken so long. He squeezed her shoulder lightly as a pal, not the doctor he'd been earlier.

'I reckon you'll fall into such a deep sleep nothing will affect you.' Hopefully, that would be the case. But this was only the first night after what had happened. There'd be plenty ahead when her fears might be realised. 'But first I'll grab a wheelchair and take you to Radiology, where we can sit in a corner while we wait for your X-rays to be done and make some calls to the banks after I've talked to Steve.'

'You've got everything covered.'

Why wouldn't he? He wasn't the one this had happened to.

'I hope so.'

'Let's do it.' Rosie sat up and swung her legs over the side of the bed. At least she tried to swing them, but the look on her face said it hurt to move.

'Take it slowly,' Lucas warned. 'We don't know for sure there's not a serious injury in your hip.' Though he doubted it. He'd seen enough fractured hips and thighs to know, but he wanted to be absolutely sure. She did not need any more pain than she was already dealing with. That was the friend side of his brain, not the medical one, which was odd considering he was a doctor first and foremost in ED.

You've signed off for the day.

True. He'd stick with Rosie while she had the X-rays and then was moved to the general ward. Because that *was* happening. Unless she would agree to go home with him.

Where did that idea come from?

Friend side of his brain, remember? It would be a lot wiser to stick to the medical side for now. Who knew if Rosie gave a fig about friends from the past?

Rosie rolled over and groaned. 'Wrong way, idiot.' The bruises on her hip had a lot to say for themselves. Thankfully, nothing else was wrong with her hip.

On the other side of the bed, Lucas chuckled. 'Want a warning sign drawn up?'

She remembered that chuckle—deep, with the ability to drag people into his aura. Everyone had liked Lucas. He just had a way of making a person feel special for the time he was with them. Even her, and she was a sceptic when it came to believing men would treat her well without turning out to be wrong about them. He'd been married to May and there was nothing behind his manner except camaraderie. May had come first and everyone knew it. Sometimes she been a little jealous of them as a couple; she'd known she and Cameron weren't as good together because she was afraid to let him that close.

What happened to May had been horrific and watching Lucas fall apart piece by piece afterwards was hard for everyone. Had he managed to move on? Reached a point where he could get through the day without reliving his time with May? She hoped so for his sake.

Carefully rolling the other way, she dug deep for a grin, because that was what she did with friends, put on a determinedly happy face to dodge the unpleasant questions they might want to ask. 'Can you make it a verbal one so if I'm asleep I'll still know to avoid my right side?'

'Onto it.' His smile faded. 'How are you feeling, really?'

She thought about it. 'Tired. Still angry. But more than anything, I'm feeling bewildered.'

Lucas straightened in his chair. 'Why?'

'To think there I was, about to unload my trolley of groceries and go home, when instead my world was tipped upside down within moments by a selfish idiot with nothing better to do than attack and rob me.'

Lucas took her hand and enclosed it in both his. It was a caring gesture that surprised her, but then she was out of kilter at the moment so could explain away the sense of belonging his touch gave her. She liked that more than she'd have believed.

'It's not something anyone expects or can imagine until it happens. You'll get through this, Rosie. You never did take nonsense from anyone, and I know this'll be the same.'

His hands were so warm and soft. It was kind of nice having him hold her when she felt so out of sorts. Good pals were the best, and hard to come by. Especially for her as she was cautious about getting close to people and then being let down. If her father could do that to her after her mother died, then anyone could, and enough had.

'You just need to get through the coming days and you'll be back to yourself. Don't be impatient, Rosie.'

He made it sound so easy. Her eyes filled. Another sign she wasn't her usual self.

'You do remember me well.' Patience had never been one of her better qualities.

'My memory's not so bad. It hasn't been that long since we were working long hours, night and day, in the ED and giving each other hell about getting everything right. Along with the others, I've missed you and those times.

We were damned serious about our work and qualifying, and always there for each other. Even our partners were part of that.'

A shadow crossed his face. Thinking about May? Or his life before he'd lost his wife in a shocking road accident? Her heart went out to him. It had been an awful time.

To fill the sudden silence, she continued. 'In the department *and* out of it.'

Yes, those were the days when it was all work and not a lot of play, but when they had played the five of them had always had a blast. Along with their partners on the occasions they'd joined in the fun. Rosie hadn't got to know May all that well. She'd been working for a large law firm and the only subject she'd ever talked about in a relaxed manner was her job. She'd always come across as perfect in all she did, both personally and professionally, sometimes making Rosie feel inadequate—not in terms of her career, but in her relationship with Cameron. She wasn't perfect in the slightest.

Cameron was a great guy, specialising in cardiology. She'd really liked him but worried he'd find her lacking in what he wanted in a life partner, so when she'd left Melbourne to work for a year in Perth to gain more experience she'd gone without him and that was the end of them. She'd hurt him big time and still felt bad about that. She'd cared a lot for him, but not enough to take that final step to for ever. There hadn't been anyone since. She couldn't seem to find it in her to find 'the one' who she could trust to settle down with, to love for ever and maybe have a family with.

After the remote way her father had raised her and her brother, Johnno, after their mother died, she didn't have it in her to trust anyone totally with her heart. If her dad could withdraw from her then anyone could, and she wasn't exposing herself to that degree of pain again. She'd only been eight, and Johnno fourteen, at the time. It had been as though their dad had died too, for all the love he'd shown them after the day of their mother's funeral. Virtually none, other than providing food on the table and money for anything they'd needed. She'd grieved for two parents from that day on. At least she and Johnno had always been close.

'I think being able to decompress together was what got us all through the difficult shifts.' Lucas laid her hand on the bed and leaned back in the chair, drawing her attention back to him and away from the past that haunted her to this day. 'Because there were certainly moments when each of us wanted to walk away and find a *normal* job.'

He was referring to those times when one of them lost a patient, despite doing everything possible, and more, to prevent that outcome. Yes, every medical doctor faced those. Lucas had faced a different pain too. Losing May had devastated him.

So had he found a new partner yet? Or was he still struggling to cope with what he'd lost? She didn't feel she had the right to ask. They had been good pals, but chances were they wouldn't be as close as they'd once been. Too much time had gone by for that. But it was so good to see him. She hadn't realised how much she had missed him. And the rest of the group. They'd had some wonderful times, unwinding over a drink, laughing and talking like there was no tomorrow. But they'd all struggled with May's death. Losing one of their own had been a huge shock.

CHAPTER TWO

LUCAS STARED OUT of the window onto the street beyond his fence as the microwave dealt with his eggs. 'Unreal' was the word that came to mind when he thought about his last patient of the day. Day? It was well after nine and he'd been home barely thirty minutes. All because he'd caught up with an old friend in unusual circumstances. Unusual in that he didn't often come across anyone he knew when working in the ED. The hospital was one of many in Melbourne, and not all his friends had gone into emergency medicine. Only those he'd known here back when they were qualifying.

His blood boiled when he thought about what that cretin had done to Rosie. He'd often dealt with victims of random crime through work, but this had happened to someone he knew and that made it more horrific. Rosie was a special friend he'd got on well with until the group had gone their separate ways to further their careers, and he'd gone away to cope with losing May. He'd feel the same if it had been any of the others coming into the ED after a similar experience. Wouldn't he? Why the doubt? Rosie hadn't meant anything more to him back then, had she? He'd been very happy married to May and hadn't looked at any other woman, hadn't wanted to. Though he had noticed Rosie's stunning looks and enjoyed talking to her about anything and everything too.

Despite the increasing arguments between them, he'd still loved May. When they married, they'd agreed to stay in Melbourne until he'd established his career in emergency medicine and so they'd bought the house. Then she'd decided there was only one way her career in law was going and that was to the top of the international company she worked for. Not that she'd discussed it with him, and when she'd told him over the phone that fatal night that she was leaving for Sydney within a fortnight and he could follow when he'd sorted his job out he'd been hurt and lashed out with angry words. That and the fact he was going to be late home to celebrate her promotion were why she'd said to hell with him, she was going to celebrate with people who mattered and hung up on him.

Beep, beep, beep.

Dinner is cooked.

Not quite. He gave the eggs a light stir with the whisk and stuck the bowl back in the microwave for thirty seconds. After buttering the toast, he took a mouthful of beer from his bottle and returned to staring outside.

Once in the ward, Rosie had fought falling asleep, but in the end the shock she'd had and the medications she'd taken had won out and she'd nodded off.

He'd stayed for another half hour in case she woke and wanted to talk about what had happened, but she'd been out for the count. It was good she'd succumbed to staying in overnight without much of an argument. It wouldn't have been wise for her to be home alone tonight. He would've offered her a bed here if that had been the case, but doubted she'd have taken him up on it. Always an independent woman, Rosie used to hate being beholden to anyone, which he'd never understood. After a particularly bad day in the ED she'd always tried to hide her emotions, but he and the others got to recognise her tell. Her little fingers would bend and straighten numerous times, as had been the case tonight.

Beep, beep, beep.

'Shut up.' His appetite was disappearing. Not that scrambled eggs were a real dinner, but he often cheated after a long day in the department. It seemed so pointless going to the hassle of preparing vegetables and steak or a casserole just for himself. Far easier to heat something already prepared from the supermarket. By the time he'd left Rosie earlier tonight he couldn't get enthused about going into the store to choose dinner from a freezer either.

His phone announced the arrival of a text. Rosie? He'd left her his number in case she wanted anything, but as she didn't have her phone she was limited on what she could do, though two of the nurses had been quick to say she could use theirs.

Not Rosie. It was Leon, his brother. He wasn't disappointed. He *wasn't*. He was not looking for another woman to come into his life. His heart wasn't strong enough to fall in love again, nor to believe everything would work out all right. If it could go bad with May then it would with any other woman he came to care about.

'Hey, dude, how's it going?'

'Not bad. The roof went on at number twenty-three today, so we can get cracking there.' Leon owned a small building company that was always in high demand. 'I've got half the guys working on the finishing touches for the other house. I've got to go over plans for the next place too. The customers want things done in the kitchen that are going to be tricky, to say the least.'

'There's always something, isn't there?'

'Makes the job interesting. How was your day?'

'Same old, same old.' Apart from Rosie turning up in his life again. But that didn't change a thing. Hopefully, they'd get to catch up a bit but he couldn't see them spending much time together. They had gone in different directions three years ago and he was looking at her as though everything had remained the same. But it wouldn't have. It hadn't for him. The time spent in San Fran had been busy with work and getting out and about in the towns further inland. He'd taken up cycling, which had led to some hair-raising rides around the city and beyond. 'I caught up with one of my friends from training days, which was cool.'

'Good. Someone else to keep you here. Are you heading out this way tomorrow?'

He had intended to, but now he hesitated. 'Not sure.' Rosie might need her car once she was back on her feet. Plus, he couldn't deny the inexplicable need grabbing at him to make sure she was recovering well and wasn't too stressed over what had happened. Strange how he felt a little lighter in the heart tonight. 'If I do, it'll be later in the day.' Unless Rosie wanted him to hang around. But then why would she ask that of him? Surely she had other friends to be there for her? He did like to make sure things were okay though. It was his doctor brain coming to the fore, not his friend side. He shrugged. Really? No idea.

'How are you feeling this morning?' Lucas asked Rosie the next morning when she took the ward phone the nurse held out to her.

Even though he couldn't see her, Rosie shrugged dramatically. 'A bit sore but otherwise all good.' The painkillers had worked a treat. Her mind was a mess about the assault and how suddenly her day had been tossed about, but that wasn't going to be sorted any time soon. Not that she intended letting her assailant screw with her wellbeing, but she understood that it mightn't be as easy as she'd like to forget what he'd done. 'I'm heading home shortly.' She couldn't wait to get out of here. It was one thing to be a doctor and look out for her patients, but quite different being on the receiving end of all the attention.

'I'll come by and pick you up.'

Hello? When did Lucas get to tell her what she was doing?

'No need. I'll grab a cab.'

'Found your wallet, have they?' he retorted.

'No, but I do have cash in my glovebox.' She'd take the taxi to the supermarket car park and collect the car. 'And before you ask, I can get into my apartment too.' The swipe card was on the same keyring as her car key. Last night she'd somehow managed to convince Lucas he didn't have to pick up her vehicle, though she wasn't sure how she'd managed that as he'd been quite persistent at first.

'Rosie, how about I give you a lift to your car this morning? It's not out of my way and I'd like to see how you're doing.' He sounded tired, as though he hadn't slept much last night.

She relented. She told herself it was because it had been good to catch up with Lucas again, and yes, she'd like to spend more time finding out what he'd been up to in the intervening years since they'd seen one another.

Returning to Melbourne at the end of her twelve-month contract in Perth had been the right thing to do. She'd missed her brother as well as her two girlfriends and their families. She didn't want to be anywhere else. Melbourne was home. Something she'd needed when she couldn't risk falling in love.

Wanting to catch up some more with Lucas had nothing to do with the fact she'd thought about him every time she'd woken during the night. Visualising his endearing smile every time she'd started to think about why she was in hospital and not curled up in her own bed had calmed her instantly. It felt good to have a friend, albeit one from a while ago, by her side at the moment. Her two girlfriends were unaware of what had happened as she hadn't been able to phone them, something she'd rectify with her laptop when she got home.

'I'll be ready and waiting when you come by.'

'That wasn't so hard, was it? Are you free to go shortly?'

'Yes, I've had the all-clear. I'll meet you outside the main entrance.' She had no idea how long it would take him to get here. 'Where do you live?'

'A few blocks away in Parkville.'

'You're kidding? My apartment's in Parkville too.' The hospital was also in Parkville. Lucas would be here shortly. 'I'll make my way downstairs when I hang up.'

'Give me thirty, will you? I'm out walking the neighbour's dog. We're not far from home so I won't be too long. Unless Molly misbehaves, that is.' Lucas laughed, that deep vibrant sound that had her skin heating when it had no reason to. Or did it? She'd always found him attractive and sexy but had ignored that because they were both in other relationships.

Reacting to him after all this time was weird. Perhaps she could put it down to the bang on the head she'd received yesterday.

'See you soon.' She hung up before she could get into a deeper mire of heat and out-of-line thinking.

Handing the phone back to the nurse, she said, 'Thanks for that. I'm going to have to do some shopping ASAP. It's weird not having a phone.'

'I lost mine for a couple of days once and thought my world had stopped. There's so much day-to-day info on it that I was lost without it,' the nurse told her.

That was the scary thing, Rosie conceded as she headed to the lift to go downstairs and wait for Lucas. There was a load of information on her phone that she needed; she was going to struggle till she had another phone and got everyone's numbers sorted. Starting with Lucas's. She wasn't losing touch with him again. Good friends were important and due to her lack of trust she didn't have many.

Johnno kept insisting she only had to get together with his best mate and she wouldn't need anyone else, but no way was she going down that path. One date with Will Clark had been one too many. He was arrogant beyond belief, and still called occasionally to remind her of what she was missing out on by not dating him. Now her brother was getting married in a couple of weeks' time, the pressure was on to partner Will to the wedding. She reckoned it was because he couldn't find anyone else who'd go with him, but he'd never admit that. Johnno really wanted her to be as happy as he was and said she'd be seated next to Will at the reception unless she brought someone else. So far, she hadn't found anyone to ask, being a bit embarrassed that she even had to do so.

Lucas.

His name slammed into her aching head. He would make an ideal partner for the wedding. Would he, though? They wouldn't come across as being in a close relationship and, bossy britches that he was, her brother wouldn't accept anything less.

Sometimes he took the older loving brother role too far. Mostly she was happy with him looking out for her and returned it in kind because they'd both lost so much when their mother passed. Turning to their father whenever they'd needed a hug and instead getting a blank stare had undermined their security and their belief that they were automatically loved without restraint by those who should have known better. At least they'd had each other to stumble through life with, until Johnno left home to go to university. Then she'd been on her own and very lonely until it was her turn to leave. She'd often wondered if her father had even noticed she'd gone.

Back to Lucas. It was too soon to be thinking of asking him to help her out of her predicament with the wedding. They'd caught up only last night. He'd regret wanting to help her out today if she put a proposition to him about accompanying her and would probably make sure he was always busy from now on so he didn't have a spare moment to play catchup. That was the last thing she wanted. It was the first time someone from her past had come back into her life and looked happy about being there. Early days, but a girl could dream of more.

She knew of people who had friends they rarely caught up with but when they did it was as though they'd never been apart.

After her few relationships she'd come to the conclusion that friendships were far safer. Longer lasting and easy to come and go with. Whereas the two serious relationships she'd had had been fun and exciting before they'd slowly become awkward because she was afraid to commit and thereby expose herself to more hurt. She'd let down the men she'd partnered up with, but hadn't been able to find it within her to open up and fall in love. It was far too risky.

'Hey, there.' Lucas was striding towards her looking so handsome in denim shorts and a green shirt that her hands tightened at her sides. Those long, suntanned legs of his were seriously sexy!

She would not think about Lucas like this. Not so soon after meeting up again. Not ever, really. He was a friend. If she did get a little closer than was wise, then she'd only lose a friend when she pulled the plug, as she always did with relationships. Okay, how about a handsome friend?

Rosie couldn't help it. She laughed.

'Glad to hear that sound. You must be feeling better than when I left to go home last night.' He gave her a quick hug.

Too quick for her liking, but he was being the sensible one at the moment. She'd get there soon.

'I've lost the dizzy head and the pain is under control.'

'Get much sleep?'

'On and off. I didn't realise how noisy hospital wards could be at night.' There'd been a young woman in the bed next to hers who'd kept pressing the bell for help with one problem or another.

'Says you, who's spent many hours in them over the years.'

'I don't think I ever thought about how noisy it got, to be honest. Something to remember if I return to hospital work.' She walked beside him to a taxi parked on the other side of the road. 'I thought you were picking me up in your vehicle.'

'This way I can drive you home in your car and then walk back to my house. It's only a few streets from your apartment.' Lucas held the door open for her.

He was being very considerate, but she wasn't incapable of looking out for herself.

'I'm good to drive. I can drop you off at your place on the way.'

'Okay.' Lucas headed around to the other side of the cab, looking unmoved by her snappy reply.

She should be grateful he hadn't made a big deal out of it. As he joined her in the back of the taxi she looked away, already regretting being short with him and embarrassed by how much she enjoyed the view of his tall, lean body and thick curly hair falling over his brow. As for the light stubble on his chin? Her fingers tightened to keep the urge to touch it under control.

'Anything you might need before we pick up your car?' he asked as the driver pulled away from the kerb.

'I need a phone sooner rather than later. I'll have to talk to the insurance company, but I can't wait until they go through the process of paying out.' Another thought crossed her mind. 'I have no idea what's happened to my groceries either. They were in the shopping trolley when

I was attacked.' What with all that had gone down, they'd completely slipped her mind. 'Hopefully, someone put the bags in my car before it was locked.'

'We'll find out soon enough,' Lucas said. 'If you do need to do another shop I'll lend you my card. Same goes for the phone.'

Rosie shook her head and instantly regretted it as pain shot through her neck. 'I don't seem to be getting my head around the consequences of what happened. I'd totally forgotten I have no access to money until I go into the bank on Monday and withdraw some. As I mentioned last night, there's a bit of cash in the car.' Nowhere near enough to buy a phone, more like a loaf of bread and something for dinner.

'How about I get a couple hundred bucks out and you can repay me when everything's back to normal? If you want to replace your phone today, I'll use my card.'

Her heart melted for this generous man. 'Thank you. I'll take you up on the offer of cash, just in case something happens and I need money urgently.'

'It's no big deal, Rosie.' He cleared his throat. 'It's what any decent friend would do.' He sounded as though he was trying to convince himself of where their relationship stood. Which made no sense whatsoever.

She might've gone off on a tangent regarding how she felt about Lucas, but she'd taken a hell of a bang on the head yesterday so anything was possible.

'You're right.' She leaned back and closed her eyes, hoping to clear her mind of anything but getting home and unwinding from the tension tugging at her from all directions. Thankfully, no image of those frightening, wide staring eyes belonging to her assailant filled her mind, as it had done during the night whenever she'd managed to get comfortable and start to doze off.

The man was ugly—and terrifying. His eyes had appeared as big as saucers. His mouth had been contorted into an evil smile. She shivered and opened her eyes to stare beyond the taxi window. It had been far nicer waking to the image of Lucas's face in her mind.

Ha, that was why she was coming up with weird and wonderful thoughts about Lucas. He'd been shoving the other man away from her thoughts.

'Think you should get some fresh milk,' Lucas noted as they checked Rosie's groceries that someone had placed in the back of her car at some point. Probably one of the cops had seen to everything. He reached for a pack of ham lying in one of the bags. 'This mightn't be too great either. It's not exactly cool in here.'

'I'll toss it when I get back to my apartment. I've still got some milk so I won't bother going into the supermarket now.' She closed the boot and headed for the driver's side. 'I just want to get home.'

That was the closest she'd come to admitting she was still out of sorts, Lucas noted. Definitely fading.

'And I'll walk from there.' He got in on the passenger's side and belted up before going for a neutral topic. 'How long have you been in your apartment?'

'Nearly two years. I bought it when I returned from Perth. It was a no-brainer as Melbourne's home for me and my brother and my closest friends are here.'

'What about your parents? Where are they?' He knew next to nothing about her private life. It hadn't been what most of the group talked about, which was usually work and the people there.

Rosie glanced at him, then turned back to stare out of the windscreen. 'Mum died when I was eight.'

'That must've been hard.' To lose a parent so young was beyond comprehension. How did a wee girl grow up and deal with life without a mother at her side? 'You still have your father?'

'He died five years ago.' She started the car and backed out of the parking bay, then drove carefully through the busy car park and out onto the road.

He didn't push for more information about her parents. It was obviously a touchy subject, and he knew only too well how it felt when people started asking questions about things he didn't want to answer—usually to do with May and his life since her passing. Even harder to take was the sympathy over his loss as it ramped up his guilt and had him wanting to hide away until everyone left him alone.

'Is your brother older or younger?'

'Six years older. He was the rebellious one. Not so much these days though.'

'Which makes you the good one.'

'Yep. Too much sometimes, I think, but it's what got me through everything until I left home to go to university. And ever since,' she added quietly.

Too quietly, but he thought he'd heard correctly. He definitely got the sadness behind what she'd said. He wasn't asking for more information and having her shut down completely. This was a side to Rosie he'd not known before. Though there were times she'd been uptight, which he'd put down to issues at work, otherwise her behaviour and attitude had always been cool and calm. Not your party all night type, despite always being there when they'd all got together to let their hair down. Nor had she been outspoken or difficult when it came to awkward situations on the job. Rosie mostly got on with what had to be done and had a lot of quiet fun when they were off work and unwinding.

'Are you saying you weren't good once you left home?' He grinned to show he wasn't being serious.

She shrugged, then grimaced. The shoulder that had taken the impact yesterday must still hurt like crazy. 'I doubt I know how to be really badly behaved, which makes me sound boring.'

Faking a yawn, he said, 'If you say so.'

Rosie was definitely not boring. Not if the way he'd spent hours thinking about her since first walking into the cubicle and seeing her in the ED yesterday was an indicator. Either that or boring was his go-to woman. Something he knew was not true. Exciting and sexy were more his style. Except this was Rosie, a friend, not a woman to start a hot fling with. Except she was so damned sexy. And stunning even when battered and bruised, once he'd got over the shock of seeing her again. How was it she was still single?

Rosie tossed him a tight smile. 'Thanks, pal.'

'Just saying.' He grinned, working on quietening the heat building in his blood. 'What do you think you'll do for the rest of the day?'

'I'll get on the laptop and email various people about what's happened. Other than that, not a lot. Unless—' She stopped.

Lucas waited, and when it became apparent Rosie

wasn't going to finish that sentence he said, 'Are you worried about how this has affected you emotionally?' Her mind had to be in overdrive, going over what had happened and how suddenly her world had been flipped. The attack had come out of the blue and would surely have her looking over her shoulder whenever she was out amongst strangers for quite a while.

'A little bit.'

'If you want to talk about it, I'm available any time.' Which meant he wouldn't go around to Leon's later if she took him up on the offer, but that wasn't a problem. Leon would understand.

'I'll be fine.' She indicated right and turned into a parking area beneath a small apartment block. 'I *am* fine.'

He doubted it, but there was nothing he could do if she didn't want to talk to him.

'I'll leave you my number anyway, in case there's anything you might need.'

'My friends will be here once they learn what's happened. So will Johnno, though I'm not sure I want to see him today.'

'Why not?'

As she parked in a space she muttered, 'He'll have plenty to say about a couple of things.'

'Are you talking about the attack?' Her brother would have to be an ass if he was going to criticise her for what had happened.

'What? Oh, no, not that. Just a family matter.' She winced as she got out of the car.

A scream rent the air.

Lucas spun around and headed for the entrance. 'What's that about?'

Rosie was right beside him. 'Someone's on the ground on the other side of the road. Looks like a young woman.' She was charging over the road, her own pain apparently forgotten.

Lucas was right beside her. 'What happened?' he asked a teenage boy as they reached the woman sprawled on the footpath, groaning and writhing in pain.

'He hit my mummy with his skateboard,' a young girl said.

'I didn't mean to,' the teenager muttered. 'I came off my board and it flew at her.'

Lucas dropped to his knees beside the woman, Rosie doing the same on the other side. 'Hello, I'm Lucas, a doctor, and this is Rosie, also a doctor.'

'My leg. The pain's excruciating,' groaned the woman as she tried to reach for her knee.

Rosie covered her hand, pulled it away gently. 'Easy. You could cause more damage by moving your leg. And more pain.' She glanced at Lucas. 'You're the one with a phone.'

He pulled it from his pocket as he studied the lower leg before him. The shin appeared to be shattered, pieces of bone poking through the skin. 'The skateboard must've hit hard.' Damned hard. The angle would have had a huge impact.

Rosie nodded in agreement. Blood oozed from lacerations where the bone had come through. Her fingers were carefully checking the shin and then the knee. 'What's your name?' she asked the woman.

'Mummy's called Freya,' the little girl said before her mother could get a word in. 'Is she going to be all right?' For someone so young she didn't appear too distressed by the sight of blood or the sound of her mother's groans, though she might come down to earth with a thud any moment.

'Mummy will need to see a doctor. Do you live near here?' Someone would need to come and get the girl.

'We were going to see Grandma when he hit her with his board.'

'I didn't hit her!' shouted the teenager.

'Hey, come and talk to me,' a passerby said to the lad and led him a little further along the footpath and away from the girl.

As he filled in the emergency services on what had happened Lucas noted a small crowd had now gathered around. 'Freya needs an ambulance ASAP,' he told the man on the other end of the phone, then shoved his phone in his pocket. 'Any pain anywhere else?' he asked Freya.

'Can't really tell with the leg. Think I landed on my left arm and shoulder when I went down. Everything's hurting.'

Rosie laid a hand on her right arm. 'You're doing so well. Once the ambulance is here they'll give you oxygen to make your breathing easier, and painkillers to help too.'

Lucas glanced at Rosie and felt a surge of admiration at her calmness, despite her own painful injuries. Something warm slid through him. No doubt about it, she was special. Mentally shaking his head at the senseless heat filling him, he moved Freya's arm, then checked the shoulder for any sign of tension. 'Shoulder's good,' he told the young woman. 'Though there are some bruises appearing.'

'Better than more broken bones,' Rosie said.

'What happened to you?' the little girl asked Rosie, eyeing her bruised face.

'Anna, don't be nosy,' Freya said, her words drawn out around the pain filling her, as though good parenting was more important than what had happened to her. Which it probably was, thought Lucas.

Rosie drew a breath and gave the girl a smile. 'I fell over and hit my head.'

'Weren't you looking where you were going?' Anna's eyes were filled with interest.

Rosie's laugh was tight. 'Something like that.'

A siren filled the air and diverted Anna from further questions.

'Freya, is there someone I can call to come and get Anna?' Lucas asked.

'Mum.' She groaned out the number for him to tap into his phone and within moments it was all sorted.

'Your mother's on her way,' he told the stressed Freya.

'Thank you.'

Lucas recognised the two paramedics leaping out of the ambulance to hurry towards them. 'Hey, Lucas, Rosie. Someone got lucky having both of you here,' said Taylor as she knelt down beside Freya. 'Fill me in.'

Lucas looked to Rosie and gave her a nod to go ahead. She was a rescue doctor and knew what was required now the paras were here.

'This is Freya,' Rosie told Taylor. 'A skateboard slammed into her shin and there are multiple fractures in a very small area.'

'Any other injuries?'

'Not that Lucas or I could find, though Freya says she hurts all over.'

'From what she's told us, she hit the ground hard,' Lucas added.

The second paramedic, Jordan, was placing a mask attached to an oxygen tank over Freya's face. 'Freya, we'll get your breathing sorted and then administer something for the pain, okay?'

Freya nodded once, then grimaced and tried to pull the mask away.

Lucas lifted it a little way from her mouth. 'Easy. Are you trying to tell us something?'

'Don't like mask.'

'Give it a minute and you'll feel a little better.' He slipped it back in place and stood up. 'We'll get out of the way and let you two get on with the job.'

Rosie was talking to Taylor. 'Do you need a hand wrapping that leg in plastic before we go?' It would keep the bone pieces from moving too much when Freya was shifted onto the trolley.

'Or help to get her on board the ambulance?' Lucas asked.

Taylor shook her head. 'Jordan and I will manage, thanks. We heard what happened to you last night, Rosie. It's appalling. Are you coping all right?'

'I'm getting there. Lucas has been great helping me with a couple of things.'

Taylor hadn't finished. 'You take care, okay? See you when you're back at work.'

Rosie straightened and rubbed her thigh. 'Monday.'

Not if that hip was still giving her trouble, Lucas thought grimly, then realised he had no say in the matter and Rosie would no doubt go to work, sore hip or not.

'Grandma!' shrieked Anna. 'Mummy's hurt.'

A worried-looking woman stumbled as Anna threw herself at her. 'Settle, sweetheart. Where's Mummy?'

Lucas and Rosie approached her at the same time. 'I'm Lucas, and this is Rosie. We're both doctors and saw to Freya until the ambulance arrived. They'll be taking her to the Parkville hospital shortly.'

'Her leg's hurt, Grandma.' Anna was clinging to the older woman's hand.

She asked, 'How bad is it?'

'She's probably going to need surgery, I'm afraid. The lower bones in one leg are broken.' That was as much as he was telling her. It was up to the orthopaedic surgeon to fill in the gaps once they knew the full extent of the injuries.

'Come on, Grandma. You've got to see Mummy.'

'Thank you for helping Freya,' the woman said as she was tugged away by her granddaughter.

'Let's go. There's nothing more we can do here.' Lucas took Rosie's hand and led her through the onlookers and across the road before realising what he was doing and dropped her hand fast. 'I'll carry your groceries up to your apartment before I head away.'

'I'll let you do that. Plus make coffee if you're interested.' This time Rosie gave him one of her soft smiles that sneaked in under his radar without any effort.

He liked it, but wasn't sure he should. It could get him into all sorts of trouble if he wasn't careful. But then *careful* was his middle name these days. Still, he wasn't risking anything by having a coffee with Rosie, surely?

'I rarely say no to a decent coffee.' Though this was one time he probably should but didn't want to. Presuming she made good coffee, it was the best pick-me-up he knew, other than a glass of cool wine after a long day at

work. But that was for another time. This was morning
and he had jobs to do when he got home. 'Make it black.'

'Pop those bags on the bench,' Rosie said when they
entered her apartment.

The place had him drawing a breath.

'This is stunning.' Like its owner. The front of the
unit was basically all glass, allowing light to flow in,
and there wasn't a dark corner to be seen. A deck ran
the length of the front wall and the worn furniture out
there suggested it was well used. After placing the grocery bags on the bench, he stepped outside and gazed at
the view. 'Not bad.'

'I fell for it the moment I walked in through the main
door.' Rosie stood beside him. 'I had to have it, and when
the agent told me there was another offer going in that
day I kind of panicked and paid over the top for it, but
I've never regretted it.'

So she could lose control over her feelings? Interesting. He hadn't seen that side to her.

'No lawns to worry about mowing. Though nowhere
to grow your vegetables either.'

'That's what fruit and veg shops are for.' She left him
standing there and went to turn on the coffee machine,
looking more at ease than he'd seen since catching up
with her last night. Home was obviously her go-to place.
She'd said she needed to get back here but he hadn't realised quite how much she'd meant it. The décor suggested a lot of input from her, modern and refined yet
comfortable and cosy, with warm pink and soft green
shades. There were two paintings of outback Australia
with the red dirt and sparse trees standing out brightly.

The emotion they brought about had him holding his
breath. 'Who painted these?'

'Dad.'

He turned to study Rosie. She was tense and her face devoid of emotion. Okay, he knew when to back off, but there was a lot he'd like to find out one day if she ever relaxed enough to tell him.

Looking around the room, he realised there were no photos. Odd, to say the least. Who didn't have some photos of family or friends to be seen by everyone? He knew she'd never shared much about herself with any of them back when he'd known her before, but this didn't add up when the apartment drew him in with its warmth and cosiness. Something wasn't right, or was he getting confused over this new awareness of Rosie? He wondered what her bedroom was like. There might be photos in there, just for her to enjoy. He wasn't even thinking about a bed. No, he wasn't.

The apartment was nothing like the house he was currently doing up—large, functional and relaxing in a simple way. The relaxing came about only when he had time to do nothing, which wasn't often. The plans he and May had had for altering the lounge, dining area and kitchen into a family space had taken a back seat. Now he was focused on making the place comfortable and modern, and easy to sell to a growing family. Though the longer he was here the more he wondered if he might stay permanently because it was great being back amongst his family and friends, who were still living all over the city. Selling might be off the cards.

Except for the memories. Those still haunted him on bad days. Last week, when he'd knocked down an internal wall where May used to hang photos, he'd had a moment of longing for the wonderful life he'd had with her. He missed the photos too. They were in a box in the attic. Rosie wasn't the only one who kept things close to her heart and away from prying eyes. But he did have snaps of his family on the sideboard.

He had got over losing May to the point that he could look forward and make decisions about where he wanted to be in a few years' time, but he was still vulnerable to memories of the past, and his fear for the future and what might lie ahead if he decided to get involved with another woman. He didn't want to go through anything like the pain he'd felt over losing May, and the guilt that went with it. That had taken everything away from him, especially the ability to make decisions involving his future and he was still a long way from getting that back.

'Coffee is served.' Rosie placed a steaming mug in front of him and sat down on one of the deck chairs with another in her hand. 'This is the life,' she murmured.

She made it all sound so easy. Except he knew it wasn't for her any more than him. Last night would stay with her for a while to come as she recovered from the mental side of being assaulted. He'd do all he could to be there and help her through the worst moments.

It was a sudden decision, but one he had no intention of changing his mind about. Everyone needed a trustworthy person in their life, and he could be that person for Rosie. It wouldn't be about a joint future; it would simply be about helping her get back on her feet to face her own again without images of what happened last night taking away her confidence. Time would show he intended sticking around for a while. Maybe along the way he'd get up to speed with making some decisions about his own future.

CHAPTER THREE

'You can't come back to work until Tuesday at the earliest,' Rosie's boss said.

'Steve, there's nothing wrong with me apart from a few bruises. It's the weekend so I can take it easy and be ready to do anything come Monday.'

She didn't want to sit at home with nothing to occupy her mind, otherwise the time would be filled with images of that evil man laughing at her as he grabbed her bag and hit her, sending her tumbling to the ground. So why had she spent so much time thinking about Lucas when her assailant wasn't taking over? Why was she seeing Lucas in a different way now to when she'd known him before? A few too many hours stood between when she'd been attacked and now for her to keep blaming the assailant for her distracting thoughts of Lucas.

Work was the only answer to her problems.

'Put your doctor hat on,' Steve growled. 'You'll feel sore and stiff for the next few days. You rarely take time off, apart from the days on the roster, so it won't hurt to use up some of your leave.' He got to his feet. 'I'm serious, Rosie.'

She stood up too, wincing when a stab of pain sliced

through her hip. 'So am I, Steve. I can do your paperwork and you can take my place on the chopper, if you like.'

He shook his head firmly. 'I saw that wince, Rosie. You're hurting more than you're letting on. Take Monday off and we'll talk again on Monday night.' He leaned in and gave her a brief hug. 'Take care of yourself. No one deserves what that man did to you. I was really shocked when I got the call from your friend last night. I didn't sleep well.'

'You and me both.' She sighed. 'All right, I'll start back on Tuesday. In the air or at your desk, I don't mind. It's only that I'm worried about having too much spare time on my hands at the moment.'

With spare time came too much thinking about things best left alone. Last night had underlined that running solo wasn't as great as she pretended. There'd been no one to call who'd drop everything to be by her side. Kelly or Simone would have come as they were her best friends, but they both had responsibilities to their own families and that wasn't the same as having her own partner rushing to be with her. Had the time come to start thinking about finally letting a man in, and not keep pushing them away? Lucas? She gasped. But why not? She knew him well enough to know he wouldn't walk away, taking her heart with him. *And* it was a big plus that he'd been there for her last night and this morning. There was more to him than she'd ever considered, which was frightening given how her priority was always to protect herself from being hurt.

'Rosie? Everything all right?'

No. She was having the strangest thoughts about a man

she'd only ever known as a friend. A very good-looking friend... 'I'm fine.'

'Call on your pals to drop by. They'll keep you busy talking and laughing.' He'd met Kelly and Simone at her recent thirty-fourth birthday party.

'I was about to email everyone to let them know what happened.' Steve had turned up within minutes of Lucas leaving so there hadn't been time to do anything about informing people of her predicament. 'I need to get onto the insurance company ASAP.' She should've used Lucas's phone while he was here. To think she'd often wondered why anyone had a landline these days. The answer had come hard and fast.

'Want me to hang around so you can use mine to call them? I can let Pam know I'll be a little while.'

Rosie couldn't do that to Pam when Steve was so often away, working or taking work calls at home.

'Thanks, but I'll be fine. I'll use one of the girls' phones when they arrive.' Because there'd be no keeping Kelly and Simone away once they read her email. 'Go have lunch with Pam and forget all about work for an hour.'

When Rosie closed the door behind Steve she sagged back against the wall. Her head pounded. Lucas turning up in her life again was almost as shocking as the assault. In a totally different way, of course, but just as overwhelming. Maybe even more so because she suspected these new feelings weren't going to disappear in a hurry, if at all. It was strange how differently she saw him now. Sucking in a long breath, she wandered into the kitchen. Perhaps because three years had elapsed since he'd lost May? But she had no idea if he'd moved on or not. Nor was she going to do anything to spoil what they already had, a solid friendship that just needed renewing again.

Another coffee while sitting out on the deck might help calm her addled brain. Or not. With her head still aching and her body painful in numerous places, stretching out on the outdoor divan was so tempting, but she doubted her brain would stop bringing up subjects she'd prefer to ignore. Plus, if she didn't get on with letting her nearest and dearest know the score, then once they did find out they'd all be around here reading the riot act for not saying anything. Opening her laptop, she sat uncomfortably at the table and tapped onto her email site. This wouldn't take long. She'd copy in everyone and keep the outline short.

Except typing the details got increasingly more difficult as unwanted images filled her head that definitely had nothing to do with Lucas and made her angry and upset. Once again she was seeing that hideous laughing face, those saucer-sized eyes, and hearing the spin of car wheels on the tarmac. Her fingers shook and too often missed the keys she needed to make sense of what she was trying to tell everyone. Tears spurted out of her eyes.

'Damn you!' she shouted and slammed her fist on the table top. 'Who do you think you are to assault me and steal my bag? Huh? Just who are you?'

Prodding 'send' hard, she shoved the laptop to the middle of the table and dropped her head onto her arms. 'What gave you the right to do this to me?' What he'd done was unbelievable.

Her shoulders heaved as the tears flowed. The attack felt unreal. But it had been real. Which made her feel utterly alone. She wasn't, of course. Steve had not long left.

She had friends and her brother to call on, and Lucas was back in her life, but this was different somehow. She'd been through something none of them had and therefore they wouldn't quite understand how it made her feel so useless. Vulnerable. Unable to protect herself. Something she'd spent her life working hard to make sure she was always capable of. Growing up without her mother to love her, and an emotionally distant father, she'd learned early on how other people could hurt her.

Yet now, after one fist to her arm and a speeding car tossing her aside, she felt so uneasy it was horrible. Her heart hadn't been involved. The man was a stranger to her. Yet he'd managed to pull the ground out from under her. Literally and mentally.

But crying wasn't going to improve a thing.

Straightening up, she blew her nose on a handful of tissues and looked around her home. It was hers, and no one could change that. But then, that was what she'd believed about going to shop for groceries yesterday. Her decision, her right, her way. Bang. Changed in a flash.

Ding-dong. Her doorbell. Who could it be? It was too soon after sending the email for it to be any of her friends. There really wasn't anyone else she wanted to talk to, unless it was her brother. As long as he didn't raise the topic of his wedding and her partner, that was. It could be Lucas, but he'd likely be busy with his chores, plus he hadn't long left here. Nor was it fair to put pressure on him when they'd only just caught up, by wanting him here with her. She had no idea where he was at with his life. Despite the time he'd spent with her, he might have a new woman for all she knew. Her stomach sank further. She needed to find out sooner rather than later, then she could either squash these feelings or do something about them. She shook her head. As if she'd ever do that. Better to keep Lucas as a friend than lose him altogether.

The bell rang again.

Sighing, Rosie pushed herself out of the chair and headed to the door. 'Hello?'

'Rosie, it's Megan, the policewoman from last night. Can I come up?'

What? And go through what happened yet again? No, thank you. But then talking about it all in a steady, un-emotional way might be the best option she had right now. Before she could overthink it, she pressed the button to let Megan into the building.

'Level three, apartment three.' On the corner so that she had one-eighty-degree views to enjoy when she was in the mood. Not today.

Late afternoon, Lucas reached the main entrance to Rosie's apartment block just as two worried-looking women turned up behind him, carrying flowers and a bottle of wine.

'I hope she's all right,' one of them said in a loud voice. 'She didn't mention any wounds, but Rosie would down-play anything that happened to her.'

'Calm down, Kelly. We don't want her seeing us stressed to the max when she's been through hell.'

Lucas hesitated about pressing the buzzer. These women were obviously friends of Rosie's. She might think two visitors were more than enough. But he hadn't stopped worrying about her all day and wanted to check that she was doing okay. He couldn't walk away without seeing her, however briefly. She'd got to him in a way he hadn't expected, which came as a shock considering he hadn't thought he was anywhere near ready to move on with his life and get out of the hole he'd buried himself in. The guilt kept reminding him he wasn't to be trusted with another woman's heart.

'Excuse me. Can you push star number three for us?' the second woman asked.

'I was about to do that myself,' he said, sounding out their reaction to him.

'You're going up to Rosie's?'

'I was, but if you're doing the same I can come back later.'

Both women were staring at him, small smiles on their faces. 'Hell, no. We'll all go up. You do know what happened to her, don't you?'

Lucas thought about how much to say.

'I'm Simone, by the way, and this is Kelly. We're Rosie's besties, if people our age are allowed to call ourselves that.' Simone laughed. Then her face straightened again. 'Sorry, this isn't the time to be joking.'

'I think you'll find that Rosie would like a few laughs at the moment.'

'So you do know what happened,' said Kelly.

He sighed. 'I was the doctor who saw her when she was brought into the ED yesterday. We used to know each other when we were doing our specialty training a few years back,' he added in case they thought he was being creepy by turning up here. 'Lucas Tanner.'

The women gave each other a nod he couldn't interpret, and Kelly said, 'Press the buzzer. We've got a friend to cheer up.'

A friend who looked as though she could do with some

company, Lucas thought as he followed the women into the apartment. There were circles under Rosie's eyes and tension in her shoulders that hadn't been there earlier, probably brought on by too much time alone filled with thoughts of the assault.

'Hey, Rosie, you look like you've gone a round in the boxing ring,' Simone said as she leaned in and gave Rosie a gentle hug with one arm. 'You all right?'

'I'm fine, though a bit tired.'

'Here's something to cheer you up.' Simone handed her the flowers.

'You didn't have to do that.' Rosie blinked and buried her face in the roses.

'How about this then?' Kelly waved the wine in front of her. 'Then there's your doc friend we found on the steps.'

Rosie glanced at him with a wry grin. 'You'll regret coming up here with these two. They never know when to shut up.'

Which could be a good thing, considering how you might need to be distracted from the images that are no doubt continuously flitting through your mind.

'I'll cope,' he said.

'So, coffee? Or wine?' Kelly asked. She looked to Rosie. 'Or are you drugged up on painkillers?'

'Haven't had any since first thing this morning.'

Lucas sent her a sharp look, which she ignored. He'd bet her hip and thigh were giving her even more grief after kneeling down to help that young woman with the smashed shin.

'So that's a yes.' Kelly opened a cupboard and got out

four glasses. 'Lucas? You'll join us?' She was already pouring the first glass.

'Thanks, but I'll be boring and stick to coffee,' Lucas replied.

Rosie made a move towards the coffee machine.

'I'll make it, Rosie. I've got one of these machines so I know what I'm doing.' He really should've turned around and gone away when he knew Kelly and Simone were visiting her. It was a bit crowded in here with the women bustling around. They seemed to gobble up all the air with their laughter and talk, trying to downplay their concern for Rosie.

He was seeing another side to Rosie he'd forgotten about—her complete relaxation around those she trusted. Not many people, if he remembered correctly, and he had to admit he could've got that one wrong because back then he'd mostly been focused on May and the state of their marriage. He glanced at Rosie. Why had she and Cameron split up? They'd been happy together and seemed on course for marriage and family.

He shook his head. Why did life get messed up so often? It wasn't always wonderful, for sure, and now he'd reconnected with Rosie he had no intention of losing her again. It would be worse this time because he was running solo and that had its lonely moments. So, was he thinking Rosie could fill those? As a friend? Or was he looking for more? No, only as a friend. For now, at least. A shiver ran down his back, making him wonder if he was trying to fool himself.

'Fill us in on everything,' he heard Simone say and he concentrated on that and not what was going on in his head. Then Simone shook her head. 'Sorry, that was a dumb thing to say. I'm sure you don't want to go over the details right now.'

Rosie pulled out a chair at the table and sank onto it, grimacing as if her hip hurt. 'Truth is, I've just spent two hours giving an in-depth statement to one of the police-women who turned up at the scene yesterday and right now I'm shattered. So, if you don't mind, let's find something else to discuss.'

'Two hours?' Lucas was stunned. 'That seems OTT.'

'Not if they want to nail him in court, apparently.' Rosie sighed. 'The cops have a good idea who attacked me. He did something similar last week to a woman in her eighties. She got a fractured arm when he dragged her along the road with his car for a few metres.'

Lucas felt his heart scrunch. Rosie had got off lightly compared to that, but he was furious all over again. Who did the lowlife think he was, attacking women as if it meant absolutely nothing? About to say something, he glanced at Rosie and kept his mouth shut. She did indeed look exhausted, as if everything was finally catching up big time. It had to happen. He was only surprised it had taken until now, but she had been busy most of the day, what with picking up her car, helping Freya, and giving that statement. He wouldn't stay long. Her friends would make sure she was okay, and she'd probably be more re-laxed with them anyway.

'You all right?' he asked quietly.

'We'll make sure she is,' Kelly answered for her.

'Have you had anything to eat since you got home?' Lucas asked.

Her cheeks reddened. 'Not really. I don't feel hungry.'

'I'll make you something. Want a sandwich?'

'That'd be nice. There's cold chicken in the fridge, and some salad in a container.'

'Consider it done.'

Rosie leaned back in her chair, trying to ignore her throbbing hip as she listened to her friends and watched Lucas clean up after he'd made her a sandwich. It was still hard to believe he'd turned up in her life after all this time, and how that had happened. He'd been nothing but supportive since he'd first walked into the cubicle in the ED where the paramedics had deposited her. Friends were the best, she had decided long ago. These two had been with her most of her life, since they'd met at school. Friends didn't turn their backs on her and leave her with a broken heart, like her dad had. What he'd done wasn't usual for a parent, or even a partner. On one level she knew that, but all those years of emotional neglect had affected her so deeply that she just couldn't face being hurt like that again. Lucas would be an amazing friend…only she suspected the warmth she felt for him wasn't only about friendship. And that was dangerous.

The problem was, she'd set herself up to miss out on meaningful relationships because she couldn't face having her heart crushed again. So how come she was looking at Lucas more often than was sensible? Feeling these mixed emotions over him? It was easy to blame the assault for shaking her up, but beginning to understand just what she'd done to herself by remaining so isolated and believing that she was keeping herself safe from heartbreak was more complicated and difficult to ignore. And unusual for her.

'Hey, sleepyhead.' Kelly nudged her. 'You should go lie down for a while.'

Even though she wasn't taking part in the conversation much, she preferred having the company to being on her own. Her friends managed to keep the ghastly memories at bay a little.

'I'm good sitting here, thanks.'

'Have you sorted the problem with Johnno and his wedding yet?' Kelly asked.

'No. The only good thing about not having a phone right now is he can't ring and nag me. I sent him the same email I sent you but chances are he hasn't seen it yet as he and Karen are up in the Yarra Valley this weekend, sorting out seating arrangements and a whole load of other things.'

Johnno would be putting his mate's name on the seat next to hers as she still hadn't come up with an alternative date to accompany her.

'I can think of an answer...' Simone grinned with a slight inclination of her head in Lucas's direction.

'Get out of here,' she muttered.

Simone stood up. 'Actually, I am about to head off now. Toby's taking me out to dinner to celebrate my promotion and I don't want to be late for that.' She was grinning like the cat with the cream.

Glancing at Lucas, Rosie saw him flinch and wondered why. But she couldn't just ignore her friend's excitement. 'Congratulations, Simone! You truly deserve it, you've worked hard enough.' All those long hours at the television station where she worked as a programme organiser had paid off.

'You bet I have.' Then she looked contrite. 'I don't really want to leave you though.'

'I'm fine,' she growled, denying the need to have someone with her for a little longer. Kelly might stay.

Kelly looked from her to Lucas and then to Simone, and grinned. 'I'll come with you. I'm going to Mum and Dad's for tea.' She flicked another look at Lucas as if to say, *Step up, man. She needs you.*

Rosie deliberately looked at the decorative clock on the wall. 'You're going to be late, aren't you?' Considering Kelly's parents had left for Singapore two days ago, she was talking nonsense. These two were stirring up trouble for her, all to do with Lucas.

Her friend just laughed. 'Probably.'

Lucas looked at all three of them and finally said, 'I'll hang out here for a while longer if you can put up with me, Rosie.' He said it with a knowing smile, as if he suspected the girls were setting him up and didn't give a damn.

Thankfully, she hadn't shared their enthusiasm—or her own—or he'd probably have been long gone, especially if he knew what was going on in her head.

'Thanks, Lucas, but I'm sure I can manage. It's not as though I'm going to be doing anything too strenuous. Might look into what's required to get a pilot's licence.' That had come out of nowhere. It had only been an idea simmering in the back of her mind, not a definite plan. Yet now she knew for sure she was going to do it. Yesterday had been a wakeup call, shown her that she'd never know what might be thrown at her so why keep putting off doing the things she wanted?

'You want to learn to fly?' Lucas looked surprised, also thoughtful.

'I do.' See? She could move forward, stop putting everything on hold, all because she was afraid to lay her heart and soul on the line. A shiver rattled her.

Slow down. You're rushing things.

Wasn't that normal after what had happened to her?

Lucas said, 'Go you. That's brilliant.'

'It sure is,' said Simone, before hugging her. 'See you tomorrow. Look after yourself in the meantime.' She winked.

Maybe it would be good to see the backs of these two as they were nothing if not trouble.

'Check I'm here before you drop by. I might be busy doing something.'

'We have a lunch date, remember?'

'I might change my mind.' No way would she do that, but perhaps her friends needed reminding they didn't control her life!

All she got in response was more laughter and a hug from Kelly. Then the door shut and the apartment was suddenly quiet.

Rosie leaned back with a sigh. She missed her friends already. Annoying as they could sometimes be, they lit up the room and made her happy.

'You all right?' the remaining person asked again.

'I wish everyone would stop asking me that. I'm a bit sore and stiff, but otherwise I am fine.' Guilt crept in. Lucas didn't deserve her curtness. 'Sorry, Lucas. I know you're just looking out for me, and I really appreciate it.'

'But you'd rather I kept my mouth shut.' He grinned.

'Want to tell me about your problem with your brother's wedding instead?'

Not really, but it was a change of topic and she'd go along with that without saying too much.

'He's getting married in two weeks and wants me to go as his best friend's date. I can't stand the guy so I've refused to oblige, but Johnno is adamant he'll seat us together unless I take someone else who's apparently important to me or that I'm in lust with, or something.'

Why hadn't she found a man to go with? It wasn't as though she didn't know any single men, and one of them would probably have agreed if she'd asked. But she hadn't been able to get enthused about that idea and hence she was still stuck between a rock and Will Clark.

'The wedding's two weeks away, you say?'

'Yes.'

'How about I go with you? I haven't got anything important on that weekend.'

She stared at Lucas. 'Everyone's going up on Friday and staying two nights.'

'No problem.'

She was still staring. So he had to be single then. 'You're serious? Did you not hear me say I have to at least look like I'm in lust with my date?' Her cheeks were heating up fast. Hopefully, no one would think she found Lucas as attractive as she did. How could she agree to him going without making an idiot of herself? Impossible.

'It's just a suggestion,' Lucas said reasonably. 'A friend helping another friend.'

Had he noticed the smug looks her *friends* had been exchanging before they'd left? If so, what was he thinking?

'I didn't mention we're staying overnight at the vineyard where the wedding's being held. We'd have to share a room.' With one bed most likely.

'I always thought you never turned your back on a challenge.' There was laughter in his voice, which irked her. Or was that the second challenge he'd just issued? Because if that wasn't one, then what was it?

'You win. I accept your offer.' Somehow, she didn't feel disappointed for giving in. Instead, it was more like excitement filling her, which was crazy. Lucas was a great guy, but she wasn't in lust or anything else with him. Or was she lying to herself about that? Hadn't she been thinking otherwise half the night? 'Are you sure you want to do this?' she pressed because she had no idea where her emotions were at.

'As strange as it may seem, I do. It's an opportunity to spend time with you and catch up on what you've been up to since we all went our own ways three years ago. I know it's going to look like we're a couple.' He highlighted that by flicking his forefingers in air quotes between them. 'But there'll be times when we'll be by ourselves without having to keep alert and can just relax.'

Not play out the 'in lust' part? Was that disappointment? Couldn't be. It was so good to see Lucas again, to have him looking out for her, she was getting carried away.

'You're right. There will be.' Though not many, as there were lots of get-togethers planned for the weekend, which was a shame because she realised she'd like a lot of time with just Lucas to sort out her mixed emotions. 'For the record, I know Johnno only has the best of intentions when it comes to pairing me up with his best friend. He thinks I'm not giving Will enough of a chance, but I haven't told him how rude and arrogant Will was the one and only time I went out with him. I didn't want to make things awkward for my brother.'

'I understand.' Lucas gave her a heart-softening smile. 'So, we're agreed? We're going to the wedding together.'

'Yes, we are.' He'd made it too easy for her to accept. Only yesterday the idea of asking Lucas to accompany her had popped into her startled mind and she'd kicked it out fast. Now she was good with the idea, though she wasn't going to think about sharing a room and therefore a bed with him. That was too much to take in right now. 'There's a dinner on the Friday night for Karen's and Johnno's families. As my partner, you'll be a part of that.' Last chance for him to bail.

'Of course.' Lucas looked thoughtful. 'Are we really going to be able to fool Johnno that we're in lust with each other? If you haven't come up with a date until now, he's going to know you weren't asking anyone else.'

'True.' Did Lucas think she was pathetic not having a man in her life, one she could've invited to the wedding anyway? 'Johnno knows I shy away from relationships and thinks I need a helping hand finding someone.' She closed her eyes. She'd gone too far. Now Lucas would be thinking the same. 'I sound pathetic, I know.'

A warm hand covered hers. 'We're two peas in a pod.'

'What?' Her eyes flew open. 'You do the same?' At least he had good reason to keep to himself. He'd lost the woman he loved. She'd lost her mother, and then her father's love. Same, but not the same.

'Yes, Rosie, I do.' He withdrew his hand and stood up to go get two wine glasses and open a bottle she had in the fridge. Handing her a glass, he said, 'Here, relax. Your wedding problem is solved.'

'Thanks.' She'd barely touched the wine Kelly had poured her and Simone had finished it off.

Sitting on the couch opposite, he breathed deeply. 'Losing May crippled me,' he stated bluntly.

'Of course it did.'

Leaning forward, elbows on his knees, he studied the floor. 'I don't know if or when I'll ever be able to move on after what happened. Will I ever reach that point?' He paused for a moment. Talking about this couldn't be easy. Yet he seemed determined to tell her where he was at. 'I have no idea what lies ahead for me in terms of another long-term relationship. I only know I'm not ready to find out yet.'

Internally, Rosie slumped. Outwardly, she worked hard at not showing that his admission rattled her when she should be relieved that she could put away these strange feelings of need and desire and get on with recovering from the attack instead of thinking Lucas might've come back into her life for a special reason.

'I suppose only time will tell,' she murmured, knowing she'd let him down with such an inane comment. But she had to protect herself too.

'So I've often heard.' His smile was crooked. 'But it's okay. If I don't know, how can anyone else?'

She could relate to that, after years of waiting for her dad to return to being the father he once was. Then a thought struck her hard. Neither she nor Lucas were truly available to put their hearts on the line. Was she relieved or not?

'We'll have a fun, friendly weekend. Thanks to you, my problem is solved.'

'Do you need to tell Johnno while he's up in the Yarra Valley?'

'You're way ahead of me. I'll email him now.' Reaching for her laptop, she opened up the email site and began composing a message, ignoring the slight shake in her fingers. Lucas was going to the wedding with her. What had she let herself in for? A lot of fun? Or more problems at a time she didn't need them? Go with the fun. Much better, and it might even lead to more good times. Except neither of them was emotionally available, remember? Therein lay the problem. She was such a worrywart.

Her glass appeared on the small table beside her. 'Get some of this into you and stop overthinking it all. Things will work out.'

'I hope so.' No, damn it, she'd make sure they had a great time without getting carried away.

She was confident about looking out for herself, but not about letting a man in to do that for her and steal her heart at the same time. Lifting her glass, she tapped it against Lucas's. 'It is so good to find you again. Given that you're working in Parkville, it was only a matter of time before we came across each other in the ED, but I'm really glad it's already happened.'

'Back at you.' Lucas settled into an armchair beside her. 'I've often wondered where everyone's living and working, what they're up to. Married, family, the mortgage. All that sort of stuff. I keep in touch with Brett. He wouldn't let me walk away when I left Melbourne, insisted we stay in contact, and I'm glad he did. I needed that. He's now working in Sydney, but he came over to

San Fran to catch up a couple of times. We went off on treks in national parks both times.'

'Laurie's in Perth, married to an awesome guy who's a nurse. They've got two toddlers, and she works part-time in an emergency department. I heard Nathan's living in London, working at one of the bigger hospitals. Whether he's married or not I have no clue.'

'That's the whole team accounted for, then.'

'It felt weird when we first went our separate ways. No one to vent to about a particularly bad day. We had a special bond back then.'

'Before it all blew up in our faces.'

Rosie grabbed his hand. 'We missed you when you left after May died. It was such a dreadful time. Everyone felt for you and would've done anything to go back to before it happened.' Which was the understatement of the year. They'd all felt guilty for not being able to help Lucas through his pain, and when he'd left Melbourne it had seemed even worse, as if they'd failed big time even though they knew he'd left not only them but his family and other friends to put space between everyone and himself.

'You'd have had to have been queued up behind me to do that.'

The sadness in Lucas's face told her how much he still carried the weight from that night. Right from the moment he'd learned that May had died he'd blamed himself for being at work instead of being in the car with her when she'd spun it out and slammed into a concrete wall. But it hadn't been his fault. He was a doctor through to his bones and couldn't have left a dying patient. But she knew from experience not to say that to him. He'd only tell her she had no idea what she was talking about, and maybe he was right. She had her own experience of losing people she loved, albeit in very different circumstances.

'I'm not surprised.'

They sat quietly, lost in their own thoughts, until Lucas finally said, 'Want me to sort something for dinner, or would you like some time to yourself?'

'If you want to hang around, then that'd be great.' She still wasn't ready to be alone with all those images from yesterday. Now she could add new, better ones about Lucas joining her for her brother's wedding, but she wasn't so sure she wanted to be inundated with those either. Lucas had admitted he wasn't over May, so she had to concentrate on remaining friends. Coming up with any number of images involving him was off-limits. 'My head's a mess, to put it bluntly.' When he started to laugh, she held up her hand. 'Stop. I'm not talking about the bruises.'

'I know that.' His laughter died away. 'It's going to take time to get over what happened.'

But I've got you to help me through it.

'Not too long. I refuse to let him win on that score.'

'Now there's a surprise.'

'Why did I offer to go to the wedding?' Lucas wondered out loud. It was another way to help Rosie out, but sharing a hotel room? A bed? When he was all over the place about what he might want from her.

'Absolutely bonkers, that's what I am.' Except there was a new bounce in his step as he walked back to his house from her apartment. The air felt lighter and the sky was shining. 'Yeah, I am totally losing the plot.'

Which went to show how much Rosie had got to him in a very short time. Not a lot more than twenty-four hours ago she hadn't been in his life and yet now here he was thinking he'd like to get to know her better. She was already starting to feel special to him.

But enough to share a whole weekend away with her?

He grinned as warmth stole under his ribs. Yeah, why not?

If it turned out he was wrong about the excitement he felt around Rosie then at least he'd have an answer. The chances were high for that to happen as he still felt he wasn't ready to engage in a full-time relationship, not even with a beautiful and wonderful woman like Rosie. The guilt and sadness over May's death still filled his heart and wouldn't be disappearing any time soon as far as he could tell.

But he couldn't help thinking he'd love to get to a deeper level than casual friends with Rosie. Was he ready for that, if nothing else? He guessed the weekend away could answer that.

CHAPTER FOUR

'CHOPPER'S FIVE MINUTES AWAY,' Chris told Lucas.

'Let's get up to the helipad now.' It was Thursday afternoon and the ED was having a quiet time, as in not every bed was full and the waiting room only had two people needing to be seen by a doctor as soon as one was free. 'I want to be there before they touch down.'

From what the Life Flight caller had said, a man had fallen off the fourth floor of a building on a construction site and was bleeding extensively, internally and externally. He'd need all the help they could give him and some. A general surgeon and an orthopaedic specialist were on standby with a theatre ready and waiting.

As soon as the chopper landed and the door began opening Lucas made his way across to collect their patient.

Rosie appeared in the doorway, looking calm and in control, though that was probably a lie. No one could be in control of what was going on with the man with his extensive injuries. 'Hey, Lucas, Chris, we need this man in Theatre ASAP. I suspect pneumothorax. We've got an oxygen tube in but it's not looking good.'

'On it.' Within minutes he and Chris were pushing the

trolley towards the door to go inside, while a nurse from the chopper held the heart monitor steady.

Beside him, Rosie was filling in the details. 'Trent suffered cardiac arrest fifteen minutes ago. Due to blood loss, I'd say. His heart rate's low. I expect another arrest any moment. Both legs have multiple fractures, likewise both arms. There's a contusion on his skull even though he wore a hard hat.'

The heart monitor flatlined.

'Here we go.' Rosie was already reaching for the defibrillator. 'Stand back everyone.'

The man's body jerked upward, sank back down.

The line on the monitor remained flat.

Lucas cursed under his breath. Compressions were out, due to the lung damage. *Hurry up, defib.*

'Stand back.'

Another electric current lifted the man's body, and this time the line moved upward.

Lucas felt no relief. There was a long way to go before Trent was out of danger. 'Move it. Fast as possible.'

The four of them focused on speed without causing further stress to their patient. Once in the ED, Rosie handed over notes and swapped over the defib for the hospital one by the bed.

'How long was Trent on the ground before medical help arrived?' Lucas asked her after telling Chris to let the surgeons on standby know their patient was in the ED.

She didn't stop what she was doing as she answered. 'An ambulance was there fifteen minutes after he fell. We were approximately another fifteen minutes after that. He wasn't brought in by road because of the peak-hour traffic.'

Lucas winced. It was a fast pickup, but still a long time when Trent was bleeding out.

'Trent's been unconscious the whole time. Observers say he took the brunt of the fall on his legs. The worst bleeding is coming from his chest. While the suspected pneumothorax is the greatest source of blood loss, I think he's also haemorrhaging in the abdominal region,' she said.

He was already checking the abdomen and coming to the same conclusion. 'I agree.'

'Heart rate's dropping,' a nurse warned.

'Get ready for another shock if needed,' he warned, even though it was already under control. Where the hell were the surgeons? The man wouldn't be able to take much more. Of course the specialists would be on their way, be here any second, but he hated these moments when most things were out of his hands except trying to keep the patient alive. They couldn't stop the bleeding in the lungs by applying pressure as that'd only push the broken ribs in deeper and cause more trouble.

'Lucas, I've got you.' Aaron, the general surgeon on standby, appeared at his side. 'Fill me in,' he said, already feeling around Trent's ribcage.

The other surgeon arrived at the other side of the bed. Lucas nodded to Rosie. 'You fill them in.'

With a grim nod, she told the surgeons all she could about Trent's injuries.

'Right, let's get to Theatre and start putting him back together,' Aaron said.

Lucas sighed with relief. No one was wasting time. 'Keep me posted.'

When he looked around after Trent had been taken

away, Rosie was nowhere to be seen. Disappointment snagged at him. But then why would she still be here? She had a job to do and that wasn't in the ED but back out amongst the busy city environs or further beyond in the countryside. He'd liked working alongside her as they got Trent's heart up and running. She was calm, focused, and didn't mess about.

Now that the case was out of his hands he was beginning to sag mentally. He didn't have to remain on edge in case he got something wrong or something else happened to Trent that caused more problems. Right then he made up his mind to call Rosie when he signed off and suggest they go somewhere for a drink to ease all the work tension.

He also wanted to catch up on how she was doing, both physically and mentally. She'd called him on Monday night to say she'd replaced her phone and arranged for new bank cards. He hadn't trusted her chirpy manner as he felt she might've been putting on a show to keep him at arm's length. It was time to stop holding back whenever he was worried about her. They were closer than that. Especially now they were going away for a weekend together.

'Sorry I'm late, but we had to pick up a child from Yarra Valley. She'd dived into the school swimming pool and hit her head on the bottom.' Rosie sank onto the stool at the table Lucas had claimed and huffed out a long breath, ridding herself of some of the tension in her shoulders, glad Lucas had suggested meeting up after work. 'What a day. How's Trent doing?'

'I'll fill you in after I've got you a drink.'

'Good man. Wine would be awesome.' It might even help her sleep tonight. There were some nights after distressing times with patients when sleep could be elusive to the point she'd be lucky to get a couple of hours. Bad cases always weighed heavily on her mind as she questioned whether she could have done things differently to get a better outcome. Along with working hard to save Trent, today's last case had been one of those. The little girl had been pulled unconscious from the pool by a parent. The head injury was severe, her lungs full of water and, from what Rosie ascertained, very likely her neck was broken too.

'Here, get that into you. You look like you're about to fall apart.' Lucas pushed a glass in front of her. 'I take it things don't look good for the young girl?'

Rosie's own neck ached as she nodded. 'Not at all.'

'Well, Trent's conscious now and fairly lucid. The hard hat saved him from serious brain trauma. Plus the fact he took the brunt of the fall on his legs.' Lucas drank a deep mouthful of beer. 'Therein ends the good news.'

'His legs are in a bad way?'

'It's unlikely he'll get full use of them back. Both lungs were perforated, and his liver needed sectioning.' The saddest emotions filled Lucas's face. 'It's one of those days when I wonder why I didn't become a truck driver.'

Shuffling her stool closer to him, she took his hand in hers. 'It's never too late to change careers. I could be your offsider so you don't have to park up when your hours behind the wheel run out.' It felt so good to be here with Lucas, her hand around his in an entirely friendly way. They understood each other and how their day had affected them as non-medical friends wouldn't.

He choked out a laugh. 'I remember the time you said you'd become a barber and shave all your clients' heads bald.'

'I don't remember that. It seems a bit extreme, even for me.'

'You'd seen a man with melanomas on his scalp that had only been found when he decided to get his long hair shaved off to raise money for a charity.'

Rosie thought back to that time. 'I still don't recall saying it, but my reaction does make sense now.'

'He'd come to town to see his girlfriend and when he got to her house she didn't recognise him. Or so the story went in the local rag.' Lucas grinned and reached for his beer again.

Slipping her hand away, she picked up her glass too, this time taking a small sip, her mind busy flipping through previous times when those available in their group got together. 'I remember when Brett said he was going to take up ironing for a living, starting with his own shirts as his current girlfriend was useless at it.'

Lucas grinned. 'I remember that too. The girlfriend didn't take kindly to what Brett said and told him he could cook dinner every night for the next month, which I think he did whenever he wasn't on night shift. He must've been in lust at the time.'

In lust. Rosie smiled to herself. That sounded like fun with no hitches. But not what she was getting into with Lucas, because something told her it wouldn't stop at that—if anything ever happened between them, which it couldn't. Right now, her hand felt warm where it had touched his skin in a way that had nothing to do with letting go of the day and more to do with how attracted she was to him. It was great sitting here laughing about nothing when both of them had had an awful day, but this connection between them was also getting a little more intense than she was prepared for.

'It's been a long time since I've been able to offload to someone like this.'

'Know what you mean. It was one of the things I missed when I headed away from Melbourne. Though I was usually struggling too much with losing May to be stressing about a bad day in the ED.' He forced a smile. 'Let's not go there tonight.'

Fair enough. They were here to destress from a bad day, not add to it.

'Why did you opt for San Francisco? I'd have thought you'd go to a smaller town.' He'd used to say when he'd finished training that he'd like to move to a town on the coast where he didn't have to grapple with traffic and lots of people every time he went shopping. Then she remembered he'd signed up for a position in Melbourne's CBD before his life went pear-shaped. Something to do with the house he and May were going to do up.

'Cities are more impersonal. I didn't have to deal with kind and caring people wanting to know too much about my past.'

Ouch. That wasn't good.

'That's sad. You were always very sociable.'

'Only because May had my back. Until I met her, I was quite introverted, stayed in the background a lot. We met in our first year at university and were together from then on.'

'Wow, that's special.'

He nodded. 'It was. Back to why San Fran. I had a

friend at school who came from there so I always had an interest in the place. His dad was Aussie and his mum was from California. While I was there, he came across to visit relations a couple of times and we'd catch up.'

'You mentioned hiking. That must've been fun.'

'There were moments when I wondered if I was mad, but mostly it was challenging and exciting. I also took up cycling as it was a great way to get around the city.'

She could just imagine those long legs pedalling away while his upper body hunched over the front of the cycle. Odd how she was noticing his physical attributes when once she wouldn't have looked at him twice in that way. Not often anyway. He was good-looking as well as tall and muscular. Her type for sure. Gulp.

Grabbing her glass, she tipped her head back and took a large mouthful of wine. Then, putting it down, she made to stand up.

'You suddenly in a hurry to go?'

Yes. I need to put space between us while I clear my head of these out-of-order thoughts.

Before she could come up with a reasonable excuse, Lucas said, 'Let's grab a bite to eat while we're here.'

She hesitated. Despite these unusual sensations, she liked being with Lucas. He was easy to get along with and had no expectations other than to enjoy her company. He didn't appear to be looking for more than friendship.

'No more talk about today or the past,' he added.

Was he lonely too?

'Good idea. The food, I mean,' she added. She hadn't thought she was too lonely, but after Lucas had spent time with her last weekend she'd begun to think it was fun having someone to do things like this with. Kelly and

Simone were often in and out of her days but they both had husbands who naturally came first. Then she shook her head as another thought struck. 'I haven't told you. Last night, the police arrested the guy who attacked me. He's behind bars for now at least.'

Lucas was on his feet, coming around the table to wrap her in his arms. 'That's the best news I've heard all day. Probably longer.'

Pressing in against him, she agreed. 'I can relax now. He's not going to find me and have another crack.'

Lucas leaned back so he could see her face, still holding her. 'Were you worried about that? It was very unlikely.'

'I know, but my head's been in some strange places lately.'

'I bet.' He stepped away, taking those comforting arms with him.

She sank onto her stool. 'Now the fun really starts, according to Megan—the cop,' she added, in case Lucas had forgotten her name. 'She warned me that getting a sentence isn't straightforward unless he steps up and admits everything he did, which includes a stolen vehicle, stolen number plates, drug paraphernalia in the car, et cetera.'

'But he'll remain locked up in the meantime?'

'Yes. He's got a history of similar crimes.' She shuddered at the thought of what else he could've done to her.

'Best they throw away the key.' He made this easier to face with his straightforward approach.

'I agree.' Picking up her glass, she said, 'I'm going to have another wine.' She only had a little way to walk home. 'Want any more beer?'

'What sort of question's that?'

Her grin widened. All because Lucas had her back. 'I'll grab some menus.' She picked up his empty glass and headed to the bar, feeling a little light-headed. She couldn't believe they'd talked about the day and come through laughing—just like old times, only better.

She was struggling to comprehend how much Lucas was lighting her up on the inside. He was something else, with that toned body and warm chocolate-brown eyes that saw too much. Not that she minded, as she hadn't given away anything about herself she didn't want him knowing. So far, anyway. To think they were going to Johnno's wedding together. That excited her. To have a date who wasn't Will made all the difference to her feelings about the wedding, even though Lucas would only be playing a role. So would she. She'd have to be careful not to overstep the mark with Lucas and have him wishing he hadn't offered to accompany her.

She'd never intended avoiding the wedding because of Will. She was Johnno's only family and she'd be there for him, no matter what else was going on. His fiancée, Karen, was gorgeous and perfect for him. Fingers crossed he didn't stuff up this time and leave her, as he did his first wife. Johnno's insecurities about love and relationships were as bad as hers, Rosie conceded. While she never lasted long with a man, Johnno went further like getting married, and then started looking for problems that weren't necessarily there. This time, Rosie intended keeping an eye on him and talking to him before it was too late, and not after everything went belly-up.

'As if I know what the hell I'm talking about,' she muttered as she placed the glasses on the bar. Why had their father withdrawn his loving side all those years ago? She'd lost count of how many times she'd asked herself that. There'd never been an answer, even when she'd asked her father directly on the day she'd left home to go to university. He'd shaken his head silently and gone out to the shed to chop firewood.

'Another wine and beer?' the woman behind the counter asked as she put their glasses in the washer.

'Thanks, and menus.' Time to stop being so glum when she was having fun. Lucas might change his mind about going to the wedding if she didn't.

'Order me the medium rare steak and chips,' Lucas told her when she returned to their table with the menus.

'You've been here before.'

'Often.'

'Me too, I'm surprised we didn't bump into each other here before.' She put the menus aside and went to order their meals and fetch their fresh drinks.

Lucas watched Rosie weave her way through the tables towards him, fighting the wave of longing swamping him. She was gorgeous. He had noticed before, of course, but purely objectively.

Because I loved May.

True. But now? Had the time finally come to move on, maybe with Rosie? The constrictions around his heart were loosening. But it wouldn't be easy to adjust to this new state. He was still afraid to give his heart away again. Nor had the guilt over the accident that took May from him vanished. Not at all.

If they hadn't argued that night, May would still be here. The disc with that refrain went round and round in his head. If he hadn't stayed back at work to save the life of a man who was bleeding out on the ED floor, May would still be with him.

Yeah, and if May hadn't told him her promotion meant moving to Sydney in a fortnight he wouldn't have got angry and they wouldn't have had that fierce argument, and she mightn't have said he was selfish and she was going to Sydney whether he decided to join her there or not. Put bluntly, she'd told him they were over unless he agreed to her demands. Demands that scrubbed him raw because they'd been on the same page when they'd bought their first house with the idea of living in Melbourne for the next few years.

'Here, get that into you and put a smile back on your face.' Rosie placed a beer in front of him. 'You look like you need cheering up.'

He did, but it was up to him to get over what had spoiled his mood. Digging deep, he leaned close and said, 'I know the circumstances were awful for you, but I'm glad we've caught up again. It's great seeing you and doing things like this.'

'I totally agree. Catching up with you has made me realise how much I've missed the group too.'

Missed the group? Not just him? That put him in his place. He pulled back and sipped his beer, but not before a heady scent of roses teased him. That was something else he didn't recall from the past. He probably wouldn't have noticed Rosie's perfume then, but now he had it wasn't disappearing in a hurry. So he breathed deep and made the most of the lovely scent. A bit like he was doing sharing this evening with Rosie herself. Making the most of everything.

They were soon going to spend a weekend together. As friends, nothing else, he reminded himself for the umpteenth time since first offering to go to the wedding with her. Except Rosie needed him to look keen on her to keep her brother's friend at arm's length. Could prove interesting. On all fronts, not least being close to Rosie without getting too intense. Interesting or difficult? Time would answer that.

'Lucas. You still with me?'

More than you would guess.

'I take it we have to be dressed to the nines for the wedding?'

He might have to go shopping for a suit and shirt. These days, he wasn't into shopping for fancy clothes but this could be fun. He could deck himself out to look good for Rosie. He grinned. That was a first in too long. Dressing up in decent gear used to be enjoyable.

'Yes, we do. Karen's parents have gone all-out to make this a luxury wedding. She's their only child and they want the best for her.'

'Why did your face drop when you said that?' Was Rosie jealous? Of course her parents weren't around to do something like that for her, but still.

'Johnno isn't into stable relationships, and tends to leave too quickly if the smallest thing goes wrong. This is his second marriage. I worry for him and Karen.'

'There's not a lot you can do but be there when he needs someone to talk to. He does talk to you?' She'd said Johnno was always there for her, but that didn't mean it worked in reverse.

'He's learning to. Takes a bit of effort, but I can be a nag when necessary.'

'Thanks for the warning.'

Rosie laughed. 'Count yourself lucky we won't be spending a lot of time together or you might get to see me at my worst.'

Not a lot of time together? Yeah, he got that, but it still grated. He wasn't ready to relinquish this bond they were rapidly forming, but he had to be careful. He might feel sparks around her but he had no idea what Rosie thought of him beyond being his friend. Hell, he didn't really know what he thought except he seemed to be falling off the rails when it came to keeping his heart under lock and key.

'I hear you. As for spending time together at the wedding, let me assure you that I will play my role to the full without overdoing it.'

Again, her face looked as if it was about to crumple, then she rallied. 'I'm not looking for anything more than regaining the camaraderie we once had, Lucas. I don't do long-term relationships either.'

Just like her brother? A leftover from growing up without a mother and their father physically present while absent in the loving parent department? The idea made his heart constrict. Rosie deserved better. So did everyone, but he especially wanted it for Rosie. In the short time since they'd reunited, he'd come to enjoy time spent with her and wanted to know her better, and yes, well, just share things with her.

No, I don't.

Yes, he did. Did this mean he truly was beginning to get over what had happened to May? *Was* the guilt quietening down after all this time? That seemed hard to believe when he still felt it was his fault she'd been so angry that she'd driven too fast that night. Of course she'd owned some of the responsibility for the crash that had taken her life, but if he hadn't stayed late at work then chances were high that she wouldn't have dumped her ultimatum on him in the way she had and then sped through the city.

'I hate to say it, but I don't intend settling down with anyone for a long while, if ever.'

'Then we have nothing to worry about next weekend. We can let our hair down, enjoy ourselves while keeping Johnno off my case.'

Again, Lucas felt his heart constricting, which made no sense at all as they were on the same page about this. 'Is the other guy likely to cause any problems now that you're going with me?'

'I doubt it. More likely he'll ignore me so I can re-alise what I'm missing out on.' Rosie pulled a face. 'That sounded catty, but I told you I don't have pleasant memories of Will.'

The buzzer Rosie had brought back to the table let them know their meals were ready.

'I'll get those.' He needed a break from those beautiful blue eyes that sidetracked his sane and sensible mind whenever they met his.

'I can't believe we live only a few streets apart,' Rosie said as they strolled towards her apartment block.

Was fate playing games with them? Lucas wondered. If so, he didn't mind. 'All I can say is I'm glad it's happened, though again, I would've preferred it to come about some other way.'

'Agreed.'

'Will you go to court to testify if the creep pleads not guilty?'

'Yes, of course. I'll do what it takes to put him behind bars. Megan said they could put up a screen so I don't have to face him, but I said no way. If he goes to trial then I'll stare him down, not let him think he's messed with me so much I can't face him.'

'I'll be there with a noose over my shoulder.' He half meant it.

Rosie laughed at him. 'That doesn't surprise me, but you'd get locked up quicker than him, I reckon.'

'True. Wishful thinking isn't always the brightest.'

She leaned in and rubbed her shoulder against his upper arm. 'Thanks for the offer. I'm not saying it'll be easy, only that I'm determined he's not winning this one.'

Slipping an arm around her waist, he held her lightly. 'Does he still keep you awake at night?'

'Not quite so often now. Where I have more difficulty is busy car parks with cars coming and going. Though not going at the speed he did, they still worry me. I also find myself keeping an eye out for women who leave their handbags or wallets in the grocery trolley while they're putting laden bags into their car. I've stopped and talked to a couple about the risks. They were surprised and then thankful, but whether it'll change anything I have no idea.'

His arm tightened. Rosie was one tough lady, but then he'd said that before.

'There's not a lot else you can do. As long as you're getting the message through to others and helping yourself along the way, then keep doing it.'

Rosie turned and looked at him. 'Thanks for being so

supportive. It means a lot.' Then she leaned in and went to touch his cheek with her warm lips.

He turned slightly at the same moment and his mouth ended up on hers, feeling the softness and warmth exuding from her. 'Rosie?' He jerked his head back. 'Sorry. I didn't mean for that to happen.'

Her eyes widened as she stared at him. The tip of her tongue did a lap of her lips.

He couldn't tell if she was disappointed he'd pulled back or taken aback at his mistake. He didn't know how he felt, except it had been an exquisite moment.

'Rosie?'

She blinked. 'Lucas.' Her hand ran down his arm. 'I'd better go inside. We'll talk during the week about the wedding.'

'Nothing's changed on my end,' he said quietly.

'Good. See you.' She flapped a hand at him before spinning around and striding across the road to the apartment building.

Leaving him with a thudding heart and feeling stupid. He had stuffed up big time. He wasn't in the market for a relationship with anyone. But hell, Rosie was something else.

Rosie closed the door and leaned back against it, arms folded across her chest. 'Wow.' The shortest kiss in history and her legs were wonky and her heart almost bursting. 'What happened there?' One moment she was about to brush a light thank you kiss over Lucas's cheek and the next his mouth was on hers, filling her with wonder.

He'd said nothing had changed. Tell that to someone who wasn't getting in a tizz about the sensations his kiss brought on. It wasn't working for her. If he hadn't pulled away when he had there was no accounting for what she might've done next.

Sliding down the door, she sat with her arms tight around her knees. 'Damn you, Lucas.' They'd been getting along so well, and now this. Except she couldn't blame him entirely. She had enjoyed having his mouth on hers, had wanted to deepen the kiss. Only she didn't usually go around kissing her friends. A bitter laugh erupted across her lips. Face it, she didn't kiss anyone much at all.

There hadn't been a man in her life for ages, and that was how she liked it because then no one got hurt. Especially her. Except she was getting tired of running solo. Friends were all very well but there were aspects of being a couple that were missing in friendships. The day-to-day sharing and caring, for one thing. Knowing she had someone to come home to at the end of a gruelling day another. With Kelly and Simone focused on their other halves these days, she was starting to see that she could end up a lonely old woman if she didn't at least try to let go of the fear she had of falling in love, only to withdraw as the relationship intensified.

But how did she do that? It wasn't as if she could just pretend nothing hurt any more and she was free to get on with falling in love with an amazing man and trusting him not to walk away. Trusting him not to break her heart and leave her to go on loving him for ever with no chance of reuniting. Which was why she'd left Cameron. He'd been getting too close and she'd been afraid of where it was going.

Lucas was in her head right now. He was wonderful. She liked him a lot. Liked? Or loved a little bit? Possibly that, she acknowledged, but friends loved each other in a different way to couples. Didn't they? She didn't know the answer to that, having walked away from every relationship she'd been in without her heart even feeling too dented. But then she was good at dampening down any feelings where her heart was concerned. The one lesson her father had taught her too well.

Her phone buzzed.

'Hey, Johnno, how's things?'

'You know what? Really good. I'm so excited about marrying Karen, Rosie. It feels different this time.'

Am I hearing correctly?

'I hope so. She's special and deserves the best from you.'

'I know. She's going to get it. I'm sick of living with the past riding on my shoulders. It's time to let it all go and forget how Dad messed with us.'

Yeah, right. As easy as that—she didn't think. But at least he was trying. Which was more than she was prepared to do.

'Go you.'

'What about you and this Lucas guy you're bringing to the wedding? How's that working out?'

'Wonderful.' If she could stop thinking how his kiss had her in a pickle, wanting more.

'Glad to hear it. I mean it, Rosie. It's time for both of us to have the lives we've always dreamed about. We can't let our family history wreck our futures.'

Thank goodness she was already sitting on the floor or she'd have crash-landed after hearing that. Never, ever, had Johnno said anything remotely close to that before. Why tonight, when Lucas already had her wondering if she could change? When his short kiss had tipped her thinking out of its usual boundaries.

'Johnno, I don't know what to say, other than it's wonderful you feel this way.'

It boded well for his marriage. As long as he kept on track.

'You can do it, too.'

Could she? She wanted to. She did? Of course she did. She'd spent her life denying how much she longed to feel loved and cared about and had instead invested in denying it was possible, yet now Lucas had started changing that. Throw in her brother's comments and it felt too much all of a sudden. She had no idea how to progress from here. It was easier to carry on as she always had, remaining untouchable.

Except she really didn't want to do that any more.

CHAPTER FIVE

'THAT'S THEM,' LUCAS said to the nurse beside him as he pointed to the moving light in the night sky above the hospital. The rescue chopper was bringing them a woman caught in a major house fire. He had a general surgeon on standby, but chances were that wouldn't be enough if the burns were as serious as indicated by the emergency caller.

Vivienne shivered as the air swirled around them as the chopper approached. 'I can't imagine being caught in a fire.'

'Terrifying, to say the least.'

Was Rosie on board? Like him, she was on nights this week. They'd talked on the phone once since he'd kissed her and she'd sounded fine, as though nothing had changed. Something to be grateful for—if he wasn't thinking he might be missing out on a wonderful opportunity to find happiness again.

Tomorrow they were heading north to the Yarra Valley and *that* shared room. Normally, he'd have said 'bring it on' if he was with a hot lady, and he wanted to now but he was wary of getting lost in all the emotions that Rosie engendered within him. Over the last two weeks she'd got to him in ways he hadn't believed possible, tapping into his guilt, his fears of making a mess of loving someone again. Could it be because he'd known her as a friend and therefore felt comfortable to let his guard down with her?

'Here we go.' Vivienne began moving towards the chopper settling on the rooftop.

The door on the side of the aircraft opened and yes, Rosie appeared, hand on the stretcher, ready to roll her patient out.

His heart running faster than normal, Lucas strode across. 'Hey, Rosie. I hear we've got serious burns. I didn't bring a bed up as I don't think it's wise to move the patient any more than absolutely necessary.'

She stepped closer. The scent of roses filled the air. 'Quite agree. We haven't strapped her to the stretcher for the same reason. She's got third-degree burns to arms, shoulders and back. Lesser degree burns on abdomen and upper legs.'

Lucas winced as he began moving the trolley towards the entry door. He couldn't begin to imagine what the woman had been through, let alone what was to come over the weeks and months ahead. 'Is she conscious?'

'Barely. I've got her on oxycodone along with oxygen as her breathing's erratic. Fortunately, her face has no burns so she can wear a mask. She was asleep when her bed caught fire.' Rosie handed him the notes she'd written up. 'Holly Green, early thirties, according to a neighbour. There are two others being taken to another hospital right now.' She drew in a deep breath, then exhaled. 'It's an absolute nightmare for them.'

Lucas touched her hand lightly. 'It sure is. Let's get Holly to the ED.' Rosie would remain with them until they'd got Holly off the stretcher and onto a bed in the high priority room.

Rosie already had one hand on the stretcher. 'I wonder if she's got burns to her lungs.'

'One of the first things I need to find out.' Breathing would be excruciating if that was the case. He got onto the phone as the lift began heading down. 'Geoff, you definitely need to see this patient.' He filled the surgeon in on Holly's condition. 'We're about to roll into the ED now.'

Rosie and Vivienne pushed the trolley carefully, making sure they didn't jar Holly. As soon as they were by the bed, where other staff waited for their patient, Rosie was preparing the woman to be transferred over. Her phone beeped but she ignored it, holding one corner of the board they were sliding Holly onto before shifting her across.

Once they were done, Rosie pulled the phone from her jacket. 'We're on our way up,' she told presumably the pilot. 'Vivienne, we've got another job. I'll call you later in the morning, Lucas.'

He was concentrating on Holly and only said, 'Do that.' She'd understand what was important here. Though last time he'd thought that, May had lost her temper at him and driven into a wall. A shudder ripped through him. Gritting his teeth, he continued assessing the burns in front of him. Right now, Holly was more important than anything else, including his feelings about one certain lady.

But four hours later, when he crawled into bed after a long shower, everything came tumbling back into his head. It was as if he had no control over what he thought about Rosie. That had been a definite wake-up call when he'd thought about May's reaction to him helping a code one patient rather than going home to celebrate with her. No way could he see Rosie losing her temper about that, because she'd be the first to stop and help someone needing her skills.

There was nothing he could do about the past and plenty to make a happy future if he was just willing to give it a chance. Was he? When he still felt so guilty over that night? Would it ever fully go away or was it something he'd have to swallow and deal with whenever it arose? He wasn't even thinking about where their marriage might've been heading at the time. There were no answers to that, though it was unusual he was even thinking this way when, only a few weeks ago, it wouldn't have occurred to him.

Lucas rolled onto his other side and tugged his pillow tight around his neck, closed his eyes and breathed long and slow, willing sleep to come.

Instead, Rosie came skimming though his mind, putting an end to that idea. Her devastating smile. Those sensuous lips he'd felt under his mouth the other night. Her sensational body that melded into him whenever he'd held her. Her warm laughter, and sudden tears when something got too much for her. Her strength after being assaulted by the drugged-up creep shouldn't have surprised him, but it had. Rosie had got to him in unexpected ways and yet he wasn't too worried. Which was a worry in itself because no, he absolutely shouldn't take a chance on finding love and happiness with her when he could end up hurting them both so badly.

'Go away, Rosie,' he muttered into his pillow. 'I need

to sleep before we hit the road for Yarra Valley. Not to mention a room that we're sharing for two nights at the resort.'

The next thing Lucas was aware of was his phone making a racket beside the bed. He had the ring set on loud because he often slept through it after hectic nights on duty.

'Hello?'

'Did I wake you?' trilled Rosie.

'You've obviously been up for a while.' She sounded chirpy, even a little excited, which was hardly surprising considering she was going to her brother's wedding.

So am I.

Grand. He tossed the cover aside and hauled himself out of bed. 'What's the time?'

Laughter was her answer, followed by, 'Relax. It's barely gone two.'

'Two?' He never slept that late, even after a nightshift. 'What time am I picking you up?' It had taken some persuading for Rosie to accept he was driving She could be stubborn at times.

'We did agree on three, but let's change that to four. I've got a couple of things I need to do first.'

'Like give me time to have a strong coffee and a hot shower, by any chance?'

More laughter. 'You're onto it. Seriously, are you okay with four or thereabouts?'

'It works for me.'

He hadn't got around to packing what little he was taking yet, but the new suit and shirt were hanging on the back of his bedroom door, and the shoes he'd bought to go with the suit were on the floor beneath, shining so much everyone would notice them. Might have to scuff them with just a little dirt... He grinned, suddenly feeling more relaxed about going away with Rosie. It had been easy to offer to be her date, but doubts had begun creeping in lately over whether he was doing the right thing for either of them. It could stretch their relationship beyond being friends, or it could kill it off totally if something went wrong.

Smile, man.

He was going away for the weekend and, while the circumstances were different, he *was* looking forward to time with Rosie. Even when she did screw with his head too much. Bring it on.

'Feel like stopping for a drink before we get to the resort?' Rosie looked at Lucas as they neared the valley. He looked good enough to enjoy in ways she hadn't done with any man for a while. 'I could do with some nibbles as I didn't have a lot for lunch.' Getting to know Lucas between the sheets would be even better.

Her face heated. Damn it. She was letting her guard down too far. It wasn't difficult around Lucas, but she had to stop. She couldn't afford to get intimate with him and then think they could carry on like they had for the last couple of weeks when they returned to the city. And that would be imperative. He wasn't stealing her heart, only for it to be broken later on when she withdrew.

'Sure thing. Do you know of somewhere to go?'

'No, but I'll have a look on my phone.' She hadn't been up this way in years. 'There are a few to choose from. Shall I keep it simple or do you want something fancy?'

'Leave fancy till tomorrow and the wedding.'

'Right. How about this one? It's a bar with outdoor dining and a view of the hills. The menu seems reasonable.'

Lucas flicked her a grin. 'Tell me where to go.'

That grin set off warning bells, reminding her she shouldn't be thinking about sex with Lucas, even when he grinned like that. It made him hot beyond description. This was not how the weekend was meant to play out and it was going to be hard sharing a room, and no doubt a bed, with him without stepping across the line from friends to something deeper. Not something more meaningful. She wasn't ready for that, and from what she'd seen, nor was Lucas. He didn't seem to have got over losing May yet.

'Take the next right.'

She was going to enjoy the stop, and then spending the evening with everyone before tomorrow's wedding. Was she going to enjoy spending time with Lucas? Absolutely. She was also going to be careful.

The bar wasn't too busy when they strolled in so they wouldn't be kept waiting for long, and for that her stomach was grateful.

'Can we sit outside?' she asked the young man behind the counter.

'Go for it. I'll bring menus out shortly. Would you like something to drink first?'

'Wine for me. One of the local Chardonnays, please. Lucas?'

'Make mine a beer, thanks, mate.'

Out under the canopy of trees, Lucas chose a table and held out a chair for her. 'Good choice.'

'Good advertising, more like it.' He was right though. The atmosphere was warm and friendly without being over the top, and the view was lovely. 'I feel like the weekend's started already.'

'It has. We don't have to be with everyone else for that to happen.' He sat opposite her and gazed around. 'I accept the circumstances are a little unconventional, but I'm looking forward to this, even though I don't know anyone else coming, and definitely not the bride and groom.'

Was he saying he wanted to spend more time with her? Well, despite that kiss and the thoughts it had raised, and the warnings going off in her head, so did she.

'Don't worry about not knowing anyone, because I don't know many of the people coming either. We'll stick together.'

'That'll fit in with the concept that we're a couple.'

The young man from the counter appeared with their drinks and menus. 'I'll give you a moment to decide what you'd like.'

'Don't rush,' Lucas told him, then lifted his glass and held it out to tap hers. 'Here's to a great weekend.'

It was as if he was being romantic. If she hadn't known why he was here in the first place she might've been hard pressed not to believe that.

'You surprised me when you offered to come, but I'm really grateful you did, and not just to shut my brother up. We get on well, and I'm glad we've reconnected. Let's make sure we don't lose touch again.'

'You're on. Now, tell me some things about Johnno so I don't make a complete fool of myself.'

'I'm going to let you suss him out for yourself.' Could be interesting to learn what Lucas thought about her brother by the end of the weekend. Johnno got very protective of her sometimes and could cross the line by being outspoken when it came to a man at her side. Which was why she struggled to understand why he'd been so persistent she hook up with Will.

Lucas shrugged. 'Fine. Why was he so intent on you being with his mate?'

'He wants me settled and happy. What he doesn't get is that I don't need him trying to set me up with his friends.'

'Especially Will.'

She nodded. 'Especially Will. I'm not incapable of meeting men and dating them as I see fit.' It sounded like Johnno thought she was hopeless, and she was far from it. She might have faults when it came to committing to a relationship but none when it came to finding great guys.

A glance at the one opposite made her draw a breath. She hadn't *found* Lucas, and he wasn't about to become her for ever partner, no matter how well they got on. It was a lot safer that way.

Lucas stared around the room Rosie had booked at the resort and pretended nothing was out of kilter. Hard to do with that huge, cosy bed taking up so much space. 'Tempting' was another word for it. How the hell was he going to stay on his side all night with Rosie lying so close he'd feel the heat coming off her? He wouldn't be able to sleep he'd be so rigid with keeping his hands to himself.

Not once when he'd offered to come along to save her from having to deal with Will had he thought sharing a bed would be so difficult. He wasn't meant to be thinking about her in any way other than someone he'd known years back and liked a lot. Certainly not as a woman who heated his blood and made his head spin with just a look. The woman who stirred him up fast. Since the night she'd been brought into the ED he'd been thrilled to see her and happy to go along with whatever either of them suggested doing outside of work but, so far, he had not wanted to bed her, to hold that sensational body in his arms and make love to her. Okay, that wasn't completely true because, more and more often, he'd been thinking about her in just that way, but nothing quite like the sensations gripping him now as he looked anywhere but at the beckoning bed.

'Not bad,' Rosie said as she hung her dress in the wardrobe. 'Give me your suit and I'll put it in here too.'

After handing his clothes to her, he stepped out onto the narrow balcony and leaned against the railing while he got his breathing under control. What the heck was going on? No way would he and Rosie have sex. They couldn't.

'Beautiful, isn't it?' Rosie stood beside him. 'So quiet too. The perfect place for a wedding.'

How had he missed her approaching? 'Shall we go down and catch up with everyone?' He needed to be busy, not standing around thinking about beds and sex.

'I guess we'd better or Johnno will be banging on the door demanding we join him.'

'Would he do that when he thinks we're a couple, staying in a romantic spot for the weekend?' Lucas closed his eyes for a moment. See what happened when he didn't think before he spoke? He'd just gone and put out there in a roundabout way what was going on in his head.

Rosie stared at him, surprise in her eyes. Then she nodded. 'You're right. He wouldn't. But still, let's go down and do the introductions.'

104 WEDDING DATE WITH THE ER DOCTOR

'Good idea.' He'd find a moment to talk to the concierge too. He'd come up with a way to put space between him and Rosie overnight.

'Hey, Rosie, there you are.' Downstairs, a tall, well-built guy wrapped his arms around her. 'Glad you made it.'

'As if I wouldn't.' She grinned. 'Johnno, this is Lucas Tanner.'

'Hey, Lucas, good to meet you.' The guy's handshake was firm, but the look he gave Lucas suggested he was going to make sure Lucas did right by his sister.

Locking his eyes on the man, Lucas returned the handshake just as firmly. 'Likewise, Johnno, and thanks for letting me accompany your sister to your wedding.'

'You're welcome. Not that I had a lot of choice who she brought.' His smile was cheeky, not annoyed, which made Lucas relax somewhat.

Lucas nodded. 'She knows her own mind, for sure.' She'd known exactly who she did not want to be partnered with for the weekend.

'How are the knocks and bruises?' Johnno asked Rosie.

'All but gone,' she replied.

Lucas studied her face and realised there wasn't any sign of the bruising that had coloured her chin and forehead after the assault. 'You're definitely looking a hundred percent back to normal.' Guess he hadn't taken a lot of notice because he'd been looking at the woman behind the smiles and tears and chatter. 'What can I get you to drink?' he asked her.

'Another wine would be lovely. Pinot Noir this time, if they have it.'

'You're in the Yarra Valley. Of course they have Pinot Noir,' Johnno cut in. 'This is red wine heaven.'

'I might try some too,' Lucas said. Not a huge wine drinker, he did enjoy most red varietals and if there was ever a time and place to indulge this was it.

'Johnno? Want one?'

'I'm good, thanks.' When Johnno followed him to the bar, he knew he was in for some questions. He just didn't know what about.

'I'm glad you were there for Rosie,' was the first thing Johnno said. 'She didn't say a lot about what happened when she was assaulted but I know she was freaking out that first day.'

'Agreed. She was, but she hid it well.'

'Give me time alone with the bastard who did that to her and he won't know what hit him.'

'You'll have to queue up behind me,' Lucas said firmly.

Johnno nodded. 'Thought I might have to.' He turned to the barman. 'Put this man's drinks on the tab, Harry. That goes for all night, along with my sister's.'

So he'd passed a test. There hadn't been any questions, but Johnno had been sussing him out in his own way.

'Thanks, Johnno. You didn't have to do that.'

'My night, my shout. Enjoy yourself.'

When Lucas returned to Rosie after a quick talk to the concierge with two glasses in hand, she took hers and nudged him lightly. 'I'll introduce you to everyone.'

There weren't many people here and they were all Johnno's friends.

'Karen's taken her lot to another restaurant for the evening. Some of the girls have been at the beauty spa this afternoon too,' Johnno told them.

Judging by her perfect pink nails, Rosie had done that back in the city at some point over the last couple of days. Lucas studied her face. 'You must be pleased with the way the bruising on your face has all but disappeared too.'

'Very pleased. I wasn't looking forward to being in the wedding photos looking like I'd been in a fight with a boxer and lost.'

'You never looked that bad,' he told her. Even when the puffy skin above her eye and on her chin was yellow, he'd thought she looked lovely. But then it seemed he was a bit off-centre when it came to Rosie these days.

'You're not good at telling porkies!' She laughed. 'But I'll take the compliment anyway. Can never get enough of them.'

There were plenty more where that one came from, but finally he'd got a grip on his mouth and was keeping it shut, except for enjoying the wine and looking around at the other guests grouped around a table at the far side of the room.

'Seems like there's a bit of a wine-tasting going on.'

Rosie looked in the same direction. 'It makes sense considering we're at a vineyard, but it wasn't mentioned in the invitation.'

'They're probably making the most of having people here. Good way to sell cases of their product. Want to try some?'

'Not at the moment. I'm enjoying this Pinot Noir and don't really want to have another flavour mixing with it. Besides, I'm tired and want to be up to speed for tomorrow. Sorry if I'm being a wet blanket.'

He was quite relieved she wasn't interested because then he'd have had to join her and right now, he was more than comfortable with what was before him. The wine, that was.

'I'm happy sitting here taking my time with this glass.'

'We do think alike about some things, don't we?' Her smile was gentle and filled with happiness.

Because they got along so well? He hoped so.

'So last night's shift wore you out too? I admit working on Holly was draining. We were with her for what seemed like hours yet wasn't. Those burns were horrendous.' Some of the worst he'd ever seen. 'She was scheduled for plastic surgery this morning. Though only to deal with the worst sites. The plastic surgeon says she'll wait a few days before doing more work on the burns.'

Rosie shivered. 'Let's not go there tonight.'

'Fair enough.' Rosie was right to suggest he drop it. They were here for a wedding and to have some positive fun time, not focus on doom and gloom. 'What time did you knock off this morning?'

'Around seven. That call we got at the ED was for an elderly gentleman who'd had a stroke. I'm not sure why we were called and not the ambulance, but that's the way it goes sometimes.'

'Not your place to ask?'

'Not really, and anyway I'd rather be busy after the previous callout than sitting in the tearoom going over it all again and again.'

'Know what you mean.' So much for not talking about it. But he understood how sometimes it was nigh on impossible to let go the details of a case. 'I see they do a platter of breads and local cheeses here. Would you like one? I know we had a meal earlier but I wouldn't mind soaking up the wine with something light.'

That gentle smile returned. 'Like I said, we do think alike.'

It would be so easy to lean in and kiss her. Too easy. How would she react? Push him away or kiss him back? If she did, would the kiss be genuine or part of the ruse to keep Johnno off her back?

Lucas stood up and headed across to the guy behind the bar. 'Is it too late to order the cheese platter?' He had to ask, though he doubted it would be.

'Not at all. For two?'

'Please.'

Turning back to Rosie, he paused and drank in the sight of her. Even tired, she looked beautiful. His kiss would've been genuine. Right now, all he wanted to do was take her in his arms and hold her close, to savour her warm and caring nature, to take away the tension that had crept into her when talking about last night's patient. And kiss her. Again, he wondered if she'd appreciate it if he did. They were doing more than acting a role here this weekend, but the thing was, he'd discovered he wasn't really acting in any way. He was happy here with Rosie, and ready to go with the flow, wherever that led.

She turned and her eyes widened when she saw him watching her. 'Lucas?'

He joined her. 'It's all right. You haven't got a mess on your chin. I was thinking you look lovely in your pink blouse and cream trousers.' There, he could put it out there and not feel he'd made a mistake.

Her head tipped to the right and her smile widened. 'Thank you.' She blinked. 'I don't know what else to say.'

He laughed. So he wasn't in trouble. Not the get-out-of-my-face kind anyway. He might be thinking she was more than a friend, but he'd keep that to himself. He picked up his glass and took a long sip. It was a damned good Pinot Noir. 'I'm going to try some of the other reds while we're here. Might even buy a case or two to take back with us.' Us? 'We can enjoy them whenever we catch up.'

Rosie's laughter filled the air between them. 'I like that idea.' Then she leaned in and kissed his cheek, much like she'd been intending to that other time. Except tonight there were plenty of people around and he wasn't going to get too hot about wanting more, or show it anyway. Thank goodness he'd ordered a rollaway bed from the concierge or who knew how he'd have controlled himself sharing that super king size bed in their room. Offering to stand in as her partner for this wedding was turning out to be the craziest thing he'd done in a long time, yet he couldn't help loving every moment.

The platter appeared between them and the barman said, 'Here you go, folks. Enjoy.'

'Oh, we will,' Rosie told him, while still looking at Lucas.

Was she flirting with him? Lucas wondered. Surely not. But she had just kissed his cheek. Could he get that rollaway removed before she saw it? No, best not. He was getting ahead of himself. He did like Rosie a lot, even felt on the precipice of something more than just friendship, but he was rushing things. For himself and Rosie. They both needed to be careful going forward so neither would get hurt.

'Here, try this blue vein cheese.' She offered him a piece of bread with a wedge of the cheese on top.

He shook his head. 'No blue vein for me.' He picked up a knife and cut into the goat's cheese to spread on the softest bread he'd seen in a long while. 'This is more to my taste.'

'You don't know what you're missing out on,' Rosie said as she munched away.

As far as cheeses went, he certainly did. It was different when it came to Rosie, and tonight he was not going to find out. Tonight was all about playing safe. That decision was made, even if he came to regret it. They had a whole weekend to get through presenting as a happy couple to everyone, especially Johnno.

A big yawn rolled through Rosie like a tidal wave. Everything was catching up with her. Arduous night shifts, sleepless days due to reruns of being attacked beside her car, and trying to get past that kiss she and Lucas had shared last week. 'I think I'd better head to bed. I need to be in good form tomorrow.'

Lucas stared at his empty glass. 'I guess you do.'

Had mentioning the bed rocked him? It wasn't going to be easy sharing one. She was so aware of him in ways she shouldn't be that if he made a move on her, she knew she'd fall into his arms in a blink. She probably wouldn't even take that long.

'Would you like another wine?' She was done but she'd stay with him if he did. After all, he'd come here to make things easier for her.

He shook his head. 'No, I'm finished for the night as well.' He stood up and held his hand out to her. 'Come on. Let's go.'

Taking his hand, she stood up and looked around for Johnno. She found him watching them and tightened her grip on Lucas. They were meant to be a couple. A good excuse not to let Lucas go if ever there was one. His hand was firm around hers. Nice. More than nice. Hot, and filling her with a desperate longing she hadn't known in a long time, if ever. She should let go, but some things were impossible.

'Goodnight, Johnno. See you tomorrow.'

''Night, both of you.'

'Don't stay up all night,' she warned. 'You've got a big day ahead.'

'You're sounding like a mother, not sister.' Lucas grinned as he led her out of the room.

'Someone has to pretend to be keeping an eye on him.'

'He's being sensible. I haven't seen him drinking anything but water for the past hour or more.'

'That's my brother. And you're the one watching him, not me.' Laughter bubbled out of her. Lucas had just made her realise how seriously he was taking this weekend and being there for her. Not that she hadn't expected him to be totally involved but not to the point of watching out for Johnno, too.

He looked embarrassed. 'Sorry, that didn't come out how I meant it to. If Johnno's anything like I was the night before I got married, he'll be excited and nervous all in one and it's easy to get distracted by what everyone else is up to. Though, to be fair, everyone's been taking it easy with the wine.'

She nudged him. 'Including us.' She was trying to take in the fact he'd mentioned his wedding. That undercut her feelings of a moment ago and put her in her place.

'Rosie—' he turned to face her, an apologetic expression coming her way '—I shouldn't have mentioned my wedding. It's history and, despite what I told you, I have moved on enough to know I don't want it coming between us.'

'How can it? We're not a couple.'

His hand tightened around hers. 'Who knows what lies ahead?'

Pardon? She hadn't seen that coming. 'Not me, for certain.'

Her mind was a shambles when it came to what she really felt about Lucas. It was definitely more than friendship. Her reaction to him mentioning his wedding proved that. So did the happiness she'd known from the moment she'd got into his car to come up here. Lucas made her feel special, which gave her hope for the future. It was obvious in the way she reacted whenever she was close to him—like right now. Sparks flew whenever they touched. As for his kiss, it mightn't have got far but it had been sensational. Like a promise of more to come—a *good* more to come.

Being together seemed so right. It was an amazing feeling. A new feeling. Had she been wrong to accept his offer to come here? With these emerging feelings, it might be too easy to be swept away on a wave of passion and wake up to cold reality afterwards. Lucas hadn't got over losing May, something Rosie understood she couldn't compete with.

Lucas opened the door to their room and hesitated. 'Rosie, I asked for a rollaway bed to be brought to our room. I don't feel comfortable about sharing a bed with you, given we're only pretending to be a couple.'

Her heart sank at that reminder, but she conceded he was being sensible. Stepping past him, she swallowed at the sight of the made-up bed pushed against the far wall. Looking over her shoulder at him, she pulled on her big girl's pants. 'It's okay. I understand.'

I also feel unwanted.

Which she knew was totally unfair. She'd been hankering for some diversion with him, and had clearly deliberately misinterpreted things he'd said or done.

'I'm being a gentleman here.' His smile was tight.

She tried to be cheerful—hard to do when her heart was heavy. 'I'm not used to that.' Then she sighed. 'Come on. Let's move on. I am so glad to have you here with me that you don't need to keep apologising for everything you do.'

If only he wasn't being cautious about their original agreement. But then if he wasn't she'd probably find fault with that too. She wasn't easy to please. Yet she felt so different about Lucas, so relaxed whenever she was with him. Was this because she'd already known him as a friend? Knew that when he'd given his heart to May it was for ever? Did that make it easier to give in to the other emotions swamping her when she was with him, unlike other men she'd spent time with? Because she felt safe to do so as he didn't return her feelings?

Right now, she had no answers. Instead of overthinking it she was going to bed. Tomorrow would be a big day. Her brother had found the love of his life, which suggested it might be possible for her too. If so, bring it on.

Sliding under the bedcover, she admitted she might be getting nearer to opening up to love. This new sense of wanting to let go and give love a chance was scary—and exciting. Because of Lucas? Was he the cause? Was it him she was willing to share her heart with? No definite answer came, instead more of a softening in her chest and a warmth settling over her. Lucas was special, either way.

CHAPTER SIX

'HERE, USE THIS.' Lucas handed Rosie a perfectly folded handkerchief from his jacket pocket.

This man was perfect. Who had handkerchiefs these days? Rosie sniffed and wiped her cheeks, where tears were slowly tracking through her make-up. Leaning close to Lucas, she said quietly as she watched Johnno walk down the aisle with a beaming Karen on his arm, 'I am so happy for him. He deserves this day.' They were sitting with all the guests in the beautifully appointed room with a glass wall overlooking the vineyards where the marriage celebrant had just pronounced Johnno and Karen married.

Lucas took her free hand and held it lightly on his thigh. 'Everyone does.'

Except the creep who'd assaulted her. She blinked. Where had that come from when she was full of such happy emotions? Could be that emotion was getting to her in more ways than she needed.

'You're right. They do.' Lucas did. She did. She'd go for that and forget the one who didn't. He didn't belong here—not today or any other day.

As everyone stood up to follow the bride and groom through to the massive outside deck, Lucas wound an arm around Rosie's waist and tucked her in against his side. 'Come on. Let's celebrate this special occasion.'

'You say that when you barely know the bride and groom.'

'I know, but there's something wonderful about a truly happy wedding—and, before you say it, there are some that are nowhere close to happy. Believe me, I went to one once and wanted to shout at the couple to see sense and go their separate ways. The angst was coming off them in waves. Turned out they were marrying because she was pregnant and he refused to let her have the baby unwed. Some history there that I knew nothing about, and still don't.'

'Where did you fit into the picture?'

'He worked at the same hospital as me in San Fran and I don't think he had a lot of friends. Most of the guests on his side were from the hospital and didn't know him well.'

'I'd rather get married with no one there to celebrate if that was the case.'

'I'll come.'

'Got to find a man to marry, yet.' Did Lucas have an answer for that? Judging by the silence that followed, he didn't. 'Actually, I haven't been looking.'

They'd reached the garden setting, where waiters were handing around glasses of champagne. Lucas took two and passed her one. 'Why not?'

'Think I've already said I struggle with risking my heart.'

'You did mention that but, to my way of thinking, if you don't give it a go, you'll never know if you can move past your fears.'

Her eyebrows rose as she stared at him. 'Really?'

'Yes, okay, I should know better than to put myself on the mat like that. But seriously, Rosie, do you truly want to remain single and miss out on what you could have for the rest of your life?'

'No, I don't.'

'I rest my case.' He gave her a gentle, almost loving, smile.

'Do you?'

His smile disappeared. 'Not really. But I have some things to get over first.'

She winced. She'd known that. 'Sorry, I should've kept quiet.'

His smile returned slowly, and it was genuine. 'It's fine.' He sipped his champagne. 'Let's drop serious and go with fun. Enjoy the moments.'

Lucas made everything seem so plausible, and so easy to do. She'd give it a crack and see how the day unfolded, because she couldn't think of anyone else she'd rather be here celebrating her brother's day with than Lucas.

'Hello, Rosie.' Will appeared in front of them.

She straightened a little more, and smiled when Lucas drew her closer. 'Hello, Will. How are you?'

'Fine, thank you.'

'Will, this is Lucas Tanner, my partner.' Weren't her pants supposed to catch fire when she lied? But it wasn't a lie, she reminded herself. Lucas was partnering her for the weekend. How Will interpreted 'partner' was his to decide.

'Hello, Will.' Lucas held his hand out to the guy.

Will ignored him. 'It's good to see you, Rosie. I'll talk to you later.' With that, he turned and strode away.

'Plonker,' she muttered.

'So that's the wonderful Will.' Lucas looked to her. 'Even if I say so, you can do much better than that, Rosie.'

She laughed. 'I already am.' Then she shivered. 'He really has an ego that needs trimming down to size.' Why Johnno thought she'd fall for Will she couldn't imagine.

She thought that again when she went to chat with Karen's mother. Will was standing to the side, watching her as though he owned her. *Creepy* came to mind. But was she being too harsh? He might have trust issues too. Still, not her problem when he'd been so rude to her the one time they had dated.

'Rosie, got a minute?' Will asked when she left Karen's mother to go back to Lucas, who seemed happy chatting with some of Johnno's mates.

Not really, but she didn't want to cause a scene or be rude. 'Sure.'

'Are you serious about that guy you came with? He's not worthy of you.'

'Will, you don't even know Lucas.' Her blood began to simmer. 'He's very much an honourable man, more than worthy of me.'

'Aww, come on. You'd be way better off with me.'

'Which bit of "I am not interested" don't you get, Will?'

'Open your eyes, Rosie. You have no idea what you're turning down. I can give you everything you want and more. I'm wealthy and an outstanding lawyer to boot.'

'You're an idiot, is what you are,' Lucas said from beside Rosie.

Thank you, Lucas.

She turned away from the arrogant man trying to loom over her and took Lucas's hand to pull him away. She didn't look back, instead moved closer to her saviour. 'Let's find somewhere more conducive to a great time.'

'How about a walk in the vineyard?'

The sun was low in the sky and the temperature balmy. Other people were already making the most of the open space and waiters were out there, refilling glasses as they wandered around.

'Let's.'

'I can't believe that man,' Lucas ground out. 'Who does he think he is?'

'William John Clark the first.' She giggled, back to happy mode. It took no time at all with Lucas at her side.

'The first? I feel for the poor little blighter that follows in the family line.' Lucas was grinning too.

'We're here to enjoy the night.'

Lucas leaned closer. 'The night is but barely started.'

Rosie sighed. He was quite something. Special didn't begin to describe him. How had she not noticed this when she'd known him before? More than likely because she'd been with Cameron and relatively happy. Just nothing like this. Anyway, Lucas had been married to May then. She didn't check out married men. Now it was obvious how considerate and kind and loving Lucas was. Loving as in being there for others, not so much as in handing her his heart on a plate. He and May had seemed the perfect couple after all, and she doubted she'd ever come up to May's standard. From the little he'd said about May and what had happened, she doubted he'd be ready for a deep and meaningful relationship for a while to come. But there also seemed to be more to his story than he was prepared to share and until he did she couldn't fully trust him. But he could be up for something hot and sexy. Like she suddenly was.

Drawing a deep breath, she went for caution. She didn't want to scare him off. As he'd said, the night was young. 'Where's a wine waiter when I need one?' When had she finished her champagne? Might be wise to slow down. But then, wise could be overdone at times and tonight was special because it was about her family. A very small family, but it had just grown with Karen and her lot becoming part of Johnno's life and therefore, in a small way, hers too.

Lucas looked around. 'Over there.' He took her hand and led her across to the young woman standing with a laden tray in hand.

They wandered along the rows of vines, still holding hands and saying little. It was a companionable silence, something Rosie wasn't used to. She felt as though this was another step in getting to know each other better. They didn't have to fill in the silence with idle chitchat all the time, and could be themselves without worrying what the other was thinking. Yes, she was usually like that with the men she'd dated, always wondering what was coming next, and if she wanted to continue being with them. If they liked her enough to stay with her and not walk out of her life just when she'd become vulnerable to them. She didn't think that with Lucas—but then they weren't in a relationship, she reminded herself.

'Excuse me, but everyone is requested to make their way to the dining room now.' A waitress had appeared in front of them. 'The celebrations are about to begin.'

'We're on our way.' Lucas grinned as they headed for the building. 'There's something special about seeing a couple sharing their most important moments, even when I don't know them.' He flicked her a brief glance, looked away again.

Her breath stopped in the middle of her chest. Wow. She squeezed his hand. 'I know what you mean.' She really did, though until now she'd never believed she might one day have those special moments herself. Since meeting up with Lucas again, all sorts of notions regarding love and permanency were taking over her mind and making her consider the possibility of letting herself be vulnerable. But then she'd immediately return to why she held herself back and bury the hope that had flared.

'Would you like a nightcap?' Lucas asked Rosie as they walked through their room to the small deck overlooking the winery. 'There's wine in the fridge or we can order something else if you'd prefer.'

'Wine's fine. A small one. I've already had more than I usually do.'

What the heck? She was having a good time with Lucas, the most wonderful man she'd known. He'd been there for her all day, had shared the fun and laughter with a complete group of strangers. And he was so handsome her mouth watered looking at him.

'You're doing fine.' His smile touched her deeply. 'How does it feel to see your brother so happy?'

'I'm thrilled. He already seems so much happier than last time. I think Karen's more his type and will be there for ever. Fingers crossed,' she added quietly.

'I'll drink to that.'

Out on the deck, Lucas leaned against the railing. Rosie joined him, letting her shoulder touch his lightly, hoping he wouldn't move away. He didn't, instead leaned in closer, his shoulder pressing against hers, his hip touching her side. Did he want more too?

Rosie took a big gulp and turned to put her glass down on the tiny table. To hell with this. Sometimes a person had to take risks, chance their feelings. It felt as if this was her moment.

Turning back to Lucas, she leaned in to kiss him, as in slide her tongue into his mouth and press her lips firmly against his like she had no intention of backing off any time soon. Her hands slid around his waist and tugged him against her love-starved body, which tightened in an instant. Still holding his wine, he hauled her in against him even more closely.

It was so good. Better than good. Amazing to feel him up against her. He was returning her feverish kiss, touch for touch, taste for taste. Then he was kneading her bottom and she was beyond thinking.

Except for, 'Bed?' Then she continued kissing him.

He must've put his glass down at some point because when he laid her on the bed both his arms were holding her firmly against that wide, deliciously muscular chest of his. She didn't let him go as she sprawled over the bed, instead held him tightly so he had to follow her. As if he wouldn't. They'd started something they couldn't stop. Winding her legs around him, she trailed kisses over his chin, neck, down to his chest, tasting him, feeling his hard length pressing into her.

A fierce need filled Lucas. Rosie was above him, unbuttoning his shirt as she kissed his chest, then his nipples, sending desire sparking throughout his hungry body.

He reached for her dress, tried to lift it over her head.

She stopped kissing his overheated skin long enough to wriggle her way out of the figure-hugging dress and reveal a low-cut lacy bra and minimal matching lace panties that accentuated her stunning body. Then she went back to running those hot lips all over his body. Chest, stomach and lower, even lower, till he had to stop her or this would be over before they'd really got started.

Wrapping his arms around her, he reversed their positions, flipping Rosie beneath him. Holding her hands above her head, he began to return the favour—kissing first one beautiful full breast then the other until she shivered and cried out. He worked his way down to her navel and beyond, feeling her body getting tighter all the way.

'Lucas,' she groaned as her hips bucked up against him. 'Lucas, stop. I can't take any more.'

Oh, yes, you can, and you will.

The words never left his mouth. He was too busy showing her.

Then her body tensed, and jerked upward. 'Lucas, join me. Now.'

'One moment.' Grabbing his trousers, he found the condom he'd placed there earlier just in case. All right, he finally admitted he'd been hoping they'd get together in bed. His need had been growing ever since they'd arrived at the resort.

'Lucas…' Those luscious lips encased his nipple, sent fire through his veins.

Then he was sliding inside her, feeling her heat engulf him, and he was lost in sensation.

Coming to some time later, he wrapped Rosie in his arms and rolled onto his back, keeping her close. A smile spread across his face. Rosie could lose control after all, and he'd seen it up close. What a different woman she was when she did. He'd like to see a lot more of that in all aspects of her life.

As she sprawled across him, she hauled her eyes open and grinned at him. 'Wow. I am so glad you came with me.'

He chuckled. 'That could be taken two ways.'

'Both ways count.' Her breath was hot on his skin.

He held her tighter. No way was he letting her go any time soon. Never had he been with a woman and felt so relaxed and yet wired all at once. This was something else. He'd offered to accompany her to this wedding as she'd needed a date and here they were, recovering from the most intense sexual encounter he'd experienced in years. Another step forward. More like a leap. Whichever, he felt good and so at ease it was incredible.

He whispered, 'Thank you, Rosie.'

Lifting her head, she kissed him lightly. 'Back at you.' Then she curled up beside him and wound an arm around his waist and closed her eyes.

Lucas continued holding her warm body against his as she slipped into sleep. Through the wide glass doors, he watched the stars twinkling above the vineyard. A perfect ending to a wonderful day. He couldn't wish for anything more.

But when Rosie woke an hour later and turned to touch him, he knew he was beyond ready for more. Far more. The scary thing being he didn't want it to ever end.

Rosie woke slowly, snuggled in against Lucas with his arm over her waist.

Wow. What a night. She couldn't remember ever feeling quite so relaxed and happy after an intimate night as she did now. There was something so easy about being with Lucas that had her feeling comfortable and not looking for trouble. He was trustworthy, which meant a lot, but she still wasn't looking for anything long-term with him. They remained friends, which was more important as there was less chance of that going wrong. Yet, after the night she'd just experienced, she had to admit to wanting to open up and let him in a little more than usual. Apart from her dad when she was very young, there hadn't been another man she'd ever felt so trusting with. Yeah, and look how her father had let her down. If he couldn't love her, then who could she trust to do so?

'Morning, sunshine. You look rather troubled.' Lucas was watching her carefully.

To get serious or relax and have some more fun? The answer was simple.

'Hello, you. I was worrying you wouldn't wake up early enough to make love again before we get ready to go to the family breakfast.' The two families were getting together this morning for a meal before the newlyweds headed to the airport to fly out to Hobart for their honeymoon.

'All you had to do was kiss me and I'd have woken instantly.' Lucas grinned and reached for her, tugging her over him, already erect.

She could get used to this, she thought as she slid down and covered him. Very much so.

They were late to breakfast but no one seemed to care. Everyone was in a cheerful mood and there was lots of laughter going around the table as Lucas held out a chair for Rosie.

'You two look happy,' Johnno called from the other end with a cheeky big brother glint in his eyes.

'Thanks for sharing that,' Rosie muttered under her breath. She might have opened up to Lucas but she wasn't into sharing her hot night with others, especially people she didn't know well. 'I think you and Karen take the award for that.' She could give as good as she got. To be fair, Johnno looked the happiest she could ever recall.

'Would you like a glass of bubbles?' Karen's father, Bill, asked her. 'We're making the most of breakfast before everyone heads off to their normal lives, except for these two, of course.' He nodded at his daughter and Johnno.

'I'd love one,' Rosie said before downing a glass of water.

'Lucas?' Bill waved the bottle at him.

'Why not?' Lucas held out a glass, then tapped it against hers. 'Cheers.'

'Cheers.' She took a small sip before picking up the menu. 'I'm starving.' Laughter broke out around the table and she could feel her cheeks heating. 'What?'

'You're not the first to say that this morning,' someone called out.

Glancing at her brother and his wife, Rosie immediately knew who he was referring to. This was getting a bit much. She hadn't been on her wedding night. It had been a wonderful experience but she and Lucas weren't exactly tying the knot any time soon. Turning to Lucas, she gulped. He looked as if he was about to burst into laughter and probably say something to make her even more embarrassed.

'What are you having for breakfast?' she asked in a hurry.

He leaned close and said quietly, 'I've had my first course.'

The heat in her face deepened and she looked away. This was getting awkward.

'Have you all put your orders in?' she finally managed.

'We were waiting for you,' Bill told her. 'Want some coffee while you make up your mind?' He looked sympathetic in an amused kind of way. 'Lucas?'

'Definitely.' Totally at ease, Lucas handed over their cups to the waiter. Obviously, none of this was getting to him. 'Thanks, mate.'

'If I ever get married, I am not having the morning-after breakfast,' Rosie decided. There again, if she ever did take the chance and tied the knot, why not have everyone there to share her happiness with? Taking a big gulp of coffee, she studied the menu, more for a distraction than to decide what to eat because she always had Eggs Benedict when out for breakfast.

'Eggs Benedict for me,' Lucas told her.

She grinned. 'Once more, we're on the same page.'

Even after an eventful night, he still looked marvellous. Knowing that sexy body better made it harder to hold onto her caution. Funny how they'd started out as friends and were now lovers. A boundary had definitely been crossed but for some reason she wasn't worried about it. Not a lot, anyway. Where they went from here was anyone's guess. Right now, she'd make the most of having Lucas with her. Sliding her hand under the table, she squeezed his thigh lightly. Touching him felt good, brought up thoughts of everything that had happened last night.

Lucas covered her hand with his and squeezed back. 'Happy?' he asked quietly.

'Absolutely.' She really was. 'You?'

'What do you think?' He grinned.

She laughed. 'Same page?'

He nodded. 'This is getting to be quite a story, isn't it?'

'I think so.'

Were they rushing things? She hoped not. Last night had been the perfect ending to a wonderful day. Lucas coming to the wedding with her had been a natural offer on his behalf. That they'd picked up their friendship when they'd caught up again had been a no-brainer. No rushing was going on. It was all a natural progression. Towards what? The answer would surely come later. Right now, she wasn't getting tied up in second-guessing herself. She was going to keep making the most of what she had.

When breakfast was over and everyone was leaving the table, Johnno came over and pulled her into a big hug. 'I like Lucas,' he told her quietly. 'You're different with him in a good way.'

'He's special, no doubt about it.' She could admit that to her brother because he'd keep it to himself. She wouldn't point out it was him who'd been insisting she hook up with his mate. 'Have a great time in Hobart.'

Johnno pulled back. 'We will, I promise.' He stepped across to Lucas and shook his hand. 'I'm glad you came with Rosie to our wedding.'

Lucas's eyes widened a little but he returned the handshake comfortably enough. 'So am I, Johnno. All the best for everything.'

'You, too.'

Rosie's heart melted a little as she watched the men. They were getting along fine, which made her happy as long as Johnno wasn't reading too much into the fact Lucas had spent the weekend with her. It had been wonderful but where to from here was anyone's guess. Yep, she was suddenly coming down off the high last night had brought on.

Lucas was an awesome man, but that whole trust thing was raising its ugly head again. How could she believe he'd stay for ever if they got into a serious relationship? The truth was, she couldn't. Couldn't trust anyone to love her for ever, not even Lucas. It wasn't in her DNA.

So she'd make the most of the remainder of the weekend and then get back to business. Friends only. Maybe friends with benefits, if that suited Lucas too. Because it was impossible to deny they'd hit it off so well in bed. Until now, she hadn't known sex could be so effortless and mind-blowing. As a lover Lucas was out of this world.

'Want to come up?' Rosie asked as Lucas parked outside her apartment building that afternoon.

He shouldn't. They couldn't carry on as if they were a real couple. Not when he still had difficulty believing he wouldn't hurt her along the way. Nor when he was still protecting his heart.

'You bet.' His tongue had a way of taking over from his mind at times, and he had to admit he wasn't unhappy with its answer to Rosie's offer. Of course she could be going to make him coffee and nothing else, but he already

knew what that wicked gleam in her eyes meant and coffee had nothing to do with it. And if he was in the tiniest
bit of doubt the sexy smile she gave him reiterated that.
The same smile that he'd seen often throughout the night
had relentlessly amped up his desire for her.

Locking his car after getting her bag out of the boot, he
did remind himself he had to be careful. He was guilty in
part for May's accident. It could happen in another way
all too easily and he did not want to lose the next woman
he settled down with.

In her apartment, Rosie led the way to her bedroom,
not even stopping to put her bag down.

Lucas had to laugh as anticipation worked its way
through him, tightening him everywhere, heating his
skin and raising his pulse. Whatever happened, they were
going to have some fun now. Fun he would not regret,
no matter what else went down. Rosie had got to him,
and he enjoyed being with her. He wouldn't look too far
ahead at the moment. Time to think about his needs, to
enjoy making love with Rosie since she was more than
willing to join him in this madness, however temporarily.

Without a word to disrupt the mood, they were under
the covers and reaching for each other in unison. They
already knew each other well and it could only get better. Couldn't it?

'Rosie, wait, let me touch you first.'

Later, when they sat up and leaned back against the
pillows, Lucas's face was warm and his body languid.
'I haven't made out so often in such a short time since I
don't know when.'

Rosie's eyes widened. 'I'm not sure if that's a compliment or an insult, being reminded you've had other lovers while we're in bed.'

He'd blown it. Now she'd send him to purgatory. Grabbing her hand, he held her lightly. 'I'm sorry, Rosie. That came out all wrong. I wasn't thinking about anyone else, I assure you. I've had a wonderful time and got carried away with it all. Plus, I'm feeling happier than I have for ages.'

'So it was a compliment?' Was she feeling uncared about?

'Absolutely. I thought you were wonderful before we went to the Yarra Valley and now I know so.' He stopped. What did he want to say? How to say it?

'I'm listening.'

What if he just shoved the past away and got on with enjoying a future with Rosie? If she wanted one with him. Taking her face in his hands, he locked eyes with her. 'Rosie, I'd love to spend more time with you. Maybe have a fling and see how we get along on a deeper level, if you're up for that?'

Her eyes widened, then blinked. A red hue coloured her face. Was that a yes or a get lost look? He held his breath, paralysed by how much he longed for her to say yes.

'Lucas, I—' She was going to tell him to go leap off her balcony and not come back. 'Lucas, I'd like to do that very much.'

Relief poured through him, quickly followed by excitement. 'No promises about the future.' He had to put it out there, just in case she read too much into his suggestion.

'Once more, we're on the same page.' She leaned in

to kiss his cheek, then his mouth, as if she was sealing a deal.

He had no problem with that. Holding her tight, he knew he couldn't have let her go completely, maybe not at all.

One step at a time.

CHAPTER SEVEN

'MULTI-CAR PILE-UP on a suburban street. Teens doing wheelies,' Rosie told Lucas and Connor, a nurse, when they had landed at the hospital next Friday night. 'Three seriously injured. Your patient appears to be in her teens. She's unconscious and has been all the time we've been with her. Skull injury on the right. Because of that we're treating this as a spinal injury and have placed a neck brace on her.'

'Makes sense.'

Rosie nodded, and continued filling him in. 'She didn't react to my touch on her feet or legs. I did get slight movement when I felt her arms and chest.'

He nodded, still checking the girl for himself. Nothing unusual there.

'There's severe bleeding from her right wrist, which also has multiple fractures. Right hip and thigh appear to have taken some impact also.'

'No idea who she is?' Lucas asked as he took one corner of the trolley.

'None. The police are onto it but it could be a while before you know anything as all the passengers in the same car were unconscious.' She glanced sideways at

Lucas, who flicked her a brief smile before returning his focus to the girl.

'It must've been one hell of a crash.'

'The car was unrecognisable. Alcohol's suspected, and possibly drugs.'

'Not uncommon,' Lucas commented. 'Right now, that's only one of our worries. We'll check for both once we've stabilised her.'

They were inside and heading towards the lift, everyone crowded around the trolley monitoring the girl's monitors and reactions. It wasn't looking good.

'Heart rate's dropping,' Connor warned.

'Get ready to perform CPR,' Lucas said while pushing the trolley inside the lift.

Rosie pressed the button for the floor the emergency department was on, all the while watching the girl and the heart monitor. Suddenly, 'Flatline.'

Connor was already onto it with the ECG attached to the girl's chest. 'Stand back.'

One charge and the line was moving up and down again. 'Phew,' Rosie said aloud.

'Too right,' Lucas agreed as he studied the monitor.

The lift slowed, stopped, and they were rolling the trolley into the ED, where they had to shift their patient from the spinal board onto the bed without any movement to her body. As soon as they were done, Rosie picked up the board. She needed to get back to the chopper. 'Right, I'm on my way. Got another patient from the same accident to collect.'

Lucas barely nodded, focused on the girl.

She leaned closer, said quietly, 'See you later.'

He nodded without looking round. 'Yes.'

'Where are we taking our next patient?' she asked the pilot once on board the chopper.

'Same hospital. Everyone's crazy busy tonight.'

'Of course they are. It's the beginning of the weekend.'

Always the worst night to be on the roster. So many people out on the town having a blast, getting tanked and then driving or brawling. Which would be why they were picking up the next patient, who wasn't in such a bad way as the last one. Every available ambulance would be out and about around the city. It was never nice dealing with the worst cases as there was often someone lurking in the background demanding attention and looking for more trouble. Thankfully, that hadn't been the case when they'd picked up the girl they'd just delivered to Lucas's emergency department.

Lucas. She hadn't once bumped into him at his work until she'd been taken there as a patient. The flights she worked on didn't often go to Parkville as the hospital was close to the CBD and the patients Rosie dealt with were more often from the outskirts of the city or rural areas. Yet now she seemed to be going to Parkville quite often. Life had a way of throwing curve balls, but in her case they weren't always bad ones. She loved seeing Lucas in the department and working on patients alongside him.

He'd definitely got to her. Something she had not expected. His lovemaking was beyond wonderful, but that wasn't her reason for starting to let go and fall for him. It was more to do with the way he'd supported her after she'd been assaulted, how he'd gone to the wedding with her, the way he treated her as an equal, as someone special, that rattled her and had her wondering if she could take a chance on having more with him than only a fling.

As in letting in the love she felt for him. But it was scary. So much could go wrong.

'Here we go. You ready back there?' asked the pilot.

Rosie glanced at Dave, the paramedic on this shift with her, who gave her a grin. 'When aren't we?'

'That's a yes,' she told the pilot. Dave was a bit of a hard case, she'd discovered. He was new to the team but very experienced after working for Rescue Flights in Sydney. 'You take the lead on this one.' It was his turn.

'Cheers, Rosie. I'll try not to make a mess of things.' That grin was ongoing.

'Hope not.' She laughed and looked out of the window as the ground came up to meet them. The scene hadn't changed a lot from when they'd lifted away before with the unconscious young woman. There were more police, but the crowd was still there.

'Jane Duncan, nineteen, probably fractured ankle and tibia.' The paramedic attending the woman stood up as they approached. 'She was lucid but has gone into shock. Admitted to drinking a lot.'

'We'll take over now,' Dave said. 'How come you're still here? I thought all ambulances were tied up with other cases.'

'They are. My lot are two streets away, dealing with a minor case at a house. I'll go meet up with them now.' He looked around. 'One of the cops is giving me a lift.'

Rosie wasn't surprised. The emergency services crews helped each other in these situations. She watched Dave as he checked on Jane. 'Ready to load up?' Sounded like she was referring to a slab of cargo. 'Jane, we're going to put you on a trolley and take you across to the helicopter. Is that all right?'

'Whatever.'

Dave gave Rosie a shrug and she reciprocated. They'd get on with the job and keep the conversation with Jane to a minimum.

When they rolled Jane into the emergency department Lucas was at a desk entering notes into the computer and looked up when she said, 'Back again. This time it's not urgent.'

'I'll be with you in a moment.' Then he winked. 'Catch up after work? Do some more...de-stressing?'

'Perfect.' Sex at her apartment, eat, get some sleep. Together. Sounded ideal.

'Sure, no problem,' Lucas answered the department head's plea for help the next morning. 'I'll be there as soon as possible.' The early day shift was down a doctor and a nurse who lived together due to a stomach bug apparently doing the rounds. Another doctor was coming in later in the morning so Lucas was going straight back in to carry on until then.

So much for putting a second coat of paint on the lounge walls. But going into work would keep his mind busy and less focused on thinking about Rosie and how much he was enjoying her company. It was hard to think of her as only a friend with benefits. Too hard. He grunted. Hard being a word he shouldn't use when thinking about Rosie. It described exactly what happened whenever he did.

The sex was amazing, and there'd be more to come. But that was only the beginning. Whenever he was with her, whether sitting over a drink or travelling to Yarra or chatting on the phone, he felt so relaxed and unencumbered with guilt, or even his fear of being hurt again. He felt alive. Like he used to feel before May died.

He hadn't always been on top of the world then, but he'd been largely happy with his life and where it was headed—until May had told him about moving to Sydney. Perhaps they hadn't been perfectly matched after all. Or they'd grown apart as they got older and found they wanted different things for their futures.

He shook his head in shock. Until now, he'd refused to really admit that to himself. When she'd told him she was moving to Sydney regardless of what he wanted and was furious at his need to discuss it, he'd been angry too. Naturally, she'd been excited about her promotion and his negative response to moving without at least talking about it must've been like having a wet blanket thrown over her. But she hadn't once paused to think about his side of things, had been so determined to take up the offer that he didn't feature in the decision. That had hurt big time.

But, looking back, he knew there'd been other incidents in the months leading up to that night where May had commented about him choosing emergency medicine instead of becoming a GP and setting up his own practice, something he'd always said he didn't want. She'd started focusing on making more money instead of what they'd agreed to do. Then she'd decided that having a family would harm their careers. That had gutted him more than the rest of her complaints. The cracks had been there in their marriage all along. He'd just denied the existence of them.

Was he remembering it all now because of Rosie? Yes, he was. Rosie was becoming more important to him every day. Even the days when he didn't see her, he couldn't stop thinking about her. This had nothing to do with a convenient and friendly fling. It was about having the whole deal. A deal he still wasn't ready to get tied into. He could still hurt Rosie. He could still stuff this all up.

Except how much of what had happened to May that night really was his fault? She'd completely lost her temper and, by all accounts, driven like a racing driver through the city. He wasn't denying he'd argued with her, but it hadn't been his decision for May to get behind the steering wheel.

Lucas spun around on his heel, looking at the room he stood in. Where was this coming from? He'd always taken more than his share of the blame so why was he changing his mind now? The answer was as clear as a summer sky. He wanted to live life fully, not half-heartedly. It seemed that might be possible with Rosie. If he was brave enough to risk it.

But right now, he needed to get a move on. Grabbing his keys, he headed out of the door. No more thinking about the woman driving him mad with desire. He had a job to do and each patient needed his full attention, and he was more than happy to oblige.

Less than an hour later, when he was sitting at the desk filling in some notes on a toddler who'd fallen out of her cot and got a black eye, the phone interrupted him. 'Emergency department, Lucas speaking.'

'Emergency response. We've got a chopper on the way to you with a male victim of a stabbing to the chest. Code purple. ETA ten minutes.'

'On my way up to the top.' He dropped the phone. 'Jason and Coop, code purple on the roof.' He didn't say any more. They knew what to do. Instead, he thought of all the symptoms the patient could be, and probably was, suffering. A stab to the chest endangered the lungs or the heart—or, worst case scenario, both. Heart failure was high on the list, as was compromised breathing. Who was the doctor on board? Because this person was going to need the absolute best there was.

The victim was getting it, Lucas noted the moment the chopper door opened. Rosie hadn't signed off yet. She was right beside the trolley being pushed by Dave, with her hands pressed into the patient's groin. There was blood everywhere.

'I thought the serious wound was in the chest,' Lucas said when he reached them.

'Yep, that too,' Rosie muttered. 'We haven't got a tally of how many wounds there are.' She was fully focused on dealing with the massive blood loss going on under her hand.

Dave was frantically keeping an eye on all the monitors while pushing the trolley towards the door.

Lucas grabbed a corner of the trolley. 'I'll take this. You keep on doing what else you're focused on.'

'Get us downstairs ASAP.' Rosie flicked him a look of desperation. 'I daren't shift my hands at all.'

The nurse who'd come up with Lucas had the lift door open and took the other end of the trolley to guide it inside.

'As soon as we get down, Jason, go sort out the suturing. This can't wait.' Lucas hadn't taken his eyes off Rosie and the wound she was trying to keep from completely bleeding out. The tension in her face told him how worried she was that the man wouldn't make it. 'The femoral vein?' he asked, though already guessed it was. He just wanted to hear her voice.

She nodded abruptly. 'I've been pressing on it for twenty minutes or more, but I don't have an accurate time for when the injury happened. The police didn't know either.'

'What about the chest injury?'

'His breathing's shallow but no sign of a pierced lung, though I've been a bit distracted.' She gave him a tight smile.

'Dave?'

'It seems the knife went downward rather than directly into the lung cavity.'

'Could've been deflected by the ribs.' The lift stopped. 'Right, let's move fast.' He didn't have to add 'carefully'. Everyone knew what was required. He'd really been talking for the sake of it. 'Jason, get onto the blood bank too. We're going to need two litres to start with.'

'Onto it.'

'Thank goodness you're here,' Rosie said. 'It's good having you here to work with on this.'

He felt a moment of pride at her words. 'How long have you got?'

'As long as it takes. The pilot's going to wait unless there's another call.'

Under the lights that lit up the bed, Lucas studied the injury site that was visible around Rosie's fists. 'This is going to be tricky.'

Jason already had the suture kit beside the man with everything laid out exactly as needed. Another nurse was attaching monitors to the exposed chest to replace the rescue helicopter's equipment.

Lucas threaded a suture needle. 'Dave, be ready to dab away any seepage the moment Rosie moves her hands.'

'Right.'

'Ready, everyone.' He held the needle close to the severed vein, where Dave had a swab. 'Rosie, take away the pressure.'

Instantly, the wound was apparent. Lucas slid the needle into the vein and pulled the edges together and tied off the first stitch. Then the next one and the next one. Another nurse had another needle threaded for the moment he ran out of thread. Once he'd done that he began on the outer wound. It seemed to take for ever to finish. Thankfully, the bleeding had slowed, making the job easier, but it was also bad news for the patient as it meant his blood level had dropped too far.

'Here's the first two litres of blood,' Jason said, already setting up the stand with the bag.

'Rosie, would you mind checking it?' He was too busy sewing and Rosie wasn't required to press on the wound any longer.

'Onto it.' Moments later, she said, 'I'm looking at the chest wound now.'

'What are you finding?'

'There was evidence of quite a lot of bleeding when we first got to the man, but it's stopped now.' Her fingers were moving over the ribs, starting with the side where the knife had gone in. If it had been a knife.

'Do we know for sure what the weapon was?'

'The cops found a knife in the bushes beside where this man lay. But no guarantees that was it,' she added. 'They'll send it to forensics. In the meantime, they're still searching the area for another likely weapon.'

He glanced at the heart monitor. 'Heart-rate's dropped.'

'I'm not taking my eyes off the screen,' one of the nurses told him. She had the defib attached to the man and she was ready to press the button for the electric shock the moment his heart stopped—if it did.

Hopefully, the machine breathing for the guy would keep everything going. He straightened up and dropped the needle in the kidney dish. 'All done. How's that blood going, Jason?'

'It's good.'

'Rosie, what have you found?'

'I suspect the two bottom ribs below the wound on the left are fractured. There's also a second wound on the same side, nearer his back. Not deep. No blood loss.'

'Too busy being pumped out elsewhere.' Lucas looked around. 'Is Sandra still here seeing the woman with abdominal pain?'

'No,' someone answered. 'She went to grab a coffee about twenty minutes ago.'

'I'll get her to come and see to this man. Rosie, thanks for everything.'

Her smile was tired. 'I'm dismissed then?'

Inside, he went all soft. He totally understood that smile. He felt shattered too.

'You know we've got this now. Go while you can.' He had the phone in his hand. 'Get some sleep.' She looked as if she could drop off right where she was standing. 'I'll catch up later.' And climb into bed with her, hold her tight.

Rolling over onto her back, Rosie slowly opened her eyes and stared up at the ceiling. What had woken her? Had she inadvertently brought her phone in here when she'd dropped into bed when she'd got home from work? Normally, she left it in the kitchen after a difficult shift left her in dire need of sleep. Glancing at the bedside table, she couldn't see it.

The apartment bell rang. Who could want to see her? Her best friends both had family commitments this weekend, and Lucas had texted earlier to say he'd be round after he'd had some sleep, which had disappointed her. He could've slept with her, but then sleep would've been out of the question.

Crawling off the bed, she wrapped her satin robe around her and dragged her feet to the door. Pressing the buzzer, she said, 'Hello?'

No one answered. Someone must've pressed the wrong number.

A yawn gripped her. Coffee. Now that was what she needed in abundance. To wake up fully and feel a bit more energetic. Last night had been full-on, no rest between patients at all, and most of them had been tricky cases requiring all her focus for every moment she was with them. Working alongside Lucas with the stabbing victim had been intense and yet rewarding, with a better outcome than predicted.

Her jaw tightened at the thought of another incident of someone hurting others with no regard for what they were doing at all. How would they feel if it happened to them or their loved ones?

Just like that man had done to her in the car park, robbing and physically assaulting her all because he probably needed money for drugs. Even seeing a number of patients who'd been deliberately injured by others, it was only now, after she'd been attacked herself, did she really understand how it changed people's ability to wander around feeling one hundred percent safe. Most of the time she was fine, but there were instances when a sudden sharp noise had her leaping out of her skin and staring around, only to find no one approaching her looking threatening. It would take a while before she was completely comfortable out and about among strangers. Thankfully, the guy was going before the judge soon and then she could move on.

As the coffee brewed she picked up her phone to check for messages. Kelly suggested lunch tomorrow since Simone was out of town with her husband. No message from Lucas. Still asleep? She'd text him shortly and see if he felt like going to the pub later on. And if he said no? Then she'd be gutted. Better to carry on as though he hadn't got into her heart.

Slinging a pan on an element, she delved into the fridge for bacon and a couple of eggs. After that she'd get dressed and go to the mall for some retail therapy.

The doorbell buzzed again. What was going on? Was someone playing games with her? It had happened before when the guy one floor down had his son to stay and the kid went up and down the building ringing bells on every door and hiding before the door was opened. Or should she be nervous? No. She never used to be and she wasn't starting now just because of her assailant.

She pulled the door wide. 'What's going—' She drew to a halt, staring at Lucas, standing there looking so good she could almost eat him.

'Hello, Rosie. Have I come at a bad time?'

Heat filled her cheeks. 'Not at all. Come in.'

He held out a bunch of flowers she hadn't noticed.

'These are for you.' He followed that up with a terse laugh. 'Of course they are. Who else would I be bringing flowers for?'

Red roses. All bound together with a red and white ribbon and looking— 'Beautiful.' Burying her nose into the bunch, she breathed deep. 'My favourite scent.'

'It's become mine since we caught up.' Lucas smiled, sending her head into a spin.

She held the door wide. 'Coffee? Or bed first?'

Stepping inside, Lucas closed the door. 'I was going to suggest we go somewhere for a late lunch and let off steam about last night, and this morning's case. Like old times, even if it's only the two of us. But—' he caught her hand '—I've changed my mind. You had a better suggestion.'

'Good. I could do with an energy fix.'

'You want coffee?' He gave her a wicked grin.

'Later.' She turned for her bedroom, a small bounce in her step. Again, Lucas was the reason.

'Got a vase somewhere I can put these flowers into before you completely crush them?'

What? Rosie glanced down and blinked. The roses were squashed hard against her chest. 'Wonderful. Now look what I've done when you went to the trouble of bringing me flowers.' No one had ever done that before. This man was definitely a romantic, even if he had said they weren't getting into a long-term relationship. 'Lucas, the flowers are just gorgeous.'

His laugh was light and warm. 'Glad you like them. Where's a vase?'

Rosie relaxed. All was good here. It might not be quite

how she wanted it, because she wasn't totally sure what that was yet, but she'd cope.

'In the cupboard under the bench. Meet you in the bedroom.'

CHAPTER EIGHT

SITTING ON THE deck of a restaurant overlooking St Kilda beach later that day, Lucas stretched his legs and leaned back in his chair after finishing some delicious fish and chips. 'Talk about perfect.' So was the company.

'Isn't it silly? I live in Melbourne but hardly ever come out here. It's not like it's difficult to get to.' Rosie was smiling non-stop, causing him to relax further. It was becoming his new normal. Should that worry him, or should he accept he was finally looking ahead, not backwards?

'Have you done anything about getting started on those flying lessons you were thinking about?'

'I talked to one of the instructors at the aero club out where I work. He said I can start any time I like, but I haven't had a lot of free time lately.' She laughed. 'Seems catching up with an old friend keeps me busy.'

He knew what she meant. Or thought he did. 'That might be the reason why I haven't got a lot of painting done either.'

'Don't blame me.'

'Of course I blame you. You're too big a distraction.'

More laughter, then her smile dimmed. 'Wonder how our girl with the back injury's getting on.'

Talk about deflating, but it was part of a doctor's life to think about cases at annoying moments.

'Her spinal X-ray confirmed a burst fracture in the mid back, so she had an MRI. It doesn't look like she'll be walking any time soon.' What a nightmare that had to be.

Rosie's hand covered his. 'Remember we always used to say no one knows what's ahead and we have to make the most of what we've got.'

Deep. Was Rosie implying that they should grab what they had and to hell with the consequences? Forget the short-term fling and go for the lot? If so, she had no idea how he could hurt her. Or be hurt himself. Though she did have a point. It was a reminder of how unpredictable life could be.

Rolling his hand over, he wrapped his fingers around Rosie's. 'I don't think I was very good at doing that.' He'd run away from his heartbreak rather than make a new life for himself.

'Back then, we didn't know how hard it might be to do that. I think you've done well, but I've already told you that.'

The tension around his heart melted a little. 'Thanks.' It would be so easy to let Rosie in and let go of everything holding him back. Too easy, which had to be good, surely?

'It must be great living out this way.' Rosie was looking out at the beach.

He relaxed further into his chair. 'I agree.' Might be something to consider once he'd got his house up to spec. He shook his head. Rosie made everything seem uncomplicated and yet she had her own problems holding her back. She was also the one complicating his life right now—because he was letting her in and falling for her hard. Talk about messed up.

'What do you want to do after we leave here?' he asked as a diversion.

Rosie studied him for a moment. 'I'd like to see where you live and how you're getting on with the redecorating.'

He hadn't seen that coming, but it was fine. He had nothing to hide in that respect.

'No problem. Just warning you there's not a lot to see really. Just lots of paint tins and covers over the carpets in the lounge and dining room.'

'Still, I'll get to see what sort of place you like living in.'

'Remember I didn't buy the house on my own. Unlike you and your apartment.' No compromises needed in Rosie's case.

'For me it was about deciding for myself. Growing up with Dad after Mum died was quite impersonal. No photos and all Mum's favourite ornaments were gone.' She paused, her finger rubbing a spot on the table top. 'Dad packed everything away the day after her funeral. When I asked if I could have some of the ornaments in my bedroom he said "no" and that was that. I don't know what happened to everything when he moved away. Probably went to the dump.'

'Blimey, Rosie, you must've been devastated.' He got up and went around to hug her. How could a father do that to his child? Lucas knew there was no way either of his parents would've been so harsh on him or Leon.

Rosie leaned into him for a moment, then pulled back. 'It's all right. I got used to it.'

Now he understood the blank spaces in her apartment,

other than those two paintings. They'd stood out as exceptional for the emotions they'd evoked within him, and he suspected the same for anyone seeing them for the first time.

'Rosie, you're better than that. You're too lovely and kind to be anything but open-hearted. You've become your own person.'

Rosie stared at him. 'You think?'

She didn't?

'I know.' He took her hand and tugged her to her feet. 'Come on, let's go to my house so you can see who I am.' An ordinary guy who worried too much about his heart, and right now he was prepared to share it with this amazing woman who'd just let him in a little. He was more than ready to do this, come what may.

On the way back to Parkville, Rosie was quiet for a while, then she moved around on the seat so she was looking at him. 'I've not really talked about my parents very often to anyone except Kelly and Simone, and I've known them since school. Not that I've told you all that much either.'

'Rosie, the fact you said anything means a lot.'

Just as well he'd stopped for traffic lights as her smile was devastating as she responded to his comment. 'It does to me too.'

The lights changed and he pulled away with a jerk. 'Something to keep doing then—whenever you're up to it.'

Rosie was still watching him. 'I know I keep saying it, but I'm glad we've found each other.'

As in 'found each other' not as friends but lovers with

a future? That sounded deeper than her usual casual way
of wording things.

'I've had an insight into you as a doctor, and you
haven't disappointed.'

'Changing the subject, by any chance?' She laughed.
'You're so damned grounded.'

'I figured you were ready for something light-hearted
to talk about.'

'I thought I was the serious one, but I'm starting to
understand that sometimes I can be flippant when I'm
not overthinking things.'

'More like enjoying yourself. Flippant is the wrong
word to describe you.'

Turning to face out of the windscreen, she laughed
again. A wonderful sound that tripped his heart. It wasn't
a sound he'd heard often from Rosie until recently, and
that it came when they were alone together lifted his
spirits further.

Looking up at the house Lucas had parked in front of,
Rosie could only feel surprise.

'It's huge.' Nothing like she'd expected, though she
didn't know why she'd thought that. Two storeys high,
with wide verandas at the front and on the right-hand side,
it made her apartment seem like a matchbox. A wide lawn
swept down to the street. 'It must take hours to mow.'

'Not at all. I've got a ride-on.'

'Of course you have, being a man's man.' Slipping her
arm through Lucas's, she said, 'Come on. I'm dying to
see the rest.'

Inside the front door, she looked around. Wide stairs

led up to the top floor. Doors opened off the entrance, showing spacious rooms with very little furniture.

'You haven't settled in fully by the looks of it.'

One eyebrow rose. 'I'm more interested in getting the place looking good at the moment. As I said, I don't even know if I want to carry on living here once I'm finished with redecorating.' He led her into what appeared to be the main lounge where there was a TV, stereo and two comfortable-looking lounge seats. 'I had intended putting on the second undercoat of paint this morning until I figured visiting you would be more fun. As it turned out to be.'

Warmth filled Rosie. They were getting on so well it was amazing. 'Definitely.' It was fulfilling too. She was falling deeper for him by the day. Scary as that was, she was okay. Lucas was worth the apprehension that sneaked in when she least expected it.

'Let's get the guided tour out of the way, then we can relax on the deck with a beer.' His grin was cheeky and told her more than anything that he also thought they were fine together.

'Lead on.' She took another look around the room. It seriously needed the paintwork done. 'You're going for a light colour with the top coat, I hope.' The windows didn't let in enough light for her.

'What would you use?'

'Dodging the question?'

'I'm interested in your opinion.' He picked up a paint chart. 'I'm using this light grey. It's already on the dining room walls and makes the room feel lighter and airier.'

'Good choice. It's very similar to what's on my walls.' Would May have approved?

Gee, Rosie, stop that. May's gone. This is Lucas's house now.

True, but it was hard to deny that May had lived here with Lucas.

'Grey's in at the moment.' Lucas moved through to the kitchen with its wide bench where stools lined up on one side. 'No need to explain this space.'

'It's where you do most of your eating,' she noted. There was an empty mug and a plate with crumbs, along with a fishing journal and a book sitting on the counter.

'No point in setting a dining table. Here, I can make a mess, wipe it up and be done until next time. Except this morning I headed out the door to visit you instead.'

'I'm glad you did.' There it was. As simple as that. She enjoyed being with Lucas, wanted more time getting to know him better. One step at a time, she reminded herself as they headed upstairs, leaving thoughts of May on the ground floor.

At the top, Lucas spread his arms wide. 'Four bedrooms and two bathrooms, all very ordinary.'

That was it? He wasn't showing her the rooms? Think again, pal. Rosie stepped through the first door on her right, looked around and walked out again.

'Yes, it does need some loving attention.'

Lucas grinned and started along the hall to the next door. 'Same in here.' Then the next, 'And in here.' Then he turned around and led her back the way they'd come and past the top of the stairs. 'This is the first room I did up.'

The main bedroom. The room he'd shared with May. Her happiness slipped. She was in May's domain.

'What do you think?' Lucas asked.

Looking around, trying to deny what was going through her mind, she noted the room was light and cheerful with wide windows and colourful blinds and bedcovering. It would've been different before he'd decorated it. It was Lucas's room now. Nothing to do with May.

'Not bad.'

'It's the first time I've ever redecorated a room and I'm pleased with what I achieved.'

'You've done a great job.' The bed looked so inviting with the plump pillows and cosy duvet that Rosie had to turn away before she got too warm and bumped into Lucas. 'Oops.'

His hands were on her elbows, holding her lightly. His gaze was fixed on her like it did when they moved in on each other.

Anticipation caused her to shiver. 'Lucas?' His name was a whisper across her lips.

'I can't resist you.'

She couldn't pull away from him either. He was too desirable to turn her back on. She could get used to this. Wanted to get used to it. Winding her arms around his neck, she stretched up to kiss him.

Before her lips had covered his, she was being swung up against his chest and taken across the room, where he lowered her beside him as he knelt on top of the bed. 'You're certain?'

This time her mouth did cover his and she kissed him like there was no tomorrow. But there'd better be, she thought briefly as their bodies moved closer and their hands worked magic on each other. Tomorrow and beyond.

Rosie slowly opened her eyes to find Lucas watching her with a tender smile softening his sensual mouth. 'Wow,' she said on a slow exhale.

'Double wow.'

Their lovemaking only got better every time. She stretched her legs down the bed and rolled onto her side to face Lucas. Her body was loose and warm, and she felt cosy tucked up beside him. It was special. More special than she could recall from the past. She really was opening up to the possibility of a relationship. One she didn't walk away from when all the doubts and fears raised their heads, or was that getting too far ahead?

Normally, she protected herself by breaking things off when she got too close. While she and Lucas were supposed to be having a fling and no more, she did worry about hurting him. He'd been heartbroken when he'd lost May and didn't deserve to go through that pain again if he came to care for her and she walked away. She sighed. Talk about doing a U-turn with her fears. But hers were still there, right behind the worry about hurting Lucas.

'What was that sigh about?'

'It was my body saying thanks for such a wonderful moment or three.' She needed to cling onto that thought and stop letting her mind raise any number of reasons for not pursuing a relationship with Lucas.

'Moments? I need to work on that.' He rolled her on top of him and held her tight. 'But not right now.' He grinned. 'I haven't got my breath back completely.'

She'd been lying beside him for a while now. 'Your chest is barely rising,' she retorted and reached between them to touch his sex. 'You sure?'

'No.' His hands were on her backside, kneading softly.

Away we go again.
'Come on, then.'

'Turn around so I can wash your back,' Lucas instructed Rosie as they stood under the shower, letting the water stream over their tired bodies. Making out with Rosie was amazing, and he couldn't get enough of her. Except right now, he was exhausted in a wonderful kind of way. Not even standing here together could bring him fully to life at the moment. She'd sapped all his energy as she shared her body and left him feeling like he'd found himself again. An amazing sense of awareness filled him as he soaped her smooth skin between her shoulder blades and down to her trim waist. He was happy. Happier than he'd been in so long it seemed unreal. But it wasn't. The woman standing in front of him was all too real. He brushed his lips over her neck. 'You're lovely.'

Rosie turned around, and rubbed a lather over his chest. 'And you're wonderful. If you hadn't gone to the wedding with me, we probably wouldn't have got so close.'

'Or we still might have but it would've taken longer to get started.'

With her determination to be strong, despite what had happened to her after her assault, and then admitting she was struggling, she had got his attention straight away.

Her soft smile nudged his heart.

For him, sharing a shower with Rosie was intimate in a trusting way, as if they were exposing more about themselves than ever before. Nowhere to hide anything. Even the fear of being hurt again backed off in here. Either that or he was fooling himself because she was coming to mean so much to him. Yes, he cared a lot, maybe too much, for this beautiful woman and it was hard to imagine not going forward with her rather than taking a backward step into safety. Hell, he'd made love to Rosie in the room, the bed, that had been his and May's. It didn't distress him to think that, or make him feel guilty.

He was moving on.

Flicking off the shower, he stepped out and handed her a towel before taking his and drying off.

'Feel like a drink out the back on the deck?' Suddenly he needed to get out of this tiny space, put some air between him and Rosie. She was coming to mean too much if he could feel that May was slipping away.

'Sounds idyllic.'

He didn't know about idyllic, but it would be less stressful. He'd added the deck when he'd first returned home. It was his idea, his work, his place to wind down after difficult days and nights. He could comfortably share that with Rosie.

'So painting's definitely off the agenda for the rest of the day. Don't let me mess with your plans.' Her grin was mischievous, as though she'd be happy to watch him do some work while she lolled around with a drink in hand.

'It's totally your fault I haven't got anything done.' He wasn't making that up. It had been because he'd wanted to see her so badly that he'd gone around to her apartment earlier, and definitely she'd been the cause of his hard-on that had led to them making love.

'You're easily distracted.' She laughed. 'I like it.'

After winding the overhead sunshade out over the deck and getting some beers, he settled into a cane chair and stretched out his legs, his earlier tension dissipating as he chatted with Rosie. 'So, what do you think of my abode?'

'Honestly?'

'Is there any other way to answer?'

'It's not me, but that could be because it's in need of the makeover you've started. There's a lot of space to be filled.'

'A family of six lived here when we bought the property.'

At the time, he and May had intended starting a family within a couple of years and then the rooms would've been filled with furniture, toys and clothes. Even when May had become fixated on climbing the corporate ladder, he'd still believed it was possible. He'd have been happy to be the primary stay-at-home parent until she'd established herself. What he hadn't understood was just how badly she'd wanted to get to the top of that ladder and what she was prepared to give up for it to happen. Now, he could admit that towards the end May hadn't been as focused on them as a couple as she had in the beginning.

'I can picture kids out here playing with a soccer ball or swimming in the pool.'

'Ahh, the pool that I haven't used once since I got back. It's a constant chore keeping it sparkling clean, let me tell you.'

'Why haven't you been in it when you've kept it so clean? I'd be in it every day if it was mine.'

He shrugged. 'No idea really. By the time I get home from work I'm more than happy to sit out here and contemplate my navel while I have a cold beer.'

Her laughter made him warm and happy. Happier. She just accepted him as he was. So good. Then a worrisome thought crossed his mind, shutting down the happy feeling. What if he did love Rosie? Would she love him back? Would he hurt her too at some point? Taking a long drink, he turned to look at the woman playing with his mind.

'What happened with you and Cameron? Everyone expected to be invited to the wedding.'

She didn't look shocked at the sudden question. 'I changed my mind.'

Lucas looked out across the lawn he'd once pictured his kids running around on and waited for more.

Finally, she continued. 'We talked about getting married but never did anything about it because I got cold feet. I hurt Cameron badly. And I hurt myself,' she added in a quieter voice.

'What changed your mind?'

'I wasn't ready.'

It didn't sound like the whole truth, which he'd like to know now that he was becoming emotionally invested in Rosie.

'But you'd been with him for a year and appeared happy.'

'I was, and then I wasn't. To have carried on would've been cruel to Cameron in the long run.' She upended her glass and drank a large mouthful, before looking at him with a tight smile. 'He's very happy now, with a lovely wife and a six-month-old daughter.'

'You keep in touch?' Seemed strange.

'Not at all. His wife, Brenda, used to work with a friend of mine in Sydney so I get the updates. Not that I particularly want them. It's over for me, and has been for a while.'

Did she mean she'd moved on and was ready for another relationship? Or was she pretending she was happy? No, he couldn't bring himself to believe that. When Rosie was happy, she was genuinely so. He'd go with the idea that she was ready for a new start. But then she did have issues about her father withdrawing from her. Did she carry those fears into other relationships? He longed to find out, but something held him back. He wanted to enjoy this time with Rosie, not stumble through his emotions with her and then have her walk away.

'Want to skinny-dip in the pool?'

'You a mind-reader? Though I'm not quite so keen on the naked aspect. Can any of your neighbours see into the yard?'

'I can't say for sure they can't. Want to borrow one of my shirts? It would come halfway down your thighs.'

'I'm on.' She stood up. 'Come on, let's do this.'

Within minutes they were in the pool, Rosie swimming short lengths while he leaned against the side and enjoyed the view. That was until she came his way and sent a wave of water over his head. He dived under and grabbed her around the legs to pull her down.

Her hair floated behind her in a gorgeous mess and the shirt he'd lent her lifted up to her breasts and higher. She dived deeper, out of his hold, and headed for the end of the pool.

He followed, swimming as fast as possible, which wasn't fast enough to catch her.

'You're really good,' he spluttered when he caught up.

'Used to swim for my college.' She grinned. 'Definitely out of practice these days.'

'I'm learning more about you every day.' What was more, he was enjoying it. He *was* waking up to new possibilities. 'Things that have nothing to do with being a doctor.'

'You said you weren't sure about staying on here once you've got the house fixed up. Any further thoughts on that?'

Looking around the pool area, then at the back of the house, the answer came to him in a flash. 'I'm going to sell up and look for another property more to my liking.' It wasn't even a shock to find he'd made up his mind. It must've been lurking in the back of his head for a while and only now, being with Rosie, though she wasn't the reason for the decision, he knew what he was going to do. 'An up-to-date house with lots of light, open-space living and modern utilities.' He was ready to permanently put away this piece of his life.

'And a pool?' She grinned.

'Don't rush me into decisions I haven't thought about.' He returned her grin. 'It's taken nearly three months to get in this one.' But now he had, he'd keep going. Hopefully, he'd have Rosie's company as he did, although autumn was fast approaching so soon there wouldn't be a lot of swimming going on.

'I could do with a drink of water. All this exercise makes me thirsty. Want another beer?' She couldn't be thinking only of the minimal swimming she'd done. It had to be the lovemaking too.

'Sure do.' He climbed out of the pool and handed her one of the towels he'd brought outside. 'I'll turn the barbecue on to heat up while you're getting the drinks.'

'I'll check out your fridge and see what I can come up with for a salad.'

'You'll find most things you need, unless you're into exotic foods.'

'Not this girl.' She wriggled her butt and headed inside.

So easy being together when they weren't trying too hard to get along. Just as it had been during the weekend up north. He could get used to it all, he decided as he turned on the gas to bring the elements up to heat on the barbecue. Face it, he already was.

Rosie appeared, wearing the clothes she'd had on earlier, and carrying two bottles of beer. 'Here, get one of these into you.'

'I'm going to find some dry clothes first. The temperature's beginning to drop.'

'Hope there's not a storm brewing.' Rosie was checking out the skyline. 'Doesn't appear to be anything heading our way at the moment.'

'It should stay that way until we've had dinner. What's it like in the helicopter when there's a storm going on?'

'Most of the time it's not too bad, even quite exciting, but there have been instances where I'd have preferred to be on the ground. Of course the pilots won't fly if it's too rough, but we do get caught out occasionally.'

'I bet they hate pulling the plug on a flight if the patient is in serious trouble.' It'd be one of those decisions where they'd feel they couldn't win.

'They don't like it, but there's not a lot they can do other than be sensible and play safe. Right, I'll go make a salad.' She headed inside again, leaving her beer on the table. She was so relaxed in his place it was as though she'd been here often.

Smiling to himself, Lucas checked the barbecue and then went to put on dry clothes.

At his bedroom door he stopped and stared at the mussed-up bed, his smile growing. They had had the most amazing sex and he still could have more. Oh, yes, he was ready for more of everything. How long could a fling last before it became something deeper and long-lasting? Not too long, he hoped.

There was no mention of Rosie going back to her apartment. Instead, she followed him upstairs to his bedroom when they were done with dinner and cleaning up, and fell into his bed, reaching for him as though she'd been here often.

When she cuddled into him, her legs entwined with his after they'd made love long and slowly, he sighed with contentment. It seemed for ever since he'd had such a wonderful time.

CHAPTER NINE

'YOU WOULDN'T BE giving me a hard time about Lucas, would you?' Rosie sat on her deck with coffee in hand as she talked to Simone over the phone.

'Absolutely. The guy's gorgeous and he obviously thinks the same about you.'

'Shut up. You haven't got a clue what you're talking about.' Rosie grinned and rubbed her aching thighs. There'd been too much of a workout for her body over the weekend. Not that she regretted a single moment of her time with Lucas. They'd come a long way since they'd agreed to a fling. 'He's a friend from years ago, nothing more or less or—'

Or what? These days, he was a lot more than a friend. Where this was going was still a mystery, but one she was ready to try to unravel as fast as possible. On the good days she didn't want to miss out on anything, and the days when she feared she'd be let down by him were becoming fewer.

Simone laughed uproariously. 'It's about time you sounded flustered over a man. It's been for ever since one got under your skin and woke you up in a hurry.'

Rosie flushed. Her friend knew her too well.

'How's the sex?'

'Shut up,' she repeated as more heat spread through her.

'Bet you're blushing right now.'

'I'm going to get changed and go to the mall. I need some new walking shoes.'

What she needed to do was to hang up on Simone before she spilled about how she was falling in love with Lucas. It was too close to the truth to be able to keep it to herself much longer. Her friends had seen her go through breaking up with Cameron and had supported her all the way, even when she'd suspected they believed she'd made a mistake.

'Which mall are you thinking about? I'll meet you there in my lunch break.' Simone worked from home a lot and could take a break whenever she chose because she always made up the time and more.

Did she want to see Simone when her friend was teasing her so much?

'The usual.' It was near where Simone and Toby lived. 'I'm working tonight so won't be there all afternoon.'

'I'll see you around one.' Simone didn't hang up.

Rosie drew a breath. She had a feeling she knew what was coming, but couldn't find it in her to cut her friend off so she waited.

'Rosie, you really like Lucas, don't you?'

'Yes, I do.' Another breath and she continued. 'More than like him, if I'm honest.'

'I'm glad. Kelly and I have only met him once, but he came across as a great guy who'd always have your back. He had it that day after the assault. Throw in how you talk about him with so much happiness and enthusiasm and I think this guy might be a keeper.'

'Whoa, slow down. It hasn't been that long since we

reconnected, and we're still getting to know each other in a deeper way than previously.'

Who was she trying to fool here? She wanted Lucas more than she'd ever have believed, and not only in bed.

'Don't put your usual walls up, Rosie. It's time to put yourself out there and take a chance on love.'

'You think I don't know that?'

'You know it all right. It's doing it that's your problem.'

Again, nothing she didn't already know and want to do something about, but what if she hurt Lucas? He didn't need that any more than she did.

'Shouldn't you be getting back to work?'

Simone sighed. 'Yes. I'll see you later. But please, please think of the future and not the past this time.' She hung up, leaving Rosie shaking her head.

And smiling. It was cool that her friend could be straightforward. There'd been a time when she wouldn't have let Simone get past the first sentence, but today she was grateful her friend had spoken her mind. Rosie drained her coffee. It seemed as though she might be finally letting go of some of her fears.

I'm ready for love and marriage and family.

She swallowed hard. Was she, really? Yes, she really was.

Time to get changed and go out. Sitting around the apartment gave her too much time to think about Lucas. There were worse things to think about, and nothing, no one, more exciting.

When she boarded the chopper for the first callout that night she wore a new pair of boots that she'd bought, along with walking shoes and a pair of heels to wear next time she and Lucas went out for a meal. There was also a new pair of jeans and a lightweight jersey in her wardrobe that she'd just had to have the moment she'd seen them.

Of course, Simone had given her a hard time while enthusiastically going through the clothing racks looking for other clothes to tempt Rosie. After coffee and a snack, they'd spent nearly two hours going through the shops. So much for Simone getting back to work on time, but then she did say she'd been at the computer from seven that morning and deserved a long break.

Her phone rang as she buckled in. 'Lucas, I'll have to call you back later. We're about to lift off.'

'No problem. Any time. I'm not going anywhere.'

Shoving her phone in her pocket, she looked out of the window at the large hangar where the rescue helicopters were housed.

'You're looking pleased with yourself,' Dave said from the other seat.

Pleased? Definitely happy anyway. Life was exciting these days.

'I had a great three days off. How about you?' She didn't want him probing into what she'd been up to. There was only so much she'd talk about and Dave would be bored silly hearing about her shopping trip.

As Dave filled her in on his weekend she thought about Lucas and how staying at his house until late last night had been wonderful for the simplicity of it. She hadn't once felt she shouldn't be there or with him. A couple of times she'd wondered about how much Lucas had loved May, but it still felt right to be with him. Cooking meals together, talking, laughing, making love and going for walks with the neighbour's dog. It was a life without complications. She hadn't queried where she stood in Lucas's estimation, had accepted they were getting on great and left it at that. She'd never be as perfect as May, but she could live with that if Lucas could.

This sense of moving forward with her life was very new. Did the fact that she and Lucas had been friends first make it easier to trust her feelings for him? She'd seen him with May and knew he gave all he had when it came to a relationship. But the problem was *she* didn't. Though she did seem to be doing so this time.

'Five minutes to landing,' the pilot called.

Time to focus on work, not a certain man. Looking out and down, Rosie could see the flashing lights of police cars in the car park beside the beach, where a crowd had gathered. A young man had rolled his four-wheel bike on a sand dune and been crushed underneath the machine.

'Looks like they've lifted the bike off him.'

'Hope they had someone there with medical knowledge before doing that,' Dave said as the wheels touched down.

Unclipping her belt, she stood up and slung her pack over her shoulders. 'Me too.' She hadn't seen an ambulance in the parking area.

'Apparently the guy was racing up and down the dunes at a ridiculous speed,' Rosie told Lucas when they caught up later on the phone. 'No helmet either.'

'Makes you wonder what these people are thinking when they go out for a ride,' Lucas replied. 'Where'd you take him?'

'South Melbourne.' Parkville had been too far away when the case was so urgent. 'How was your day?'

'Much like any other, though without any heart-wrenching cases. I've been talking to a home decorator about getting the house finished. At the rate I'm going, it'll take till I retire to get it done.'

'So you're serious about selling and moving?' She'd wondered if he might change his mind when he thought about living there with May.

'I am. It's time. Not that I've spent a lot of time here since May died, but this place is part of a different life.'

Wow. These days, Lucas could talk about his past in small bites without hesitating. He *was* moving forward.

'Any idea where you might move to?'

'Not yet. I'll leave that for now.'

'I had a phone call today from Megan, the cop. She told me the guy who assaulted me is going before the judge on Friday and if I wanted to go along I could.'

'It might give you some closure. I'll go with you, if you like.'

No surprise there.

'Thanks, Lucas. You always have my back, don't you?'

'I try. Think about it and let me know what you decide.'

'I'm going. I want to face him, show I'm not a blithering mess because of him.'

'That's my Rosie.'

Her heart warmed. His Rosie. She loved it, loved Lucas. She did? Yes, she did. Not that she was quite ready to put it out there though. The fear of being rejected hadn't completely disappeared. Would it ever? Damn, she hoped so, or life ahead looked lonely.

Dave appeared in the doorway. 'We're on.'

'Sorry, Lucas, I've got to go. Talk tomorrow.' It was after eleven and he'd probably head to bed soon.

She really loved Lucas? Yes, for better or worse, she did.

'Take care.'

'I will.' Now she had someone to spend her free time with she'd be ultra careful. A sudden image of her assailant filled her head, those wide staring eyes and ugly grin reminding her that being safe wasn't as easy as she'd once believed, but she was prepared to face him. *And* she'd have Lucas with her while she did.

It was the night before Rosie was going to court to hear the judge sentence her assailant and Lucas had kept her company all day in an attempt to take her mind off tomorrow.

She was grinning in that way that always tightened his gut, and his crotch. 'We're together a lot of the time outside work, so I guess it doesn't matter that I don't come to your department often. I have been there twice in the last two weeks. There are some other nice doctors working there.'

'Nice? I'm nice?' He leaned in and kissed her cheek. 'Try again.'

'Okay, you're sexy whereas they're not.'

'Phew.' Not that he felt he'd let her down in that department.

They were sprawled over her bed after mind-blowing sex. They'd spent most of the day at Phillip Island, where they'd walked the beach and ate fish and chips, trying not to get sand in the food. Returning to the city, he'd come up to her apartment and here they were, sated and relaxed. Being with Rosie got better by the day.

Rosie got off the bed and headed to her en suite bathroom. 'I'm going to grab a shower and then throw something together for dinner.'

Should prove interesting as there wasn't much in her fridge. When he joined her out in the kitchen after his shower, he couldn't smell anything. 'What are you making?'

Handing him a beer, she said, 'Seafood pizza.'

'Put together by the outlet down the road?'

'That's the one.' After pouring herself a wine, she wandered through to the lounge and stood staring at one of the paintings that had stirred him deeply the first time he'd seen them.

Moving up beside Rosie, he took in the brilliant colours and soft shapes of the outback setting. Once again, he was drawn in and could feel his heart beating a little faster.

'Have you ever been to the Outback?'

'No.'

'What did your father do out there?'

'Opal mining. When he died, I learned he'd worked on his own, miles from anyone, which is dangerous. He had a heart attack and might've been saved if he hadn't been alone.' Rosie took a mouthful of wine and turned to him. 'Dad became a complete loner after Mum died.'

Now he was beginning to understand even more about what made Rosie tick. It would be a big hurdle to get over if they were to have a future together. He waited.

Rosie paced across the room, then turned to face him. 'The day Mum passed, Dad withdrew from everything and everyone. It was as though he'd died too. Johnno and I never went without any of the basics. We were well fed, clothed and housed. Our university fees were paid for, as was anything we required. But…' her chest rose high, dropped low '…he never again showed us love. Up until then, he'd been as loving a father as any kid could wish for. It was as though he was afraid to love us in case we were lost to him too.'

Lucas struggled to keep from hugging her, to hold her close and comfort her, but he sensed it would be the wrong thing to do. Rosie had said she never talked about her father and now that she was the last thing she'd want would be sympathy.

'I can't imagine what you both went through.' Were still going though, by the sound of it. His parents had never backed off from him or Leon, were still always there whenever they might be needed.

'Be thankful you can't.' Bitterness laced her words. Then she glanced back at the paintings. 'Yet I question his feelings because of these paintings. He created them and left them to us. They have our names on the back. He always made sure we never went without a thing. Yet when I left home to go to university he was quick to head away. As far as I know, he never returned home. He missed both our graduations and Johnno's first wedding.'

What a mixed-up man he must've been.

'It's hard to understand what was going on inside his head. Obviously, he adored your mother.'

'Too much if he could do what he did.' Rosie moved to sit down.

Joining her, Lucas reached for her hand, held it on his thigh. 'You've done well, despite everything.'

Tugging her hand away, she shuffled around to face him full-on. 'Have I? When I struggle to get close to anyone, to trust a man with my heart? I've never been able to, and sometimes I doubt I ever will.'

His heart hit the ground. She was hurting now. Telling him what had gone on in her past was causing her pain. He didn't want that. She was also warning him to be aware of what she could do to him, how she could hurt him.

'You're better than that. I've seen you with Simone and Kelly, with Johnno. Your smiles are soft and loving, your eyes shine. You *do* let others in.' He drew a breath and put it out there. 'You're the same with me. I don't ever feel as though you're worried I might let you down.'

'You don't understand, Lucas. I'm afraid to open up entirely, afraid of being hurt, not just by friends but by any partner I might have.'

That explained why she'd called off her relationship with Cameron. She'd been afraid he'd leave her.

'Do you think you look for problems that aren't there when you're in a relationship?'

'I have to protect myself.'

In other words, yes. That was scary. Perhaps he should explain where he was at with May the night she'd died.

'May and I had an awesome marriage, were very happy together.'

'I know. It was obvious all the time.'

Not behind the scenes, it wasn't.

'Actually, things were already changing. We were beginning to argue a lot. May was moving to Sydney, whether I agreed to it or not. I would've moved if she'd talked it through with me instead of saying that's what we were doing or she'd just go on her own, without me.'

Rosie's eyes widened. 'Truly? That's not how it goes in a relationship. Not how I'd approach it anyway.'

Sadness touched him. 'Me either. Nor would May in the beginning. She seemed to get caught up in making it to the top of the corporate ladder to the extent that nothing else mattered, including our marriage.'

Rosie's hand was warm on top of his. 'I would never have guessed you were going through that. You always seemed so happy with her.'

Go on. Tell her everything then there'd be no comeback if they continued this relationship. That was a big *if* since she'd warned him she got spooked easily and wasn't great at staying around.

'What I'm saying is that there's always risk in any relationship, no matter how loving it starts out. Looking back, I think my love for May had already begun to fade a little, and I'm certain hers had for me. I was no longer as important as her career and I probably locked down a little and made things worse. There were other problems too. We'd always talked about the kids we'd have, then she changed her mind about wanting a family, said they'd get in the way of her career, which isn't what she'd said when we first got married.'

'You must have felt guilty over the accident that took her life.'

'I still do. We argued again on the phone that night about me not being able to celebrate her promotion with her, but if I'd gone home instead of helping a critically ill patient...' He paused, started again. 'There are a lot of ifs. Basically, I should've been patient and waited till we were together to celebrate her promotion and then talked about what we were doing next. I didn't. I was angry with May for saying she didn't want children any more, and that we were moving, whether I liked it or not, and I just pulled away.'

Rosie was staring at him as if something was wrong.

'What's up?'

'Nothing.'

'Come on, Rosie. There is, and you know it. Don't hold out on me, whatever you do.'

Like May used to. Oh, no. No, no, no. This couldn't be right. Rosie was not May. He'd loved May with all he had. He was falling deeply for Rosie, but he struggled to understand his feelings at the moment. Maybe he was there. And now he'd shown Rosie he could withdraw from the woman he'd loved more than life, and she was always on the lookout for that exact thing happening to her. Basically, he'd put a big warning sign on his forehead.

Watch out. I'm not to be trusted.

He reached for her hands. He needed to explain how he felt, to show he could be trusted. He loved her. But he'd failed last time with May, so she'd think there wouldn't be any guarantees that his love could last for ever. Did anyone have those? He didn't think so.

Pulling back before he could say a word, she said, 'I need time to think about what you've told me.'

'Talk to me. Ask whatever you want to know.'

'I don't need to. I get the picture, as clear as can be.'

Clunk. A dart hit his heart. She was seeing the worst of him, not the best. He wanted to fight back, explain how he'd changed and wouldn't repeat his mistakes, but her face was closed off, her body erect and tight. The barriers were in place.

'Rosie, you can trust me.'

She stared at him. There was a high chance she'd walk away, unable to love him because of her fear of being discarded. 'You should go now.'

He said quietly, 'I mean it, Rosie.' Even though she'd

told him to go he had to stay or she'd believe she was right about how he could walk out of her life.

Pain filled Rosie's face as she snapped at him. 'This is the first time I've ever let a man get so close to me, let him into my heart, and you're doing exactly what I was afraid of. Walking away.'

'I'm not walking away. I never said that. *You* asked *me* to leave.'

Maybe he had to go so she had time to calm down and think it all through.

'I've spent my whole adult life looking for love and walking away before it could happen, and now when I want to take a chance, look what happens. You tell me you weren't as happy with May as I believed…that you were arguing all the time and by the end your marriage was just a sham. That you locked down, pulled away from her.'

He froze at the despair in her voice. 'I was telling you the truth about what happened, not hiding it.' His mouth was dry. 'May and I had a terrific relationship but we met when we were eighteen and I think, as we grew older, we wanted different things from our lives.' That was the conclusion he'd finally come to. 'Whereas you and I are adults and established in our careers and it's time for more—together.'

She winced at his honesty. Not used to it from the men she got close to? Or looking for more problems?

'You mean the world to me, Rosie.'

'You can have whatever future you want without me, because I'm not risking getting hurt. I cannot commit to you, knowing this. I can't face being dumped by you in the long run, because I don't believe in myself. I tried before and had to get out. I'm totally messed up, Lucas, and I know it. I'm so sorry but we're done. Please go now.'

For a long moment he watched her, now fully understanding just how much he loved her and just how hurt she'd been by her father's actions. But to tell her how he felt would bring another verbal dart to his heart. She wouldn't believe him.

Heading for the door, he could feel his heart sinking lower and lower with every step he took. It felt as if he was leaving Rosie for good. Which he probably was.

''Bye, Rosie.'

Silence followed him out of the door, which he closed carefully behind him.

'I love her,' he murmured to himself. 'I'll be back. She needs me beside her, backing her. Showing her she can trust me and let my love in.'

Wrapping her arms around herself, Rosie held on tight in an attempt to prevent herself from falling into little pieces. Lucas had gone. As she'd told him to. What had happened there? They'd been sharing their pasts and then suddenly it had become tense and awkward.

Lucas saying he'd started to fall out of love with May had shocked her to the core. He was the one man who she'd always believed had committed to one woman for ever. Of course she was being naïve. Not all relationships lasted for ever. It was a dream to believe that.

Not all parents loved their kids unconditionally or for ever either. Was she bitter or what? Bitter or covering her resentment that her father hadn't loved her enough to be part of her life in all aspects? She'd resented him hugely for withdrawing from her and Johnno. So why had she done the same thing to Cameron when she'd known he'd loved her? Why do it to Lucas before she'd really given them a chance? Because he'd got too close to her fear when he'd talked about May and how he hadn't loved her as much towards the end. In showing his vulnerability he'd cranked up hers, sending her instantly into self-protection mode.

Staring sightlessly out of the window, she could feel her heart splintering. Yes, she had fallen in love with Lucas when she hadn't been looking. Believing he was only a friend had made it too easy to pretend nothing was going on in her heart. But she did love the man. More than she'd ever have believed possible. To the point she'd stick by him and push all her doubts aside, come what may?

More than anything, she wanted to believe she would. That she could. But old habits didn't just go away because she wanted them to. Loving Lucas didn't mean she could instantly let go of all her fears. But she should because he always had her back, and he *wouldn't* let her down. It was hard to believe he thought he might not have loved May as much towards the end. There'd been no sign of that years ago. Guess it wasn't something to be put out there for everyone to see though.

Her phone rang.

Go away, whoever you are.

It might be Lucas.

So?

So she wanted to hear his voice.

I can't talk to him.

Crossing to get her phone, she stared at the screen.

Kelly.

No way was she answering. Kelly knew her too well

to believe she was fine and having her girlfriends dropping by tonight was the last thing she needed. Time alone thinking about Lucas mightn't be best either, but it was what she'd do. Face it, she wasn't about to fall asleep the moment she climbed back into her messed-up bed with all its memories of making love with Lucas.

The doorbell clanged.

What now? Had Lucas returned to tell her he wanted to be a part of her life?

Hauling the door wide, she stared at the teenager holding two pizza boxes. Dinner. Not Lucas. She needed to pay the kid.

'Just a moment.' Her mind was a blank. Where had she left her bag?

The teenager held the boxes out to her. 'It's all right. A man paid me at the main door and then let me in to come up.'

Lucas. Had to be. Who else would do that?

'Thanks.' She had no idea if she was thanking the teenager or Lucas. Closing the door, she took the pizzas to the kitchen and dropped them on the bench. Her appetite had long vanished, along with Lucas.

At home, Lucas tossed his shoes into the wardrobe and threw himself on the bed to stare up at the ceiling. What had happened at Rosie's? For a moment there he'd thought they were making progress and Rosie understood him so he could stop worrying about letting her down if they got into a deeper relationship. Then he'd admitted to the problems he'd had with May in their marriage and that had been like proving to Rosie that he wasn't to be trusted to stay around for ever, even if he loved her.

'I do love her.' He loved everything about Rosie. She was amazing and special and beautiful and tough. The list was endless. Then tonight he'd gone and blown it. Rosie was never going to abandon her fear of rejection, even if he managed to sneak into her heart.

Just because he had fallen for her didn't mean his feelings were reciprocated. Yet she always gave herself completely. Like when they made love. Yes, they made love, they didn't just have sex. It had always been special with Rosie. She was one incredible woman who he adored. Totally and utterly.

So why was he here and not at her apartment telling her this?

Not because she'd told him to go but because he was an idiot. When the going got tough he'd backed off fast. Because he'd told himself he had to protect Rosie by giving her space, but in reality, he was also protecting himself. The guilt over not being there for May when she'd been thrilled with her promotion and wanted to celebrate with him was real, but it had diminished over the years since. He couldn't hold onto it for ever as an excuse not to step out and try again to have love and a family. No one wanted to have their heart broken, but to have loved and lost was far better than not to have tried at all.

He'd told Rosie about him and May because he knew he loved her now. She hadn't seen that he'd never deliberately let her down. Life threw curve balls for sure, but they could talk through those together. They had to. Did Rosie care about him at all? He was certain she did. Did that mean she loved him? He wasn't so sure, but he wasn't going to find out unless he fronted up and laid his heart on the line.

Which he would do. Decision made. He had nothing to lose and a lot to gain. Sitting up, he checked his phone. One a.m. Okay, not the best time to turn up at Rosie's door and ask to be let in. He had to wait till the sun came up around seven. What to do in the meantime? Sleep was out of the question. Impossible with how his mind wouldn't shut down. Rosie this, Rosie that. Damn, but she'd got to him in a big way. A way he did not want to give up. He loved her, as simple as that.

Then he remembered the creep was appearing before the judge in the morning and he knew immediately what he was going to do.

Rosie rolled over and buried her face in the pillow. What was she supposed to do with herself until she went to court to see the man who'd messed with her get his sentence? Call in and see if there was any work she could do? Yeah, and have Steve give her a hard time about not having a life outside her job. Maybe she didn't. No way. She did, and it centred round Lucas.

Because he was everything to her. And she'd let him walk out of here last night. They both needed to think about things, he'd said, and she'd agreed. What had she been thinking? She hadn't been. That was the problem. Other than for reasons to keep Lucas at a distance, which really was the last thing she wanted. She loved him. End of. No, not that. It wasn't an ending. It was the beginning of something special—if she had the guts to tell him how she felt. Why wouldn't she if it meant finding what she'd been looking for most of her life?

Groaning, she hauled herself out of bed and went to stand under the shower until the water ran cold. Then she went through her wardrobe to find an outfit that was serious without being boring. A navy trouser suit was the best on offer. Adding a red blouse to the mix lifted the dark blue and added colour to her pale face.

Lucas had said he'd go with her to the sentencing. After last night she had no idea what he intended doing. She wasn't phoning him to find out. It was his decision to make and not one she wanted to influence. If he cared for her as much as he'd indicated then he'd be there. He'd have her back as he had other times, and hopefully today would be no different. It might be the game changer she needed if he turned up.

Or she might be a fool even thinking like this. For all she knew, he might've walked out of here for the last time, never to come back and enjoy sitting on the deck, sharing a wine and talking about their day.

She was such an idiot for letting him go. For kicking him out of her apartment. She should've reached out and told him how she felt about him, said she loved him and was still afraid but willing to do anything in her power to be worthy of him.

I do love you, Lucas.

If nothing else had come from last night, that had. It was the truth, and she was ready to step up and show him how much. Ready to put all her fears aside and have a wonderful life in love with Lucas. To stop doubting herself and finally have that happy life she craved.

She glanced at the watch on her wrist. It had been her mother's and she wore it most days. Blink. What was going on? Had it stopped? Less than an hour had passed since she'd crawled out of bed. How was she going to fill in the hours till she went into the courtroom?

Go see Lucas.

He wasn't home when she tentatively pushed the door-bell. Her heart skipped a couple of beats as her mind came up with a dozen reasons for that. He'd got called into work, was out walking the neighbour's dog, had gone to the supermarket, gone around to see her and she wasn't there.

Swiping at the tears slipping out of the corners of her eyes, she turned around and headed back the way she'd come. Lucas wasn't at her apartment. Her heart dropped further. She'd been crazy to think he might've been.

She couldn't stay around here wondering if she'd ever get a chance to tell Lucas how she felt. Might as well head into the city early.

Other than lawyers, there weren't many people in the courtroom when Rosie sank onto a seat near the front. Looking around, she shivered. This was where people's lives were decided upon with little input from themselves. It was nothing like how she'd got to where she was, be-coming a doctor because she'd wanted to and prepared to work hard to get there. Mind you, the man who'd at-tacked her had made a decision to do that to her, and de-served whatever punishment he got. Hopefully, the judge wouldn't be too soft on her assailant.

A court official stood up. 'Call Gerald Blackmore to the stand.'

A guard led a man in, handcuffed to his wrist.

Rosie gasped. That was the man, right there, looking almost pathetic now he wasn't drugged to the eyeballs and leering at her.

'You okay?' Lucas sat down beside her and reached for her hand.

'I am now.' Her heart was beating erratically and she didn't think it had anything to do with Gerald Blackmore.

'He's quite disappointing, isn't he?' Lucas said quietly.

Damn it, she was smiling. 'Very.'

Lucas was here—with her. What more did she need?

'He's looking this way.'

Rosie sat up straighter and stared back at the man who'd attacked her. He wasn't going to undermine her strength again.

The smirk on his face faded and he looked down at his feet.

Lucas squeezed her hand. 'Go you.'

Glancing at her man, she beamed at him. 'I'm tough when you're with me.'

A gavel banged, interrupting her happy moment, and for the next few minutes they listened to the judge comment on Blackmore's crimes before sentencing him to two years behind bars.

Outside on the footpath, Lucas took Rosie in his arms. 'How does that make you feel?'

'Two years doesn't seem long enough, but it's better than a slap on the hand, I guess.' She was smiling. 'Lucas, I have to tell you something.'

'Let's go somewhere less busy.' It was lunchtime and there were crowds heading in all directions around them.

'To heck with private. I want the whole world to know I love you, Lucas. With all my heart, I love you, and I'm sorry about last night.'

He stared at her as hope and excitement flared, and

grew into wonder. 'Me too.' Shaking his head, he tried again. 'Last night was a mess. It probably had to be got out of the way, but I'm sorry for how it went down. I love you too. My heart is yours to keep.'

The wonder in Rosie's face had him pulling her in for a hug that quickly became a kiss that even the elbow-knocks from passers-by didn't detract from.

When they came up for air, Rosie was beaming. 'I won't walk away, Lucas. This is for real and I can't imagine not having you at my side for ever.'

'I won't change my mind about how much I love you either, unless it grows even more.' Without another thought, he dropped to his knee and took her hands in his. 'Marry me, Rosie, and make me the happiest man on the planet.'

Leaning down, she brushed a sensational kiss on his mouth. 'Try stopping me. That's a yes, in case you're wondering.'

He stood up and swung her up in his arms. 'Let's go celebrate, my darling. And start planning a wedding.'

'I already know where I want to go for that.'

'The place we got together.'

'I'm not getting married in an emergency department.' She grinned.

'How about the same vineyard in the Yarra Valley where Johnno and Karen tied the knot?' He grinned back.

'You read my mind.'

EPILOGUE

Five months later

LUCAS STOPPED BREATHING as he stared at the beautiful woman watching him as she walked towards him with the biggest smile ever. She held a large bouquet of red roses and wore a white wedding dress that highlighted her stunning body as it flowed out behind her. His heart lifted.

Rosie.

Her brother had her arm tucked firmly in his and looked happy for her, which gave *him* a sense of relief. He'd hate to get on the wrong side of Johnno. But the guy was with his sister for this special occasion, and standing up with him and Leon afterwards. He guessed that meant he'd made the grade.

Rosie.

They were getting married, were committing to for ever, and making him the happiest man possible. His heart was in a frenzy, beating madly while his mouth was dry and his head light.

Rosie.

She was all he wanted, needed and loved.

Rosie.

She looked to him as she and Johnno reached the end of the aisle, her smile so wide and open and loving that Lucas felt his heart squeeze, something it did a lot these days.

Life couldn't get any better than this.

The marriage celebrant cleared her throat. 'Let's get you two married, shall we?'

Karen's mother, Sheree, had offered to marry them when she'd heard about the wedding and they'd both been more than happy to accept.

'Karen's family is mine now too,' Rosie had said at the time.

Now she grinned. 'Bring it on.'

'Take it slowly, enjoy the moment.' Sheree laughed. 'This only happens once so you've got to make some special memories.'

Lucas was certain his head was already full of those. Seeing Rosie in her stunning gown and holding her favourite flowers had torn at his heart, tightened his gut and made him happier than ever. If that was possible.

Sheree became serious. 'Lucas Tanner, do you promise to love Rosie for ever, to protect her and care for her, be the best partner for her?'

'Absolutely I do. I will always love you, Rosie.' He hadn't kept to the short script, but hey, this was his marriage ceremony.

'Rosie Carter, do you promise to love Lucas for ever, to have his back and care for him, be the best partner for him?'

'I do with all my heart.' Rosie stretched up and brushed a kiss on his chin.

'Hang on, you two. We're not quite done yet,' Sheree admonished through a big smile. 'Leon, have you got the wedding rings?'

'Lucas would have my hide if I didn't.' Leon grinned as he took a ring box from his pocket.

Lucas took the etched gold band from the box and turned to Rosie. 'This ring marks my dedication and love to you.' He slid it over her finger and kissed the back of her hand. Nearly there.

A tear trickled from the corner of Rosie's eye. This was the best day of her life. Never had she believed she'd get here and feel so completely relaxed about handing her heart over in front of family and friends, knowing she'd never get cold feet.

'Rosie?' Sheree said quietly. 'Your turn.'

She blinked, grinned. 'Just making the most of the moment, making those memories you mentioned.'

Kelly and Simone laughed beside her.

Reaching for the other ring, she took Lucas's hand in hers. 'Lucas, with this ring I give you my heart for ever.' Then she slid the ring in place and stretched up to kiss him lightly.

As their families and friends applauded and called congratulations, she leaned in close, still grinning, and said quietly, 'There's more. I'm two months pregnant.'

His head jerked upward and his eyes widened as a stunned smile appeared, and grew and grew. 'And I thought things couldn't get any better.'

She kissed him. 'Shows you don't always get it right.' But he had been right in loving her and making her dreams come true. 'I love you, Lucas Tanner.'

'Back at you, Rosie Tanner.'

* * * * *

*If you enjoyed this story,
check out these other great reads
from Sue MacKay*

Brooding Vet for the Wallflower
Healing the Single Dad Surgeon
Paramedic's Fling to Forever
Marriage Reunion for the Island Doc

All available now!

MILLS & BOON®

Coming next month

NURSE'S DUBAI TEMPTATION
Scarlet Wilson

Theo's presence in the room made her catch her breath. She tried not to notice how handsome he was, or the way her body reacted to the smell of his aftershave.

He looked up in surprise at Addy. 'What are you doing here?'

She raised her eyebrows. 'You mean you aren't part of the plot to destroy me?'

He sagged down into a seat with a look of bewilderment.

'I've not been here long enough to plot anything,' he said easily. 'And I'm not important enough, and I don't have enough hours in the day. But—' he took a breath and looked amused '—I might be up to plotting some kind of coup at a later date.'

She leaned forward. 'And why would that be?'

He sat back and folded his arms. 'Let's just say I'm watching and waiting. Biding my time.'

'Are you planning on becoming leader of the world?'

He shook his head and grinned at her. 'You forget I have a three-year-old. Leader of the world is tame. He'd expect me to be leader of the universe.'

Continue reading

NURSE'S DUBAI TEMPTATION
Scarlet Wilson

Available next month
millsandboon.co.uk

COMING SOON!

We really hope you enjoyed reading this book.
If you're looking for more romance
be sure to head to the shops when
new books are available on

Thursday 24th April

MILLS & BOON

LET'S TALK

Romance

For exclusive extracts, competitions and special offers, find us online:

- **f** MillsandBoon
- **X** @MillsandBoon
- **⊙** @MillsandBoonUK
- **♪** @MillsandBoonUK

Get in touch on 01413 063 232

FOUR BRAND NEW BOOKS FROM
MILLS & BOON MODERN

The same great stories you love, a stylish new look!

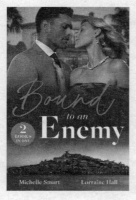

OUT NOW

Eight Modern stories published every month, find them all at:

millsandboon.co.uk

Afterglow Books is a trend-led, trope-filled list of books with diverse, authentic and relatable characters, a wide array of voices and representations, plus real world trials and tribulations. Featuring all the tropes you could possibly want (think small-town settings, fake relationships, grumpy vs sunshine, enemies to lovers) and all with a generous dose of spice in every story.

♪ @millsandboonuk
⊙ @millsandboonuk
afterglowbooks.co.uk
#AfterglowBooks

For all the latest book news, exclusive content and giveaways scan the QR code below to sign up to the Afterglow newsletter:

SCAN ME

afterglow BOOKS

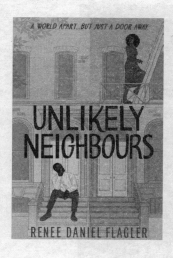

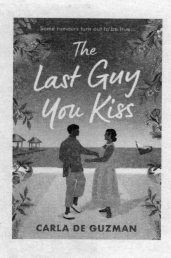

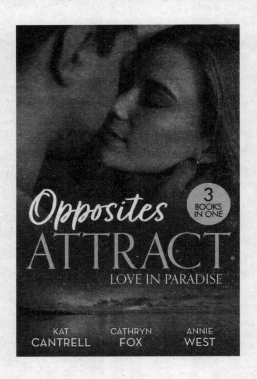

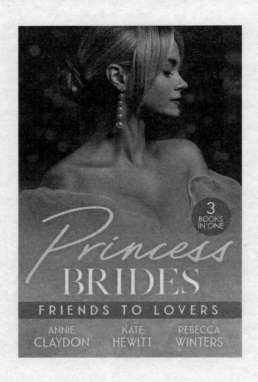

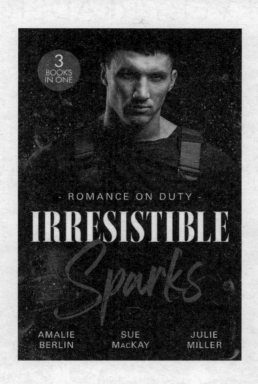